The New Criticism

The New Criticism

Munir

ADHYAYAN

ADHYAYAN PUBLISHERS & DISTRIBUTORS
NEW DELHI (INDIA)

Published by
ADHYAYAN PUBLISHERS & DISTRIBUTORS
4378/4B, 105, J.M.D. House, Murari Lal Street
Ansari Road Darya Ganj, New Delhi - 110002
Ph.: 011-23263018, 011-23277156, Fax: 011-23280028
Email: adhyayanpublishers@yahoo.com

The New Criticism

Edition 2011
ISBN 978-81-8435-251-1

Printed in India

Published by Harish Chandra Yadav for Adhyayan Publishers & Distributors, Laser Typeseting at A.V. Rao and Printed at Tarun Offset Printers, Delhi

To

Charu Sheel Singh—

Poet, Philosopher, Critic

Foreword

Dr. Munir Khan's book, *The New Criticism*, is an in-depth examination of the key texts from this literary critical movement in English literature. The author has clearly read widely and judiciously, and he provides his academic audience with a useful introduction to this important historical phase of textual analysis. Munir rightly notes that a century ago, the practice of literary criticism, post-Matthew Arnold and pre-F. R. Leavis, suffered from a sense of inferiority and disorientation in the wake of new scientific, psychological, and sociological discoveries. Munir accurately explains how a new generation of mostly Modernist critics and poets successfully reacted to these historical changes.

Munir notes how these writers and thinkers turned science to their advantage by using its analytical tools. At the same time, as Munir shows, these critics preserved and celebrated the inherent aesthetic value of literature. It is worth noting that a few decades later, in 1959, the novelist and scientist C. P. Snow famously pondered the implications of a cultural divide between the "two cultures" of science and the humanities. While Munir does not directly address this later (and continuing) conflict, the New Critical ideas he discusses implicitly reflect the early twentieth century efforts among British and American literary critics to negotiate the period's profound ideological shifts, scientific as well as social (including the tragedy of World War I). By engaging with these significant developments rather than evading them, literary critics called attention to the vitality of art in an age that generated a growing sense of alienation.

Munir provides clear, brief introductions to the important New Critical precursors—Hulme, Pound, Eliot, Richards, Empson and Ransom. He then devotes chapters to the exponents of New Criticism: Ransom, Tate, Brooks, Blackmur and Wimsatt. Although the influence of mostly French-based ideas in the 1960s, '70s and '80s led many to disparage the tenets of New Criticism, more recent scholarship has come to acknowledge, and sometimes even champion, the value of close textual reading and aesthetic evaluation.

This book's short chapters provide basic insights into these important ideas, and will therefore be useful to students of English literature. Munir's introduction to the New Criticism will provide a salutary companion to introductions to more recent and more influential theories of literary analysis.

Alan Johnson

Professor of English

Dept. of English and Philosophy
Idaho State University

PREFACE

In the opening decades of the twentieth century, the entire critical climate appeared to be confused and chaotic. There was nothing like pure criticism, as its sanctity was molested by the undue encroachment of science, history, social sciences, religion, and interest in other fine arts. Consequently, there emerged a crowd of critical approaches—philosophical, psychological, biographical, historical, social etc. The function of these approaches was to hunt ideas and philosophies from the poem, not to explicate the aesthetic and poetic traits which contribute to the creation of a literary work. The age was crying for an order, pattern, structure, and aesthetic values missing in both society and art. Then the New Criticism, sharply reacting to the preceding and existing condition of poetry and poetics, dawns with an intellectual and aesthetic light to clear the blurred vision of the contemporary poets and critics.

The New Critics with their new tools, new methods, and new theories make serious efforts to vivify the vitiating poetic language. They offer a cluster of critical concepts of criticism: Richards's "emotive" and "referential" meanings, Eliot's "objective correlative," Brooks's "paradox" and "heresy of paraphrase," Ransom's "structure" and "texture," Blackmur's "gesture," Tate's "tension," Warren's "irony," Wimsatt's "verbal icon" and M. C. Beardsley's "The Intentional Fallacy" and "The Affective Fallacy." Though they all carry heterogeneous views towards the objectivity and ontology of the poem, yet their goal is one and the same i.e. to explore the intrinsic factors of a work of art. However, through these yardsticks, they determine the quality of a poem. They contend that the language of the poetic discourse is quite different from that of science. The poetic language lends a complete knowledge to understand human emotions and attitudes. The New Critics hold that a poem is a complex linguistic artifact with full anatomy and autonomy. Their emphasis is always on the unity, concreteness, complexity, inclusiveness, and wholeness of the poetic language. They also raise very genuine questions about literature and criticism: what a poem is; how it is produced and read; its poetic effect, the semantic and poetic meaning, intuition and experience, the validity of mythical and allegorical presentation, and many other related matters which come in for close examination.

Since the New Critics are primarily philosophers and cultural critics, they incisively react to the modern commercialized, industrialized, urbanized, and technological civilization founded on scientism and secular knowledge. They intensely experience the topsy-turvy condition of the modern age—the loss of spirituality, religion, culture, social, and moral values. They encounter utter chaos, confusion, disorder, and fragmentation in society as well as in the psyche of the individual in the West. They have a great challenge to restore and reorganize the fractured human self and society, because nothing can offer any solace to soothe and restructure their disintegrated self. But the New Critics are quite sure that no other forces than the aesthetic beauty of an art can perform a therapeutic function. They embrace poetry as an art and its immense organizing capacity of imagination to define and reestablish the contemporary sensibility.

The New Critics are committed artists and warn that poetry is not a pastime, but a very serious act of mind. It is produced out of perspiration, not of inspiration. Poetic creation is achieved through a life-long labour, through perpetual process. It demands mental rigour, control of the senses, contemplation, and meditation. It is a sort of *sadhna*. Wimsatt believes that poetry belongs to "a psychological discipline, a system of self-development, a yoga." It lends mental peace, harmony, and joy, organizing warring ideas and emotions crowded in the mind. The New Critics, therefore, are endlessly in quest of hidden meanings of a work of art, placing it on the pedestal of surrogate religion. They cherish a firm faith that the world, history, and chaotic and fragmented human self can be restructured through the organizing capacity of poetic imagination. And thus human self can become free of all conflicting feelings.

This book containing ample background material is structured with seven chapters, dealing with the critics of both continents—five from England and five from America. Divided into seven sections, Chapter I entitled "Precursors to the New Criticism" pieces together T. E. Hulme, Ezra Pound, T. S. Eliot, I. A. Richards, and William Empson, who play a decisive role in the development of the New Criticism.

They effectively reacted to the deplorable condition of the contemporary literary criticism. Their main aim was to liberate it from the non-literary approaches and give a new shape to English criticism with the sharper tools and idioms creating an intellectual and aesthetic canvas. In "Romanticism and Classicism" and "A Retrospect" Hulme and Pound respectively discard romantic sentimental poetry, as it had become 'blurry,' 'messy,' and 'poppy-cock' full of 'rhetorical din and luxurious riot.' They anticipate and call for classical poetry through the use of hard, clear, concrete, and concentrated image without the decorative and the didactic. Hulme intends to see everything in terms of an adequate image, which, as Wyndham Lewis believes, is the 'primary pigment' of poetry. Pound also strongly recommends image in poetry. Though it is a tough job, yet, "it is better to present one image in a life time than to produce voluminous works." He injects Chinese ideogram, Japanese *Haiku* and *Tanka*, voriticism, phonopeia, logopepeia, and melopeia in poetry to invigorate its anemic condition. In his "Tradition and the Individual Talent," "Hamlet and His Problem," "The Metaphysical Poets," and "The Function of Criticism" Eliot demands a complete overhauling of English poetry through tradition, impersonality, objective correlative, unification of sensibility etc. Richards also propounds his two basic theories—theory of value and the theory of communication, boldly facing the challenges posed by the scientific discoveries. When William Empson comes to know the enigmatic role of language playing a variety of games, he theorizes that the literary use of language is related to a particular type of ambiguity.

Chapter II entitled "The New Criticism" is divided into nine sections and dwells upon the different views of the New Critics regarding the nature and function of the poetic discourse. But they all converge on the one common meeting ground i.e. the intrinsic quality and ontology of the poem. The chapter deals with the origin, scope, dimension, characteristics, moral values, and the decay of this movement. It also details how the numerous influences and inspiration, social and cultural milieus operate in its flowering. They are the British critics—T. E. Hulme, Pound, Eliot, Richards, and Empson; the philosophical background of Coleridge and Kant; and the outlook of the Fugitives and the Southern Agrarians.

Chapter III, "J. C. Ransom," dealing with Ransom's two representative essays—"Poetry: A Note in Ontology" and "Criticism, Inc." exposes the plundering and mutilating effect of science, which slays the spirit of religion and poetry. Differentiating poetic knowledge from scientific, Ransom contends that the truth of poetry is grasped through the contemplation of the aesthetic symbol, iconic nature, and contextual quality, the universals and the particulars. His poetic theory based on structure and texture is related to the problems of ontology or beingness of the poem discussed in "Poetry: A Note in Ontology." Ransom divides poetry into three kinds—physical, Platonic, and metaphysical. The essay also describes Ransom's basic credo that art is based on the second love. He argues that human experience undergoes three stages—the first is pre-categorical experiences, purely sensuous devoid of the working faculties of the mind; the second is a period of thought, categorization, and concept formation; and the third is the moment of making poetic image, in which sensuousness and reflection combine together. In his another essay "Criticism, Inc.," Ransom suggests that there should be a proper formal training for criticism which can be achieved very well by university teachers. He also says that criticism is neither a summery nor synopsis nor paraphrase, but a study of the techniques of art.

Chapter IV, "Allen Tate," correctly presenting Tate as a social, cultural, and literary critic, contains three of his essays—"The Present Function of Criticism," "Tension in Poetry," and "Understanding Modern Poetry." "The Present Function of Criticism" delineates the predicament of twentieth century man on the one hand and the decaying condition of literature and criticism on the other. Tate's main concern is the expressive theory and the theory of communication, and scientism in literature and criticism. He finds that the scientific discoveries and positivism have made a deep encroachment upon literature and have 'kidnapped' criticism. In "Tension in Poetry" Tate defines the nature of poetry. He argues that all types of poetry good as well as mediocre—have certain common characteristics that can be designated as the name of a single quality i.e. "tension." He explores a common poetic element in the nature of language itself. Just as the language of poetry is irony and paradox to Brooks, so is tension to Tate. In "Understanding Modern Poetry" Tate concentrates upon the characteristic difference between romantic and modern poetry. The readers are so badly habitual of reading romantic poetry, Tate asserts, that they refuse to read modern poetry, because they are untrained. In addition, modern poetry demands a new taste, a new perception, and a new intellectual exercise.

Chapter V analyses Cleanth Brooks's "The Language of Paradox," "The Heresy of Paraphrase," and "Irony as a Principle of Structure." These critical essays reveal how Brooks is perpetually concerned with "the interior life of the poem" throughout his life. Metaphor, paradox, intellect, gesture, irony, wit, and dramatic attitude are the main tools in his concept of poetry. In "The Language of Paradox" Brooks makes an unmistakable distinction between the language of science and that of poetry. Unlike the scientist, the poet directs and controls the dictionary words according to their own way, disturbing their normal meanings. A very close reader of the poem, he discovers the truth only in terms of paradox, and finds the richness, depth, and power of the poems issuing from the paradoxical situations on which they are based. In "The Heresy of Paraphrase" he further explains that the beauty of a poem never lies in its paraphrasable content, statement, diction, and imagery, but in its structure, and structure itself depends on irony, paradox, ambiguity, and complex of attitudes. The patterning sound, pauses, and rhythm of the language of poetry also condition, control, and create various mental waves, psychological states, and emotional feelings, whereas the paraphrasable content fails to yield such characteristics. In "Irony as a Principle of Structure" Brooks highlights the four aspects of his poetic theory: (i) the function of metaphor, (ii) an organic theory of form and content, (iii) irony as a principle of structure, and (iv) the role and pressure of context.

Chapter VI focuses on R. P. Blackmur's four essays—"A Critic's Job of Work," "Language as Gesture," "A Featherbed for Critic," and "A Burden for Critic." Blackmur theorizes that a critical object has two parts—"facts" and "gesture." The former is concerned with reason, while the latter with imagination. If "A Critic's Job of Work" discusses the conscious critical act of the critic, "Language as Gesture" examines the role of imagination in the critical act. Blackmur defines gesture as quality—an added meaningfulness to words. Through this process, language gets layered with multidimensional potentiality and acquires poetic meaning. Like other New Critics, in

"A Burden for Critic" Blackmur expressing his deep fury at the corrupted state of current criticism suggests both the artist and the critic to bear shared responsibility to maintain a continuity of cultural and literary values. His "A Featherbed for Critics" discovers that the general impact of writing in America is very despairing and disheartening. It is the duty of the reader, the writer, and the society to brood over its fate.

The final chapter, "W. K. Wimstt, Jr." is devoted to the study of his four famous essays—"Intentional Fallacy," "The Affective Fallacy," "Explication as Criticism," and "Organic Form: Some Questions about a Metaphor." Primarily known for his *The Verbal Icon*, Wimsatt holds the poem a pure linguistic artifact, a verbal icon, independent of all external factors operating on it. His two fallacies discussed in two different essays—the 'intention' of the poet and the 'affection' of the reader—expose the erroneous ways of analyzing a work. They are supposed to be main hurdles to appreciate a poem as a poem, because they are purely based on psychological and impressionistic form of criticism. In "Explication as Criticism," therefore, he suggests that criticism should be formal, analyzing each part of the poem in the direction of the total value i. e., the organic whole. His theory of organicism finds its full articulation in "Organic Form: Some Questions about a Metaphor." Wimsatt's contention is that a poem like painting and other visual arts embodies an organic order, aesthetic beauty, and secret of life of the creative human spirit. He establishes analogies between a poem and the human body and the plant to demonstrate the concreteness, beingness, and organic whole of the poem. These two metaphors for the poem are repeatedly and emphatically argued in the modern organic literary theory.

This book primarily written for the university students of the Indian subcontinent aims at providing with clear, concrete, and concise material on the New Criticism logically organized at one place. Students of literature, particularly Indian, often fail to avail this critical material in one book easily in the market. They have to consult one library after another perspiring to solve their problems, but come back with a little success. Removing such difficulties, this volume certainly increases its market value. The striking feature of this book lies in my impersonation of students to understand their problems. I made an earnest effort to study the ten critics of both continents: England and America. The representative critical essays with an extensive analysis mark a departure from other than this book. The second noticeable characteristic of this book is that the critical essays dealt with are hardly interpreted individually anywhere else, but found scattered in the books written from historical perspective. In Indian academic scenario, students and teachers approach to literary theory and criticism with a scared look unnecessarily. They refuse to realize that a right way to study literature is to apply critical tools on it. The book assiduously tries to clarify the critical concepts, so that the scholars could get to the relevance of criticism. This study hardly pretends to be complete in its magnitude and scholarship, but it has definitely been a long felt need to cater to their requisite.

After the completion of this book taking a long period of eight years, I arrived at this conclusion that literary criticism is a branch of philosophy, which enables me to be free of all petty things and evils: cast creed, colour, religion, status, prejudices, and infinite other conflicting desires and feelings. The study also helps maintain a psycho somatic balance. Hence, I can also offer a humble suggestion to the students who lack concentration, mental equilibrium, and seriousness to the mystery of life. They should embrace theory and criticism, which will decisively turn them an analytical and reflective man.

In the end, though least aspirant of any recognition from anyone, I would like to pour out my heartfelt anguish that I made this study in the most adverse circumstances of my life. At every step, I was denied to pursue my research work with a free mind. This warring gesture would sometimes deplete my faith in the goodness of human beings, but finally it made me more and more struggling, exacting, and above all, dignified.

I am deeply grateful to Dr. Alan Johnson, Professor, Dept. of English and Philosophy, Idaho State University, who got ready to go through the manuscript to write an illuminating foreword to this book. During my stay at Osmania University Centre for International Programme, former American Studies Research Centre, Hyderabad, I learnt a lot from a number of scholars and Professors well-versed in their own areas. I would like to express my deep thanks to some of them: Prof. R. S. Sharma, Prof. Gopal Rao, Prof. Sukhbir Singh, Dept. of English, Osmania University, Dr. G. Thirupathi Kumar, Prof & Head, Dept. of English Literature, The English and Foreign Languages

University, Hyderabad, Prof. K. Purushotham, Dept. of English, Kakatiya University, Warangal, Prof. Thirunumeli, Dept. of English , Presidency College, Madras, Dr. Balesh Y. Naik, Prof & Head, Bangalore University, Dr. Ram Badode, Prof. & Head, Bombay University, Dr. B. S. Korde, Prof. & Head Pune University, Dr. Hameed Khan, Prof. & Head, Dr. Babasaheb Bheem Rao Ambedkar Marathwada University, Aurangabad, Dr. Ved Prakash Sharma, Prof. & Head, Himanchal Pradesh University, Shimla, and Prof. Mohd. Toha, Dept. of Sociology, Banaras Hindu University. I should mention with gratitude the always helpful encouragement and critical insight of my friend, Vijay Kumar, I. G. Agra. Likewise I am greatly benefitted by my friends Dr. Sushil Kumar Awasthi, Nagar Sawasthya Adhikari, Azamgarh, who is also a Hindi poet and satirist and Dr. R. P. Singh, Joint Director, (P M S) Azamgarh. My due and deep acknowledgment is also to the publisher, Mr. Harish Chandra Yadav, a meticulous person, who took a keen and enthusiastic interest in publishing this book. I cannot but express my feelings to my younger brothers— Yasin Khan and Amin Khan who bore pain in composing and providing me with technical facility to send the book to the publisher in time. I also record my gratefulness to the critics and scholars whose views have been quoted and commented upon this book. Lastly, the loving support of my wife, N. Tasneem, and my sons—Reyan Munir and Zaryab Munir—who kept me most of the time free from the burden of the family, made this book possible.

Munir
Shibli National College
Azamgarh (U P)
India

Contents

1

Precursors to the New Criticism

I

At the turn of the twentieth century, on both sides of the Atlantic, literary criticism was in a very sad state of affairs. Engulfed in chaos and confusion, it had gone down to very low ebb. Literary works, after the explosion of the new theories of physical and social sciences, were chiefly studied in terms of historical, philosophical, biographical, psychological, and social purposes. We, therefore, witness multifarious approaches of criticism—philosophical, historical, impressionistic, academic, periodical, and textual—overlapping one another. It is quite clear that the ideas or contents ingrained in the literary works were of main consideration of study, not the characteristics which contribute to the composition of a literary work. In fact, all kinds of criticism distracted the reader from the literary work, the poem itself. Moreover, critics were perhaps not aware that literary discourse is quite different from other types of discourse such as physical or social sciences. It is the New Critics who highlight the difference between the language of poetry and that of science. They focus their earnest attention on the complexity, organic unity, autonomy, and the cognitive status of poetry, rejecting all the approaches of criticism which overlook the artistic values of a work. This book is mainly an introduction to the New Criticism, which thrived in America between 1930s and 1960s, but its favourable path is paved in England during the 1920s. Some of the seminal features of this critical movement find their genesis in the literary criticism of these intellectuals—T.E. Hulme, Ezra Pound, T. S. Eliot, I. A. Richards, F. R. Leavis, and William Empson. They create an intellectual climate, unchain art from unliterary tendencies, and give a new shape to English and American thinking about literature. I am, therefore, constrained to deal with their views and principles before plunging headlong into the New Criticism. These critics deserve to get their full share of attention in this chapter.

II

In the opening decades of the twentieth century, a plethora of critical approaches made the whole of the critical canvas nebulous and flustered. Eliot observed that "the twentieth century is still the nineteenth century."[1] It was unsystematic, muddle-headed, and blind to the literary worth and excellence. It was characterized by partiality, fixed ideas, cultivated taste, bigotry, prejudices, eccentricities, and personal likings and dislikings. The critics would indulge in virulent and vicious fault-findings. Most of them were unknown, irresponsible, and non-literary. There was nothing like pure criticism in the Victorian era, as politics, economics, science, history, religion, passion for social reform, interests in other arts—all jumbled together with literary criticism. They were detriment to it. No objective or scientific method was formulated to judge a work of art. Eliot rightly discovers in "The Function of Criticism":

> Criticism...is no better than a Sunday Park of contending and contentious orators, who have not even arrived at the articulation of their differences. [2]

In this cloudy environment of criticism, Darwin, Marx, Frazer, and Freud revolutionized the system of thought about man and society. These heroes shook the very foundation of the "genteel tradition" changing the whole approach and forming the basic assumption of modernist criticism. With the scientific discoveries and explosion of knowledge, the introduction of new ideologies, the twentieth century created a violent tremor of interrogations that fractured almost all the existing values—socio-economic, political, religious, and literary. The new era yielded a concept of a new man—complex and bewildered—and manifested "a symptom of change in modern art." The whole of the contemporary poetic landscape—dull, flimsy, and hazy—compelled the modernists to think deeply over the new aesthetic of poetry. They had in common a furious contempt for this debased poetic state. Imbued with the spirit of modernism, a group of powerful critics—T. E. Hulme, Ezra Pound, T. S. Eliot, I. A. Richards, F. R. Leavis, and William Empson—emerged with their objective and scientific theories. They headed for a new direction in a sharp disagreement with the preceding and existing schools of criticism. They also changed the direction of criticism on the other side of the Atlantic. That is why the New Criticism was deeply indebted to these English critics. In their hands, the literary criticism became more a science than an art, because the development of new ideologies of psychology, anthropology, linguistics, sociology, economics, and politics left a tremendous effect on the critical approach, magnifying its scope.

The scientific civilization surcharged with a new intellectual outlook posed a challenge to both the poet and the critic. Now the poem became more important than the poet. Therefore, in the realm of criticism, the main focus shifted from the poet to the poem. The job of the poet became more exacting and demanding. Against the Georgian prolixity, he cultivated very precise and concrete methods to portray his emotions and experiences through imagism and symbolism. Similarly, "criticism turned away from pleasure principle and resumed a scholarly habit as in the case of T. S. Eliot or as in the case of I. A. Richards".[3] They wielded a tool of the analytical method against the biographical and impressionistic criticism. Stanley Edgar Hyman aptly remarks:

> Modern criticism could be defined … as the organized use of non-literary techniques and bodies of knowledge to obtain insights into literature…. Modern criticism does a number of things that criticism has always done: interpreting the work, relating it to a literary tradition, evaluating, and so on….[4]

Poetry leveled with a general charge of being an imaginary literature without having any relevance to practical life has been bearing biting remarks from many directions almost all the time. But during the nineteenth century onward, with the extraordinary growth of the physical sciences, it finds itself standing at a crucial crossroad facing special challenges as to what the truth and value of poetry is in the modern era. It is now valued from utilitarian perspective. It has to exist independently of its creator, and justify its own merits, as an end in itself and as a means. Thomas Love Peacock comments the position of poet and poetry very ruthlessly. To him a poet is "a semi-barbarian in a civilized community." He "lives in the days that are past." Peacock furthermore remarks that poetry is "the mental rattle" and "the jingle of silver bells." It is ridiculous to say that poetry gives insight into the mysteries of the universe. He interrogates very rationally the validity, existence, and future of poetry in the face of stiff competition of modern scientific knowledge. It, therefore, becomes inevitable to respond to the temperature of the time to verify the validity and utility of poetry. Modernist poetic theories stem from the demands of such modern scientific truth, investigation, inquiry, and discovery of reality. Rejecting the views of traditional rhetorical theorists, they hold that they are only a collection of set rules for communication, which is supposed to be extraneous for the twentieth century. In *The Philosophy of Rhetoric*, Richards writes that the study of rhetoric should be "a philosophic inquiry into how words work in discourse."

In the Victorian age, Matthew Arnold also gets confronted with the religious predicament caused by the Darwinian theory of evolution and technological development. Religion is put to scrutiny and facts. Disillusioned, Arnold seeks to find value and meaning in poetry. But his theoretical canon is of general nature; it is least concerned with the creative process of poetry and its operation on the mind. Inspired by Arnold, Richards and others accept the challenge of Love Peacock and justify precisely the relevance and purpose of poetry in life, testing it on the touchstone of the scientific truth. To achieve this end, they seek the help of modern science itself to analyze the exact nature and function of poetry. Richards wields the tools of psychological scientism to examine as to what actually goes on in a poem and how it affects the mind of the reader. In this respect, Richards is more theoretical and analytical than Arnold.

In such a utilitarian civilization, it was unreasonable and anachronistic to overlook intellect and rationality and lay emphasis only on feeling. Eliot boldly faced this trial and pleaded the utility of poetry in new contexts. He proves that poetry does not lack logic at all. The poet examines, evaluates, and chooses with care 'the significant emotions' which he wants to shape into poetry. Before the poem takes its shape, it exists only in imagination. Before putting forth his ideas and feelings into verbal patterns, the poet has to struggle with not only appropriate experience but also with appropriate expression. It is difficult for those who believe in the theory of inspiration to imagine how much labour is involved in shaping a poem. The poet wrestles with every word lest he should miss the nuances of its meanings and musical possibilities. Through constant practice and experience only comes control over language. He sweats to find an adequate idiom for mature and significant thoughts and feelings. In "Function of Criticism" Eliot holds that a poet's critical acumen is more developed than his creativity, since he is the first listener of his own poetry. If his critical sense is not sharp, he will not be able to produce art. This is why Eliot called his study room 'a workshop' where he manufactured his poetry and said that the greatest contribution of Ezra Pound to the contemporary poetry was his stress on conscious training that a poet was unavoidably supposed to undergo. Therefore, while writing poetry neither does he discard his mind, nor does he put aside his heart while creating criticism. Thought and feeling are inseparably related and are the obverse and reverse of the same personality.

The modernist criticism is not based on character interpretation as done by Coleridge and Goethe (according to Eliot in "Hamlet and His Problems") nor the feeling nor the content nor the message conveyed by the work. It is also not concerned with the interpretation between the work of art, its creator, and its reader. Much of the endeavour of the modernist criticism from 1920s through1950s was to deal with the structure, organic unity, meaning, and the language of the work itself, particularly how the language works in a piece of work. Cleanth Brooks holds that the modernist criticism is a part of "the general intensification of the study of language and symbolism."[5] Dissatisfied with the impressionistic criticism, the Victorian morality, the inadequacy of the aesthetics of the nineties and the vagueness and wooliness of the Edwardian and the Georgian poets and critics, the modernist critics rejected their metaphor, poetic idiom, timid approach and the evasive attitude. Their aim was to develop an adequate and contemporary idiom and a theory of living criticism that would not only stand the test of veracity and maturity but would also supplement their attempts of forming a new taste in poetry. So they began to redefine the poem, the poetic process, emotion, the place of thought and action in a work of art; and criticism, its nature, aims, forms, scope in a changed literary, intellectual, and cultural context. This critical tendency is sown by T. E. Hulme, Ezra Pound, T. S. Eliot, I. A. Richards, and William Empson. They opened a new vista of critical activity broadening the horizons of the analytical understanding of literary works.

III

It is Thomas Ernest Hulme (1883-1917), a robust individual, philosopher, aesthetic theorist, soldier, and imagist poet, who develops characteristically a pugnacious proclivity to intellectual debate. With his rowdy behaviour, argumentative nature, and tough-minded attitude, he exerts a deep and direct influence on the eminent London modernists— Wyndham Lewis, Ezra Pound, and T.S. Eliot—in the early years of the twentieth century. His reputation largely depends upon the foundation of imagist poetry with its strong contempt for romanticism and earnest advocacy for hard, clear, particular, and visual images. One of the first critics to write about modern painting and sculpture, Hulme makes a prophecy of a hard-edged geometric art of Pablo Picasso and Wyndham Lewis as a potential expression of the new art in opposition to the Romantic formlessness of impressionism.

T.E. Hulme, "the key thinker behind the Pound-Eliot revolution in English poetry,"[6] gets extremely fed up with the ideas and nature and function of romantic poetry and rejects that poetry is akin to religion. With his meager output, a volume of critical essays entitled *Speculations* (1924) edited by his friend, Herbert Read, he exercises a paramount influence on the development of the new poetic aesthetic, and prepares a ground for the New Criticism, too. Hulme discards romantic sentimental poetry, exposing its inadequacies and shortcomings. He discovers that the wonder of romanticism has come to an end, because its tools have got rickety to express the complex modern sensibility. Influenced by the French Symbolists, the ancient Greek lyrics, Chinese poetry, Japanese *Haiku* and *Tanka*, the modernist painting and sculpture, and the Bergsonian philosophy, Hulme advocates and prophesies a new convention, a new attitude, and a new kind of poetry with an infallible method and an accurate poetic idiom. He calls for a more subtle and sophisticated technique for the clarity of expression. Hulme strengthens Imagism and Voriticism by insisting on a concrete style and formulating a new taste for verse.

Hulme's critical essay "Romanticism and Classicism," a kind of a manifesto of his poetic theory, "has assumed the status of sign-post to a literary revolution."[7] It reveals that his poetic tenets are based on the theory of knowledge, fancy, tradition and organization, and rejects the spirit of emotion, inspiration, imagination, and humanism in verse. He provides an aesthetic basis to verse by introducing the two terms "classicism" and "romanticism" and interprets them in the light of his dogmatic 'antihumanism,' the French Revolution, the philosophies of Rousseau, Weltanschauung, and Kant and the theories of Darwin and De Varies. Hulme traces the basis of romantic taste back to the Renaissance and the humanist tradition which bank upon the false premises such as the sentimental viewpoint that human beings are without fundamental limitations and imperfections. The Renaissance rejects the medieval order of life and ethical values and substitutes anthropocentric values instead. This substitution starts a wrong conception about the values in arts, religion, economy, and the whole range of human activities. Hulme's definition of romanticism is liberty—the liberty of man. This ferment about the ideas of liberty created mad enthusiasm. Though a positive virtue, it degenerated into "a good solid practical war-cry"—the French Revolution. Hulme considers it "so essentially negative a thing." Rousseau is held responsible for inculcation of this principle or concept of man in the French who, overlaid with the ferment of human rights and liberty, make the revolution practically 'a new religion.' He teaches that man is basically good when he comes from the hands of the author of nature but degenerates in the hands of man. It is bad laws and customs that have enfeebled him. If this "oppressive order" is destroyed, there are immense possibilities of his potential and progress. The root of all romanticism is that man is "an infinite reservoir of possibilities." This romantic concept of man is more reinforced with the evolutionary theory of Charles Darwin. Its hypothesis is that "new species came into existence by the cumulative effect of small variations—this seems to admit the possibility of future progress" (p.94). To Hulme classicism is quite contrary to the concept of romanticism. He postulates his creed in *Speculations*:

> A man is essentially bad, he can only accomplish anything of value by discipline—ethical and political. Order is thus not merely negative but creative and liberating, Institutions are necessary.[8]

With its pre-Renaissance philosophy and a dogmatic Christian pessimism about the imperfectability of man, classicism sees man as an extraordinarily fixed and limited being whose nature is absolutely constant. It is only by tradition and organization that anything decent can be got out of it. Man is never exaggerated, "man is always man and never a god."[9] In the classical attitude man is always faithful to the conception of a limit, because he knows that he can never "go blindly into an atmosphere more than the truth, an atmosphere too rarefied for man to breathe for long"(p.96). Hulme also keeps up his classical view with the scientific backing of De Varies's mutation theory. It tells that each new species comes into existence, not by the accumulation of small step, but suddenly in a jump, a kind of sport, and that once in existence it remains absolutely fixed.

Hulme further identifies his classicism with the normal religious attitude—the Christian dogma of Original Sin—the nub of human predicament. Man is imperfect, limited, weak and finite, whereas God is perfect and infinite. Wyndham Lewis is very pertinent when he says, "no one thinks of Hulme without thinking of an original sin."[10] It is the belief in the Deity that man's nature is fixed. The fixed human nature means appetite, the instinct of sex and all other fixed qualities. When these natural instincts are suppressed, they burst out in some abnormal instincts. Similarly, when man's religious instincts, under the influence of rationalism, are suppressed he gets perverted into an agnostic. And he starts thinking man a god and believing in heaven on earth. This very concept forms the spirit of romanticism. It dislodges all concepts that are placed in their own right and proper parameters. They are messed up, falsified, and scattered, and the whole clear-cut ideas or facts of human experience get blurred. "It is like pouring out a pot of treacle over the dinner table" (p.95). Thus, the best definition of romanticism, as Hulme assumes, is "spilt religion." To the romantic "man's nature is like a well" and "a reservoir full of possibilities," to the classic "like a bucket" and "a very finite and fixed creature." With these political, philosophical, scientific, and religious backings, Hulme wants to prove that man is finite and limited being. And beauty can be conceived in order, tradition, organization, and fancy. This is what the crux of classicism. The difference between romantic and classic is that between exuberance and restraint; the former "an awful disease," and the latter "a living thing."

These two attitudes and temperaments—classical and romantic—which are towards man and cosmos, are well reflected in English poetry. In the classical verse even the most imaginative flights there is always holding back, a reservation. The classical poet never forgets the limitedness of man. He always remembers that he is mixed with earth. He may jump, but always returns back. The aim of the classical verse is dry, hard, accurate, and definite description. On the other hand, the romantics always delight in some form of vagueness roaming in such a land where they come across a strange light—a light neither on land nor on sea. They crave for a beyond of something and express metaphors of flight. In place of accurate description in verse, the general tendency of the romantics is to pour out their unsatisfied emotions that are "grouped round the world infinite." They think that without sentiment verse cannot be written. Hulme has a perpetual fury to this damp romantic poetry: "I object to the sloppiness which does not consider that a poem is poem unless it is moaning or whining about something or other" (p.98). Thus, the effect of romanticism on them is that of 'drug.' Verse strictly confined to the earthly and the definite might seem to them "to be excellent writing, excellent craftsmanship, but not poetry." Romanticism has so much debauched that a classical revival means the prospect of an arid desert and the death of poetry. Eliot writes in the same vein in his "Dryden":

> The nineteenth century had...limited tastes and peculiar fashions; it... was unaware of its own limitations. Its tastes and fashions had no place for [the classicists.][11]

Hulme holds that it is a bad metaphysical aesthetic that the best verse should be serious and the act of judgment an instinct. The romantics influenced by the idealist theory of Kant define beauty or the nature of art by dragging always in the infinite. Romantic aesthetic collates all beauty to an impression of the infinite and claims the identification of human being in absolute spirit. Even in the smallest thing of a beauty they have a total intuition of the whole world. The romantics try to deduce their critical opinions from a fixed metaphysical principles i.e. the transcendentalist theory of inspiration. It is Germany where the metaphysical theories of aesthetics are first created, and a total intuition of the whole world is discovered even in the tiniest element of beauty. Every artist becomes a kind of pantheist. It is very topsy-turvy. The ultimate reality can be comprehended through knowledge—"the hurly-burly, the struggle" of life.

Hulme makes a clean sweep of "series of mixed and bastard phenomena" of the modern world such as "Romanticism in literature, Relativism in ethics, Idealism in philosophy, and Modernism in religion."[12] His emphasis is on dry and hard expression, a new role for fancy, beauty in finite things, the revival of the qualities of the eighteenth century verse, and the medieval concept of man and life. It was a new and different poetic neatly worked out. With these propositions Hulme presents various prescriptions concerning the attitude and style of the expected classical poetry. In matter of judgment of beauty, no artist can keep himself aloof from the traditional order. He is governed by the literary history that comes before him. No man is physically born as an abstract entity; he is a child of particular parents. His existence is known by them whom he is related with. Similarly, in matter of literary judgment no artist exists by himself. His value is judged when he is placed in the line of literary history. Eliot also holds the same view in "Tradition and Individual Talent":

> No poet, no artist of any art has his complete meaning alone. His significance, his appreciation is the appreciation of his relation to the dead poets and artists. You cannot value him alone; you must set him, for contrast and comparison, among the dead. I mean this as a principle of aesthetic, not merely historical, criticism.[13]

There are two theories—theory of image and theory of language, which issue forth from Hulme's "Romanticism and Classicism." His new theory of 'phonopeia' is based on a theory of knowledge rejecting theory of inspiration—an idealist theory of the universe. He tries to show that beauty can be conceived in definite and finite things. He remarks: "It is essential to prove that beauty may be in small, dry things" (p.101). Inspired by aesthetics of sculpture, he believes that poetic idea should not be expressed, stated or commented upon, but be suggested and presented through the use of hard, exact, concrete, clear, and concentrated images without the decorative and the didactic. It is an image, in Wyndham Lewis's phrase, which is the 'primary pigment' of poetry; and the poet who uses it is by that very fact differentiates from other men. The poet should embody his feelings in specific physical analogies that exactly convey his meaning. A doyen of the imagist group, Hulme wants to see everything in terms of an image. His "Above the Dock" reflects the use of exact efficient imagery:

> Above the quiet dock in midnight,
> Hangs the moon. What seemed so far away
> Tangled in the tall mast's corded height,
> Is but a child's balloon, forgotten after play.[14]

A vital change or excellence in poetry depends on the ruthless rejection of the traditional poetic values. His most notable poem, "Autumn," no doubt, exhibits his new style—fresh, forceful, direct, and braided with new metaphors. It presents a self-contained depiction of a single event by means of sustained metaphor without explanation and commentary. "Autumn" exemplifies his theory in practice:

> A touch of cold in the Autumn night—
> I walked abroad,
> And saw the ruddy moon lean over a hedge
> Like a red-faced farmer.
> I did not stop to speak, but nodded,
> And round about were the fistful stars
> With white faces like town children.

This seven-line poem presents a vivid picture with a great accuracy, simplicity, and directness, shorn of all romantic ornamentation, vagueness, and abstraction. In his short poem, "The Sunset," there is a single metaphor that expresses the equation: the sun is a ballet dancer. This metaphor is elaborated or extended to capture the moment when the sun finally tips over the horizon, giving a graphic snapshot of the sunset. So, the sun is seen to linger on the horizon's stage, showing off her skill. Clouds reddened by the sun's final beams are likened to the dancer's fine costume. Such condensed and concentrated lyrics written under the influence of the imagist movement reminds the Japanese Haiku: [15]

> A crow is perched
> Upon a leafless withered bough—
> The autumn dusk.[16]

There are two main things required for such "cheerful, dry and sophisticated" classical poetry. First, the artist has to develop the particular faculty of mind to see things as they are, freeing himself from the conventional manners and attitudes in which he has been trained to see them. Though it is in itself very difficult in all consciousness. Secondly, the concentrated state of mind in the actual expression of what he sees. If an artist cherishes this sincerity, he can achieve a sufficient justification for poetry and the aesthetic pleasure. An artist has to attain a keen interest in a thing—"an intense zest which heightens a thing out of the level of prose" (p.102). Contemplation means a detached interest, not identification with the absolute spirit. The artist remains in an actual physical state when he contemplates the nature of language and technique. In this way, the poetic aesthetic can be externally detected.

The language an artist can use in verse is that of analogy. He has no material clay to mould to the given shape. The only thing which he has for the purpose, a kind of mental clay that produces certain metaphors modified into theories of aesthetic and rhetoric. The analogy is every bit of it necessary for accurate description in verse. Analogy requires fancy; though it is inferior to imagination, yet it does not mean that it is not serious in the effect it produces. If it is sincere in its accurate sense, the whole of the analogy is necessary to get out the exact curve of feeling or thing he wants to express. At that time he has the 'highest verse.'

The language of poetry is a 'visual concrete one' that suggests hard to avoid the language of prose. The poetic language "hands over sensations bodily" and always makes one see the plastic images—

solid, concise, and clear. It prevents from gliding through an abstract process. "Visual meanings can only be transferred by the new bowl of metaphor; prose is an old pot that lets them leak out" (p.102). Poetry chooses fresh epithets and fresh metaphors because worn out epithets and metaphors "cease to convey a physical thing and become abstract counters" (p.102). Images in verse are not mere decoration, but the very essence of an intuitive language.

To achieve an accurate and definite image, an artist has to wrestle terrifically with language. He searches for infallible words to depict the thing, because plain language is always unconvincing and inaccurate to express exactly what one feels, thinks, or perceives. Real communication is rare. Hulme remarks:

> ...language is by its very nature a communal thing; that is it expresses never the exact thing but a compromise—that which is common to you, me and everybody. But each man sees, a little differently, and to get out clearly and exactly what he does see he must have a terrific struggle with language, whether it be words or the technique of other arts. Language has its own special nature, its own conventions and communal ideas. It is only by a concentrated effort of the mind that you can hold it fixed to your own purpose (p.101).

Avoiding the conventional language of prose, the poet flounders about in a series of metaphors in order to enliven it and delineate the exact curve of idea, and the exact curve of emotion. It is the nature of language and technique which determines the highest quality of verse. In poetry, subject matter, intensity and kind of emotion produced is not as important as the visual objects which delight the reader. Any subject matter may be taken up for treatment. "It does not matter if it were a lady's shoe or the starry heavens" (p.103). A poet's main concern should be with his craft severed form religion and morality.

Advocating suitability and appropriateness of French *vers libre*, Hulme points out metaphorically: "To put the modern conception of the poetic spirit... into regular metre is like putting a child into armour."[17] Gustave Kahn explains that the free verse refuses the regular number of syllable. "The length of the line is long and short, oscillating with the images used by the poet; it follows the contours of his thought and is free rather than regular." Hulme concludes with a call to arms:

> ...a shell is very suitable covering for the egg of a certain period of its career, but very unsuitable at later age. This seems to me to represent fairly well the state of verse at the present time... [It] has become alive, it has changed from the ancient art of chanting to the modern impressionist, but the mechanism of verse has remained the same. It can't go on doing so. I will conclude... the shell must be broken.[18]

Hulme rejects the mechanical complexity and believes in the vital or organic complexity. The former is product of intellect while the latter of the supra-rational or intuition. The mechanical complexity has an analytical approach, and can only make diagrams; and diagrams are essentially things whose parts are separate one from another. The organic complexity is a metaphor. With an intense zest, the poet seizes and combines at the same times all the important ideas of its poem or picture. The organic complexity is of different kind; in it the parts cannot be said to be elements because each one is modified by other's presence and each one to a certain extent is the whole. For example, the leg of a chair is by itself a leg but a human leg by itself would not be. Hulme presents an appropriate and interesting analogy of the vital complexity in the following words:" ...the motion of a snake's body goes through all parts at once and its volition acts at the same instant in coils which go contrary ways"(p.104). The whole process (the original feeling expressed through a bowl of fresh and new metaphor) envisages another theory of language—'intensive manifold.' It is based on the central philosophy of Bergson, who calls the vital complexity 'intensive' and the mechanical complexity 'extensive.' The fact is that the intellect can deal with the extensive multiplicity and intuitions with the intensive, producing a new organic metaphor.

Hulme imbibes inspiration from Ayn Rand, George Sorel, David Bomberg, Gaudier Brezeska, Jacob Epstein, and Welhelm Worringer. They all are a guiding force to prepare his critical mental make-up. Like Eliot, Hulme believes in cyclical pattern of history, and is assured that any tradition or convention in art cannot last for a long time. The nature of a particular attitude in art is like the course of human life. It is bound to change like organic life. "It grows old and decays. It has a definite period of life and must die. All the possible tunes get played on it and then it is exhausted; moreover its best period is its youngest" (p.96). It is very well reflected in the astounding poetic flowering in the Elizabethan period. A new medium, namely, blank verse, is introduced to play with. "It was new so it was easy to play new tunes on it". (p.96) But with the passage of time it got drained and enfeebled because "Each field of artistic activity is exhausted by the first great artist who gathers a full harvest from it" (p.97). Naturally, the spirit and period of romanticism is badly used-up and "it is the business of every honest man to clean the world of these sloppy dregs of the Renaissance." A new technique, or new convention or another classical revival is required for new efflorescence of poetry. But the classical revival does not mean, Hulme warns, the anticipation of a return to Pope. For Hulme, and even Eliot, the words 'romantic' and 'classic' are very pliable. They represent, Hulme tells, five or six different kinds of antithesis, but he uses them in a "perfectly precise and limited sense." He could have concocted a couple of new words, but they were then very much in vogue in literary circles. For Hulme, new classical verse simply is to be based on the theory of image, fancy, and organic complexity.

Hulme discards liberal individualism, infinitude, mystery, emotion, and loose and facile texture of romantic poetry. He has no belief in the Arnoldian view of 'high seriousness' in poetry dealing with specific subject matter. He pleads that the essence and excellence of verse lie in fancy and free verse rather than in conventional metrical forms. The poet has to deal with fleeting and fragmentary impressions, which cannot be transcribed in smooth regular verse. The poetic aesthetic is possible by being only classical. Hulme calls for simplicity and directness but with subtlety of suggestion, a tendency to understatement, avoidance of sentimentality, close and careful organization, tradition and order, architectonic balance of composition, musicality, and conformity to certain fixed standard forms. Hulme, a pioneer and one of the flag bearers of modernism, holds a secured place, not so much for his own poetic output, but for his catalyzing influence upon the radical innovators and the imagist poets—Ezra Pound, T. S. Eliot, H.D., F. S. Flint etc.

IV

Ezra Pound (1855-1972), "an iconoclastic poet," "a solitary volcano," is perhaps more than any other single man responsible for the emergence of an authentically modernist literature in England and America of his time. With his perpetual enterprise in artistic revolution, he creates some of modern poetry's most enduring and inventive techniques. He has always been committed to a sheer integrity of craft. F. R. Leavis writes: "he (Pound) is in the most serious sense of the word, an aesthete." Pound, like T. S. Eliot, wants a modernism that brings back to life the highest standard of the past. His constant reading of the past in English and Romance literatures, his early contact with Europe, and meetings with the contemporary European writers lead him to range widely through the verse of half a dozen languages—Latin, Greek, French, Italian, Spanish, Provencal, Anglo-Saxon, Chinese and Japanese *haiku* and *Tanka.* In search of his own tentative skills and laconic precision, he has been defining and promoting a modernist aesthetic in poetry. Almost from the beginning, Pound has a deep desire to build a mastery of his craft accompanied by a vision of the social usefulness, considering a poet as a "guide and lamp of civilization." The greatest works of every accessible tradition define his craft. He endeavours to resuscitate the "dead art" of poetry and "make it new" by stylistic experimentation. Early in his career, Pound turns away from Victorian verse, which seems to him too rhetorical, too much given to generalization, and too moralistic. Experimenting in imitation of Browning, Yeats, and the verse of the English decadents, Pound, inspired by T. E. Hulme, Ford Madox Ford, Wyndham Lewis, and Henry Gaudier-Brezeska, and Henry Bergson, has been modernizing his style to shape his language and poems with a craftsman's zeal. He speaks a style and seeks a symbolic language capable of expressing the values, which were beginning to cohere for him. In his drier intellectual air "as clear as metal," Pound's verse takes on new qualities of economy, brevity, clarity, and having the density of masses of sculptures. Discarding the descriptive mode of verse, he uses concrete details and exact visual images to compare concentrated moments of experience.

According to Ezra Pound, the conception of poetry is a 'pure art,' a serious work, and a result of a long contemplation. Pound assumes that previously poetry has been merely the vehicle for transmitting thoughts. It was a wrong conception. Poetry demands knowledge of technique—technique of surface and technique of content. The technique of an artist reveals his sincerity; the more he is sincere, the more his work gets refined and sophisticated. The mastery of poetry is a gradual long process of a life-time—not a pastime. Pound thinks that the present state of chaos in poetry is because it was not inculcated in mind that after a long struggle would poetry attain such a degree of development or modernity. So any sensible man cannot be deceived by a 'mediocre-verse.'

However, Pound is not a student of philosophy and therefore his criticism is not a systematic treatise but is in the form of letters, and practical advice to other writers. His "most vigorous and most influential criticism is ad hoc and occasional.... Pound has not aspired to system-building...."[19]Pound's reaction to the existing English poetry is sharper than that of T. E. Hulme. Pound looks back on the nineteenth century poetry as 'blurry,' 'messy,' 'sentimentalistic,' 'mannerish,' and 'poppy-cock' full of 'rhetorical din and luxurious riot.' He seeks a new precision and explicitness in rendering in nature and emotion in W. B. Yeats, because Pound considers: "Yeats knew more about poetry than anybody else."

> Mr. Yeats has once and for all stripped English poetry of its pardonable rhetoric. He has boiled away all that is not poetic—he has made our poetic idiom a thing pliable, a speech without inversions.[20]

The sad state of writing, absence of a suitable poetic idiom, crisscross of literary and cultural values, the helplessness of Britons in a situation which offer no promise or direction, shock the abject passivity of the Edwardians. Pound finds that Wordsworth and Coleridge or Tennyson and Arnold, too, could serve no purpose. Milton with his "noise tradition" has aggravated the dissociative process and thus could not be taken as a reliable guide. Pound describes him as "a thoroughgoing decadent in the worst sense of the term."[21] His language is

> ...a dialect which imitates the idiom of the ancients rather than seeking their meaning, a state of mind which aims at 'teaching the boy his Latin' or Greek or whatever it may be,

> but has long since ceased to care for the beauty of the original; or which perhaps thinks 'appreciation obligatory,' and the meaning mere eccessories.[22]

Pound further describes Milton and Virgil as "concerned with decorations and trappings, and they muck about the moral."[23] The Latinism of English is a wrong practice on Milton's part, and 'blight' influence on others, as Pound notes:

> Not only does such usage—with remnants of Latin order-ruin the word order in English, but it shows a fundamental miscomprehension of the organism of the language, and fundamental stupidity of this kind is bound to spread effects through the whole fibre of a man's writing.[24]

It is obvious that in an age that had dethroned the ideal of the "sublime," the literary direction could be given by some novel aesthetic only—a fresh language and true perception on nature. Like Hulme, Pound also predicts that the poetry of the next decades will be based on new methods and innovative skill. "It will be harder and saner, it will be...'nearer the bone.' It will be as much like granite as it can be, its force will lie in its truth, its interpretative power...we will have fewer painted adjectives impeding the shock and stroke of it....I want it so, austere, direct, free from emotional slither" (p.66). So Pound wrote in 1971 in *A Retrospect*, repeating that he had first published in *The Poetry Review* in 1913. He declares:

> Poetry is a sort of inspired mathematics, which gives us equation, not for abstract figures—triangles, spheres, and the like, but equations for the human emotions.[25]

On this basis Pound in collaboration with Richard Aldington and Hilda Doolittle propounds imagist theory holding that poetry is the highest of arts. His bold theories and poetic experiments set the fashion of modernism.

1. Direct treatment of the thing whether subjective or objective.
2. To use absolutely no word that does not contribute to the presentation.
3. As regarding rhythm: to compose in the sequence of the musical phrase, not in sequence of metronome (58).

Pound makes out that these "three simple presentations will throw out nine-tenths of all bad poetry now accepted as standard and classical: and will prevent you from many a crime of production" (62), as committed by Walt Whitman—"an exceedingly nauseating pill."

Pound hates abstraction. With his great fascination for the concrete particularity of the Chinese ideogram, he wants to write everything in a concrete and clear manner, deeply influenced by Ernest Fenellosa's *Chinese Written Character as a Medium for Poetry.* He has been called the 'inventor' of Chinese poetry of our time. Brooks remarks that "the Chinese ideogram provided Pound with a screen upon which to make a vivid projection of his ideal for a poetic language."[26] Influenced by the Japanese *haiku* and *tanka,* he upholds that the proper and perfect symbol is the natural object to present in a concrete style, but the symbolic function must not dominate poem so much that it should exclude all other possible readings –including the literal. So "a sense, and the poetic quality of the passage, is not lost to those who do not understand the symbol as such, to whom, for instance, a hawk is a hawk" (p.63). In addition there should not be any intermingling of an abstraction with the concrete. Such an expression as 'dim lands of peace' should not be used because it enfeebles the image.

Pound's emphasis on image is so much that, it seems, without it poetry cannot be written. That is why he says: "It is better to present one image in a lifetime than to produce voluminous works" (p.59). He defines that

> 'An Image' is that which presents an intellectual and emotional complex in an instant of time....It is the presentation of such a 'Complex' instantaneously which gives that sense of sudden liberation; that sense of freedom from time limits and space limits; that sense of sudden growth, which we experience in the presence of the greatest works of art (p.59).

The properly chosen image must communicate intellectual meaning as well as emotional force, and it must do so instantaneously, and in a highly condensed way. Pound understands the image to be complex, which might be received with a yearning to transcend the limits of the mundane world. And thus the image attains a vision of unearthly beauty.

Imagery is not visual only. Even visual images are not to be looked for exclusively in descriptive poetry, and a few who have attempted to write 'imagist' or physical poetry have succeeded in restricting themselves to the pictures of the external world. Ezra Pound defines the image not as a pictorial representation but a 'unification of disparate ideas.' The imagist credo also asserted: "we believe that poetry should render particulars exactly and not deal in vague generalities, however...sonorous." Middleton Murry, who thinks of 'simile' and 'metaphor' as associated with the formal classification of rhetoric, advises the use of image as a term to include both, but warns that one should never think that the image is solely or even predominantly visual. The "image may be visual, may be auditory" or "may be wholly psychological."[27]

The greatest misunderstanding of imagism, by readers as well as by poets who quickly began to imitate it, is that it demands visual images to the virtual exclusion of everything else. For Pound, however, imagism means the achievement of a precise, economical verbal equation and idea. Though he often uses visual image, the image is not a picture, but a structure of words. In his three initial rules, he asks for a rhythm free of artificial constraints, a ruthless pruning of all unnecessary words, and "direct treatment is far more flexible and subtle than some of his imitators understand."

Pound is recognized as a formidable critic. Along with his essays outlining imagist tenets and Chinese poetic technique, Pound contributes three concepts to literary criticism: melopoeia, phonopoeia, and logopoeia. Each of these terms isolates a method by which poetry imbues language with significance. In melopoeia, meaning is conveyed by the musical qualities of word; phonopoeia is the "casting of image upon the visual imagination." And logopoeia is described by Pound as the dance of intellect among words." The last term is voriticism. He believes the image to be "a vortex, from which, through which, and into which, ideas are constantly rushing." By 1914 Pound perceived limitations inherent in imagism and disparagingly termed the movement "Amygism" after Amy Lowell, the editor of several subsequent Imagist anthologies. He believed in her but she devalued the term to connote only free verse. With sculptor, painter, and writer Wyndham Lewis and sculptor Henri Gaudier Brezaska, Pound creates voriticism, a dynamic amalgamation of visual and literary arts.

Pound is interested in how the world can be known through images that fuse and focus the enormous complexities of external object and internal emotion. He says that an image "is more than an idea. It is a vortex or cluster of fused ideas and is endowed with energy."[28] Vortex is a process by which the indefinite variety of experience might be known concretely. There is continuity in Pound's thought which critics have sometimes tended to obscure with their descriptions of periods—preimagist, imagist, voriticist—which are not as distinct as they appear. The conceptual theories of Pound's voriticist period are less a departure from the previous thought than they are an elaboration and refinement.

Pound calls for a crystallized form of prose. In a letter to Harriet Monroe, he writes: "Poetry must be as well written as prose." There should not be any unnecessary ornamentation or any otiose word in a good poem; every word must have meaning and proper function in it. He says: "use no superfluous word, no adjective which does not reveal something" (p.60). Both contents and expression are complements with each other. "Form is expressive of meaning: ideally, form is meaning."[29] Unlike the vague and indefinite poetry of romantic school, an ideal poetry has simplicity, economy, and hardness of good prose:

> There must be no book words, no periphrase, no inversions. It must be as simple as De Maupassant's best prose, and as hard as Stenhal's.... It can't be merely a careless dash off, with no grip and no real hold to the words and sense....There must be no cliché's set phrase, stereotyped journalese. The only escape from such is by precision, a result of concentrated attention to what (one) is writing.... Objectivity and again objectivity and expression: hindside—beforeness, no straddled adjectives ("as addled mosses dark") no Tennysonianess of speech; nothing—nothing that you couldn't, in some circumstances, in the stress of some emotior, actually say.[30]

To Pound, the entire question of language is a matter of technique, involving the considerations of rhyme, meaning, syntax, and the introduction of the conversational tone. Perpetually concerned with the power of language, Pound compares it with modern sculpture.

Pound writes: "Great literature is simply language charged with meaning to the utmost possible degree."[31] He discovers the unavoidable fact that language is constantly changing, and that poet must change with it. "Neither can anyone learn English, one can only learn a series of Englishes. Rosetti made his own language. I hadn't in 1910 made a language, I don't mean a language to use, but even a language to think in."[32] The shape of language is not mere a fashion, but a part of how one thinks. To change the form of language is to change one fundamental way of knowing the world. The language should be precise, restrained creating an impression. Pound emphasizes the language of common speech, but always the exact word.

Pound calls for 'melopeia' or 'absolute rhythm' in poetry. "Rhythm must have meaning."[33] A rhythm must convey the exact meaning of the emotion or nuances of emotion expressed in poetry. The artist must interpret rhythm to reveal exactly the same idea and sense. In image Pound expresses the musical aspect, Hulme the visual. For Hulme word is a sign, and for Pound a musical curve. If an artist exercises his full sincerity rendering rhythm, his rhythm will be original, "uncounerfeiting, uncounterfeitable" (p.65). A poet should cultivate all those qualities which a good musician retains. Just as the latter is supposed to know harmony and counterpoint, and all the preliminary details of his craft, so the former should know assonance and alliteration, rhyme immediate and delayed, simple and polyphonic; and should master all known forms and system of metric.

Pound holds that *vers libre* has been used in a very loose manner, with certain shortcomings of its own. His campaign is directed against prolixity, verbosity, and flaccidity. The words are shoveled in to fill the metric pattern or to complete the noise of a rhymed sound. Sometimes Pound comes across a "marked meter in *vers libre,* as stale and hackneyed as any pseudo-Swinburnian, at times the writers seem to follow no musical structure whatever"(p.59). His interpretation of free verse is based on a musician's constant need, and erosion of rhyme. If it is used at all it must have in it some slight element of surprise to give pleasure. It should not be strange or curious. Pound is of opinion that a poet should use vers libre "only when the 'thing' builds up a rhythm more beautiful than that of set notes or more real, more a part of the emotion of the 'thing,' more germane, intimate, interpretative than the measure of regular accentual verse; a rhythm which discontents one with set iambic set anapaestic" (p.66). T. S. Eliot says: "no *vers* is *libre* for the man who wants to do a good job" (p.66).

Therefore, prose should not be chopped into separate iambs. Each line should not be made stop-dead at the end, and begin every line with a heave. The beginning of the next line should catch the rise of the rhythm unless a definite longish pause is needed. The music in the best verse is a sort of the residue of sound that lingers for a long time in the ear and functions like an "organ-base." Though Pound encourages rhythmical variation in modern poetry, yet the rhythmic structure should not destroy the shape of words or their natural sound, or their meaning. For a young artist, in the beginning, "it is very difficult to achieve a rhyme-structure because he gets trapped by all sorts of false stopping due to line ends and caesurae" (p.61).

Pound insists that a young poet has to practise his craft with the same discipline as the young musician gives to the study of harmony and counterpoint. A large number of people should be writing poetry, just as lots of people learn to play a tune or two on the piano. But publication is entirely different matter, because the art of poetry is the business of a lifetime and no one ever writes very much poetry that really matters. It should be kept in mind that an artist cannot deceive the reader for long. Therefore, he should be honest and sincere, following the way of the scientist rather than the way of an advertising agent for a new shop. Pound compares an artist with a scientist. A scientist never talks of himself nor wants to be a charming fellow personally. He shows his discovered thing after a long constant labour and learning. If he discovers something, he goes from that point onward. Similarly a poet should also keep on learning to create a lasting work.

In fact, Pound wants a theory of poetry based on the "non-discursive concetto," in which words would not discourse, and would present physically the experience or sensation bodily. Pound's analogy of poetry with music is given, again, for the reason that "in music it is all form and no-discourse." An artist should fill his mind with the finest cadences he can discover. But Pound further cautions: "It is not necessary that a poem should rely on its music, but if it does rely on its music that music must be such as will delight the expert" (p.60). However, Pound's experiments with rhythm are often considered the first substantial twentieth century effort to liberate poetry from iambic patterns.

According to Pound another remarkable point is that a vast number of subjects cannot be precise and therefore can be properly rendered in symmetrical forms. There are two types of content—'fluid' and 'solid.' Some poems may have as a tree has; some as water poured into a vase, though nothing is dull or poetic for verse. In the words of David Lodge, *A Retrospect* "conveys the flavour of Pound's thought and personality in his role as pundit and patron of modern poetry in the second decade of the century" (p.58). Really the essay is an epitome of Pound's poetic theory underlying rhyme, rhythm, *vers libre*, language, imagery, and subject matter. He emphasizes that poetry is a very serious work of art, and it is an artist who knows how difficult it is to write. Therefore, one should not pay any attention to the criticism of men who have never themselves a notable work. For Pound, criticism is a healthy process, not a set of prohibitions. It may "startle a dull reader into alertness" (p.59), and force to bring a change. He tries desperately to fulfill this motto with "a few pearls of unexpected wisdom," extending a sense of generosity to W. B. Yeats, Robert Frost, William Carlos Williams, Marianne Moore, H. D., James Joyce, Hemingway, and T. S. Eliot. That is why Pound is called the "poets' poet." Depreciating the common reader, he also argues that poetry is not "entertainment," but is a record of the poet's spiritual quest for transcendence and intellectual search for worldly wisdom.

V

T. S. Eliot, the creator of a new taste for reading and writing poetry, marks a watershed with his objective modus operandi in the history of English literature. Repudiating almost all established poetic canons, right from the sixteenth century with an exception to the Jacobean dramatists and the metaphysical school of poetry, he propounds his own principles and theories in the light of scientific temper. He does not attach any importance to the inspirational and pleasure-giving function of romantic school of poetry. As a conscious artist, he explores the scientific process of the creation of poetry, which demands exertion, labour, and sweat. The crux of his all theoretical views are outlined in his four famous essays—"Tradition and the Individual Talent" (1919), "The Metaphysical Poets" (1921), "Hamlet and His Problems" (1919), and "The Function of Criticism" (1923).

In "Tradition and the Individual Talent" Eliot objects to romantic subjectivism, freedom, and direct emotional expression, while laying emphasis on the poem rather than on the poet. He gives a slogan for objectivity, neither for originality nor for individuality, in poetry. He is sure that any distinctive original quality of an individual artist is already best dealt with or shown by his predecessors. He deduces that "the poem which is absolutely original is absolutely bad."[34] Eliot remarks:

> ...we shall find that not only the best, but the most individual parts of his work may be those in which the dead poets, his ancestors assert their immortality most vigorously. And I do not mean the impressionable period of adolescence, but the period of full maturity.[35]

Eliot topples down the Wordsworthian poetic theory that "poetry is a spontaneous overflow of powerful feelings" and aims at achieving impersonality or depersonalization in poetry. This characteristic is possible, he contends, through only the cultivation of tradition. Eliot tells that English people would always take out the meaning of tradition with negative overtone or sheer imitation, but his use of tradition fosters a positive and creative aspect of poetry. In "Tradition and the Individual Talent," he interprets these two terms—(i) tradition and (ii) the individual talent or individual artist—in his own way.

Eliot's concept of tradition is very agitating; it demands a great mental exercise to understand. First of all, tradition is never used in a narrow compass, e.g. just to imitate the past blindly. It is neither a mere collection of past practices, monuments, beliefs, standards nor a slavish inheritance to fixed rules and models of the past. Tradition has a broad spectrum. It is dynamic and living; it has an organic growth; it is a living current, continuity and developing from the past into the present and future. It is not inert or dead; it lives in the present. Tradition is based on regular give and take system. Eliot traces the concept of tradition in the writings of different writers and discusses in his writings at several places. In his early phase it refers to literary tradition, in later phase, its dimension gets widened and takes on the extra-literary complexion applying to several disciplines such as literature, culture, education, philosophy, and politics. In "What is Classic?" Eliot defines tradition as "the collective personality realized in the literature of the past." He believes that literary creativeness of the present or the individual artist depends upon the collective personality of the literature of the past or tradition. In his poetic creation the two pillars—objectivity and impersonality—are constructed on the pedestal of living tradition. And there is a direct interplay or dynamic relationship between tradition and the individual artist. Tradition is a paramount quality that plays a vital role in the creation of every new work of art. In this essay, Eliot defines 'tradition':

> Tradition is a matter of much wider significance. It cannot be inherited, and if you want it, you must obtain it by labour. It involves, in the first place, the historical sense, which we may call nearly indispensible to anyone who would continue to be a poet beyond his twenty-fifth year; and the historical sense involves a perception, not only of the pastnesss of the past, but of its presence; the historical sense compels a man to write not merely with his own generation in his bones, but with a feeling that the whole of the literature of Europe from Homer and within it the whole of the literature of his own country has a simultaneous existence and composes a simultaneous order. This historical sense, which is a sense of the timeless as well as of the temporal and the timeless and of the temporal together, is what makes a writer traditional. And it is at the same time what makes a writer most acutely conscious of his place in time, of his own contemporaneity.[36]

If we read the essay carefully, we notice that there are several features involved in Eliot's notion of tradition, which claim clear clarifications e.g. what is the historical sense? How tradition is living, dynamic, and organic? How does the historical sense create an ideal or simultaneous order and how does it create a sense of timeless and temporal together and separately? And how is tradition a two-way track? These are basic questions to be solved. In the first place, tradition never comes easily or automatically, it must be obtained by a good deal of toil and moil to become a poet in a true sense. Tradition entails the historical sense, which means a writer should have the knowledge of the past European literature from Homer down the present age. This knowledge or the feeling of the past literature should be functional and have its relation or relevance to the present. An individual artist should cultivate an awareness of the qualities of the 'living past'—an entire pattern of emotions, feelings, morals, forms, rhythms, and words; he should imbibe or assimilate these characteristics into his individual work. Eliot describes this special awareness and assimilation of the past as 'the creative eye':

> We need an eye which can see the past in its place with its definite differences from the present, and so lively that it shall be as present to us as the present. This is the creative eye.[37]

In this way, the present is modified by the past. Conversely, the past is also modified by the present when the past writer is interpreted, defined, and understood by the present state of knowledge of the individual artist. In this way, the past and the present become one unit; they cannot be separated. This process goes on and on changing and developing constantly and in this change and development, it is the very new work of art has to play its role.

The historical sense also involves that a poet should not only be well-saturated in the literature of the past but also generate in him the 'feeling' of the past. While living at the particular point of the present, he must feel the pulse of the past. To appreciate the literature of the past, he has to transport himself to that age and imagine, feel, and think like the writer of that age, but at the same time he has also to keep in mind his location and time where he happens to be living. There must be a simultaneous temporal sense of his own age and the age of the writer he happens to be reading. The divisions of time into present, past, and future are abolished and the poet achieves a sense of timelessness and at the same time temporality, too. This historical sense brings about a fusion of the past and the present in his sensibility and emphasizes that tradition is not like "a dead weight" or "a lifeless corpse."

The historical sense also reveals that the past literature should be considered as on 'organic whole,' not merely "collections of the writings of individuals." It creates a simultaneous order which is an organic whole. For Eliot tradition or the past means the whole and the individual work or present means the parts. The relationship between the past and the present or the whole and the parts is organic which is inextricably related to each other. Coleridge himself remarks: "Depend on it, whatever is grand, whatever is truly organic and living, the whole is prior to the parts."[38] Here let me clear the concept of the whole and the parts through an example of the human body. The human body is an organic whole and its limbs are the parts; both are equally important; they cannot be separated or amputated because both will get affected and deformed. The whole and the parts act and interact upon each other, but the whole, or human body, or tradition comes first, and the parts, or the limbs, or the individual work comes later. This is what Eliot wants to say that tradition gets galvanized with the introduction of a new work of arts. The whole is all the time readjusted or reordered whenever a new work of art arrives. Thus the whole or tradition forms an ideal order.

> What happens when a new work of art is created is something that happens simultaneously to all the works of art which preceded it. The existing monuments form an ideal order among themselves, which is modified by the introduction of the new (the really new) work of art among them. The existing order is complete before the new work arrives; for order to persist order after the supervention of novelty, the whole existing order must be ...altered; and so the relations, proportions, values of each work of art towards the whole are readjusted; and this is the conformity between the old and the new[39]

Eliot further admonishes that the cultivation of the historical sense is not a period of one or two year, but it is a life-long process. The important point is also to be kept in the mind that the shadow of the historical sense should not be reflected directly in the individual work. Eliot views the contemporary scene with a full consciousness of the past. A writer cannot be evaluated or appreciated in isolation, but he must be compared and contrasted with the past writer. This compare and contrast is essential for forming an idea of the real worth and significance of a new writer and his work. But he is not judged either to prove good or bad, worse or better than the past writer. Judgment means analysis and to know the facts of works. Eliot further points out that the relation of a poet to the past does not mean that he should know the past as a whole. But he must be familiar with the main literary currents and the significant parts of the works of the past.

The current of the past history of a poet's culture must guide his whole being, and monitor his private mind, which keeps itself away from indulging in the wayward fancies of the personal or subjective and whimsical outburst. The poet acknowledges the superiority and significance of tradition over the individual mind. Tradition paves a path for the formation as well as the restraint of the individual talent.

The other aspect of "the Impersonal theory of poetry" is the process of poetic creation and depersonalization of emotion. Eliot epitomizes his poetic creed in these words: "Poetry is not a turning loose of emotion, but an escape from emotion; it is not the expression of personality, but an escape from personality."[40] He is solely concerned with the poem not with the personality of the poet because "Honest criticism and sensitive appreciation are directed not upon the poet but upon the poetry."[41] When the poet's mind gets charged with tradition, he proceeds to create poetry. Eliot presents an analogy between the process of poetic creation and that of chemical reaction. When the two gases—oxygen and sulphur dioxide—are mixed in the presence of a filament of platinum, they form sulphurous acid. This reaction takes place only if the platinum is present. It functions as a catalyst and helps form a new combination. But the filament remains inactive and unchanged, and even there is no trace of it in the new formation. The mind of the poet, which is like the catalyzing agent, is already charged with the sense of the past. His tradition-oriented mind starts combining, like the filament, the experiences and impressions in a peculiar and unexpected way. A new creation takes place without having anything of the poet's personality. His mind becomes a medium, which digests and transmutes the passion perfectly, while it remains completely detached like the filament of platinum. In short, according to Eliot's logic, a traditionless mind will not be "platinum shred." Creation becomes impersonal only insofar as the creator's feelings are under firm control; and the mind must be properly trained, like "a bit of finely filiated platinum."

Eliot further compares a poet's mind to a container in which a large number of feelings, images, and phrases are stored and they remain inactive until the poet's mind unite them to form a new compound. And in the creation of the new compound, the intensity of the emotions and components is not important, but the intensity of the poetic process and the way the fusion takes place, that is to be considered. This is the process of achieving impersonality in the poetic creation. Eliot's another engaging theory "objective correlative" in the essay "Hamlet and His Problems" is an extension of the Impersonal theory of poetry. He writes:

> The only way of expressing emotion in the form of art is by finding an 'objective correlative;' in other words, a set of objects, a situation, a chain of events which shall be the formula of that particular emotion; such that when the external facts, which must terminate in sensory experience, are given, the emotion is immediately evoked.[42]

The "objective correlative" theory can be conceptualized in a better way by framing the following equation:

C	=	**E**	=	**O**	=	**E E R**
↓		↓		↓		⏟
Cause		emotion		objectification		emotion evoked in reader

The equation represents that there should be an exact balance between cause and emotion (effect) in the form of an art. This particular emotion should be presented through objectification or sensory facts. And through the external sensory facts the particular emotion is aroused immediately in the mind of the reader. A poet's duty is not to communicate his emotion to the reader directly, but he should embody it in a hard, concrete, and definite image or any object, scene, character, action, event or situation. Through these paraphernalia, he should evoke the particular emotion in the mind of the reader. The best way of transmitting a poet's emotion to the reader is to externalize, depersonalize, and dramatize it through outer symbols. To achieve this artistic perfection there must be a complete balance between the emotion of the character and the emotion generated by an external concrete manifestation. And this manifested emotion in the reader should be equal to that particular emotion of the poet. Shakespeare finds this exact equivalence (correlative) in his successful tragedies, particularly in *Macbeth*. The mental state of Lady Macbeth in Sleep-Walking Scene is not directly described, but a set of sensory facts is presented—candle, perfumes of Arabia, smell of blood—and immediately a vivid picture of her emotional and mental state is reflected. Macbeth's philosophical outburst—"tomorrow and tomorrow and tomorrow"—after the fall of Lady Macbeth from the tower is quite infallible and natural in the sequence of events.

According to Eliot, *Hamlet* is an artistic failure because here Shakespeare fails to find the "objective correlative" for Hamlet's emotion. Hamlet (the man) is overburdened with an emotion which is inexpressible. His emotion is "in excess," suffused, all-pervasive, overflowing, and thus is uncontrollable because it is more than the cause. Hamlet's disillusionment is caused by the guilt of his mother, but neither his mother nor the plot is the adequate equivalent for his emotion. His disgust envelops and exceeds her guilt. It is this feeling which he cannot understand; he cannot objectify it, and it, therefore, remains to poison life and obstruct action. None of the possible action can satisfy his emotion. There is no object, character, situation or incident which adequately expresses the inner anguish of Hamlet. In other words, just as in practical life the reaction of emotional and sensitive people is sometimes in excess to the fact or cause and they suffer a lot, so also Hamlet's reaction is excessive or unjustified. This over-reaction poisons his life, frustrates him, and obstructs his action. It is the root cause of his neurosis.

"Objective correlative" theory is subject to severe criticism. First, there is no question that there should be a balance between cause and emotion (effect). Human behavior cannot be reduced to a formula or bound in mathematical calculation. Human behavior cannot be fully measured. The psychic make-up of an individual varies all the time. It is always in a state of flux, flow, and stream of consciousness. How can the magnitude of an emotion be in proportional to the cause? It may be more or less but not exactly the same, because human mind is controlled and determined by a number of variables. Eliot develops this imbalanced notion being influenced by positivist philosophy and naturalistic sciences, and he wants to apply the same theory in social sciences that is perhaps not possible. Eliot is deeply influenced by Ezra Pound's *The Spirit of Romance.* Pound remarks: "poetry is a sort of inspired mathematics which gives us equations, not for abstract figures, triangles, shapes, and the like, but equation for the human emotion."[43]

Secondly, the emotion, Eliot states, should not be communicated to the reader. There should be mediation, a transaction between the reader and the poet. This is done through object or situation or incident, in other words, through "empirical referents." First of all, no object or situation in advance is in itself a formula for an emotion, but depends for its emotional significance and effect on the way it is rendered by the poet at the time of composition. Secondly, how is it possible that the emotion of the poet in the same magnitude should be embodied in the "empirical referent?" They may embody more or less, not the same emotion in the same magnitude. The same question arises how the empirical referents evoke the same emotion of the poet in reader's mind. Lastly, how it is possible that as soon as the reader reads a poem and comes across scene, image, character or situation, the same emotion is *immediately* evoked in the mind? It may be possible that he may or may not conceptualize or perceive the "empirical referents" instead of being evoked by them. In fact, Eliot's theory of objective correlative is marked by the fallacy of scientism.

In "The Metaphysical Poets" Eliot discusses another very popular phrase "dissociation of sensibility," pointing out the deficiency of English poetry from the later seventeenth century to the first decade of the twentieth century. He discovers a split or separation of thought and feeling. He finds an absence of "a direct sensuous apprehension of thought, or a recreation of thought into feelings."[44] The neo-classical poets can think but not feel; the romantic can feel but not think. Tennyson and Browning are also incompetent to harmonize thoughts and emotions: "they think, but do not feel their thoughts as immediately as the odour of a rose."[45] Eliot, therefore, always lays emphasis on the "unification of sensibility"—a trademark of good poetry. Gifted with a 'refined sensibility,' he has a capacity to harmonize all diverse experiences and fuse them into one whole, by finding "the verbal equivalent for states of mind and feeling." Therefore, a poet must transmute his thoughts into sensations to achieve an end of good poetry.

Eliot holds that "criticism is as inevitable as breathing," but it must be objective, analytical, and scientific, not impressionistic or interpretative. He is opposed to the "lemon squeezer" school of critics, who try to squeeze every drop of meaning out of words and lines. In "The Function of Criticism" Eliot calls the impressionistic critics corruptors of the taste; they supply merely opinions and mislead the reader. He further says:

> *Qua* work of art, the work of art cannot be interpreted; there is nothing to interpret; we can only criticize it according to standards, in comparison to other works of art; and for 'interpretation' the chief task is the presentation of relevant historical facts which the reader is not assumed to know.[46]

First of all, Eliot says that poetry is an art, not an expression of ideas. A work of art never demands interpretation, but analysis. Interpretation cannot fulfill this purpose as it presents only opinions and historical facts which corrupt the taste, instead of educating. It presents a rather arbitrary attitude and tends to be wayward, erratic, and unbalanced because it cannot be argued or demonstrated on the solid rational ground. Even it does not guarantee the competence of an artist. On the other hand, fact does not corrupt because it is analytical, not interpretative. The fact can be achieved by applying two important tools—compare and contrast and analysis. Eliot's 'fact' does not mean the sociological or historical or biographical facts but the technical aspects of art—its genesis, condition, structure, setting, and theme.

A good critic is always a good artist. The criticism of a trained and skilful writer on his own work is the most vital and highest kind of criticism. In the process of creation of his writing, his critical faculty also remains conscious and he works a hard critical labour—"the labour of sifting, combining, constructing, expunging, correcting, testing."[47] That is why some creative writers are greater than others only because their critical faculty is superior. This critical activity comes "in the heat of creation," that is rare and apparent in the work. Eliot finds justification that the only critics worth reading are the critics who practice the art they write and fuse criticism with creation.

VI

Richards, with his critical issues, fosters a complete new attitude towards literary criticism. He develops, like T. S. Eliot, T. E. Hulme, and Ezra Pound, distaste for the past poetic criticism and calls it "an empty garner." A many sided man, imbued with his profound knowledge of philosophy, psychology, aesthetics, the fine arts, and the new theories and principles of various sciences, he plunges into literary criticism without any formal training of literature. With his interdisciplinary learning, he comes to the conclusion that the study or specialization of literature in itself or isolation has no meaning at all unless a scholar also makes a study of a cognate field such as philosophy, rhetoric, psychology, aesthetics, linguistics etc. He, therefore, makes a systematic and fresh attempt to formulate a theory for the better way of teaching and reading poetry. Exploring the power and function of language, especially literary language, he analyses some of the smallest and simplest words.

Richards's *The Principles of Literary Criticism* (1923), "a machine for thinking with," a reply to the scientist's objection to poetry, contains his arguments chiseled with scientific rigour. Discussing the historical development of literary criticism, Richards raises question after question about the nature, value, and place of poetry and its effect on the mind of the reader in day to day life. These pragmatic questions are almost ignored or unanswered scientifically by the critics of the previous generations. He, therefore, criticizes the existing principles of poetic theory to enunciate his own two important poetic theories— theory of value and theory of communication.

Richards, first of all, topples down the old-fashioned concept of 'Beauty' based on "phantom aesthetic experience." The traditional aestheticians cherish a general notion that in human psyche there is a distinct instinct, which functions a unique kind of mental activity. This instinct is called the aesthetic experience or the experience of beauty, considered to be quite different from other experience. It means Beauty with its specific appeal constitutes a special category and possesses an absolute value. It is also quite incompatible with any other kind of appeal. In a nut-shell, the prevalent theory of Beauty is that the artistic experience is something *sui generis*—something matchless, mystic, and mysterious, something without any counterpart.

Rejecting this theory of Beauty, in *The Principles of Literary Criticism*, Richards argues that the aesthetic experience is not distinct in any way. Rather, it is only a part of total human experience associated with other human experience. The difference between the two is that the aesthetic experience is more unified and characterized by greater intensity, vividness, and complexity. It is capable enough to organize a greater variety of impulses to have been stimulated. To justify this contention, Richards propounds the theory of the value of poetry. He first investigates the working of human mind from modern psychological perspective i.e. *Gestalt* psychology and neurology. He discovers that the human mind is a system of impulses. It is generally fraught with a number of conflicting instincts, desires, and wants, and so on so forth. He technically calls them "appetencies" meaning unconscious impulses. These opposing instincts always disturb and disorder the human mental peace, whereas the human mind itself craves for a harmony, order, and systematization of the warring instincts and emotions. Nevertheless, the human mind has also got a natural gift, a capacity i.e. an inherent power and tendency to restore mental equilibrium by ordering and organizing the conflicting impulses. But with new experience, all the time, the human mind gets disturbed and it has to readjust itself the different instincts in a fresh manner to attain the desired system or poise. Consequently, the mind often remains in a disturbed state. It means the ideal state of the mind can be achieved when all the instincts, prodded into action by some stimulus, are satisfied, but it is not possible in practical life. The next alternative to keep the mind poised is to satisfy the maximum number of impulses and frustrate the minimum number of impulses. It is art that performs this function quite well. It enables the human mind to organize itself more quickly and completely than it could do otherwise. It should be noted here that the mental reconciliation and organization happens through an unconscious process.

In *The Foundation of Aesthetics* (1922) and later in *Science and Poetry*, (1926) Richards and his associates, C.K. Ogden and James Wood, formulate a new definition of beauty based on psychology. Art has a power to adjust and organize conflicting impulses, creating a mental state full of peace, pleasure, and harmony. This peaceful and pleasurable state of mind is called synaesthesis. Richards's concept of beauty is based on the "synaesthetic equilibrium" but it should not be confused with inertia, because in the process of harmonization all the mental faculties are alive and active, and the pleasure results from their harmonious adjustment.

Richards's theory of synaesthesis has a practical value in the individual as well as in communal life, because it does the function of psychic therapy. Art has a capacity to order and harmonize simultaneously a variety of complex human impulses—thoughts, feelings, desires etc.—into a pattern, into an aesthetic whole, yielding a lasting mental peace and pleasure. It is always conducive to maintain the psychological well-being of the reader and the poet. Though the human mind has a natural tendency, a principle to systematize opposite impulses, yet art increases very effectively the intensity of the coordination of the impulses. This systematization led by art makes an individual psychologically balanced and determines the pattern of human behaviour that definitely plays a vital role not only in his personal behaviour but also in the social life. When the adjustment of impulses becomes difficult or impossible, there is resultant unrest and psychological disorder. Richards widens the scope and value of art, elevating it to a moral level. He intends to establish relevance and need of art that has a direct relation with the society. A society, blind to the significance of art, lacks harmony, peace, cultural refinement, the elegance of life, and above all visionary spirit. On the other hand, the society where art finds its full cultivation, articulation, and reception breathes an air of mental equilibrium, peace, and joy and may escape chaos, disorder, and segregation. Great art always vitalizes human soul and outlook, brings the redemption of the oppressed and expands our sympathies with each other. Richards sums up the value of art in these words: "...it has something of the soul of humanity in it, and finds its logical, its architectural place, in the great structure of human life."

Art, naturally, Richards holds, produces a state of mind where all the warring tensions are ordered and adjusted harmoniously. This harmonization brings tranquility in human mind, which is responsible for tragic pleasure. In other words, Richards refutes the Aristotelian theory of purgation of emotions i.e. *Catharsis.* His assertion is that pleasure always emanates from the systematization of conflicting emotions, not from their purgation.

Richards's another poetic theory is the theory of communication or the concept of poetic language. It emerges out of these five books—(i) *The Principles of Literary Criticism* (1923), (ii), *The Meaning of Meaning* (1923), (iii) *Science and Poetry* (1926), *The Practical Criticism* (1929), and *The Philosophy of Rhetoric* (1936). He holds that poetry is communication, not expression. Communication is possible through the medium of language. He, therefore, makes a very systematic and scientific study of language. Studying the subtleties and nuances of words, he divides language into two categories: (I) scientific or referential or symbolic language and (ii) emotive or evocative or pseudo-language. The scientific use of language makes a direct, logical, and factual statement; it is either true or false. It lacks ambiguity and gives only one meaning—no more than a reference to a corresponding object in life. Referential word faithfully recalls the object. Emotive use of language is a distinct type of language. It is a language of poetry or literature. It, therefore, does give a distinct type of knowledge, too. Emotive use of language is never concerned with the fixed and only one meaning, but evocates emotional effects and certain attitudes in the reader to whom it addresses. For example, the word 'rose' yields only one referential meaning, 'a flower,' to a botanist, but in this line: "My Love is like a red, red rose," 'rose' never conveys a referential meaning; it goes beyond the corresponding object. It produces the effects of emotions—emotions of love and beauty of the sweetheart, who has been likened to the characteristic traits of a rose—its softness, its rosy colour, its fragrance, its delicacy, its smoothness, and above all its entire fascinating look. It gives an image of the lover's charming face. In addition to this, the repetition of the word 'red' is not merely a repetition but the increase of the emotional intensity of the lover's beauty in the reader's mind. Emotive language produces and manipulates emotions and attitudes.

Richards points out that this kind of 'truth' i. e. poetic knowledge is gained through emotive language— not through scientific. Scientific truth presents "true statements" in a technical sense, whereas the poetic truth deals with values, meaningfulness, and human emotions. In *Science and Poetry*, Richards differentiates scientific truth from poetic truth. The poetic truth has capacity to organize and give a vent to pent-up human impulses and attitudes. It thus overcomes chaos, disorder, and unrest and saves humanity and human civilization. Scientific truth is subject to verification, while the poetic truth is beyond verification because it is concerned with emotional reactions and attitude. Richards states: "...only the very foolish would think of attempting to verify. They are not the things which can be verified."

In *The Meaning of Meaning*, Richards further explores that the total meaning of a word, particularly poetic word, depends upon the four factors. They are sense, feeling, tone, and intention. These four cardinal factors or components of a word function four types of contributory meaning simultaneously in the poetic discourse. First, *sense* means simple, plain, and literal statement. Sense is the referential meaning. It seeks a similarity between the impulse and the object which stimulates it. Secondly, *feeling* speaks of the feelings, emotions, emotional attitudes, will, desire, pleasure etc. of the poet about the object or state of affairs he is referring to. Feeling is a state of mind, which warps language to produce emotional reactions into the object. When a poet wishes to express something, he cherishes a feeling, a personal flavor about it and then embodies his feeling into the object along with conveying referential meaning. *Tone* means the attitude of the poet towards his reader. It reflects a consciousness of the relation between the two. A writer changes his language according to the standard of the reader. If he is addressing a scholar, his language will be marked by profundity; and if he communicates children, his diction will definitely be simple, direct, and easily grasping. He always keeps in his mind the type of reader who he is speaking to. In other words, there is always a variation as his readers vary. The last component is *intention*, bearing the aim of the writer. In every piece of writing, the writer, consciously or unconsciously, has some purpose which he wants to tell his reader. His purpose may be of any kind—didactic, inspiring, exciting, moving, convincing etc. The purpose of the writer modifies the language and determines the worth of his writing.

In *The Meaning of Meaning,* Richards and Ogden discuss very minutely the semantic aspect of language. They think that words are simply signs or symbols. So far as the referential meaning is concerned, they are capable enough to relate the reference with the referent. But to fix the true meaning, the reader has to lean on the crutch of psychological and contextual theory. Therefore, the meaning of a poem, Richards contends, is never fixed, objective, or absolute. New, fresh, and something different meaning is created in every case by each reader. Words work in association and their meanings depend upon context. Context means the word what comes before and after a particular word, phrase, statement, and circumstance. They all help to determine the true meaning of a word. If a word is used out of context, the meaning will definitely be changed. In poetic discourse, words are never shoveled in indiscriminately but are used with a great care and in a particular context. Richards states: "Words are not oiled and naked thieves that infest railway carriages in India."

In *The Principles of Literary Criticism*, Richards tells that poetic meaning is also modified by metre and rhythm. They depend upon repetition and expectancy. Rhythm is created by the repetition of particular sounds and this repetition arouses expectancy in the mind. Expectancy means an unconscious psychological tendency to anticipate the repetition of the same sound. Metre is not only a series of sound sequences made more regular and organized in pattern, but also it has an importance in creating music which has great psychological properties. Rhythm is not simply a mechanical contrivance, but has a direct appeal to emotions. The actual rhythmical sounds of words in poetic language convey the meaning of word. In this way, metre and music or rhythm is an organic and integral part of the poem. And music and meaning cannot be separated, but exists together to form a single system. Wimsatt and Brooks write:

> And if we want to praise or condemn the rhythm of a particular poem, we shall not be able, except in the loosest sort of way, to deal with rhythm apart from meaning.[48]

In furtherance of his concept of language for the purpose of communication, Richards asserts an indispensable and all-pervasive role of metaphor. In *The Philoscphy of Rhetoric*, he rejects the traditional theory of metaphor that considers it simply a verbal matter, "a shifting and displacement of words," and "a grace or ornament or added power of language." It was in too exclusively grammatical and rhetorical manner and, therefore, had a limited application. Richards expands the scope of metaphor and discovers that it is required at every step in the process of communication. He states:

"That metaphor is the omnipresent principle of language can be shown by mere observation. We cannot get through three sentences of ordinary fluid discourse without it."[49] Richards is of the view that metaphor is an indirection or deviation or "a carrying over of a word from its normal use to a new use." He further says that metaphor is "a transaction between contexts." Its function is generally not very apparent, but works rather stealthily. The interaction of sense, tone, feeling, and intention contribute to the understanding of metaphor.

Richards's stress is that thought works basically through metaphor. A metaphor has two components—(i) tenor (idea) and vehicle (image). *Tenor* is the subject to which a metaphorical expression is applied. In a metaphor like "life is a brief candle," 'life' is the tenor, while the metaphorical expression, 'a brief candle' is the *vehicle*. The total meaning of a metaphor is the product of a complex interaction between them. There are two types of metaphors—(i) sense-metaphor and (ii) emotive metaphor. In a sense metaphor, there is a direct resemblance between the original object and the new one. There is but one point of resemblance between tenor and vehicle. On the other hand, an emotive metaphor depends upon the speaker's attitude and his feelings aroused in the mind. It mounts one identification upon other. A truly poetic metaphor is never decorative or logical or explanatory, or illustrative. Rather it lends a quality of dynamism, density, gesture, richness, irony, paradox, and multi-layered meanings to the poetic language, which would not be possible otherwise.

Keeping in view all these paraphernalia, Richards proceeds to make an experiment in his class room. In this respect, he is a Columbus to the technique called "the practical criticism" or "applied criticism." It is after the name of his epoch-making revolutionary book, *The Practical Criticism*. It is a brilliant empirical document, perpetuating more vigorously Eliot's critical approach that "Honest criticism and sensitive appreciation is directed not upon the poet but upon the poetry."[50] Being a Professor at Cambridge, he is fully aware of the current unscientific method of teaching and reading of literature, particularly poetry. He, therefore, makes a fascinating experiment based on pedagogy to place literary criticism on the scientific pedestal. He distributes some short anonymous poems to his students to analyze them. The poems are unannotated and stripped of all the information about authorship, date, circumstances of compositions, titles of the poems, biographical, historical, and linguistic contexts. With this clinical isolation from all contexts, the students are left to analyze the 'words on the page' to form their judgments and comments. This method of the analysis of the poem is highly analytical because the reader remains free of all preconceived notions about the text. It is not a study, say, the romantic age a distinct literary movement, with its characteristic outlook, social formations and so on.

The objective of this study is to disengage the ideas and emotions contained in the poem. The figures of speech, the special words, and significant sounds are discovered in the expression of the poem. Broadly speaking, the critic has to find out for himself how a poet has expressed his ideas in the poem. This is possible, if one does not read a poem but also read it between the lines and even between the words. Reading a poem critically is a serious activity demanding attention of the mind to letters, words, phrases, comparisons, and shades of meaning. A poem is not a simple composition but a complex of feelings, ideas, and images presented in a form of its own. The achievement of this decontextualized and text-oriented analysis is that a critic fails "to offer a vague, flowery, metaphysical effusion and call it crirticism"[51] His practice of close-reading marks, as it is thought, the beginning of modern literary criticism. Richards intends to create a new kind of reading habit "for those who wish to discover for themselves what they think and feel about poetry" and reform the teaching of poetry. Richards argues that the focus of the reader should always be on the text and the text alone— the bedrock of practical criticism. These days it is treated as an ancillary skill rather than the foundation of a critical method. It is asked in many examinations in literature at almost all levels, and is used to test students' responsiveness to what they need and write the way poems create their effects.

In the 1930s and 40s, this critical approach is warmly welcomed in America and establishes some basic connections between Richards and the theoretical cohesion of the New Criticism. Richards, therefore, is called "the father of American New Criticism." Ransom acknowledges:

> Discussion of the New Criticism must start with Mr. Richards. The New Criticism very nearly began with him in right way, because he attempted to found it on a more comprehensive basis than other critics did.[52]

Richards paves a ground for evolving a technique of verbal analysis of literary work of art. Though the New Critics downright disregards his effective theory of value, they have received from him the unique concept concerning the nature of literature. Some of Richards's incipient ideas of poetry are to be developed by the New Critics incorporating into their main critical idioms. They are those of "complexity," "ambiguity," "irony," etc. Despite his seminal theoretical assertion, Richards is not free of numerous charges leveled on him. His introduction of excessive psychologism i. e. the effects produced on the mind of the reader by the poem reveals his lop-sidedness.

VII

William Empson (1906-1984), "a critic of genius," is one of the pioneers of the New Criticism. Like all the modernists, he is also devoted to modernist experimentation by founding a literary magazine, *Experiment.* Gifted with a highly analytical mind, as he has a fascination for mathematics and science, Empson is best known for his literary criticism and in particular his analysis of the use of language in poetical works. Empson is influenced by the philosopher, Ludwig Wittgenstein, who was concerned with the nature of language in its relation to the world and to its speakers. In *Tractatus,* he first assumes that language is used to play one kind of game only, i.e. a perfect logical language to describe facts with clarity and precision. Later he argues that language plays a variety of games. However, critics were also previously aware with this indeterminate and playful aspect of language and its tendency to slip constantly from denotation to connotation. But after Empson's benchmark critical study, *Seven Types of Ambiguity* (1930), the term "ambiguity" enters into the critical vocabulary. Empson's main concern is that literary use of language is related to a particular type of ambiguity, though he later admits that it is not a suitable term to have used for a full-scale investigation of multiple significances that occur in the use of words in poetry. It is ambiguity that is the essence, according to Empson, of all great poetry. The worth of a poet does not depend on the emotional quality evoked by the ideas, but the devices of ambiguity which demand a lot of mental activity of inventing reason. This process of analyzing poetry lends pleasure to the reader.

Empson categorizes arbitrarily seven types of ambiguity over-lapping one another:

1. "When a word, a syntax or a grammatical structure, while making only one statement, is effective in several ways at once.
2. When two or more meanings all add to the single meaning of the author.
3. When two ideas, which are concerned only by being both relevant in the context, can be given in one word simultaneously.
4. When two or more meanings of a statement do not agree among themselves, but combine to make clear a more complicated state of mind in the author.
5. When the author is discovering his idea in the act of writing, or not holding it all in his mind at once, so that, for instance, there is a simile which applies to nothing exactly, but lies half way between two things when the author is moving from one thing to the other.
6. When a statement says nothing by tautology, by contradiction, or by irrelevant statements, if any; so that the reader is forced to invent statements of his own and they are liable to conflict with one another.
7. When the two meanings of the word, the two values of ambiguity, are the two opposite meanings defined by the context, so that the total effect is to show a fundamental division in the writer's mind."[53]

Generally "ambiguity" bears a pejorative overtone meaning an obscure or vague expression but in the hands of Empson, it achieves a special poetic device in literary criticism. If a word or expression gives two or more distinct references or diverse kinds of connotation, it is marked by ambiguity. Multiple meanings and plurisignation are also the terms for such use of language. Empson, therefore, never uses the term "ambiguity" in its ordinary sense. It is not used just to convey the casual sense of "mere possession of double meaning," as in the case of pun or concision. His definition of "ambiguity" calls for the alternative reactions produced by any verbal nuance. Empson epitomizes this method in these words in the Preface to the book:

> An ambiguity, in ordinary speech, means something very pronounced, and as a rule witty or deceitful. I propose to use the word in an extended sense, and shall think relevant to my subject any verbal nuance, however slight, which gives room for alternative reactions to the same piece of language….A word may have several distinct meanings; several meanings connected with one another; several meanings which need one another to complete their meaning; or several which unite together so that the word means one relation or one process. This is a scale which might be followed continuously. "Ambiguity" itself can mean an indecision as to what you mean, an intention to mean several things, a probability that one or other or both of two things has been meant, and the fact that a statement has several meanings.[54]

Empson feels that generally readers of the poetry reduce the meaning of a given word to a single denotation. They do not realize that poetry is an aspect or condition of language. Certain attributes differentiate the language of poem from other language. Poetry should be explained or studied in terms of its medium. Empson, therefore, displays his skill in discovering a rich variety of interpretation of poetic literature. He presents the astonishing riches of linguistic ambiguity. His studies unearth layer upon layer of multiple puns, ironies, suggestion and argumentation in various literary works. He carries the hunt for hidden meanings in great poetry further than ever before. He argues that it "is not just that an individual word is open to various readings, but also that sentence-structure from line to line allows of alternative syntactical and grammatical readings."[55] Robert Graves and Laura Riding's *A Survey of Modernist Poetry* is a main influence on Empson's sophisticated analysis of the works of Chaucer, Shakespeare, Milton, Pope, Donne, Marvell, Eliot, etc. His fundamental position is that all great poetry is complex; and it is nuances of words that make it complex. In *The Structure of Complex Words* (1951) Empson suggests that it is the colloquial not the official language which embodies the thought of a period.

Empson leaves a marked impact on the close-reading of the New Criticism, though his model to the New Critics is very tough, and demands their full alertness to the verbal subtlety involved. Moreover, he refuses to be called a New Critic because he refers to this critical movement as a "campaign to make poetry as dull as possible." Some critics also hold that Empson's *Seven Types of Ambiguity* and *The Structure of Complex Words* anticipate Darrida's deconstruction, but he dismisses with derision Darrida's work as "very disgusting." In addition to the deep analysis of the language, Empson's contributions lie in other domains i.e. his concern for political and psychological ideas in literature. He is interested in explaining the human or experiential reality in great works of literature: the emotions of desire and love; the sensibility and intentions of authors; and deep truth communicated to the reader. In *Some Version of Pastoral* (1935) Empson adopts historical, comparative, and analytical method.

Through this mode of word-by-word explication, Empson expands the scope of the complexity and richness of poetic language, but at the same time, he heaps a lot of condemnations on his head. Some critics realize that his seven types of ambiguity are "unnecessary and mistaken," because the risk of this literary phenomenon is that the intensive search for the ambiguities easily leads to head-scratching and over-reading that violates the norms of language. William York Tindall finds the division into seven types "pretentious." J. C. Ransom remarks: "the ordinary critic cannot read them (Empson's analyses) and be the same critic again." *The Princeton Encyclopedia of Poetry and Poetics* also writes: "A weakness in the method, which Empson himself does not always avoid is that it invites overly complicated, ingenious, and finally irrelevant reading."[56] However, all these comments cannot dwarf his high stature in modern criticism, particularly, his influence on the New Critics galvanized into fresh thinking, creating a "landmark in the shift to modernism."[57] In this way, the main ingredients for the verbal study of the poem are—metre, rhythm, metaphor, the components of the poetic meaning (sense, feeling, tone and intention), verbal and structural analysis, irony, balance, tension etc. This orientation of study becomes a source of inspiration to the New Critics and finds a fertile expression in their critical theories.

References:

1. T. S. Eliot, *The Sacred Wood* (London: Faber & Faber, 1963), p. 305.

2. *Ibid.*, p. 25.

3. A. C. Ward, *Twentieth Century Literature1901-1950* (W. C.: EIBS Methuen, 1963), p.217.

4. Stanley Edger Hyman, *The Armed Vision: A Study in the Methods of Modern Literary Criticism* (New York: Vintage Book, 1955), pp. 3-4.

5. R. W. Stallman,ed., *Critique and Essays in Criticism1920-1948* (New York: Ronald Press,1949), p. xix.

6. David Lodge, ed. *20th Century Criticism: A reader* (London: Longman, 1972), p. 92.

7. Harry Blamires, *A History of Literary Criticism* (London: Macmillan Education Ltd., 1991), p. 311.

8. T.E. Hulme, *Speculations* (London: R. K. Paul Ltd., 1960), p. 47.

9. David Lodge, ed., "Romanticism and classicism,"*20th Century Criticism: A Reade*, p. 99. The subsequent references to this book will be indicated by the page number of this edition in the bracket.

10. Herbert Read, ed., *Speculations* (London, 1924), p. 45.

11. T. S. Eliot, *Selected Essays* (London: Faber and Faber, 1963), p. 305.

12. Herbert Read, ed., *Speculations* p. 10.

13. T. S. Eliot, *Selected Essays*, p.15.

14. Quoted in Munir, *An Autopsy on English Literature* (Varanasi: Vishwajana Adhyayan Sansthan, 1998), p. 77.

15. In Haiku feelings are suggested through natural images rather than directly stated. In its three-line poem, it gives a picture and a mood. It is elliptical in nature. *Princeton Encyclopedia of Poetry and Poetics* states that Haiku's most important lessons were

condensation, definite imagery, and freedom from didactic comment...Haiku has encouraged a style in which imagistic techniques give order to poems, passages, and sequences" (p. 334).

16. Alex Preminger, ed., *Princeton Encyclopedia of Poetry and Poetics (*London: The Macmillan Press Ltd., 1974), p. 427.
17. T. E. Hulme, *Further Speculations*, ed., Sam Hynes (Minneapolis: University of Minnesota Press, 1955), p. 73.
18. "A Lecture on Modern Poetry," Wikipedia, the free encyclopedia. http://en. wikipedia. org/wiki/ A_Lecture_on_Modern_Poetry. 8/5/2006
19. D. D. Paisge, ed., *Letters of Ezra Pound* (New York, 1950), pp. 48-49.
20. David Lodge, ed., *20th Century Literary Criticism: A Reader*), p. 65. The subsequent references to this will be indicated by the page number of this edition in the bracket.
21. T. S. Eliot, ed., *;Literary Essay of Ezra Pound* (London, 1960), p. 216. The subsequent references will be mentioned by the title of the book.
22. *Ibid.*, p. 232.
23. *Ibid.*, pp. 216-7.
24. *Ibid.*, p. 169.
25. Ezra Pound, *The Spirit of Romance*, (London, 1910), p.5.
26. Wimsatt & Brooks, *Literary Criticism: A Short History*. (New Delhi: Oxford I B H Publishing Co., 1964), p.664.
27. J. M. Murry, 'Metaphor,' *Countries of the Mind*, second series, (London 1931), pp. 1-16.
28. William Cookson, ed., *Selected Prose* 1909-1965, (New Directions, 1973), p. 375.
29. Quoted in Wimsatt & Brooks, *Literary Criticism: A Short History*, p. 663.
30. *Letters of Ezra Pound*, pp. 48-9.
31. Ezra Pound, *Polite Essays*, (Norfolk, Conn., 1939), p.167.
32. *Literary Essay of Ezra Pound*, p. 194.

33. *Letters of Ezra Pound*, pp. 48-9.
34. T. S. Eliot, ed., "Introduction," *Selected Poems*, pp. x-xi.
35. David Lodge, ed., *20th Century Literary Criticism: A Reader,* p. 71.
36. *Ibid.*, pp. 71-72.
37. T. S. Eliot, *The Sacred Wood* (London: Methuen: University Paper backs, 1964), p. 77.
38. S. T. Coleridge, *Philosophical Lectures* (London: The Pilot Press, 1949), p. 192.
39. *20th Century Literary Criticism*, p. 72.
40. *Ibid.*, p. 76.
41. *Ibid.*, p. 73.
42. T. S. Eliot, *Selected Essays* (London: Faber& Faber Limited, 1932), p. 145.
43. Ezra Pound, *The Spirit of Romance*, p. 5.
44. *Selected Essays,* p. 286.
45. *Ibid.*, p. 287.
46. *Ibid.*, p. 142.
47. *Ibid.*, p. 30.
48. Wimsatt and Brooks, *Literary Criticism: A Short History*, p. 642.
49. I. A Richards, *The Philosophy of Rhetoric* (New York: Oxford University Press, 1965), p. 92.
50. T. S. Eliot, *Selected Essays,* p. 17.
51. Peter Barry, *Beginning Theory* (Manchester: Viva Books Private Limited, 1988), p. 15.
52. J. C Ransom, *The New Criticism*, p. 111.
53. William Empson, *Seven Types of Ambiguity* (Harmoundsworth: Penguin, 1961), pp. 2-3
54. *Ibid.*, p. 1.
55. Harry Blamires, *A History of Literary Criticism*, p. 339.
56. *Princeton Encyclopedia of Poetry and Poetics*, p. 19.
57. Harry Blamires,*A History of Literary Criticism*, p. 339.

2

The New Criticism

I

The New Criticism, an American movement in literary criticism, is an objective and text-oriented approach to analyze and evaluate a work of art. It is also called the trans-Atlantic critical movement, which develops in the 1920s and dominates the critical landscape till 1960s with a tremendous success. The heroes of this critical movement are J. C. Ransom, Donald Davidson, Allen Tate, R. P. Warren, Cleanth Brooks, R. P. Blackmur, and W. K. Wimastt Jr. The New Critics, shrouded in the commercialized, industrialized, urbanized, and war-ridden society, condemn the split and specialized nature of the modern technological civilization founded on scientism and secular knowledge. They grope into the dark of emotional and spiritual bankruptcy only to encounter utter chaos, confusion, and disorder. Bewildered and dejected, standing at a crucial juncture, they ultimately turn to take a shelter under the bower of poetry. They cherish a firm faith in poetry as an art and its immense organizing capacity of imagination. With the new critical attitudes of European modernism and literary mannerism and experimentalism, the New Critics, thus, set out to propound the theory of the New Criticism to soothe and structure their fragmented psychic phenomenon. They try their level best to bring an order, pattern, structure, and aesthetic values in a work of art, which are almost missing in the modern fractured society. In this context, Pritchard aptly comments:

> Opposed as they were to escapist literature, they nevertheless unconsciously found relief in sailing with Yeats to Byzantium or speculating with Kant upon aesthetic knowledge.[1]

In the world of insensitivity and disintegration, it becomes the responsibility of the critics to define and organize the contemporary sensibility.

The New Critics emerge with their heterogeneous views regarding the nature and function of poetic discourse, but their focus always remains on the intrinsic values of the work—its internal complexity, organization, and harmony. They believe in the organic growth or the whole of the poem. which has its own autonomous and self-contained entity. Anything outside the poem, they feel, is not going to help in understanding the aesthetic values. The New Criticism, therefore, brush aside all the existing critical approaches—philosophical, moralistic, impressionistic, biographical, historical, psychological, and socio-economic and political. They frown upon these extrinsic sources, as they have done a great harm to the understanding of a poem as a poem. These approaches distract the reader from exploring the vital parts contributing to the formation of an aesthetic objec.. The main intention of the New Criticism is to cultivate an artistic sensibility, sharpen an aesthetic perception of the reader, and educate him as to what a poem is, how it is produced, and how it be read, interpreted, and evaluated. The New Criticism, also known as a textual, aesthetic, formalistic, objective, ontological, and even practical criticism, proves to be a benchmark for the evolution of the modern literary criticism, dominating the academic prospect of the American schools and colleges from 1920s to 1950s.

The New Criticism has its origin in the South and is affected by diverse aspects such as economic, political, cultural, and literary. In order to understand its full significance, origin, characteristics, scope, and dimension, it is essential to have a clear-cut knowledge of the philosophical and cultural background of the New Critics—J. C. Ransom, Allen Tate, Cleanth Brooks, Davidson, R. P. Warren, and W.K. Wimsatt. It should be kept in the mind that they are primarily philosophers and cultural critics, and literary critics later. It, therefore, warrants me first to delve into the cultural and social milieu out of which their literary canons are formulated

II

In the early decades of the twentieth century, the canvas of American literary criticism was as blurred and rudderless as in the then England. On both sides of the Atlantic there was an urgent need to ameliorate and uplift the miserable condition of criticism. In England, T.E. Hulme, Ezra Pound, T. S. Eliot, I. A. Richards, William Empson, etc. reject the study of socio-political and biographical background of literature in the name of criticism. They did their level best to propound some new critical canons by introducing such tools as ambiguity, tradition, imagism, dissociation of sensibility, connotation, denotation, objective correlative, etc. These critical idioms help these critics understand and evaluate a work of art from a fresh perspective. It is discussed in details in the First Chapter of this book. In America also there emerges a group of very potential and enthusiastic philosopher intellectuals—J. C. Ransom, Allen Tate, Donald Davidson, Andrew Lytle, R. P. Warren, Cleanth Brooks, W. K. Wimsatt—who are called the new critics. Their criticism is parallel to that of British counterparts. In establishing the textual and objective approach to literature, they take inspiration from numerous sources. They are the writings of the above mentioned English critics, Remy de Gourmont, the French *explication de texte*, the Imagists, Immanuel Kant, S. T. Coleridge, and above all the Southern Agrarianism. In this way, a close relationship between the Cambridge critics and the American new critics can be perceived, because some of the common critical tenets can be explored between them. But over this issue, there arises a dispute and the two schools of thought get branched off. The first lays emphasis on the British critics and hold them the forerunners of the New Criticism and tries to ignore its origin in the Southern Agrarian Movement. The second school gives prominence to the regional character and keeps its Americanness intact. However, the New Criticism is not free of the varied sources and it cannot be denied that it owes a good deal of debt to English critics and German transcendental philosophers. That is why it is safe to state that the New Criticism is an Anglo-American or trans-Atlantic movement in criticism.

Of course, the New Criticism has also its origin in the South and wears a regional garb in its inception, but soon it achieves a national and international status, undergoing several stages before it achieves its fullness. In this context Yiannis Stamiris says: "American New Criticism underwent three distinct phases: the Fugitive, the Agrarian, and the New Critical, in all at which Ransom, the philosopher of the movement played the leading role."[2] The New Critics are neither expatriate nor cosmopolitan nor even urban; they belong to a particular region coming from the Agrarian background of the South. They assemble with a mission in the small city of Nashville at Vanderbilt University. Disenchanted and distressed with the contemporary culture based on the technology, capitalism, industrialism, and scientism of the North, they cherish a sense of deep nostalgia for the cultural life of the Old South. Therefore, like the romantics, they escape into the past and adopt their names "Fugitives." The name itself suggests a withdrawal from the mechanized, industrialized, and dehumanized society of the North.

III

In the second phase, the Fugitives acquire another name "The Agrarians." They join the movement of The Southern Agrarianism in 1930s to protest against the inroads of commercialism and protect the Southern heritage. The New Critics, therefore, are also called the Southern critics. The Fugitive-Agrarians, who are called the new critics, are led by Ransom, Tate, Warren, Brooks, Wimsatt etc. They nurture a profound sense of the past history, an awareness of tragedy, fallen and sinful state of man, the sustaining spirit of patriotism, moral values, religious beliefs, and observations. They want to maintain the agrarian culture and society of the South. Though the South is economically and politically backward and ridden with racism and superstition, yet it is blessed with rich folkways, a strong sense of pride and tradition, the secured and supportive family life; the familiar settled community and the natural and eternal rhythms of nature that guide the planting and harvesting on the farm. The Fugitives reject the North and its urban commercial values, which they feel, have taken over American life. Despite its outward gaiety, modernity, and unparallel prosperity, the North manufactures the urbanized "lost generation." Without a stable tradition and structure of values, the individual loses a sense of identity and feels disoriented in time and place. They are forced to live under the pressures and dilemmas of modern life—the loss of belief, the barrenness of philosophy, the spirit of scientism, the vulgarization of the industrial society, the break-down of the communication, the cliché-ridden language of romanticism, and the propagandist tone of mass communication.

The essentials of the Agrarian outlook are very well described by Ransom in *God Without Thunder* (1930) and in a more effective manifesto in *I'll Take My Stand* in the same year, written collectively by the Fugitives. Extremely worried with the vanishing agricultural society, they make a general cultural analysis of the South. They adopt an inimical flight from the values of the North and recommend the Southern agrarian culture based on the classical values and the idea of a society encouraging tradition, rituals, and the rigorous and analytical reading of the literary texts. In a nut-shell, the Fugitive-Agrarian movement is a social, cultural, and regional movement with its conservative ideas. These Southern agrarians champion religious and rural social order in which family, kinship, and custom constitute the grounds of community as they are aware of the crisis that science and industrialization of the North has brought about at the turn of the century.

In this way, we witness that the agrarians are haunted by a dream of the revival of the old agricultural values, aristocracy, and feudalism, and react sharply and consciously against the technological and political domination of the North. However, their dream of agrarianism gets failed and shattered by the development of science, the commercial values of life, and the emergence of the big factories, which create the problems in the name of 'progress.' Consequently, arts make desperate attempts for survival. In the face of this new reality, they fail to restore and establish a society founded on the pedestal of leisure, natural beauty, agricultural economy, and feudal life. Yet their failure and defeat does not destroy their spirit and ideas. They turn their direction from cultural criticism to the realm of aesthetics and literary criticism, depicting the image of the Old South in their literature and arts. For them literature is an escape from modern life to an ideal realm of true humanity. The aesthetics and motivation of the New Criticism, thus, filters out of the human interest and has a direct relevance, but the academia generally unjustifiably fail to capture the human interest in the formulation of its aesthetics. The New Critic acclimatize themselves with the established reality of science and industry through their commitment to aesthetic sensibility. In this context, Fekete remarks: "From the time of the Agrarian failure, the progression is an inexorable one toward the integration of critique into dominant rationality."[3]

IV

In the New Critical Phase, the third phase, the New Critics adopt an attitude of reconciliation, because they find themselves helpless to curb the current of scientism and commercialism. Acknowledging the primacy of science, they realize that they cannot check the changing process of the world, but can change themselves at least. They set out in quest of the ideal land of philosophy, spirituality, aesthetics, literature, and criticism. They hope that they can achieve order, pattern, communication, love, and the binding force of humanity over there. Cut off from the urban culture, experiencing a sense of rootlessness, they portray their self-image in ideal realm of aesthetics, in "the idealization of an interiority that is externalized and shared in the form of works of art."[4] They try to confine themselves within the limits of literary criticism that protects art from being molested by the non-aesthetic life of the society. In the world of science, it is literature which carries and represents the desired cultural standards. Rick Rylance states:

> The significance of the Agrarian movement, therefore, was its articulation of a perception of the world which created a modern role for literary study. In response to a culture increasingly scientific and industrial literature was to act as the communicator for the preserver of central human value.

Ransom's theoretical expression in *The World's Body* is a fury against the abstraction of science. Science, a foe to innocence and beauty, through its rationalism has dissected the body of the world reducing it into a skeleton. Science has bared the body of nature, which is full of variety and delight and beauty. It is arts that give us the concreteness and particularities of the world's body which science fails to provide. Science, for Ransom, is devouring and art is health giving and 'restorative.' The key words—'self-sufficiency' and 'autonomy'—yielded by Agrarian South movement refers to Ransom's 'ontology' and Brooks's 'heresy of paraphrase.' Allen Tate pleads for the moral and spiritual condition of the Old Southern culture favourable to poetry. Terry Eagleton rightly writes in his *Literary Theory: An Introduction* (1983) that the New Criticism is "an ideology of an uprooted, defensive intelligentsia who reinvented in literature what they could locate in reality. Poetry was the new religion a nostalgic haven from the alienation of industrial capitalism."

The social, political, and cultural presumptions operate on the rise and completion of the New Criticism. The New Critics retreating from the real into the ideal define their position as the champions of metaphysical and aesthetic values, and lend a mythic dimension to the history of the New Criticism. Fekete points out:

> As Fugitives they had tried to insist their social dislocation on the grounds of culture, for which, as Agrarians, they attempted and failed to gain a socio-economic basis. Their defense of culture, in the absence of socio-economic content, was empty reaction referring back to an idealized past.... Art and values were now caught in the crisis of the transformation of the South from the old agrarian culture to the New Industrial culture.... New Criticism, as an academic specialization, preserves the escapist Fugitive movement no longer as an abstract negation but as integrated tension.[6]

V

When the New Critics get disillusioned by the culture of the North and receive a defeat of the Southern Agrarianism, they seek backing for their literary and critical arguments in the philosophical aesthetics of Kant, Schopenhauer, and Coleridge. Ransom, the most philosophical of the New Critics, calls himself 'post-Kantian.' His repugnance to science, reason, and logic is supported by Kant. In "The Concrete Universal: Observations on the Understanding of Poetry"

Ransom states: "I am obliged to think of Kant as my own mentor." Kant, therefore, is responsible for introducing philosophy into the literary discussion, particularly into modern criticism. He believes that science and reason is unable to comprehend man's experience embodied in a piece of work. Human experiences, says Kant, provided by science are confined, and even twisted, but the unique language of art goes beyond the limitations of the scientific language. The main concern of the New Critics is also the structure of the poetic language i. e. a precise difference between scientific formulations and artistic formulations. Poetry for Kant is a symbolic construct of man's experience in terms of concrete particulars completely shorn of abstraction. He knows that the job of a poet is to clothe the incomprehensible abstract rational ideas into the concrete and sensuous words. Poetry presents a wealth of thought, which we cannot express in other language; it, says M. A. Habib, "raises the mind above the phenomenal sphere of natural determination."[7] In Kant's words: "We have a faculty of mere aesthetic judgment by which we judge forms without the aid of concepts."[8] Ransom also affirms that the poetic discourse has an ontological status, which cannot be compared to scientific discourse. Habib cites:

> Hence poetry can produce emotions which cannot be expressed by our ordinary, definite concepts, and it is poetry above all, according to Kant, which can manifest the power of aesthetic ideas.[9]

To express this concept, Kant introduces a technical phrase, 'the universal concrete.' The concrete universal means the universal abstract ideas, feelings, and thoughts are transformed into the concrete sensuous form. The universal of a poem is a moral universal and its concrete is its sensuous detail. The moral universal uses nature for its sensuous particularities or for images and metaphors. The relation of the universal moral with concrete is significant for both Kant and Ransom.

Kant elevates art to metaphysical stature by distinguishing artistic communication from the rational one. According to him, artistic consciousness is quite different from the rational consciousness. An aesthetic judgment is formed without the help of concepts. The New Critics such as Ransom, Tate, Brooks, and Wimsatt are modern Kantians who try to investigate and prove that poetry is a distinct form of knowledge. Kant says, "If we estimate objects merely by conceptions, all ideas of beauty is lost."[10] He further says "The beautiful in nature belongs to the form of a thing which consists in having boundaries."[11] For the New Critics, he sets the principle that the value of art is not a conceptual experience but a perceptual and contemplative one. Rene Wellek has rightly pointed out that Kant has defended the aesthetic realm from all sides, against moralism, intellectualism, and didacticism.

VI

Coleridge, with his radical mind, imbibing the intricate philosophy and theory of the German idealist thinkers—Immanuel Kant, the Schlegels, and Schilling, lays a philosophical foundation foı the New Criticism. Reposing full faith in the Bible, actual history and culture, and the human potential, he vehemently opposed the current philosophies of Enlightenment—"the principle of abstract reason"—derived from such as Hume, Locke, and David Hartley. He holds that truth cannot be understood by focusing only on the present, on the immediate or on the material. He believes in the principles that would comprehend past, present, and future. He, therefore, expresses his deep hatred for the principles which erect "immediate utility" and the gratification of the sense at the cost of value. Coleridge laments the forces of commerce, industry, technology, and science, which innervate the diverse potential of human beings. All these ideas boost up the thinking and approach of the Agrarians in shaping their cultural criticism.

So far as the influence of Coleridge's aesthetic and literary theory is concerned, it leaves a tremendous impression on the New Critics. His concepts of organic form, symbol, and imagination and fancy are transmitted to them which facilitate to construct the tenets of the New Criticism. A. H. Tak observes: "Though the forefather of this ... critical tradition is Aristotle, the work oı the exponents of this tradition in the twentieth century is closely based on the Coleridgean formulation of Aristotle's notion of organic form."[12] Formulating a "non-mechanistic" aesthetics of the creative process, Coleridge lays emphasis on the over-all structure of a work of art and its interrelationship of the parts with the whole. He holds that a poem is an independent object with a living organism. It is like a plant or human body. A poem, says Coleridge, grows like a "seed" or "germ" in the creative imagination of the poet. While dealing with the mental creative process and the production of a given poem, he shows a genetic interest. He takes an example of a plant which coalesces to its substance various external elements of air, earth, light, and water. An act of this assimilation exhibits a spontaneous evolution, growth, and genesis of the plant. In the evolution of the plant, there runs an inner source of energy, an inherent vital force, a natural life, a soul, and a self-generating power. It functions invisibly and is responsible for the secret growth, extension, and the proper form of the plant. The achieved structure of the plant is, thus, an organic unity. The parts of the plant—its stems, leaves, twigs, roots etc. are as important as the whole plant in itself. The parts cannot be separated; if done so, they lose their existence. Their existence in isolation, therefore, is unthinkable. For example, if a leaf is removed from the parent plant (the whole), the leaf dies. The part cannot exist independently of the whole. Similarly, at the same time, the whole also dies, as the part is taken away from it. The parts and whole are complementary with each other. The survival of the one depends upon the other. Each part simultaneously serves both as an end and a means sustaining the harmonious existence of the whole. However, the being of the whole is more important than the sum of the parts. M. H. Abrams quotes Coleridge that "the whole is primary and the parts secondary … the living whole is prior to the parts." The parts of the plant are also in its tight integration, interrelation, and interdependence, unlike the combination of discrete elements in a machine. The same thing again is with the human body. If one takes away a part of it, it may die.

Coleridge extends from the plant to the mind and points out the relationship between the poem (the product) and mental creative imagination (the process). He holds that imagination is a pivotal force behind the creation of a poem. It has a deep meaning, and is quite different from fancy. Before Coleridge, people used imagination and fancy as though they were the same word, but he for the first time makes a distinction between the two and tells that they are not synonyms. Imagination, a faculty which is distinct from conceptual thinking, is a vital creative and transforming power. It has a capacity to dissolve, dissipate, and unite images into new forms; it also reconciles opposed qualities into a new reality. Imagination is the mind's capacity to generate images of objects, states, or action without being felt or experienced by the senses. Coleridge defines imagination as "an affirmation of eternal Being in which subject and object are one." On the other hand, fancy is merely "a mode of memory emancipated from the order of time and space." It is a mechanical process and can only combine, reassemble, and again dislocate the component parts. Its capacity is only to unite readymade images in new spatial and temporal arrangements, but not able to dissolve and unite them in new creations as the imagination could. Fancy is attributed to the interior faculty of the mind. It is "passive," "mechanical," and "a lesser, limited power."

Coleridge takes a deep interest in the mysterious power of imagination which lends an organic unity and natural growth to the poem. To understand the nature and function of imagination clearly, he divides imagination into two parts—the primary imagination and the secondary imagination, as he does between imagination and fancy. The primary imagination, an involuntary act of mind, subjective consciousness, receives impressions of the external world of objects through the sense. It is an echo of the infinite in the finite mind. Inspired by the absolute universal power, possessed by all, the primary imagination perceives sensations and impressions from the outside world unconsciously, and enables the mind to form an image. But it has no power to re-create and unify them into an organic whole in a new way, because it is static. The secondary imagination is a creative power, a perceptual power, mysterious power, and a spiritual power. It has a dynamic quality to fuse ideas, images, impressions, and sensations into a new organic whole. As a chemical reaction, it synthesizes multiple things into a single whole. It takes the raw materials given by inspiration and reshapes it into a new and vital form.

The growing process of a poem taking place in the mind of the poet is referred to the synthetic power of the creative imagination i.e. the secondary imagination. Just as a plant assimilates automatically the most diverse materials of air, earth, water, etc., so the mind has an "automotive" power of imagination and receives images and words and feelings from a number of realms of human endeavour and thought and bring them altogether into a poem he writes. This requires a huge effort of the imagination, which Coleridge calls the 'esemplastic' power of the poetic imagination. He coins this word borrowing the Greek. It has the three component parts:

> es (into) + en (neutor of eis 'one') + plastic = to shape into one

The esemplastic power of imagination has a characteristic property to mould or shape into one and creates three things—(i) organic whole, (ii) symbol, and (iii) the concrete universal. These three characteristics immediately arrest the mind of the New Critics. That is why *Princeton Encyclopedia of Poetry and Poetics* observes that "the real father of practical criticism is Coleridge. In him we can for the first time see the qualities of the best of the 'New Critics.'"[13]

The esemplastic is an organic and self-evolving power, which organizes a number of and diversity of component parts and help bring the tightness of their integration into the whole. In organic unity, there is a complex, interrelation of living, indeterminate, and endlessly changing components. This diversity into unity refers back, in Coleridgean words, to the Pythagorean definition, "the reduction of many to one."[14] Coleridge defines organic form as 'innate':

> It shapes as it develops itself from within, and the fullness of its development is one and the same with the perfection of its outer form. Such is the life, such the form.[15]

The synthetic power of esemplastic, in the words of Coleridge, "reveals itself in the balance or opposite or discordant qualities." Eliot also talks of this faculty, or mental creative process, or sensibility and calls it "an essential quality of transmuting ideas into sensations, of transforming an observation into a state of mind."[16] Eliseo Vivas offers a very much similar definition of aesthetic experience when he says:

> An aesthetic experience is an experience of rapt attention which involves the transitive oppression of an object's immanent meanings in their full presentational immediacy.[17] Coleridge's organic theory is based on the inseparability of form and content. The relationship between form and content is inherent, natural, not imposed from outside.

Now we should come to the difference between a symbol and an allegory. To Coleridge, a symbol is superior to an allegory. Right from the beginning, an allegory is used to denote abstract ideas; it is merely a translation of abstract notions into picture language. There is no essential link between the idea and the picture. In other words, we can use another picture and it would make no difference. There is no organic and synthetic relationship between idea and the picture. On the other hand, a symbol comes closer to the ideal of the organic whole. Invested with the mystical spirit, it "is characterized by a translucence of the universal in the general." The symbol is specific and general, temporal and eternal, and the concrete universal meet and fuse in an almost mystical incarnational way. Coleridge again echoes Aristotle and Kant in the phrase, the concrete universal. It denotes the highest forms of organic wholes and symbols of a poem. To call a poem a concrete universal is to say that within the microcosm of the poem, universal idea has been fully realized in a concrete form. The concrete universal affects a full fusion of an abstract non-physical idea in a specific physical image.

VII

In the course of its development, the New Criticism traces first the inspiration from the British critics—Hulme, Pound, Eliot, Richards, and Empson; secondly, from the philosophical background of Coleridge and Kant; and thirdly, from the outlook of the Fugitives and the Southern Agrarians of the movement. John Pritchard, therefore, remarks: "The origins of the movement are diverse."[18] With such a rich heritage of knowledge and diverse influences, the New Critics appear on the horizon of literature, aesthetics, and criticism. And there occurs a dawn of "the Southern Literary Renaissance." But here also they encounter numerous challenges. The entire atmosphere of literature and criticism breathes an air of stagnation, unrest, impurity, hybridism, and interdisciplinary approaches. Arts are making desperate effort for their survival. There are various prevalent modes of interpretation and evaluation such as historical, philosophical, moralistic, biographical, and psychological. There is a tradition to deal with the information about the work, not with the work itself. In addition to this, literature is allied with physical sciences. History, sociology, and science have become the handmaids in the North. Critics and reviewers make all-out attempts to minimize the humanistic literary and aesthetic values. That is why the New Critics attack the conventional and traditional ways of viewing life and art. They protest against romanticism with its doctrine of self-expression, its expressive theory of art, its philosophy of perfectibility, the impressionistic adventures of the soul in criticism, and the Marxist attempt to use literature as propagandas. They also react against scholarship and the ethical and didactical emphasis of the New Humanism of Babbitt and Thomas More. In this way American literary criticism is flooded with such kinds of approaches as deal with the extrinsic aspect of a work of art in the early decades of the twentieth century. Almost none was to talk about as to what poetry and literature technically are, but there was a wide-spread dissatisfaction in the critical climate and it had become inevitable to bring a radical change. It is Joel Spingarn who bugles a clarion-call against the current situation in his lecture "the New Criticism" at Columbia University in 1910, which is as follows:

> We have done with all the old Rules.... We have done with the genres, or literary kinds.... We have done with the comic, the tragic, the sublime, and army of vague abstractions of their kind... We have done with theory of style, with metaphor, simile, and all the paraphernalia of Graeco-Roman rhetoric.... We have done with all moral judgment of art as art. We have done with the race, the time, the environment of a poet's work as an element in criticism.... We have done with the "evolution" of literature.... We have done with the old rupture between genius and taste.[19]

Spingarn appears as an iconoclast to sabotage all existing rules and seriously calls for a new criticism based on the formal and aesthetic aspects of a literary work. Though the term New Criticism is first introduced by Spingarn, it is credited with Ransom and comes into general use after the publication of his book *The New Criticism* (1941). It surveys the poetics of T. S. Eliot, I. A. Richards, William Empson, and Yvor Winters and calls for objective or ontological criticism. In this way, the New Criticism vigorously maps out to establish a text-oriented criticism. Stanley Edger Hyman views that the New Critics "rose passionately against the organized use of non-literary techniques and bodies of knowledge to obtain insights into literature."[20]In the words of R. W. Stallman, their basic aim is to "illumine the centre" of the work.

VIII

This section proceeds to offer the basic map of the New Criticism. The New Critics view that a poem is an independent object with a living organism. It has a self-contained verbal medium held together by a unifying principle dictated by the poem itself. A poem is an organic unit, with each part working to support the whole. It has its own anatomy and autonomy and exists for its own sake like "a tree which you can admire, you can sit in the shade, you can pick bananas, you can cut fire-wood, you can do as you fully well please."[21] The New Critics believe in the total experience of the work. Its various components are integrated and interrelated into a satisfying organic whole whereby one element balances another. Cleanth Brooks declares:

> One of the critical discoveries of our time—perhaps it is not a discovery but merely a recovery—is that the parts of a poem have an organic relation to each other.... The parts of a poem are related as are the parts of a growing plant.

The poem is like a complex living entity, in fact, like life itself. Its aesthetic effect depends on the parts-whole relationship. The parts of an artistic whole have qualities, meanings, and effects so long as they are inseparable from the whole. When all the distinguishable parts of a whole are essential and in proper order and when the whole lacks no part necessary for its completeness, the parts are "organically related" and the whole has an "organic unity."

A poem cannot be paraphrased. The paraphrase of the poem means the demolition of the internal harmony of structure; like the chopping off the branches of a tree or an amputation of human limbs. How can a reader paraphrase the patterning sounds, pauses, and rhythm of the language of poetry which create various mental waves, psychological states, and emotional feelings? The paraphrased content can never fulfill these requirements. Brooks concludes that the core meaning of the poem depends upon structure, and further structure depends upon "paradox," "irony," "ambiguity," and "complex of attitude." Brooks remarks:

> The structure meant is a structure of meanings, evaluations, and interpretations; and the principle of unity which informs it seems to be one of balancing and harmonizing connotations, attitudes, and meanings.[22]

Here it should be kept in the mind that the term 'structure' is used by Ransom in a different sense. For him it means the argument or content of the poem. It is always isolated from texture and creates a dualism in the poem. But for Brooks structure combines the conflicting ideas or opposites and discordant elements in the poem, producing an organic whole. Structure also never denotes the meaning of 'form' in traditional sense i. e. the external form. It is not just a kind of envelop which "contains" the "contents," nor is it a form like ode, elegy, sonnet etc. in which ideas or subject-matter are dressed. Traditionally, when we analyze a sonnet, we define its external form—-poem with fourteen lines of iambic pentameter, a conventional pattern of rhymes, and a conventional division into two parts as a sonnet. But the New Critics centre their concentration upon the linguistic organization of the poem rather than on any alleged over-all structure independent of words. They do not begin an analysis of Gray's 'Elegy' by discussing the elegy as a traditional form of literature with a particular purpose and with certain devices appropriate to it, rather they study the words in the poem and find the form in the total pattern of language, image, irony, paradox, and ambiguity. Their primary concern is to discover the intrinsic worth or the literary aspects of the text at the level of language and its working, not to the history of literary genres, plots, characters, and thoughts. They are concerned with the structure of works or art than feeling, content, or message. However, in actual practice the New Criticism has most often been applied to the lyric. It has been less successful when applied to extended works of fiction or drama.

The New Critics hold that a poem is neither an idea nor statement, nor philosophy nor history. It is a verbal construct, an object made by human, or a concrete entity like a painting. Therefore, they ruthlessly attack those approaches of criticism which give information about the work of art. When we look at a painting, we never take an external and extra recourse to appreciate it. We do not need any information outside the painting to experience its aesthetic beauty. We do not need any biography or personal information of the artist because his painting is an autonomous, self-contained, and self-sufficient concrete object. Similarly, a poem, like painting, is an art. It has its own "universe of discourse," its own meaning and significance, and its own ontology and being. In Ransom's view poetry is an independent autonomous unity. Laying stress on the study of poem as poem, in his essay, "Poetry: A Note in Ontology," he is concerned with the reality of the poem's being. To treat a poem ontologically means to treat it as an autonomous objective structure. The being of the poem or its quality of beingness is that which is designated by Ransom as ontology. Borrowing the term from Kant, he considers a poem "a concrete universal" in which universal abstract ideas such as death, God, sin, etc. are manifested through concrete images and sensuous word. Ransom states that the essential quality of a poem "is that it shall be objective, shall site the nature of the object and shall recognize the autonomy of the work itself as existing for its own sake."

A poem does not require any extrinsic values. It should be treated, as T. S. Eliot says, "primarily as poetry and not another thing." Its merits and demerits, success and failure, and beauty and repulsion are explored within the work itself, not in the life of the author, the history of his times, or the socio-economic and political implications of the literary work. They think that literature is not to be judged as ethics, science, theology etc. Criticism is an act of analyzing and evaluating a work of art, and is neither concerned with the intention of the author, nor with the reader's emotional reaction. Though the New Critics are deeply inspired by I. A. Richards's most influential book *The Practical Criticism* (1929), yet they differ from his emotional or psychological reaction of the perceiver or reader. The New Criticism finds its full articulation in the two essays—"The Intentional Fallacy" and "The Affective Fallacy"—in *Sewanee Review* by W. K. Wimsatt Jr. and M. C. Beardsley, both collected in *The Verbal Icon* (1954). Intentional fallacy means an author's declared or supposed intention in writing a work. The New Critics reject the assumption that the meaning and value of a work is based on the author's expressed or implied intentions. They argue that if once a work of an artist gets published, it is beyond his control and belongs to the public. It acquires an objective existence and author's original ideas are thrown into the background. The second phrase, the Affective fallacy, is an erroneous ways of interpreting a work. When the critic or reader reflects his own personal, emotional, and psychological bias, it influences the interpretation of the work and the emotion of the impressionist critic makes the text merely as an occasion for pleasurable excitation. In this way, the objectivity of the work gets confused with its subjective colouring. The reader-response critic, however, asks how the critic, who is a reader first and has read the text he is criticizing, can discount his experience of the text if it makes his criticism possible to begin with. However, the New Critics consider the text as the final authority, independent of extra literary categories. The extrinsic values mar the aesthetic experience, because they distract the attention of the teachers, critics, and readers from the essential matter i. e. the intrinsic quality of the work.

The New Critics employ the objective theory of art and concentrate on the work of art itself and examine it through a process of close-reading and detailed analysis. It is like the French method known as *explication de texte*, which has long been a formal procedure for teaching literature in French schools. The New Critics with their variable views vary in their approach to analyze and study literature, but they all have a meeting ground i. e. to focus on the work of art and lay bare its intrinsic characteristics. Their aim and intention is thus to see hitherto unseen relationship between various parts and aspects of the poem—between word and word, between phrase and phrase, between line and line, between stanza and stanza, between image and image, and even between idea and idea. They make a detailed and subtle analysis of the complex interrelations and ambiguities of the component parts within a work. This internal and reflexive part-whole relationship constitutes the form and structure of the poem, interpreting multiple layers of meanings. Probing the connotations and permutations of the words and their complex interactions, the New Critics make a very close scrutiny of diction, syntax, symbols, metaphors, and imagery and then arrive at a critical judgment. They respect the text as a "verbal icon" which retains its internal tensions, irony, paradox, and rhetoric. Along with its linguistic organization and complexity, a text has to achieve a "reconciliation of diverse impulses," or "equilibrium of opposed forces," or an organic unity. The aim of the New Critics, remarks Peter Barry, has been "to show the unity beneath apparent disunity."[23] The New Critics also raise very genuine questions about literature and criticism: what a poem is; how it is produced and read; its poetic effect, the semantic and poetic meaning, intuition and experience, the validity of mythical and allegorical presentation, and many other related matters which come in for close examination.

The New Critics are deeply concerned with the function of language and the different nuances of words. Therefore, they, first of all, make two categories of language—(i) scientific or logical language and (ii) poetic language. Though both of them bank upon verbal medium, yet are poles apart. Scientific language or discourse only yields denotative, factual, or fixed meaning as the language used by philosophy, science, history, social sciences or any other expository prose does. On the other hand, the nature, aim and effect of the poetic language are different, because it does not employ words the way other verbal forms do. Poetic language is important for its verbal organization, not for its content, philosophy, moral lesson, nor historical facts. A poem, therefore, is a complex linguistic construct. It carries human emotions and attitudes which cannot be scientifically verified. The 'truth' or knowledge of poetry is relative to the perspective of the reader as well as universal. It reveals a specific type of knowledge which is neither scientific nor factual; it has both qualities temporal and timeless. Its language manipulates emotions and experiences, which is more 'true' and 'complex' in its use than science is. Poetic truth, therefore, is not possible in any other forms of language. Science focuses on truth in terms of abstractions or generalities, whereas poetry in terms of concreteness. Poetry communicates something significant about human experience by its special kind of language made up with the help of metaphor, figures of speech, metre, rhythm, imagery, irony, tension, and paradox. They all create a unified whole or a complex structure working internally and organically. To achieve this end, a poet wrestles with each and every word to convey the poetic meaning—a meaning which is inseparable from organic embodiment. This creative language gives a unique kind of pleasure and a higher kind of truth than that conveyed by abstractions of scientific language. To this end the New Critics arrive at this point that the essential components of any work, whether drama, lyric, or narrative exists at the level of language and its working.

The New Critics fed up with the verbosity and ornamentation of the existing poetic discourse take up the gauntlet to curb the vulgarization and corruption of language. Eliot in "The Metaphysical Poets" strongly suggests: "The poet must become more and more comprehensive, more elusive, more indirect, in order to force, to dislocate if necessary, language into his meaning."[24] He further argues that "there is a perpetual slight alteration of language, words perpetually juxtaposed in new and sudden combinations" in poetry. Ransom's basic poetic theory is based on structure-texture relationship. Structure is the central statement or argument or idea of a poem, whereas texture is the quality of language decorated with the appropriate metaphorical devices the poem contains. The texture gives full particulars of concrete knowledge. Conversely, science lacks texture and, therefore, has no rich particularity; science has only content with pure structure. The debased and deteriorating condition of the language makes Brooks worry: "I am concerned with what is happening to our language." He further states: "The dying flesh of language may produce a spiritual gangrene. One of the uses of literature is to keep our language alive—to keep the blood circulating through the tissues of the body politic."[25] He discovers that "the language of poetry is the language of paradox."[26] A scientist conveys the truth through a language which is quite direct. Clear, and shorn of all figures and paradox—"a language purged of every trace of paradox."[27] But a poet on the other hand, reveals very closely line by line and considers that paradox is one of the common structural properties. Allen Tate advocates liberating poetry from the traditional poetic paraphernalia and adopting different diction and poetic idiom. He calls for a dislocation of language connoting strange and unexpected domain of meaning. Tate argues that all types of poetry have certain common characteristics that can be designated as the name of single quality i.e. "tension." The equilibrium of two forces—denotative quality or 'extension' and the connotative value or 'intention' produces 'tension' in poetry, which gives the poetic meaning. R. P. Blackmur is also called "a botanist of the stanza, verse, phrase, even the single word." His poetic theory ingrained in "Language as Gesture" weighs the density of words. He contends that gesture is a quality—an added meaningfulness to words. To enlarge language with gesture, numerous devices are adopted such as simple repetition, complex repetition of words, puns, alliteration with rhyme, refrain, metre etc. The gestural language acquires new dimensions, depths, and nuances, while the language used in the common life or the ordinary definitions of words lack these qualities. In Blackmur's view, language has also capacity to go beyond the denotative and connotative activity and takes the reader into the realm of myth, history, religion, and even silence.

In this way, each critic of this group appears yielding a new tool, a new method, a new theory to vivify the vitiating poetic language. They all formulate a cluster of different concepts of criticism: Richards's "emotive" and "referential" meanings, Eliot's "objective correlative," Empson's "ambiguity," Tate's "tension," Brooks's "paradox," and "heresy of paraphrase," Ransom's "structure" and "texture," Blackmur's "gesture," Warren's "irony," Wimsatt's "verbal icon," and M. C. Beardsley's "intentional fallacy" and "affective fallacy." These are the yardsticks to determine the quality of a poem. They place emphasis on the unity, concreteness, complexity, inclusiveness, and wholeness of the poetic language. However, it is urgently important to note that the New Criticism, sharing their common orientation towards the invigoration of language and the close textual analysis, fail to subscribe their views unanimously. They do not agree upon a single methodology or a set of principles. For example, Kenneth Burke, R. P. Blackmur, and Yvor Winters are other noted critics who are generally associated with the group of the New Critics, but their work is really too individual and diverse to accommodate into this category. Winters especially has in fact attacked the New Criticism. In this context, Pritchard rightly comments that "there exist sharp cleavages among them."[28] Therefore, the two critics Kenneth Burke and Yvor Winters have been deliberately excluded from this study because they fail to fit comfortably into the scheme of this book.

IX

The New Criticism, enjoying its flowering and fruition, is on the wane from 1950s. It faces charges and accusations of the various emerging critical movements, particularly the Chicago School of Criticism. Even some of the New Critics themselves begin to revaluate and broaden their critical premises and procedures. The first charge is leveled that the New Criticism is too restrictive, dogmatic, narrow, and reduces literature to a formula or a form of monism. It is too arbitrary in its emphasis on complexity, excessive preoccupation with individual word, image, irony, paradox, and metaphor. R. S. Crane, therefore, in *Critics and Criticism* (1952) rules out that there is only one approach possible to understand a work of art. He rather supports different approaches and methods to apply to take out the meaning. Elder Olson also asserts that there should be a synthesis of both the intrinsic and extrinsic approaches. Secondly, the New Criticism is mostly applicable to short poems and ignores dramatic and narrative forms, though F. R. Leavis uses brilliantly this approach of close reading in fiction, too. Thirdly, cut off from the sociological, historical, psychological, and philosophical approaches, it lacks social and ethical content of literature. It is totally separated from the practical concerns of human life. Fourthly, the extreme negation of the reader's emotional response undermines the value of the work. Sixthly, it also rejects the genre study, which is very important for the development of the literary history.

Of course, it is quite true that the New Criticism has certain limitations and drawbacks, but it is also irrefutable that this movement offers a number of techniques and methods to read and teach poetry at a time when there was a complete chaos in critical procedures. Unfolding the density, gravity, and multi-layered meanings of words, it educates the sensibility of the reader and cultivates a new taste for appreciating a work of art. The main credit of the New Criticism is that it shifts the importance from the author to the text. Finally, it leaves an indelible mark on the evolution of the modern literary criticism in America. Later the form of the New Criticism is found in structuralism and deconstructionism. However, the traditional methods of criticism and analysis are still widely employed, because structuralist and deconstructionist practice tends to be inaccessible to many.

References:

1. John Paul Pritchard, *Criticism in America* (Ludhiana: Lyall Book Depot, 1956), p. 233.
2. Yiannis Stamiris, *Main Currents in Twentieth Century Criticism: A Critical Study* (New York: Whitson Publishing Co., 1986), p.158.
3. John Feket, *The Critical Twilight* (London: Routledge and Kegan Paul, 1977), p. 45.
4. *Ibid.*,
5. Rick Rylance ed., 'The New Criticism' in *Encyclopedia of Literature and Criticism* (London: Routledge, 1991), p. 724.
6. John Fekete, *The Critical Twilight*, p. 47.
7. M. A. R. Habib, *A History of literary Criticism and Theory* (Blackwell Publishing, 2008), p. 380.
8. Immanuel Kant, *The Critique of Aesthetic Judgment*, trans. By J. H. Bernarms.
9. M. A. R. Habib, *A History of literary Criticism and Theory,* p. 380.
10. E. F. Carritt, *The Philosophies of Beauty* (Oxford University Press, 1952), p.112.
11. *Ibid.*, p. 117.
12. A. H. Tak, *Coleridge and Modern Criticism* (Delhi: R. P. Publishing Corporation, 1985), pp.114-143.
13. Alex Preminger, *Princeton Encyclopedia of Poetry and Poetics* (Princeton University Press, 1974) p. 159.
14. John Shawcross, ed., *Biographia Literaria* (Oxford, 1907) p. 238.
15. T. M. Ratsore, ed. *Coleridge's Shakespearean Criticism* (1930), p. 224.
16. T. S. Eliot, "The Metaphysical Poets," *Selected Essays* (London: Faber & Faber, 1972), p. 290.
17. *Philosophies of Beauty*, p. 253.
18. John Paul Pritchard, *Criticism in America*, p. 231.

19. Joel Spingarn, "Introduction: Criticism in America," *Literary Opinion in America* (New York: Harper Torchbooks, 1962), p. 22.

20. Stanley Edger Hyman, *The Armed Vision* (New York: Alfred Knoff, 1948), p. 3.

21. Ray B. West, Jr. ed., *Modern Literary Criticism* (New York: Renehart & Co.) pp. 4 &115.

22. Cleanth Brooks, *The Well Wrought Urn: Studies in the Structure of Poetry* (New York: Harcourt, Brace and Company, 1947), p. 195.

23. Peter Barry, *Beginning Theory* (New York: Manchester University Press, 2007), p.72.

24. T. S. Eliot, "The Metaphysical Poets," *Selected Essays*, p. 289.

25. Cleanth Brooks, *Shaping Joy*, p.16.

26. ——————"The Language of Paradox," *20th Century Literary Criticism,* ed., David Lodge, p. 292.

27. *Ibid.*

28. John Pritchard, *Criticism in America*, p. 233

3

John Crowe Ransom

John Crowe Ransom (1888-1974) — a critic, theoretician, poet, teacher, and editor— is one of the seminal American men of letters of his time. The founder of the *Kenyon Review* and an associate of the two important movements in American literary history—The Fugitive Group and The New Criticism, he articulates his critical approach in *God Without Thunder* (1930), *The World's Body* (1938), and *The New Criticism* (1941). A salubrious personality propounding the basic tenets of the New Criticism, he is mainly concerned with the objective or 'ontological' criticism of a work of art and discusses it as a thing in itself. He directs his concentration on the central plank of the New Criticism i.e. text-as-text or an objective and close analysis of the text itself. Ransom considers poetry an independent autonomous unity and lays stress on the study of poem as poem, celebrating its verbal procedures. He holds a poem "…as assembling a small universe of objects and actions, in which a thing in order to exist must coexist with many other things which are quite unlike it…."[1]

Ransom is very ruthless to science, because it inflicts damage on religion, myth, culture, and poetry. It is science that plunders the agrarian society and that lays the foundation of industrialism, creating an environment of artificiality, glamour, and illusion. In *God Without Thunder*, Ransom expresses his deep dissatisfaction at the sharp development of science and rationalistic attitudes. Science is "a death drive" with an appearance of "a life force," which shatters the older values of the agrarian society. Scientific knowledge topples down modern man from the pedestal of peace, prosperity, serenity, and leisure to the world of illusion—an illusion that he has conquered the universe and himself. "His arts and religions wither and he lives miserably in a rectilinear jungle of factories and efficiency apartments."[2] Science, Ransom argues, is a great foe to the leisurely southern agrarian society. It is a root cause of the decline of modern man, and this decline still continues "in which an old body of thought is being progressively disbelieved and a new body of thought is progressively governing our conduct."[3] Science more and more banking upon rationality for all phenomena has thrown religion into the background or diluted it:

> This diluted religion posits an amiable and understandable God who is the embodiment of general benevolence and social welfare. He is a God without Thunder, demanding nothing extraordinary or supernatural.[4]

Science, "a new religion," is "an order of experience in which we mutilate and prey upon nature." Man gets dispossessed of himself and achieves his own doom and destruction in the course of over coming nature. His reliance on scientific concerns leads to a steep fall, slaying the spirit of poetry and religion. John L. Stewart writes: "Trouble arose when man supposed that the representations of science, which lacked the 'fullness of the natural,' were the only valid ones."[5] But *God Without Thunder* is not as much concerned with religion as with myth, symbol, culture, and human love for transforming abstract ideas into concrete sensory objects. With nostalgia for social stability and order, Ransom wishes to recapture the virtues of the vanished past through a programme that demands "de-industrialization." Monroe K. Spears states:

> He [Ransom] protests against the abstracting intellect because he believes it to be, as embodied in modern science, a present danger; the danger is that it may win too complete victory, drying up or denying the pleasures of the innocent sensibility.[6]

Science, Ransom contends, is abstract and has made the world skeleton through its abstractions, but the body of the world can be restored through the sensuous particularity of poetry. Science appeals to "the reason," whereas poetry and other fine arts satisfy "the whole man." Poetry is primarily aesthetic; it is a redemptive force, a source of knowledge, and establishes an order. It is an inexhaustible "utterance of the whole soul of man." The function of poetry, Ransom theorizes, is to restore human feelings. It can become a discipline for that ordering of the soul that the Greeks called *paideia*. Ransom asserts that the essential features of poetic language are its concreteness and aesthetic value. His poetic theory personifies and concretizes abstractions.

Ransom makes a difference between science and poetry. Poetry proves knowledge or truth quite different from the knowledge supplied by science. The realities presented by the scientific discourse are "reduced, emasculated, and docile versions" of the world in which we live. On the other hand, "Poetry intends to recover the denser and more refractory original world which we know loosely through our perceptions and memories."[7] The truth of poetry is grasped through the contemplation of the aesthetic symbol, iconic nature, and contextual quality. Poetry, like myth or religion, functions as a symbol or a unified complex and reveals truth in a metaphorical way. It is a living entity. Through its *structure* and *texture*, it gives knowledge of the universals as well as knowledge of the particulars. Science, on the other hand, has a utilitarian relation to the animal life of man; and it gives a limited and rather incomplete knowledge of reality. It is poetry that provides a vital knowledge and makes man a full human being. Poetic activity is cognitive and complementary to the knowledge furnished by science. In this way, poetry can open our eyes to the riches of the "world's body." Science or prose discourse deals with "universals" reducing nature into abstract formulations, but poetry deals with "particulars" recovering reality in its full concreteness. Poetry asserts reality because of its concern with the 'Being' of reality.

In *God Without Thunder*, Ransom's other generative idea is myth, which is a mode of concrete presentation that preserves the particularity of nature. He supports and recommends myth, because it serves as a remedy for the predicament of the Western mind. Ransom observes:

> A myth is a fable; it calmly alleges a miracle or impossible occurrence; it leaves its natural history altogether and yet attempts to imply the whole of that history. Myth restores to the supernatural in order to represent the fullness of the natural.[8]

Myth, Ransom further defines, is the "psychic necessity" for modern rationalists, though they would refuse to believe in the supernatural. They see "myths as lies or at best incorrect attempt to explain natural phenomena."[9] But for Ransom, myth is the symbolic presentation of truth. It is "a symbolic projection of fundamental human feeling," rather than "the theological or metaphysical reality." Louise Cowan rightly remarks that myth is "the only remaining means available at present" [10] to restore and organize the human psyche and give full knowledge to it. Eliot also adopts the mythical technique in *The Waste Land* to show the present spiritual predicament—an ever-recurring phenomenon. He applies myth to give control, order, shape, and significance to the chaos, anarchy, and disintegration of the contemporary civilization. Myth saves from modern scientific abstractions. "Modern scientific man…has ignored those individual matters so vital to poetry; in viewing the forest he has overlooked the trees."[11] Though the Enlightenment causes damage to myth, yet the New Critics try to restore its lost meaning. However, Ransom makes it clear in the preface to *The World's Body* that he opposes science only so far as it claims exclusiveness. Being a dualist, he sees art and science as "equal and apposite" activities; both producing valid and necessary knowledge of the world, and he makes no more important claim for arts than it is necessary to counterbalance science. Monroe K. Spears also comments: "Ransom never repudiates logic or science; he would not give a complete victory to emotion, texture, play, innocence, and usefulness even if he could."[12]

In *The New Criticism*, Ransom holds that criticism is the study of *structure* and *texture*—rather the dialectical interpretation between the two. Literature provides a high emotional content, but this passion is always mediated by the poem's formal structure and particular details. These details are a system of tensions which may operate without ultimate solutions, and this process proves to be a merit of a great work of art. Inferior or popular works offer simple solutions or messages, whereas mature works resist easy satisfaction. However, quality literature never remains incomplete or indecisive, because it may ironize or complicate; the various components are integrated into a satisfying 'organic whole,' whereby one element balances another. The poem is, thus, like a complex independent living entity—in fact, like life itself. This critical interpretation of a poem reveals the integration and balancing force of the two components—*structure* and *texture*.

Ransom's basic concept of poetic theory is based on the dialectical interplay between *structure* and *texture.* He defines a poem as "a logical structure having a local texture." No poem can exist without both *structure* and *texture.* The combination of these two goes to make the meaning of the poem. And a critic's job is to analyze or study a poem keeping in view these two terms. He "must examine the prose-object which the poem celebrates and the form in which that celebration is cast." To conceptualize *structure* and *texture*, Ransom presents an image of a living room:

> A poem is a *logical structure* having a *local texture.* These terms have been actually though not systematically employed in literary criticism. To my imagination, they are architectural. The walls of my room are obviously structural; the beams and boards have a function; so does the plaster, which is the visible aspect of the final wall. The plaster might have remained naked, aspiring to no characters, and purely functional. But actually it has been painted receiving colour; or it has been papered, receiving colour and design, though these have no structural value; or perhaps it has been hung with tapestry, or with paintings, for "decoration." The paint, the paper, the tapestry are texture. It is logically unrelated to structure.[13]

Structure, the term, suggests that in every poem there is an object which can be stated in prose "which any forthright prosy reader can discover...by an immediate paraphrase."[14] The central statement or argument or idea of a poem is its structure. Its content may be of any sort 'a kind of story, character, thing, scene, object,' situation, which gives us the argument of the poem. Structure of the poem is the framework of meaning. Ransom writes: "The structure proper is the prose of the poem being a logical discourse of almost any kind, and dealing with almost any suitable content."[15] It is more comprehensive and includes the argument or the development of the theme in a poem. Structure has its arguable, analyzable, abstract, and universal framework on which the poet creates a texture of poetic meaning. It gives the poem such shape as it has; "it regulates the assemblage of sensory data, providing order and direction," [16] but reveals no rich particularity. Ransom speaks of structure variously as 'a logical object,' 'the logical construct,' 'a universal,' 'the prose object,' 'the core-object,' 'the prose-logic,' 'the presentable object,' 'the constant element,' 'plot,' 'argument,' and 'the primary interest of the poet.' Logical construct carries an overtone of "the world of affairs." It is "ethical," "social," and useful, but reveals an undistinguished and commonplace argument. This logical structure is controlled by irrelevant or unrelated matter or details, which is called *texture*. Texture restores order. It is a differentiating principle of a poem, not the content, or the logical sequence of thought. This peculiarly poetic kind of order is to be created by an ontological 'law.'

Texture is the aesthetic of the poem. It is the thinginess of the things by which it is particularized. Though it has no functional role in the sense of providing utility or moral principles; it is "impractical;" it is "a luxury yet it determines the form of a poem and forces "us to take in the rich particularity of experience."[17] The texture is the quality of expression embellished with the appropriate metaphorical devices constituting heterogeneous elements like metaphors and rhythm which the poem contains. The texture gives full particulars of physical knowledge. Conversely, science lacks texture and, therefore, has no rich particularity; science has only content with pure structure. The argument of the poem is complicated, hindered, and diverted because of texture. The poem "develops its local particularities while it progresses towards its functional completion."[18] The local particularities are called texture. It is used to designate the individual concrete qualities of a poem that cannot be paraphrased. It is opposed to the paraphrasable structure or abstract argument or the ideas of a poem.

The verbal surface of a poem, its sensuous qualities, the density of imagery, the words, the connotations suggested by 'the inload' of words, the particular pattern of sound: its assonance, consonance, alliteration, euphony—these local values or properties are applied to *texture*. Ransom incidentally also uses texture to refer to the variation on the basic metrical pattern. Thus, texture, the identifying character of a poem, is its flavour, mode, mood, tone or voice, which provides "a private character" to the poem. In this way, the poet forces his words to convey many layers of meaning simultaneously. If a critic has nothing to say about the texture of a poem, he has nothing to say about specifically as poem. A vivid texture is essential for criticism.

Though, Ransom says, texture is irrelevant to structure, yet he places the strongest emphasis on it. Texture is irrelevant in contradiction to prose, which is rational. Ransom rejects science, abstraction, the universals, and the Platonic world of ideas because they do not give any 'texture.' They are not dense but thin and deal with the conceptual world only. A critic treats a work only in so far as 'increment,' 'superfluity,' and 'tissues of irrelevance residue' is concerned. The "intent of the good critic becomes, therefore, to examine and define the poem with respect to its structure and texture."[19] "Structure" or the argument of a poem gives pleasure to the reason, while "texture" delights the sensibility. It is very important to note here that the relations of words and phrases, sounds and images with each other in a poem are grouped by other New Critics under the heading "*Structure*." To Ransom they form the *texture* of the poem.

Texture, Ransom holds, is the aesthetic of the poem without playing any functional role, because it lends no utility or moral principles. It is really deplorable that the two elements—structure and texture—are separable entities in a poem. There is an unresolved dualism in Ransom's poetic form:

> The poem actually continues to contain its ostensible substance which is not fatally diminished from its prose state that is its logical core or paraphrase. The rest of the room is x which we are to find.[20]

This citation reveals that the texture is super-added, "an increment" or decoration of "local details" to the structure. In other words, the two are "logically unrelated." Texture or irrelevances proves impediment in precise expression of feelings and thoughts. The poet has to wrestle with the indeterminate at every stage. Sometimes the poet gets indulged in the textural details so much that he deviates from giving a right impression to the thought-core. Thus, in the clash between the intention and execution, between the determinate and the indeterminate, there emerges a poem that is quite different from what the poet intends at the very outset of composition or creation. This indeterminate of Ransom may be called 'a new determinate,'[21] as Lee T. Lemon says to emphasize its relevance to the total structure of the poem. But Ransom fails to explain convincingly how the two elements are integrated into the single unity or the objectivity of the poem. That is why Murray Krieger discovers a lack of organic view of form. Ransom rejects the theory that everything in a poem is "functional" and must merge with the 'whole.' The independence of details, "texture," must be accepted as the very ontological nature of poetry. Thus, prose is "one-valued" and the poem is "many valued."[22] Cleanth Brooks, however, refuses to agree to this view about the irrelevance of local texture: "in a good poem, as in a good drama, there is no waste motion and there are no superfluous parts."[23] Ransom's view is dialectical, whereas Brooks's is organic: "the beauty of the poem is the flowering of the whole plant." [24] Ransom is primarily anti-rationalistic with all his anti-abstractionism. He thinks that the poetic mode of thought replaces scientific abstraction, but he lays emphasis on the logical meaning in his poetic theory. He argues that poetic knowledge is not unrelated to life in general. Hence, he reacts against Cleanth Brooks's objection to the paraphrase of a poem and Blackmur's refusal of ideas in a poetic structure. Ransom's approach towards "the poetic world-view is Aristotelian and realistic rather than platonic and idealistic." Ransom States:

> No faith, no passion of any kind is originated in a poem; it is brought into the poem by the 'imitating' of life (to use Aristotle's term); it is the fact which is the heart of the action.[25]

Ransom is called a dualist. His tenet is that in a poem the prose meaning or "a logical structure" is made to submit to an apparently unrelated and independent body of sense particulars of both sound and imagery, the "texture." This combination of "a logical structure" and "texture," he calls, is a "miracle of equilibrium," which remains a cornerstone in Ransom's aesthetic position and finds a recurrent expression in his writings, poetic and critical. All of his other generative ideas—myth, form, metaphysical poetry, and the extinction of the personality of the poet are related with this structure-texture reconciliation, a theme to which he has returned again and again throughout his career.

In *The New Criticism*, Ransom extends the theme of *Dinglichkeit*, or sensuous particularity of poetry developed in *The World's Body*. Stressing the concreteness of poetic language, he moves his theory to the extreme of iconicism. That is why he has a very serious objection to Charles W. Morris's categorization of sign into three separate parts—*semantic*, *syntactic*, and *pragmatic*, corresponding to science, art, and technology. Ransom rejects this qualification and points out Morris's weakness to distinguish art from science on the ground of the difference between symbol and icon. The difference is "that the object symbolized by a scientific sign would seem to be abstract...whereas the object symbolized by an iconic sign must be a whole object...." In brief, under the iconic sign, the abstract item is restored to the body from which it was taken. Thus, the language of poetry is quite different from that of physical and social sciences. It is a magical view of poetic language that the iconic sign is identified with an object in nature. In childhood, man knows the world in its primordial beauty, but as he grows older, his perception gets dim and abstract by "science." Then it is reconstructed and restored through the iconic language of poetry. Ransom states: "Science deals exclusively in pure symbol, but art deals essentially, though not exclusively in iconic sign."[26] Thus, iconicism is the distinguishing feature of his poetry.

In 1953 Ransom gets conscious and makes a frank confession of the deficiency in his structure-texture formulation and discovers the term texture incompetent. The texture is "a flat and inadequate figure for the vivid and felt part of the poem which we associate peculiarly with poetic language."[27] He, therefore, coins a new term "organism"[28] to conceive a fusion of three aspects—head, heart, and feet. These three aspects are three modes of experience: the first rational experience; the second, the experience of feeling and desire; and the third, the experience that cannot be stated, but only sounded; it is a measured rhythm—metre. The poetic creation is a complex model. Though the dualism between intellect and sensibility or structure and texture maintains its balance, yet there is a third part in the poem, which sets in motion. It is the metre. Ransom continues

> ...another interpretation, involving a third part in the poem. It is the meter, and the musical phrasing. Here the relation is between the prose rhythms of the language and the imposed meters, and that opposition is fruitful too. The resultant language has an access of authority which is almost miraculous.[29]

With the tools of his poetic theory—its nature, concept, and function—Ransom dismisses all the poetry of the nineteenth century, romantic as well as Victorian. It is the poetry of escapism, the poetry of opium dream, and poetry of emotional eruption. He observes:

> The poetry I am disparaging is a heart's desire poetry. If another identification is needed, it is the poetry written by romantics, in a common sense of that term. It denies the real world by idealizing it: the act of a sick man.... It indicates in the subject a poor adaptation to reality; a subnormal equipment in animal courage, flight and escapism, furtive libido. [30]

Romantic poetry is the pathological symptom of mental, moral, and spiritual disease. In idealizing or improving the world, it is lost in that world and even loses the touch with the real world. It is a pseudo poetic activity. Ransom, therefore, discovers lack and thinks romantic poetry is not worthy of serious consideration. He looks down upon the subjective expression of grief, desire, and agony in poetry; it is "a simple and mistaken theory of art." He writes aptly:

> The century outdid itself in the non-sense melodies of Swinburne, and the similar naiveté of the pre-Raphaelite. But going back into the century... it is evident that not Byron nor Keats nor Shelley ever became quite sophisticated or grown up.... Nobody in the whole century knew how to put his whole mind and experience to work in poetry, as had Chaucer, Spenser, Shakespeare and Milton.[31]

Ransom warns that the composition of poetry is not a diversion of an idle hour or an exalted subject or spontaneity. It is more conscious, more intelligent, and more effective exploitation of the technique. Poetry, therefore, is an art—every word has to justify in its use and place, every image has to show and perform its function. It has to prove its strength and perfection. Ransom writes:

> If to be conscious of his art is a higher form of accomplishment than to be an untutored singer warbling native woodnotes, the poet himself has developed.[32]

Ransom downright rejects poetry that reveals sentimentality, moralism, and love for the ornate phrase, and unfunctional beauty of language. Like Eliot, he advocates for an extinction of the poet by putting on "fictitious personality." He considers that a good poem intends as a work of art to lose the identity of the author," and assumes "an ideal or fictitious personality." A poem is basically constructed, not expressed with emotional outpouring; and the attachment from the self is the aesthetic attitude.

In Ransom's view there are two clear categories of poetry—(i) the pre-scientific and (ii) the post-scientific. The former is produced out of myths and belief, while the latter banks upon facts and demonstrates truth. Poetry of the pre-scientific era is not possible, because the poet cannot retreat into the past, nor the past can be brought back again. Moreover, he has to face the real world—a world of rationality, logic, and scientific inquiry. He knows the limitations and shortcomings of scientific contemplation. Thus, post-scientific poetry is born out of disillusionment of success, discontent, frustration, and failure. The poet is deeply dissatisfied with the existing life and suffers problems of the world. "He therefore invents a private world where such injustice cannot be, and enjoys it as men enjoy their dream....[33] He gets indulged in prayers, requests, and beseechments, and tries either to idealize or improve the world. Ransom disapproves such poetry—the romantic and classical (in the sense of didactic). He writes in his preface to *The World's Body*:

> The true poetry has no great interest in improving or idealizing the world, which does well enough. It wants to realize the world, to see it better. Poetry is the kind of knowledge by which we must know what we have arranged that we shall not know otherwise.[34]

Ransom recommends a poetry that should be difficult, strange, and shocking to the men who are deeply conditioned with the prose view. The modern poets, guided by the symbolists and the imagists, should consistently set out in quest of aesthetic effect irrespective of moral or useful ideas, casting away the decorative ornaments. He accepts only the Metaphysical mode of poetry, which intends to know and realize the world better. Thus, the three phrases: (i) idealize the world (ii) improve the world, and (iii) realize the world—stand for the three different kinds of poetry i.e. the romantic poetry, the didactic poetry, and the metaphysical poetry.

Ransom's *The World's Body*, a benchmark in modern criticism, consists of fifteen essays, centering on the poetic mode of knowledge and the nature and function of poetry. Of them, the two noteworthy essays—"Poetry: A Note in Ontology" and "Criticism, Inc."—deserve special attention to understand his viewpoints regarding poetry.

Poetry: A Note in Ontology

The concept of the autonomy of a poem is the bedrock of Ransom's poetics. He uses the term 'ontology' to describe the autonomy of a poem. It is a Greek word combining two roots "onta" meaning existing thing and "logos" meaning knowing. Ontology is concerned with the reality of the poem's being. To treat a poem ontologically means to treat it as an autonomous objective structure which has its own world of meaning and own mode of being. The problem of ontology is related to Ransom's ideas on "structure" and "texture." The being of the poem or its quality of beingness is that which is designated by Ransom as ontology. In "Poetry: A Note in Ontology," Ransom divides poetry into three kinds. First, there is "physical poetry" which tries to capture the precise qualities of things by using the kind of hard, clear, and accurate images advocated by the Imagist poets. His second kind of poetry is "Platonic poetry," which seeks to move reader to take a particular ethical attitude. He considers this as "bogus poetry," not poetry at all. His third kind of poetry is "metaphysical poetry," which is poetry that uses metaphorical and other kinds of figurative language to shock the reader into new and exciting perceptions on its subject. Ransom, like T. S. Eliot, observes a rupture between reason and sensibility, and also aligns English poetic tradition with the metaphysical school of poetry.

Physical Poetry

Physical Poetry or the poetry of things is about things and employ images, which are endowed with "a primordial freshness which idea can never claim." Man is temperamentally more interested in things than in ideas. Though, for some time attracted by science, he shifts his attention and interest from things to ideas. But very soon, he always gets fed up with the theories of science, and again he turns to his primeval objects or images. His dreams and memories corrode his mind for the loss of things for the sake of the scientific generalizations. It is in his memories he finds the first images still quite alive and intact. The scientific abstractions or theories after all fail to diminish or distort the original freshness of things. He revives his love for the things. In the modern age, Ransom admits, some poets witness everything so ravaged by the prose of science that they return to the first phase of his experience and take shelter in it. The revived love for the things is an outcome of the poetic contemplation of objects or images, creating the pleasure of recognition. In this way, Ransom propounds a new concept i.e. Art is based on the second love for things, not on the first love. In the beginning a child loves things, not because of the trailing glory of heaven in the sense of Wordsworthian philosophy, but he has no systematic ideas. When he acquires ideas, his love for things begins to die, but again his love for things gets born, when he finds himself totally dissatisfied and frustrated with the scientific activity of the mind.

Ransom's basic credo of second love in the poetic theory of the aesthetic process is ingrained in his unpublished manuscript entitled "The Third Moment." He argues that the order of human experience can be divisible into three moments. The first moment is the original experience of life. It is concrete, intense, unfallen, and complete; it is pre-categorical experience, pure of all intellectual content, unreflective and singular. The first moment is purely sensuous and beyond the limits of the working faculties of the mind. The second moment is a period of thought, of analysis, of recording experience; it is the moment of categorization and concept formation through abstract ideas from the total experience. The second moment Ransom associates with science, logic, and history. The third moment begins with memory and a sense of loss; it is the moment of making poetic images in which sensuousness and reflection combine together. Thus, the third is a moment of mixture which recovers qualities through images. To achieve the third moment, imagination plays a vital role; it is the faculty of Pure Memory, or unconscious mind; it unearths the original experiences from the dark storeroom. The fullness of the first moment can be recaptured only by the creative agency. The artists construct dreams, fancies, morals, art, religion—all images made in an attempt to recapture the "fugitive first moment." The result of the construction of images is a "mixed world" in which images co-exist with formed concepts. In this way, there is interplay between idea and image, between the conceptual and the concrete. Ransom states:

> We have elected to know the world through our science and we know a great deal, but science is only the cognitive department of our animal life, and by it we know the world only as a scheme is abstract conveniences. What we cannot know constitutionally as scientists is the world which is made of whole and indefeasible objects, and this is the world which poetry recovers for us.[35]

The lost world in the first moment is recovered through the agency of poetry. It is concerned with the act of perception, which proves that the object is physically remarkable. This formulation of his theories is important to Ransom's critical thought throughout his career.

In the modern age, ideas are considered important by which science becomes paramount. But the modern poets and the New Critics like Ransom fully condemn the poetry of ideas, because it suffers from "dissociation of sensibility" in Eliot's phrase. That is why the imagist poets wish to liberate themselves from science and logic, which play havoc with other faculties. They immerse in images to drive away abstractions. Consequently, the poetry of things is born, but Ransom notices that the reading public through the nineteenth century is so badly conditioned with ideas that they look into poetry for them of any dimension and range. It has become their habit to prefer ideas to things. Their only motto and interest is to take out ideas from things. In this process, they squeeze every drop of idea from things and ultimately mutilate the whole image. According to Ransom: "Their game is the images or the things, and they acquire the ability to shoot them as far off as they can be seen, and do." To them if there are no ideas in poetry, there is no important poetry. Deeply dissatisfied with this predisposition of the people, in modernism, the imagist poets not only reject ideas but also abhor the poetry of ideas. They lay deep emphasis in their manifestoes on the concrete, hard, and precise poetry of sharply defined images. There is an honest accuracy in expression, devoid of moral platitudes and sentimental clichés and language unborrowed from any school of poetry. Ransom supports T. E. Hulme's theory of image that every word should present an image or set of images and not an idea. The imagist poetry claims to be 'Pure Poetry' because it depends on "the faculty of present images so whole and clean that they resist the catalysis of thought." George Moore also pleads for physical poetry as 'pure poetry' where image is important not the idea. Ransom illustrates through quotation from Shakespeare:

> Full fathom five thy father lies
> Of his bones are coral made.

Here the idea or thought is drowned in the configuration of image. Ransom admires this essential quality to silence logic to enjoy good health of the soul, but refuses to accept imagist poetry fully as pure poetry. Though image is the first qualification of any poetry, but the imagists practice it crudely by introducing the free verse and eliminating traditional metres. All true poetry is a phase of physical poetry. Moreover, pure poetry is not as innocent as it appears to be. It is a product of deliberate and conscious art, and demands rigorous discipline. The poet cannot enjoy a certain amount of license—that privilege is gone. Pure poetry is nicely metred and the images in it are carefully ordered. Pure poetry demands order, which makes the logical arrangement of things, involves dramatic "form," reflects things, brings out their appropriate qualities, and carries them through a systematic course of predication. In this way, the total impression is achieved. It is not merely a solid lump of thing-content.

> Technique takes the thing-content and meters and orders it. But meter is not an original property of things. It is artificial, and conveys the sense of human control, even if it does not wish to impair the thinginess of things.[36]

Platonic Poetry

Ransom calls the poetry of ideas Platonic Poetry, which has a quality of poetry, but a discourse which makes use of only abstract ideas without any images would be nothing but a scientific document. It cannot be called a poem; not even a Platonic Poem. Platonic Poetry is also extremely steeped in the colour of the physical poetry. Just as the Physical Poetry, though it apparently looks innocent of ideas, carries secretly some ideation, so Platonic Poetry also possesses the properties of physical poetry. Thus, the poetry of ideas is teemed with images, and sometimes more than the reader desires. But the main intention of the images pictured in Platonic Poetry is to explain or propagate the ideas; the images function as examples of ideas or precepts, or a note of didacticism. Ransom cites an extract of Browning's "Pipa's Song" to point out the shortcomings of Platonic Poetry:

> The year's at the spring
> And day's at the morn;
> Morning's at seven;
> The hill-side's dew-pearled;
> The lark's on the wing;
> The snail's on the thorn:

In this extract, there are six lovely images, but they are all sacrificed, like six little lambs, at the cost of the message in the two concluding lines:

> God's in his heaven—
> All's right with the world!

Platonic Poetry is like a medicine hidden in the sugar candy—a note of didacticism in the garb of objects or images. Ransom calls it a "pedagogical trick," and even idealists like Hegel consider such poetry unworthy, because it will be spurious, when mankind achieves maturity and enlightenment.

Platonic Poetry, Ransom discovers, is an exercise of mental faculties, a science, but remains in the disguise of poetry, and pretends to have a concern for physical objects. He gathers all the genuine charges leveled against Platonic Poetry by Allen Tate published in *The New Republic*. First of all, Platonic Poetry is an allegory, a disease in things and after a close study, things can be translated into ideas at every step. Generally, the ideas are concerned with such popular causes as patriotic, religious, moral or social. In fact, Platonic Poetry is a celebration of ideas but behaves like Physical Poetry. It introduces physical properties for the sake of ornaments after the style of Physical Poetry. It is simply rhetoric, which turns to ideas seeking images to illustrate them. Platonic Poetry becomes positive when the poet believes that the ideas are produced effectively, but it becomes negative when he feels that ideas are not cared attentively. Consequently, romantic poets like Shelley pour out their personal lament:

> I fall upon the thorns of life! I bleed!

Ransom calls it "Platonic Irony," but such variety of poetry stiil falls under the category of Platonism. It generally suggests some new ideas which are quite incompatible with the prevalent ones. In "Ode to the West Wind," Shelly introduces some novel idea i.e. the spirit of revolution to root out the whole social, political, religious evils or systems or even sometimes "scientific optimism." But such ideas are not welcomed and he starts wailing.

Platonism, Ransom defines, is an 'impulse,' a nature, which is found in all human beings. It frequently gives too much emphasis on rationality and reasoning faculty and submits two important forces—(i) the love for the truth and (ii) the zeal of human improvement. The explanation of modern man is rational and by exerting rational power he can control the whole of the universe. Under the universal or scientific ideas, he is perennially in quest of the truth, nature, and world. Ransom thinks that this Platonic view is ultimately the predatory, reducing to the scientific. It does make man masterful but not righteous. That is why he regularly defends poetry against the encroachment of science. He defines:

> The Platonic Idea becomes the Logos which science worships, which is the Occidental God, whose minions we are, and whose children, claiming a large share in His powers for patrimony (p.123).

Ransom advises the modern man to know the limitation of his potential and be content in the sort of world he is placed in. But it is science that

> ...spins its project for human improvement at the expense of nature, which it scorns, and of God, who is its spirit. Science is always abstracting some arbitrary essence from the whole and will not care if it loses the whole for the part.[37]

Ransom has deep disparagement for ideational poetry, because an idea is deprived of another one. It is "derivative and tamed." "It has to be discovered there, not put there, obeying its own law and none of ours." The fine Platonic world of ideas does not match or keep in harmony with the "original world of perception...populated by the stubborn and contingent objects" (p.123). So the poetic sensibility always dominates the scientific truth. George Moore defends the poetry of things and calls it "pure poetry" because the things are constant and ideas even change. Ransom recommends Moore's condemnation of Victorian poetry—the poetry obsessed with ideas and never ends without speaking of the soul. Moore's strong dislike to Victorian ideas is because of their moral overtone. The ideas relate everything to the human soul in Platonic sense. This sense of morality always blurs and dulls perception. Modern man places high value on the scientific morality to achieve the more perfect possession or control of nature. The scientific morality appears to be inevitable for the general public, but it has no value for the aesthetic experience. A very pertinent question arises as to why people express ideas through poetry; they can adopt other means to express them. Some Hegelians think that they are hired to do so. By doing so, science cannot become poetry. Rather science becomes "less effective as a science when it muddies its clear waters with irrelevance, a sermon becomes less cogent when it begins to quote the poet" (p.125). It is the propensity of the moralist, the scientist, and the prophet of idealism to sum up their conclusions in poetry. Though these conclusions could not reach the desired end and are killed by poetic elements. The Platonist, Ransom suggests, can be cured by two ways. The first treatment is by the Platonic ideas themselves, when they become ineffective to work on because of treachery, love, and economics. In this way, the Platonist gets defeated and bewildered. The second treatment is by education in fine arts, which erases his Platonism more smoothly and effortlessly and tells that man is not habitual of generating abstract ideas to cloud perception.

Some artists define art as "the reference of idea to the image and intend to prove ideas through the image," but it is also not right way to express them because

> The ideas will not cover the objects upon which they are imposed, they are too attenuated and thread like; for extension is thin while intention is thick (p.126).

Here Ransom brings two other significant terms to describe the dual presence of the conceptual and the perceptual in the aesthetic object. In the poem, an idea exists thread-like and tends to expand beyond the particular object in the poem. According to Ransom, genuine poetry is always in the form of thesis or argument in the mind of a poet. It is developed through the characters and the situation or the images, but what happens is that images and characters develop faster than the idea automatically, and when the desired goal is achieved or the end is reached, the thesis or ideas disappears, and only the images are perceived. This image Ransom designates as texture of the poem, and the idea as structure. Though the structure may be almost forgotten, no poem exists without both texture and structure. To the end, Ransom passes a very harsh remark to Platonic poetry:

> Platonism is steady and malignant. This poetry is an imitation of Physical Poetry and not really a poetry. Platonists practice their bogus poetry in order to show that an image will prove an idea, but the literature which succeeds in this delicate mission does not contain real images but illustration (p.128).

It should be noted here that Platonic poetry includes both romantic and classical poetry. Ransom calls classical poetry in the sense of didactic poetry. The former tries to idealize the world, while the latter improves the world. Thus, romantic, Victorian, didactic, and even poetry with the ideas of Plato—all are under the category of Platonic poetry.

Metaphysical Poetry

In the third section of the essay, "Poetry: A Note in Ontology," approving metaphysical poetry as pure or good poetry, Ransom discusses the nature, creative process, and function of poetry. He constructs his poetic theories quoting George Moore's assertion:

> Most men read and write poetry between fifteen and thirty and afterwards very seldom, for in youth we are attracted by ideas, and modern poetry being concerned almost exclusively with ideas we live on duty, liberty, and fraternity as chameleons are said to live on light, and air, till at last we turn from ideas to things, thinking that we have lost our taste for poetry, unless, perchance, we are classical scholars (p.128).

On this framework, Ransom builds his theoretical formulations. He argues that it sounds so nice to hear that many men become poetic minded in order to atone for having been hard practical men and hard theoretical scientists. They withdraw from Platonism and come back to things from ideas. But it is not absolutely possible, because the mind is a little bit molested by Platonism. Despite all possible effort, it remains defiled; it never remains chaste and intact as it was in the first moment. The aesthetes wish to achieve the state of childhood or the original experience, but they do not succeed fully because the mind is still associated with the ideas of youth. Ransom holds: "It cannot be exactly a volte-face." Even in the third moment, the moment of image-making, poet's impulse is not free from science, because Platonism is always 'militant', 'sciencing,' and 'devouring.' The poetic impulse has to struggle hard against it, "to constitute the world of perception," and enjoy the image. Ransom epitomizes this assertion in these words:

> Science gratifies a rational or practical impulse and exhibits the minimum of perception. Art gratifies a perceptual impulse and exhibits the minimum of reason (p. 130).

The aspiration of the poetic impulse, ever in the clutch of logic and science, ventures to be fully free to attain innocence. The innocence of this aesthetic attitude cherishes an extreme desire which automatically reveals itself. But this innocence of the aesthetic attitude, Ransom holds, cannot be achieved, but demands a scrutiny. It is

> ...the most objective and the most innocent attitude in which we can look upon the world, and it is possible only when we neither desire the world nor pretend to control it.[38]

Innocence of knowledge or "knowledge without desire" in Schopenhauer's terms poses some question and examination. Man is an efficient animal species. When his biological appetites are fulfilled, he wants to control treasure and piles up "power and wealth for beyond the capacity" of his desires. Before he comes to the aesthetic moment, he shows that "every act of attention...is conditioned by a gross selfish interest." Thus, the aesthetic moment appears as curious moment of suspension, not the moment of innocence—suspension between Platonism and innocence. There generates a conflict between the poetic and Platonic impulse. There is a reconciliation or modification between idea and thing. Neither pure ideas nor pure things can make pure or good poetry. It is the integration of the two that creates the objective form of an aesthetic artifact. The pull towards ideation inhibits the perceptual impulse and leads to conceptual generalizations. The pull towards the simple physical sense of thinginess inhibits the cognitive impulse and leads to naked realism. The aesthetic pleasure lies in the complexity of poetic cognition. Ransom suggests that when the poet achieves the aesthetic attitude of the suspended moment he should cultivate many technical devices to increase the magnitude of the "percipiendia" and "sensibilia." These characteristics are best recorded in metaphysical poetry.

Ransom prescribes three important devices to enrich the perception and sensibility of artists:

1. Metre
2. Fiction
3. Tropes

According to Ransom, poetic form gives a shape to the shapeless emotion. The specialty of a poem does not consist in its balance between structure and texture or mere musical phrasing, fiction and tropes which are called the third part of the poem. The poet "must reckon with the meters too. And the poem assumes the form of a trinitarian existence."[39] Ransom puts special accent on metre and calls *it sine quo non* of poetry and defines rhythm as a variation on metrical pattern. He considers metre as "the most obvious device" (p. 130). About the duality of words in poetry, he writes: "Words which make sense...also make a uniform structure of accents and rhymes."[40] He calls the sound pattern "symbolic rhythm," and asserts that "the rhythm of the meters envelops....like an atmosphere, a constraint, and a blessing too. For it is sounding all the time."[41] Metre may impede the flow of language, but it is also correct that once an idiom is put in metre it glistens. Ransom is not content with the diction, imagery, and tropes, but he calls for the necessity of regular metre in poetry. It is not enough that the feeling be expressed precisely in a well-formed phrase; the phrases must also have a rhythm to fit into the chosen metre.

Fiction is another very important device in poetry. It means an artist adopts an aesthetic distance in art by introducing a fictitious object or hypothetical situation. Every poem looks like a sign without treating the actual situation. Kant also asserts that aesthetic judgment is not concerned with the existence or non-existence of the object. It is generally easier to obtain the aesthetic pleasure from art than from nature. Arts, with a view to aesthetic distance, create "the illusion of reality," and remain "true to life." The artists present such sort of truth with dignity in arts. In this way, arts perform their work with much fidelity to the sensuous world.

Trope or figure of speech is the third device, which a scientific discourse never uses for its exact language. Figures of speech, Ransom defines, deviate from normal course of writing to lend sensuous touch and cripple the tyranny of science over the senses. They shockingly reveal the limitation of rationality running in the prose discourse. Brushing aside other figures of speech, Ransom focuses his attention only on metaphor—'the climatic figure'—which has been exploited very strikingly in metaphysical poetry. Dryden uses this term metaphysics for the first time to refer to the poetry of a group of poets, particularly John Donne. He "affects the metaphysics, not only in his satires, but in his amorous verses." From the middle ages through Shakespeare till Dryden's time, the meaning of the term 'metaphysics' was simply supernatural or miraculous. Dryden notices miraculsim in metaphysical poetry and condemns it. He permits it only in satires where it is possible for witty effects. Though Dryden himself, Ransom says, employs miraculism wittily. He avoids it his level best.

Ransom has a very high opinion of metaphysical poetry where he explores miraculism. He gives a new definition to it: "'Metaphysics' or miraculism informs a poetry which is the most original and exciting and intellectually perhaps the most seasoned..." (p.135). Metaphysical effect may be found at two levels: large scale and small scale. Milton's poetry embodies the large scale effect, while metaphysical poetry the small effect. To Ransom, Milton's *Paradise Lost* is both 'heroic and miraculous.' The virtue of a long poem on a metaphysical subject consists in dramatization of all parts. *The Paradise Lost* incorporates all such characteristics everywhere:

> Thus Adam to himself lamented loud
> Through the still Night, not now, as ere man fell,
> Wholesome and cool, and mild, but with black Air.
> Accompanied, with damps and dreadful gloom,

> Which to his evil Conscience represented
> All things with double terror: on the ground
> Outstrectcht he lay, on the cold ground, and oft
> Crush'd his Creation, Death as oft accus'd
> Of tardie execution, since denoune't
> The day of his offence. Why comes not Death,
> Said hee, with one thrice acceptable stroke
> To end me?

Metaphysical poetry is fraught with conceits that constitute its staple. Ransom sets out a difference of the use of conceits between Donne and Cowley in the following two different extracts:

> Our hands were firmly cemented
> By a fast balm which thence did spring;
> Our eye-beams twisted, and did thread
> Our eyes upon one double string.

But Cowley's use of conceit is more powerful:

> Oh take my Heart, and by that means you'll prove
> Within, too stor'd enough of love:
> Give me but yours, I'll by that change so thrive
> That Love in all my parts shall live.
> So powerful is this my change, it render can,
> My outside Woman, and your inside Man.

Ransom defines that "a conceit originates in metaphor," and "the conceit is but a metaphor." The difference between the seventeenth and the nineteenth century poetry depends upon the use of metaphors. The former used them boldly and effectively, while the latter half-heartedly and was rather content with simile. Ransom comments:

> The difference between the literary qualities of the two periods is the difference between the metaphors and simile.... One period was pithy and original in its poetic utterance, the other was prolix and predictable (p.137).

Ransom illustrates examples from Shelley and Tennyson to show how they miss the effect of metaphysical miraculism. In Shelley's *Adonais*:

> Thou young Dawn,
> Turn all thy dew to splendour....

Here splendour is not an exact correlative of dew; it has a flat tone of Platonic idea rather than a conceit. On the other hand, Tennyson also introduces conceits in "Come into the Garden, Maud":

> The red rose cries, "She is near, she is near;"
> And the white rose weeps, "She is late;"
> The larkspur listens, "I hear, I hear;"
> And the lily whispers, "I wait."

This is a technical conceit, but too complicated, with a plurality of images, without maintaining individuality. The flowers stand for lover's thoughts, but their distinctness is too arbitrary, and these are childish metaphors.

Ransom compares Tennyson's conceit with Humbert Wolfe's in his "Green Candles:"

> "I know her little too," gray carpet said:
> "Who but I should know her light tread?"
> "She shall come in," answered the open door,
> "And not," said the room, "go out any more."

Wolfe's conceit is striking, while Tennyson's not. Though his [Wolfe's] conceit is not very daring or important, yet it is pleasant. He employs the technique of conceit correctly, because he knows that the miracle must have a likeness to reality.

Metaphysical poetry, Ransom argues, is the extension of a rhetorical device. It deals with things but introduces the miraculism. The miraculism is a variety of figure which ignores the credible surface of life and expresses the fullest possible reality in life. But it is quite different from simile, which says "as if" or "like," and is accurate to keep the identification partial. It "arises when the poet discovers by analogy to identify between objects which is partial, though it should be considerable and proceeds to an identification which is complete" (p.139). Ransom further sates: "...there is a miraculism or supernaturalism in a metaphorical assertion if we are ready to mean what we say, or believe what we hear" (p.139). From the literary and critical point of view, it must be noted that the miraculism which produces the humblest conceit is the same miraculism which supplies to religions their substantive content. In religious context, just as Christ, through his miracle, turns water into wine, so, in poetry, when the Metaphysical poets employ the miracle, things are transformed into ideas, and ideas into things. The effect of the miracle is seen wonderfully when it becomes extremely difficult to distinguish the thing and idea apart. But Hobbes, the naturalist, strongly objects to the use of metaphoricai language, because it creates confusion and ambiguity in such phrases as "faith infused;" infusion means "pouring into," but nothing can be "poured" which is abstract or immaterial.

The myth is a device of expression which has its relevance and sanctity because of its public and social importance. The myth is a conceit born of metaphor. The metaphysical poets recognize myth, as they recognize the conceit. They admire the methodology of science and virtually copy it. Their phrasing is often technical, spare, and polysyllabic. Though they do not repeat actual science, yet make those metaphorical substitutions that are so arresting. There are two main aims of metaphysical poetry. First, it is a complement to the scientific knowledge, and secondly, it also improves poetic discourse through a rhetorical device, conceits, metaphors, and myths. On the other hand, naturalistic discourse is incomplete. In it there is a dearth of physical content and sensibility or an excess of it. Platonic poetry is full of ideas and didacticism, whereas Physical poetry is only teemed with concrete images. The former is too idealistic and the latter too realistic. Realism is monotonous and, therefore, cannot cherish interest for a long time. Ransom, thus, advocates the third category of poetry i.e. Metaphysical poetry. It employs the psychological device of fusion of thoughts and feelings, ideas and emotions. It is just like the chemical reaction in which the elements lose their properties and become very difficult to distinguish one from the other. It suggests that the object is perceptually or physically remarkable. It is not true like history but true in the pragmatic sense. Metaphysical poetry, Ransom holds, is one of the most brilliant successes in English poetry. That is why it deserves a long and thorough examination, and demands a more ontological criticism.

Criticism, Inc.

Wedded to the dignity, status, and elevation of criticism, Ransom abruptly commences the essay, "Criticism, Inc.", pouring out a phial of fury on the so-called critics who are without any training and qualification to it. His deep dissatisfaction and despair at the plight of English literary criticism ushered in revolution. He discovers its existing condition quite frustrating and rudderless, enveloped in chaos and confusion. It is really a very sad state of affairs that no one critic is capable enough to explain as to what the proper business of criticism is. It is in the grip of amateurs. Without any training, specific qualifications, or professional background, they plunge into criticism. Consequently, what they produce is not real criticism. Ransom considers three types of persons, who are supposed to have competence and qualification for criticism: (i) the artist (ii) the philosopher, and (iii) the university teacher of English literature. The artist should know good art while making a criticism of it, but he has also his limitation; "his understanding is intuitive rather than dialectical."[42] He fails to explain his theory convincingly. With his good command of language, a literary artist proves himself to be a better critic of his own art than other critics; "probably the best critics of poetry we can now have are the poets," (p.228) but an artist's commentary or criticism in art is valuable until he focuses his attention on its technical effects, and definitely he can do it. Secondly, the philosopher is quite familiar with the function of fine arts, but his theory is very general and his acquaintance with the particular works of art is not persistent and intimate, particularly their technical effects. He lacks the capability of close criticism. Thirdly, the university teacher of literature, who is professional, should undertake the charge of the critical activity. He can discharge his duty as a critic more efficiently than a philosopher or an artist. But it is a pitiable thing that the professional morale of the university professors of English in this regard is very low. They escape from their responsibility, while their real business is the "erection of intelligent standards of criticism" (p.229).

Criticism, Ransom holds, must become more scientific, or precise and systematic, and should be developed by the collective and sustained effort of learned persons. Its proper seat is in the universities. In psychology, sociology, economics, chemistry, theology and architecture, it is taken for granted that criticism of the performance is the prerogative of the man who has had formal training in its theory and technique. But the contemporary literary criticism is not at all in the hands of those who direct the English studies, and, therefore the "contemporary literature...is barely officialized as a proper field of serious study." Contemporary literature is crying for its criticism. It, therefore, should also be dealt with utmost seriousness by the professional English teachers. Ransom states: "...what we need is Criticism, Inc., or Criticism Ltd.," (p229) because criticism has become more an industry than human pursuit. The wave of opposition must start from the present incumbents of the professional chairs. The duty of the department of English is to communicate the understanding of the literary art.

Ransom has a very high opinion of Professor Ronald S. Crane of the University of Chicago, who argues that historical scholarship has been overplayed heavily in English studies. He advocates that emphasis must now be shifted to the critical. The students of literature must study literature, not about literature. In fact, good students want to study critically but they are denied, because the history of criticism in America has a "comic history." Professor Ronald wants to raise the academic standards. Ransom revolts against the New Humanism of Irving Babbitt, W. C. Brownwell, and Paul Elmer More, who are active in the early decades of the twentieth century. They are moralists, more accurately, historians, and advocates of a certain moral system. "Criticism," Ransom argues, "is the attempt to define and enjoy the aesthetic characteristic values of literature" (p.231). But the Humanists would shudder at "aesthetic." Babbitt consistently discusses the terms of classical and romantic. Like the New Critics, the New Humanists also condemn the romantic school of poetry and criticism, but his approach is quite different from that of the New Critics. The former repudiate on the ground of technical and aesthetic ground, while the latter on the moral. Babbitt makes war on romanticism for purely moral reasons; and his preoccupation was ethical, not aesthetic. Ransom supports the moralist to attack romantic literature on the ground that it deals with emotions rather than principles; or the poet reveals himself as flabby, intemperate, escapist, unphilosophical, or simple, adolescent. This objection, Ransom pleads, is also valid, because the romantic period fails largely to adapt to the social and political environment. But T. S. Eliot, as a critic, objects to romanticism not on this ground. His charge is aesthetic—imperfection in objectivity or "aesthetic distance," its weakness of structure, death of aesthetic attitude, and artistic purity.

A moralist's disapproval of a romantic work is quite different from that of a literary critic.

Ransom also mentions the other diversion from the traditional orthodox criticism i.e. the Marxist criticism. The Marxists try to analyze a piece of work to discover class-consciousness in literature, and tc make literature serve the cause of loving-comradeship, as for the Humanists to revive the Aristotelian moral cannon. The Humanist and the Marxist never debate on aesthetic ground, for they are equally intent on ethical values, which give a great jolt to the conventional historical studies. Ransom rejects all the three—the New Humanism, Marxism, and the historical criticism. He suggests that the department of English should maintain its own self-respecting identity. Its duty and responsibility is to understand and communicate literature, an art.

In "Criticism, Inc.," J. C. Ransom registers a list of exclusions, which are not within the purview of criticism. Despite his philosophical and religious orientation, he completely rules out the moralistic, historical, social, biographical, philosophical, and psychological approaches to criticism. He designates such varieties of criticism as "shapeless miscellany." Ransom is opposed to the psychological jargon to evaluate the attitudes and emotions of the poems. *In The New Criticism,* he makes a thorough rummage of Eliot, I. A. Richards, and Yvor Winters. Richards, for instance, too scientific in outlook, reduces poem to a level of psychology, and gives too much attention to the reader rather than the work. So, his criticism is too affective; that is oriented towards the feelings the poem arouses in the reader rather than the calm description of textual details. To Ransom the proper function of poetry is not to arouse and communicate passions. He, therefore, objects to record the subjective effects of a work. Critics should evade 'personal registration.' It means the effect or response of the work of art upon the critic or reader. Criticism, Ransom contends, should be objective and cite the nature of the work-art (object) rather than its effects upon the reader (the subject). Readers' impulse or the psychological effects are inappropriate for a well-founded critical understanding. Ransom is not concerned with the effects, because effects generate tears, joys, ecstasy, reflection etc. and provoke to pass such sweeping comments as moving, exciting, pitiful, admirable, and even beautiful. These words are actually uncritical, because they deal with properties explored in the reader, not in the literary object. Criticism, Ransom holds, focuses on the poem itself, not on the reader or author, and dismisses receptionist criticism. Criticism is not subjective impressionism nor "any other special studies which deal with some abstract or prose content taken out of the work." A critic's approach to the poem, Ransom maintains, is "to read and remark the poem knowingly—that is with the aesthetician's understanding of what a poem generally is."[43] F. R. Leavis also argues that the business of critical intelligence is "to determine what is actually there in the work of art."[44] That is why in "Wanted: An Ontological Critic," Ransom declares: "I think it is the time to identify a powerful movement that deserves to be called a new criticism."

The second strong objection of Ransom is that criticism is not the procedures of a "synopsis or paraphrase" of a poem. With a scorn, he remarks that these activities are to make up the delight of high-school classes and women's clubs. The value of a work never depends upon the summary of the content of the text but on the form. The third negative item of criticism is what Ransom calls "historical studies," in fact including historical, biographical, and bibliographical ones. Literature furnishes material for almost any domain of knowledge, but the critic's business is to dwell on 'the technique of art'—the device which distinguishes it from prose. The proper concern should be with literature as an art with its own constitution and structure.

Criticism certainly is concerned with the technique of the art—the unique form of the art. The technical studies of poetry means its metrics; its inversions, solecisms, lapses from the prose norm of language, and from close prose logic; its tropes; its fictions, or inventions, by which it secures 'aesthetic distance' and removes itself from history, or any other device or systematic usage which violates the norms of prose is a poetic device. A true critic is not only content with the demonstration of the separate devices, but also speculates on poetry as to why it differs from prose, and what it represents cannot be done by prose.

One of Ransom's strongest aesthetic presumptions is that the poet writes a poem in a state of agony and labours, not in inspiration. It "is born of experience not of innocence;" it is "post-scientific," rather than "pre-scientific—not the work of a child or of "that eternal youth that is in some women." It is not the expression of the feminine or of the childish. It is not written by sentimentalists or innocents or holy fools, but by those who have struggled with the word. This attitude is the governing factor of Ransom's own work. That is why he calls for reading a text closely, line by line, giving a close attention to its verbal ambiguities and details of metre, rhyme, and syntax. He gives an order of existence to his poem, which in real life constantly crumbling beneath his touch. His poem celebrates the object which is real, individual, and qualitatively infinite. The poet knows that a poem is 'a living object,' but if the practical or scientific interests are applied, it will be reduced to a mere utility. The sciences will disintegrate this 'living object' for their convenience into their respective abstracts. And the poet, therefore, protects his 'object's existence or ontology against its foes—sciences. The critic, therefore, should regard the poem not as a desperate ontological skill. Additionally, his function is to find out a total poetic or individual object in the poem. The poetic object can be evaluated in terms of "the universal or commonplace object" out of the "tissue," or totality of connotation, which holds the poetic object secure. The former is called the structure and the latter the texture. The structure is "the universal object," which "any forthright prose reader can discover to him by an immediate paraphrase; it is a kind of story, character, thing, scene, or moral principles" (p. 238). The texture or the tissue, which holds the quality of the poetic objects, is the superfluity or irrelevance of the 'prose logic' or the structure.

A poet is known by his style—the general character of his irrelevances or tissues. His technical devices contribute to his style, elaborating the universal, the core-object. In each poem, there is a logical object and a tissue of irrelevance. The critic has to analyze the poem in order to exhibit these features. Though it demands a delicate skill, yet "it is rude and patchy business," and without it the value of poetry cannot be understood. However, the critic should keep two terms in his mind—(i) the prose core, which can be reduced to a total object, and (ii) 'the differentia,' 'residue,' or 'tissue,' which keeps the object poetical. The character of the poem resides in its way of exhibiting the residuary quality. The character of the poet is defined by the kind of prose object and his way of involving it firmly in the residuary tissue.

M.A.R. Habib remarks that "'Criticism, Inc.' expresses a core of New Critical principle."[45] Ransom deplores the poetry that reveals sentimentality, abstraction, generalities, love for ornate phrase, and the unfunctional beauty of language. He is perpetually concerned with only the formal analysis of the technical and aesthetic values. He calls for a criticism which must be specialized, technical, scientific, systematic, and precise, and make an analysis of structural organization and textual details. It leads to the analysis of those factors which signify "sensuous particularity" to the poetic language. It is this 'sensuous particularity' that distinguishes poetry from other modes of expression. With this emphasis on concreteness, on verbal analysis, and close-reading, Ransom attempts to distinguish the language of poetry from that of science. He, therefore, engages himself with each and every poetic line and its meaning before him.

References:

1. John L. Stewart, *John Crowe Ransom* (Minneapolis: University of Minnesota Press, 1962), p. 36.
2. J. C. Ransom, *God Without Thunder: An Orthodox Defense of Orthodoxy* (New York: Harcourt, Brace and Co., 1930), p. 4.
3. Louise Cowan, *The Southern Critic* (Texas: The University of Dallas Press Irving, 1972), pp. 24-25.
4. *Ibid.*, p. 36.
5. Monroe K. Spears, *Dionysus and The City: Modernism in Twentieth Century Poetry* (New York: Oxford University Press, 1970), p. 158.
6. *The New Criticism,* p. 281.
7. Quoted in *The Southern Critic,* p. 27.
8. John Paul Pritchard, *Criticism in America* (Ludhiana: Lyall Book Depot, 1956), p. 238.
9. *The New Criticism,* p. 27.
10. *Criticism in America*, pp. 238-239.
11. *Dionysus and The City,* p. 158.
12. "Criticism as Pure Speculation," in R. B. West Jr. ed., *Essays in Modern Literary Criticism* (New York, 1952), p. 233.

13. J. C. Ransom, *The World's Body* (Baton Rouge, 1968), p. 348.
14. J. C. Ransom, *Beating the Bushes,* p. 2.
15. William K. Wimsatt Jr. & Cleanth Brooks, *Literary Criticism: A Short History* (Oxford & IBH Publishing Co.; 1957), p. 627.
16. *Ibid.*, p. 629.
17. J. C. Ransom, "Criticism as Pure Speculation." In Moton S. Zabel (ed.) *Literary Opinion in America,* 2nd ed. Harper, New York pp. 639-54 (essay first published, 1941).
18. J. C. Ransom, *The Intent of the Critic,* ed., Donald Stauffer (New York, 1966), p. 89.
19. *The Intent of the Critic,* p. 86.
20. Lee T. Lemon, *The Partial Critics* (New York: Oxford University Press), p. 121.
21. J. C. Ransom, "Criticism as Pure Speculation." *Literary Opinion in America,* ed. Morton Dauwen Zabel (New York, 1951), p. 650.
22. "Irony as a Principle of structure," *Literary Opinion in America,* ed., Zabel, p. 730.
23. *Ibid.,* p. 729.
24. J. C. Ransom, *Poems and Essays,* p. 107.
25. *J. C. Ransom,* The New Criticism, *p. 114.*
26. "The Concrete Universal: Observations on the Understanding of Poetry," *The Kenyon Review,* 16 (1954), p. 559.
27. *Ibid.,* p. 554.
28. J. C. Ransom, *Poems and Essays,* pp. 103-4.
29. J. C. Ransom, "Preface" to *The World's Body* (New York, 1938), p. ix.
30. *The Fugitive,* iv, 1 (March, 1925), p. 28.
31. The Fugitive, iv, 4 (Dec., 1925), p. 127.
32. J. C. Ransom, "Preface" to The World's Body, p. ix.
33. *Ibid.*, p. x.
34. *Ibid.*, pp. x-xi

35. *The World's Body,* p. 119. Hereafter references of this edition will be given in brackets after the page number.
36. *God Without Thunder,* pp. 139-140.
37. *Ibid.,* p. 173.
38. J. C. Ransom, *Poems and Essays* (New York: Vintage Books, 1955), p. 151.
39. *The Fugitive,* (February, 1924), p. 2.
40. "Humanism at Chicago," *The Kenyon Review,* 14 (1952) p. 658.
41. David Lodge, ed., 20th *Century Literary Criticism* (London: Longman, 1972), p. 228. Further references of this edition will be given in brackets after the page number.
43. J. C. Ransom, *The Idea of Great Poetry,* p. 70.
44. F. R. Leavis, *The Common Pursuit* (London, 1952), p. 224.
45. M.A.R. Habib, *A History of Literary Criticism and Theory* (Blackwell Publishing, 2008 p. 622.

4

Allen Tate

A compelling and driving intellect, Allen Tate (1899-1979), one of the leading exponents of the New Criticism, is "the most aggressively modernist in his poetics,"[1] as the title of one of his works, *Reactionary Essays on Poetry and Ideas* (1936), displays his revolutionary and hard-hitting gesture. With his sharp wit, deep philosophical grounding, and a certain acerbity of judgment, he shares a number of critical canons with Ransom and stands next to him in prominence. His critical essays fraught with dicta reveal that "he had a lot of wildness and he had a lot of construction," which distinguishes him from his contemporaries. His emphasis on the hollow, secularized, valueless, and irrational modern society is epitomized in the preface to *Reason in Madness* (1941) in such words as "a deep illness of the modern mind." Monroe K. Spears speaks of Tate: "He is always concerned with the diagnosis and cure of this deep illness."[2] Though there are various factors responsible for the modern "dehumanized society of secularism," yet it, Tate considers, is occasioned mainly by the "dissociation of sensibility" resulting from isolation of thought from man's total being. He, therefore, nourishes nostalgia for the organic society and archaic civilization of the preindustrial South. Immersed in the Southern history and haunted by a vision of agrarianism, he shows his perpetual concerns for culture, religion, and tradition of the Old South. Tate also deals with the social, economic, and political problems of the South, but he holds politics in cultural rather than in economic terms. Paul Bindings comments: "He has constantly—and frequently with scathing wit—attacked cultural vulgarities, shoddy values and ungenerous attitude."[3]

Allen Tate treats modernism not only in poetry and criticism but also in culture and society. He discovers his tradition in the culture of political conservatism, the agrarian south, and later in Roman Catholics. He, therefore, suggests the writer to adhere to a tradition in his criticism and poetry as well. With his classical, detached, and modernist objective, his essays deal with both literature and society. George Hemphill states:

> The essays can be classified under three heads—criticism of society, literary theory, and judgment of particular authors and works. The three sorts of essays cohere. They cohere because they proceed from a single recognition: the imperfectability of man.[4]

Frank Kermode also demonstrates very well the relationship between the literary and social criticism of Tate. Tate's social criticism means his "refusal to accept the modern world," where the omnipotence of the reason in the form of demon flatters intellectual pride and pillages the good of nature. To present a correct evaluation of Tate as a literary critic, it warrants me first to study him as a critic of society, culture, and values.

Like T. E. Hulme, Tate's concept of man bears the religious overtones. He is quite conscious of the past, the fallen nature of man, and the power of evil and sin. He believes in the limited and imperfect nature of man, and in his vicious imbecility. With this religious awareness, the condition and understanding of human nature is possible. Without a recognition and fear of evil, man cannot be explained merely by social theory or social programmes. But the modern material society based on the doctrine of man's perfectibility thinks that through education and environment progress can solve all the problems. Therefore, modern man sacrificing his moral nature to gnosticism has become abstracted, empty, and blind to the world. Without a sense of God, his emotions, indeed his entire life, have been drained to abstract science. At this crucial juncture, religion, which unites all the aspects of reality, is extremely essential for the development of psychological and spiritual wholeness. Only through the establishment of a Christian society and accepting the knowledge of evil and sin, man can become human again and thus capable enough of receiving God's grace. Modern man driven by lust of power and wealth has undone the order of civilization. He wallows in a world that reduces morality to society. Tate, thus, comes across a clash between the perfectibility and the imperfectability of man. Imbued with this concept of man, Tate's entire body of his works explores a search for order and unity through history, religion, and tradition. Haunted and wrecked by religious predicament and inner turmoil throughout his life, he finally explores his psychic unity and integrity through an embrace of Roman Catholicism. It represents a secure moral and religious structure, resolves the spirit in human consciousness, and ends his spiritual dilemma.

With his agrarian enthusiasm, a hero of the American Old South, Allen Tate, bears an unmistakable mark of the Southern history, sharing with Ransom and Davidson. His preoccupation with the antagonistic attitude of science in a traditional society becomes quite obsessive. Realizing its limitation, he is quite sure "that science has very little to say for itself." Deeply interested in the region's distinctive cultural identity, Allen Tate sharply opposes the destructive power of science, because it leaves a deep scar on the southern culture and shatters a wholeness of human sensibilities. His "agrarian view of industrialism recognized only the evils, not the benefits, not worse, saw no way of combating the evils except by abandoning the industrial system. Industrialism meant tyranny. To work for industry meant slavery."[5] Tate escapes into the world of the Old South, medieval culture, and religion to nurse his unflinching faith in Catholicism and promulgate the Southern doctrines, which mould the character, thought, and being of a man into a wholeness. This wholeness, Tate finds, is necessary for a good society. In the traditional society, people blessed with the historical imagination and the memories of the past experience a wholeness of life and sensibility with all its eventualities in all sections of society. The Southerners, Tate finds, are devoted to a set of values, however irrelevant to the contemporary life, which gives them a steady view of the universe and man's role in it. Characterized by a community of belief and an individuality of function, the traditional society cherishes a glorious past as a heritage and offers a moral vision, a code of manners, and property to the present. Robert S. Dupree observes: "The Southerner can be comfortable as neither believer nor unbeliever. He is forced into a trap, the only escape from which is the invention of a past that never existed."[6] The economic life of the South is also basically based on the soil out of which human experience takes a form of wholeness. The traditional society is based on the land, and its past serenity, integrity, happiness, and beliefs are not for itself, but provides sustenance to the present. It is the duty of men not "to put aside their normal natures."

Tate, like Eliot, is aware of the animating and controlling force of religion, which survives and enlivens any culture. Haunted by a deep religious dilemma throughout his life, he embraces Roman Catholicism, which represents a secure moral and religious structure. His approach to religion is considered rational rather than ecstatic or mystic. He expresses his animus over the contemporary South, because it lacks faith, despite its religious life. In "Religion and the Old South," he finds that the Old South fails to provide a healthy ongoing tradition because Southerners "had a religious life, but it was not organized with a right mythology. In fact, their national life was not powerfully united to the religious experience as it was in medieval society...."[7] Another problem with the South is its Protestantism that is more suited for trading and commercial society rather than one built around non-materialistic value. Sometimes Tate's religious enthusiasm turns into fanaticism and speaks in "Christ and Unicorn" like a staunch supporter of faith: "There can be no culture for us in the true sense, without our unique Revelation.... Either we are a Christian civilization or we are nothing." However, he is quite conscious that "civilizations rise and fall as they hold fast to or lose an active faith."[8]

Unfortunately, science engenders a great havoc to the blessedness of traditional society. As an enemy, the industrial North, based on greedy self-interest or the positivistic knowledge of the twentieth century, invades the unity of life and unvacillating belief and tradition; and finally brings serious defects to the society. The unity of social and economic life is dislocated after the Civil War. Man escapes from life, as work becomes drudgery; the modern or rather the untraditional society gets deprived of "the forms of human action." After the demise of the American South, there comes a decay of morality, religion, and manners in the wake of violence and chaos. The untraditional society does nothing but manufactures the chaotic behavior. In this way, it "can bequeath nothing from one generation to another."[9] Caught in the empirical world, modern intellectuality is muddled and disjointed. It can be restored through the subjective wholeness of the individual. But the recent wealth amassed creates an upper-class life style of self-consciousness and often bogus luxury, which undermine the traditional social order of the South. There is discovered "the serpent in the garden disguised as science and industrialism."[10]

The rise of "New Knowledges" produces a wave of cosmopolitanism, which disturbs Tate as much as T. S. Eliot in "Gerontion." Both of them hold that the new discoveries, new inventions, new theories, new philosophies, and above all, the incipient globalism—they all try to establish a standardized society, which is responsible for disorder of the traditional society and disintegration of self. In his another essay "The New Provincialism" (1945), Tate is perturbed with the loss of regionalism and rapid construction of "One world." The cosmopolitan men—cut off from their roots, memories, and the past culture and heritage—live in the society of "industrial capitalism" and Utopian politics," where they are confronted with the problem of communication. "They have no memory; they have only response to present stimuli."[11]Tate perpetuates his anxiety of the deterioration of the health of culture in his telling essay "What is a Traditional Society?" Here he demonstrates how sensibility declines step by step:

> First, there is the religious imagination, which can mythologize indiscriminately history, legend, trees, the sea, animals, all being humanly dramatized, somehow converted to the nature of man. Secondly there is the historical imagination, which is the religious imagination *manqué*—an exercise of the myth-making propensity of man within the restricted realm of historical event.... The third stage is the complete triumph of positivism.[12]

In this way, Tate thinks long and hard about the fate of the South, the prospects for its traditional culture and the phenomenon of Southern literature. He earnestly contributes to the symposium *I'll Take My Stand* (1930), a manifesto defending the cultural traditions of the agrarian society of the South against the industrial North. Tate's modernism relies on the revival of patterns of thought older than rationalism and scientism. However, he is not as much critical to science as knowledge as science as a mode of abstract thought dominating religion and discarding tradition. Of course, positivistic knowledge is valid in science itself, but it presents partial view of reality; it has only pragmatic approach. On the contrary, a poet's transcription of his experience is marked by fullness and totality. His experience is more composite and full than that of a scientist who aimed at only one set and stratum of meaning and knowledge. The definitions of a scientist are abstracted and reduced to the minimum, to denotative meaning of words; whereas the poet forces his words to convey many layers of meaning simultaneously.[13]

Obsessed with movement, speed, and power, the moderns are dehumanized, bloodless, and the living dead; theirs is an abstract and meaningless world. The Second World War stamps the worst foreboding. The modern art also reflects that "social man is living without religion, morality, or not...in a mere system of money references through which neither artist nor plutocrat can perform as an entire person."[14] Tate further states:

> If we think of the actual world as either a deep lump or a whirling wind somewhere outside us, against which we bump our heads or which whirl us around, we shall never be able to discover it.[15]

This chaotic and tragic world, Tate confirms, should be approached through poetry. Steeped in the spirit of the poetic power, he is sure that poetry is capable enough to diagnose the integrity of the individual consciousness.

Tate's view is that literature is particularly a form of knowledge. The poem yields true and real knowledge. He holds that "if the poem is a real creation it is a kind of knowledge that we did not possess before."[16] And this knowledge through a new order of perceptual reality is engendered in poetic form. It is in this sense, Tate declares: "form is meaning and nothing but meaning."[17] The critic, therefore, should first of all, determine the literary work as a particular object. Without its specific objectivity neither criticism nor literature is possible. The distinct objectivity of a poem retains its formal properties, which are "the focus of the specifically critical judgment."[18] The creative act and the critical judgment hinge upon poetic form; and this poetic form becomes the viewpoint through which both the creative act and the critical object are realized. To be very clear, nothing is relevant to art outside its form.

Tate, "the recognized champion of the moderns,"[19] is a confluence of philosophy, theology, culture, criticism, and poetry. He is deeply influenced by T. E. Hulme's theory of discontinuity, modernist painting, and Eliot's hard-edged *The Waste Land*—an arresting commentary on Western decadence. His models are Baudelaire whose Theory of Correspondence is "the backbone of modernist poetic and the character."[20] Tate admits: "I began to connect with the modern what I have already learned from Baudelaire first through Arthur Symons then from Baudelaire himself."[21] With his modernist sensibility, he cherishes a powerful historical sense that shapes all of his best creation. To him, like Eliot, "poetry is not a solitary art" but an ongoing tradition in which the dead retain their living voices." Therefore, traditional literary and religious symbols have special values for him. Robert H. Brinkmeyer points out:

> ...three disparate traditions—the Old South, Roman Catholicism, and Modernism—most clearly shaped his art and thought. Each tradition appealed to Tate as a way to establish order and meaning in his life; throughout his career, he explored the value and significance of each tradition, working with the three forces in various combinations and playing certain aspects of one against aspects of the others.[22]

Tate also bases his aesthetic on distancing himself from the feelings in order to explore the fundamental emotional and intellectual issues underlying passing sensation. Along with a technical ability, he is genuinely concerned with the power of language—its content, its sound, and its rhythm. He liberates it from "mass language."

Though Tate resembles and learns from Ransom immensely, yet his aesthetics differs from the latter on many points. In an age of fragmentation and incoherence, Tate makes a heroic quest of wholeness and harmony. To achieve this end, the traditional techniques and tools, he feels, help no longer; they are quite inadequate to give holistic knowledge. He is quite sure that neither the past can be recaptured nor the heroic mode nor the lyric voice can be used to render the modern complexity. Traditional metres and the ordinary poetic idiom could not be used without radical dislocation. Concerned with the nature of poetry, Tate makes a marked departure from the framework of narrative or logical sequence and displays supra-rational elements of suggestion and dislocation. Just as modern paintings, liberate itself from the "tyranny of representation," so modern poetry should also get rid of hackneyed poetic diction and idiom. There should be dislocation of language connoting strange and unexpected domains of meaning. Tate rejects Ransom's belief that the content of poetry is identical with that of prose. Ransom assumes that poetry, like prose, is exclusively concerned with rational order or exposition, which controls the poem. But Tate holds that modern poetry must embrace "the entire range of consciousness." He admits: "Poetry is to me successive instances of the whole rhythm of thought, and includes reason, emotion, extra logical experience, or… the entire fantasy of sensation." Tate emphasizes the poet's role of giving individual form to an experience of the common sense world.

Tate also differs with Ransom on the points of metaphor and rhythm. To Ransom, these two elements are not accountable for the fullness of poetic being. The figurative language as textural element is the poem's aesthetic and constitutes only a part of the whole poem; the other part is the "paraphrasable content." On the other hand, Tate considers metaphor and rhythm as the active agents of poetic organization. Metaphor and rhythm cannot stand aloof in the poem; they embody or carry the feelings, emotions, and experiences. The language of poetry is metaphorical and rhythmical or metrical, and the experience in the very act of choosing metaphors and the metre. This view reminds the theory of "tension," because poetic form is a "body" rather a result of "increment;" the awareness of the body is the awareness of experience embodied in the poem. Tate's notion of metaphor is also identical with I.A. Richards's theory of metaphor. In *The Philosophy of Rhetoric* (1936), he argues that the total meaning of a metaphor is the product of a complex interaction between 'tenor' and 'vehicle.' This position of Tate gives the poetic experience an identity and the poem becomes a concrete object. In this way, what is expressed in the poem can never be abstracted as "literal statement."

The Present Function of Criticism

In the essay, "The Present Function of Criticism," Tate delineates an alarming condition of literature and criticism on the one hand and the predicament of twentieth century American man and culture on the other. With his deep distress, like other New Critics, he reveals the present sad state of affairs of American literary criticism. It has become a handmaid of the culture created by scientism—a very destructive force to it. Tate expresses his concern on the existing mode of criticism i.e. the theory of communication. This approach is also called historical or scholarly criticism communicating ideas—sociological, political, historical, psychological, and moral ideas to the reader. It starts in the early nineteenth century by the romantics who pour out their emotions and experiences direct to the reader, but it is more reinforced and perpetuated by the positivist school of critics in the early decades of the twentieth century. This approach is so strongly rooted in the existing criticism that critics are not ready to accept any new approach to look at literature. In fact, they have "invaded the field of letters and kidnapped criticism." They emerge as foes to literature, because they would interpret it from all possible branches of knowledge except from formal literary qualities.

Allen Tate discovers that the contemporary world-view fully banks upon modern science, rejecting superstition, religion, and metaphysics as pre-scientific or unscientific forms of thought. The moderns think that pre-scientific ideas hinder the progress of mankind and human salvation is only possible through scientific based knowledge. This state of mind is called positivism, evincing that all knowledge is based on sense-experience. Except this, there cannot be any other kinds of knowledge. All genuine inquiry is concerned with the description and explanation of empirical facts. This intellectual method of knowledge enjoys its heyday and leads modern scholars quickly to "find a procedure, a program, an objective"[23] to express their point of view. Positivism "assumes that the communication of ideas towards the formulation of truths is irrelevant to action; the program is an end itself" (p.3).

The title of the essay "The Present Function of Criticism" is very deceptive. It purports that Tate is going to discuss the function of literary criticism in the present time, but he talks of two other things, though very important; the condition of twentieth century American culture and various approaches towards criticism. He realizes that the greatest tyranny to literature is done by Enlightenment and positivism. Literature is not treated as literature—an artifact or a complete organic unit, but is reduced to a system, method and a general statement. With the rise of the knowledge of social sciences, poetry is read as a sociological, historical, psychological, and moral treatise. This deviation from poetic to philosophical or didactic or pragmatic sources puts the immediate function of literature to an end. It becomes something else—a tool for propaganda. Tate, therefore, rejects the historical approach to criticism based on the scientific mood. He warns: "On principle the sociological and historical scholar must not permit himself to see in the arts meanings that his method does not assume" (p.5).

Positivism is a scientific movement, a moral attitude and a temper of the age. It has wide implications encroaching upon American politics and education. In such a consumer-ridden society—a society conditioned by the scientific programme and procedure, the fate of literature is in a deep crisis. It is a society where the tradition of free ideas is dead because everything has been reduced to "a method." This scientific, industrialized, pragmatic, and empirical society plays a more destructive role to literature than the official Nazi censorship. The Nazis are open foes to men of letters but the positivistic society is just like a hidden snake in the grass. It sucks the vitality, free thinking, aesthetic sense, and the critical intelligence of the profession of letters.

Deeply influenced by T. E. Hulme, Allen Tate, every inch a modernist, finds a deliberate and radical break with the traditional Western culture and Western arts. He observes the old simple verities and certainties—traditional religion, traditional morality, and traditional Western ways of behaviour—crumbling down. The vexing issues and corroding problems create a complete rupture between physical and spiritual orders. The positivist claims that all human experiences can be ordered scientifically. Consequently, this assumption reduces the spiritual realm to irresponsible emotion or irrelevant feeling; it is irrelevant because it cannot be verified to the empirical facts. Tate's contention is that in such a crucial moment, "the high forms of literature offer us the only complete and thus the most responsible, versions of our experience" (p.4).

Allen Tate makes a prophecy of the future of criticism worsening in the United States, as it is under the pressure of positivists who are guiding American education. The rise of the social sciences and their influence on education create a pseudo-democratic intellectual tradition, supported by the monopoly of capitalism. Under the degraded version of the myth of reason, the positivists collect the data of social behaviour, social control, and social dynamics, building "a pseudo-mystical and pseudo-democratic utopia." The intellectual movement variously known as positivism, pragmatism, and instrumentalism is an expression and creation of the middle-class culture. It is this culture that forms the major proportion of American society and remains in the clutch of the exploiting conditioning intellectual society. It feeds and nourishes industrialism and the positivistic school of knowledge. Tate is reminded of Matthew Arnold who discovers the chief weakness of the middle class that it lacks intelligence because industrialism has "materialized the upper class, vulgarized the middle class, and brutalized the lower class." This utilitarian attitude not only exploits and conditions the life of the middle class but also influences other levels of its intellectual activity.

Allen Tate categorizes the tradition of the two types of knowledge—(i) the knowledge of the Pre-Enlightenment and (ii) the knowledge of the Post Enlightenment. The former establishes "the humane tradition" while the latter "genteel tradition." The humane tradition informs the independence of judgment, the belief in intelligence, and the confidence in literature, but these things are no more; they are blasted by the sterility of sheer intellectuality. On the other hand, under the genteel tradition, the scholars exhibit timidity of judgment, disbelief in intelligence, and suspicion of the value of literature. These attitudes in the modern age thrive in historical and scientific scholarship. Allen Tate comments: "it is now commonplace to observe that the uncreative money-culture of modern times tolerates the historical routine of the scholars" (p.9).

In this society, people have surrendered their humanity to the predatory impulses and get deprived of enjoying a natural life. This conditioning process boosts up hypocrisy, affecting American thought and feeling at every level. It only teaches the present generation that intelligence has no role in the modern age. The main thing is man's adjustment to society—to a mechanical society in which the modern man has to be conditioned for the realization of gadgets and of the consumption of commodities, which is quite beneficial to the state. In this way, the public education becomes a slave to the professional "educationists" and "sociologists," leaving a deep effect on literature. With this irresponsible and destructive bias towards the profession of letters, the positivists establish a utilitarian-oriented tradition of literary criticism. They play, Tate says, a role of the state agents, because their approach towards criticism is always to fulfill the requirement of the state.

Tate discovers a great misconception among the contemporary literary critics who hold the meaning of a work of literature identical with the positivistic method—"a method that dissolves the literature into its history" (p.10). He fails to understand as to why these scholars study literature, if they have to deal with it in the light of social sciences. They are obsessed by politics and are guided by the social determinism of literature. In principle, they consider themselves academic scholars, but demonstrate literature as a non-existent thing. According to them, literature is simply history, and must be studied as history is studied through certain scientific analogies. They are deviated, Tate thinks, from the main track of the tradition of literary criticism viz "the tradition of literature as a form of knowledge." In fact, the critics look at literature as merely one of the forms of social and political expression. With indignation, Tate asks to curb the leaning of those critics who have been intent on declaring literature as "only politics" or try "to convert literature in sciences" (p.10). Though they study literature, yet completely avoid focusing their attention on the literary characteristics. In fact, they are hypocrites and pretenders. Tate says: "This is scholars' contribution to the intellectual hypocrisy of the positivistic movement." (p.10). He points out the role of criticism very clearly:

> The function of criticism should have been, in our time, as in all times, to maintain and to demonstrate the special, unique, and complete knowledge which the great forms of literature affords us. And I mean quite simply, *knowledge*, not historical documentation and information (p.9).

After the generalized notion, Tate comes to the individual critic, I. A. Richards, whose critical focus is "the powerful, semi-scientific method of studying poetry" (p.10). Despite 'errors,' 'evasions,' and 'a certain ambiguity' in Richards's criticism, Tate is impressed by him and particularly by his *The Principle of Literary Criticism*, a curious, ingenious, and seminal work of criticism. In one respect, this book, Tate thinks, is valuable that it is free of sociological, political, moral, and historical criticism and deals at least with the language of poetry and, provides profound insights into the art of reading poetry. But Richards raises literature to the scientific position, which irritates the New Critics. Tate comments Richards's views in these words: "literature is not really nonsense, it is a special way, a kind of science; ....poetry is a kind of applied psychology" (p.11). However, like Ransom and Blackmur, Tate disapproves psychological criticism, because Richards interprets poetry in terms of 'impulses,' 'stimuli,' and 'responses.' His charts of nerves, nerve-systems, organizing impulses, and scientific jargons show that "poetry is at least a laboratory science" (p.11).

Testing poetry scientifically, Richards makes another very candid confession that poems are compacted to *pseudo-statements*; they are "false statements," or "just plain lies" because they could not be verified by any of the known scientific procedures. Tate describes about Richards:

> As a good positivist he saw the words of a poem as referents, and referents have got to refer to something—which the words of even the best poem failed to do (p.12).

In *Science and Poetry*, Richards also subscribes his views to Matthew Arnold's belief that the future of poetry is immense and it would replace religion. "It would perform the therapeutic offices of religion" (p.13). Though poetry is false, it would order human minds. On the other hand, science is true, but it fails to bring intellectual order. While translating *Coleridge on the Imagination* (1935) into naturalistic terms, Richards fails to do it, and then realizes his weakness in the psychological and philosophical approaches toward criticism. He develops an entirely different outlook to poetry and remarks that "it is an independent form of knowledge, a kind of cognition, equal to the knowledge of the sciences at least perhaps superior" (p.13).

The next approach towards criticism, Tate discusses, is the Doctrine of Relevance. It is also called biographical or scholarly criticism. It simply means that the subject matter of a literary work cannot be isolated from the form. In other words, historical critics ignore the form of literature and mainly focus their attention on the content, interpreting it in the light of social, political, religious, and historical perspectives. They verify the work whether it represents truly and authentically or not. They also test scientifically the scene, the action, and the relations of the characters in a piece of work. This criterion is very difficult to apply to poetry, because it has a medium, which is the most complex and least reducible to any set of correlations. But with the novel the case is different, because it points with some directness towards history or to the historical process.

From the historical point of view, Tate considers David Daiches's *The Novel and the Modern World* an important book. It prescribes the precept that literature is to be understood chiefly as a part of the historical process. Quoting and commenting his doctrine of Relevance, Tate raises a volley of questions:

> Yes: but relevant to what? And are they *equally* relevant? The quality of relevance points to historical documentation; or may we assume here that since the "main object is to indicate relevance," the critic must try to discover the relevance of history to the work? Or the work to history? What Mr. Daiches seems to me to be saying is that the function of criticism is to bring the work back to history, and to test its relevance to an ascertainable historical process. Does relevance then mean some kind of identity with an historical process?

After analyzing the prevalent approaches towards literary criticism one by one, Tate gets quite confident that the positivist school of critics does not study it as such because it is "unreal." They, therefore, treat literature as a document of sociology, Marxism, or history and rule out the characteristics and qualities which contribute to the literariness of a writer's work. Towards the end of the essay, Tate submits the crux of the nature of literature:

> Literature is the complete knowledge of men's experience, and by knowledge I mean that unique and formed intelligence of the world which man alone is capable (p.19).

Historicism, scientism, psychologism, and biologism deeply affect human thoughts and feelings, bring a loss of religion and sensibility, and create a mental make-up to think only within that parameter, and behave like a wound-up watch. Consequently, literature and literary criticism suffer a lot and disappear into abstractions. They become a lump of ideas of positivism, a document, and propaganda. To overcome this fatal deficiency in American letters, Allen Tate suggests the readers to cherish common animating ideas such as religious belief and organizing capacity of sensibility. They will help order fragmented human psyche and disordered spiritual realm. With the restoration of such beliefs, the critics should treat literary works as objects with their individuality, objectivity, and formal qualities. The artists should present their ideas along with their artistic presentation and believe that the poem should be a complete organic unit. They should also maintain and demonstrate that literature is a form of knowledge— special, unique, and complete.

Tension in Poetry

"Tension in Poetry" (1938), one of the most celebrated critical essays of Allen Tate, defines the nature of poetry, leaving a seminal effect on the other critics. With his penetrating understanding of poems, he argues that all types of poetry good as well as mediocre— have certain common characteristics that can be designated as the name of a single quality i.e. "tension." He explores a common poetic element in the nature of language itself. Just as the language of poetry is irony and paradox to Brooks, so is tension to Tate. The key term "tension" deserves a special attention to be clarified to understand his poetic theory. About tension Tate explains:

> I am using the term not as a general metaphor, but as a special one, derived from lopping the prefixes off the logical terms extension and intension. What I am saying, of course, is that the meaning of poetry is its "tension," the full organized body of all the extension and intension that we can find in it. [24]

Tate holds that the use of words in poetry is made in such a planned and organized manner that the artifact achieves an effective whole, and this wholeness or organization depends upon "tension." In the essay, he clarifies the term by introducing other two logical terms—

extension and *intension.* "Extension" means the abstract and denotative quality of poetic language and "intension" the concrete and connotative values. The former refers to "things" and the latter to "attributes." The equilibrium of these two forces produces "tension" in poetry, which gives the poetic meaning. When the polarities of the qualities of extension and intension are balanced in any particular set-up of language, tension is produced which alone reveals "poetic knowledge." The more the denotative aspect of language extends, the more the connotative values should also expand in the same proportion at the same time. Ferman Bishop comments: "By creating this special word [tension], he implies the necessity for both qualities in poetic expression and at the same time shows that both qualities are inherently related" (p.129). Tate's concept of poetic theory is kinetic, whereas Ransom's structure-texture concept static.

It is quite apparent that the language of a poetic work has a distinct quality and its meaning depends upon the ultimate effect of the whole and this whole grows out of a configuration or structure of meaning. With this critical approach, the duty of a critic is to evaluate and examine the poetic work. The critic while evaluating and examining the qualities of tension should not completely ignore the "earlier method" or other qualities. The analysis and interpretation of general ideas implied in the poetic work should also be highlighted. Commending a poem of Hardy, Tate lays a deep emphasis on rhythm, metre, rhyme and other conventional supplements. These poetic accessories are not merely adornments but are important vehicles to convey the shades of thought, emotion, and feeling. Denotative and connotative potentialities of language alone cannot fulfill this job, however ingenious their use is in the poem. Tate makes an explication of Donne's "Valediction: forbidding-mourning" and though he explores poetic tension, yet he always keeps in his mind the function of rhythm in the poem "which is of the essential meaning" (p.75). Like Brooks, Tate does not believe in the monistic critical approach. He remarks: "no single critical insight may impute an exclusive validity to any one kind" (p.62).

Tate's poetic theory of tension completely condemns the poetry of communication—the poetry which expresses only ideas and feelings and experiences for the purpose of propaganda. Though there are various types of the poetry of ideas—love, religious, patriotic, and didactic, yet the most common sort of poetry is generalized personal poetry. It usually results from sentimental and inaccurate observation and is mainly responsible for the deterioration of the poetic language. The personal poetry corrupts and strips the language of the possible subtleties. It arouses affective state or feeling in the reader. Instead of bringing to formal order, it becomes the language of the mass. Tate writes:

> Mass language is the medium of "communication," and its users are less interested in bringing to formal order what is today called the "affective state" than in arousing that state (p.63).

That is why many poets invent their private languages because public speech has become heavily tainted with mass feeling. Tate is also doubtful of the effect of his poetic theory on long poems, as he has confined himself with the "slighter effects" or with certain immediate qualities of language. Ultimately a poet's reputation rests on the quality of his language—"the quality of his language is the valid limit of what he has to say" (p.76), however deep is his philosophy or meaning in the work.

Allen Tate cites and interprets poem after poem of different poets—Miss Millay, James Thomson, Abraham Cowley, Marvell, Donne, Dante etc.—to demonstrate the frailty of the fallacy of communication in romantic poetry and the powerful working of tension in metaphysical poetry. First, he cites a stanza from Miss Millay's poem "Justice Denied in Massachusetts" to show how the "fallacy of communication" in poetry corrupts language:

> What from the splendid dead
> We have inherited—
> Furrows sweet to the grain, and the weed subdued—
> See now the slug and the mildew plunder.
> Evil does overwhelm
> The larkspur and the corn;
> We have seen them go under.

The stanza reveals that the poet's glorious ancestors make the earth yield crops, fruit, and vegetation. In a sense there was complete prosperity, peace, and happiness; the life was worth living. Now the condition is worsened; evil rules everywhere, as the very title of the poem displays. Tate fails to understand as to how Massachusetts could cause a general desiccation. Moreover, it is also not made clear how the two persons—Sacco and Vanzetti—mentioned in the poem are compared to the rotting of the crops. It is quite an illogical comparison. They have nothing to do with the rotting of the crops. In fact, these lines written in mass language arouse an affective state in the reader and make them sentimental. They communicate certain feelings about social justice and these feelings are admired by only those who share with them and the poet. But those who do not share with, the lines or the entire poem are "impenetrably obscure." Tate observes:

> I am attacking here the fallacy of communication in poetry. (I am not attacking social justice.) It is no less a fallacy in the writing of poetry than of critical theory (p.65).

Tate rejects the theory of communication in poetry, which achieves its bloom during romanticism after the publication of *The Lyrical Ballads* in 1798. Such poetry seeks to arouse an affective state of didacticism, patriotism, religious belief or of lovesickness in the mind of the reader. Tate remarks: "The whole nineteenth century English verse is a poetry of communication" (p.65). The romantics handle verse as a vehicle to convey ideas and feelings which they felt, but they (ideas and feelings) could have been better presented by natural or social sciences. They prefer to communicate ideas in poetry to prose organized on scientific principle, because the scientists are difficult to understand. They also share with this view that the poets are 'tender' and pay attention to verse, not to other social and pragmatic problems. This tradition continues even after the nineteenth century as they more often dwell upon sociology (e.g. Shelley). However, they lose their position as poets by doing so.

Tate points out that another very noticeable characteristic of the poetry of communication is obscurity. It is so heavily tainted with the rationalism of the social sciences that however easy the verse looks on the page, it gives up all claim to sense. That is why Tate finds Miss Millay's poem obscure, whereas Donne's "Second Anniversaries" does not. To justify his point, he further displays obscurity in a nineteenth century lyric, "The Vine" by James Thomson:

The wine of love is music,
And the feast of love is song:
When love sits down to banquet,
Love sits long:
Sits long and rises drunken,
But not with the feast and the wine;
He reeleth with his own heart,
That great rich Vine.

The language of this lyric, Tate holds, arouses an existing affective state. It means the emotion created in the minds of the readers is of topical issues. It can be relished as long as the immediate events are concerned but never for a long time. As the contemporary problems come to an end, the emotional vehemence of the people also gets subdued. The poetry itself loses its significance because it does not have a universal appeal and high order. This is another flaw of the poetry of communication. Tate argues: "what I want to make clear is the particular kind of failure not the degree in a certain kind of poetry" (p.67). The poem "The Vine" also lacks a coherent meaning either literally or in terms of ambiguity. It can be simply changed into its several paraphrases hidden in the minds of the readers. The imagery has no functional role to do with the general idea that it tries to uphold. Of course, there emerges a confused image of "a self-intoxicating man-about-town." Tate says: "the more closely we examine this lyric, the more obscure it becomes; the more we trace the implications of the imagery the denser the confusion" (p.66). But good poetry has every word, phrase, and line examined literally and closely.

Dismissing the poetry of communication, Tate approves metaphysical poetry in which his theoretical equation of extension and intension is harmoniously balanced, producing perfect tension. In metaphysical poetry, "the logical order is explicit; it must be coherent; the imagery by which it is sensuously embodied must have at least the appearance of logical determinism" (p.68). The imagery should have a logical appearance on the surface, though there are numerous ambiguities and contradictions beneath it. The logicality of the imagery should be maintained at least outwardly. The development of imagery by extension is the leading feature of metaphysical poetry. Tate also quotes Ransom's view of this kind of poetry: "The impulse to metaphysical poetry...consists in committing the feelings in the case...to their determination within the elected figure" (p.68).

Tate is also quite aware that all metaphysical poems are not good, but a bad metaphysical poem is better than a romantic one. While comparing Thomson's "The Vine" with Cowley's "Hymn: to light," Tate makes a very frank confession that both are "equally bad poetry." But he prefers "Hymn; to light" because it has a firmer use of language without arousing an effective state. With its analytical proposition, the main statement is expressed very clearly that God is light, and light is life. However, both of the poems have an equal defect. "The Vine" is failure in denotation and "Hymn: to light" failure in connotation. That is why Tate maintains "that good poetry is a unity of all the meanings from the furthest extremes of intension and extension. Yet our recognition of the action of this unified meaning is the gift of experience, of culture, of, if you will, our humanism" (p.7).

Tate rejects either extreme denotation (extension) or extreme connotation (intension) in poetry. He considers metaphysical poetry of a high degree, because it is the poetry of the centre—the poetry of tension. The metaphysical poets are rationalists. They begin with the literal statement and gradually develop the complication of metaphor. At every point, they wait to reveal the meaning so far grasped, and at every stage the meaning becomes coherent. But the meanings taken out at different points along with the infinite line between extreme intension and extreme extension also vary from man to man with his personal "approach" or "interest." For example, the Platonist, who is a fanatic in morals, may determine that Marvell's "Coy Mistress" is the recommendation of immoral behaviour to the young man. Of course, it is one true meaning, the denotative meaning, but the complete meaning is not possible without full tension of the poem. The critic should also give equal weight to an intensive meaning. It is so valuable that it lifts the lover-mistress convention into an insight into one phase of the human predicament—the conflict of sensuality and asceticism. Tate spells out metaphysical technique or in Ransom's phrase "metaphysical strategy" that indicates

> ...the point on the intensive-extensive scale at which the poet delays his resources of meaning. The metaphysical poet

> as a rationalist begins at or near the extensive or denoting end of the line; the romantic symbolist poet at the other, intensive end; and each by a straining feat of imagination tries to push his meanings as far as he can towards the opposite and, so as to occupy the entire scale (p.76).

Allen Tate's illustration and elucidation is not a canon of criticism. Adopting the touchstone method of Matthew Arnold, he cites several extracts from different poets as touchstones and is fully convinced that meaning in poetry depends on "logical extension of imagery," which is found in good metaphysical poetry. Tate cites a four-line stanza of Donne's "Valediction: for bidding mourning":

> Our two soules therefore, which are one,
> Though I must goe, endure not yet
> A breach, but an extension,
> Like gold to aiery thinness beate.

Here Donne develops the imagery of the unity of two lovers' souls—the souls equated with a gold leaf. The lover, while parting with the beloved, assuages that their separation is not possible, because their united souls are non-material and non-spatial. Donne presents the logical contradiction by embodying the unitary, non-spatial soul in a spatial image—the malleable gold which expands mathematically by one half towards infinity at every beating. It means the more separation (beating), the more closeness (expansion). Every subsequent parting with the beloved is similar to every beating of the gold leaf. The farther the lover goes from the beloved, the closer the unified souls come to infinity. There is no separation between them at all. Tate explicates

> ...the clear denotation of the gold contains, by intension, the full meaning of the passage. If we reject the gold, we reject the meaning, for the meaning is wholly absorbed into the image of the gold. Intension and extension are here one, and they enrich each other

Towards the end of the essay, Tate quotes a tercet from Dante's *Divine Comedy* to demonstrate an example of perfect tension in it. The illicit lovers—Paolo and Francesca—fails to control their incontinence. First, Dante watches them whirling in a high wind, the symbol here of lust. But as Francesca begins to talk with the poet, the wind calms down and she depicts her birth-place in these translated lines:

> The town where I was born sits on the shore,
> Whither the Po descends to be at peace
> Together with the streams that follow him.

But the third line does not convey the exact sense. That is why Professor Grandgent translates it like this: "To have peace with its pursuers." He comments: "The tributaries are conceived as chasing the Po down the sea." The streams are conceived of as pursuers, not merely followers. Otherwise the beauty, density, and the extension of logical imagery will go away. Francesca describes her abode vividly and picturesquely, yet the description connotes something more. She fuses herself with the river near which she is born. In these three lines, there are three noticeable qualities. Firstly, the metaphor of pursuit extends to the metaphysical conceit. Francesca identifies herself with the river Po personified. The pursuer and the pursued become one. Soon Dante's poetic imagination encounters the pursued river as Francesca in Hell. The figure has completely absorbed the substance of her sin: she has become the sin. The second merit of the verse is the identification of the streams of the Po with the winds of lust. The third quality is that the visual image is transformed into an auditory image by the introduction of the sound of sibilants in the following line:

> ...discende
> Per aver pace co sequacisui.

The sibilants are the hissing of the wind. The streams of the Po are not only the winds of lust by analogy of visual images, but they are also identified by means of sound. Tate concludes:

> The river is thus both a visual and an auditory image, and since Francesca is her sin and her sin is embodied in this image, we are entitled to say that it is a sin that we can both hear and see (p.81).

Tate's theory of tension is immediately concerned with the poetic language which should have a perfect fusion of emotional and intellectual contents. The harmonious blending or oneness of all meanings arising out of extreme extension or denotation or literal statement and extreme intension or connotation or figurative values creates poetic tension. It lends an organic and logical development of imagery. In this way, the poetic knowledge always emanates from the coherent structure or configuration of meaning in the poem. It can be likened with a chemical reaction producing a new whole. Tate's concept somewhat matches with Ransom's "miraculism or supernaturalism in a metaphysical assertion." On this ground, Tate condemns the poetry of communication, which corrupts the language, expresses only ideas for the purpose of propaganda, makes the reader sentimental, presents confused and frequently undignified imagery, lacks the unity of thought and emotion and literate statement and figurative devices. It is poetry of a low degree, unlike the poetry of metaphysical school.

Understanding Modern Poetry

In the essay "Understanding Modern Poetry," Tate expresses his genuine anguish at the "gloomy" poetic landscape engendered by those "historical villains" who have completely lost the taste of poetry or do not have any education of reading it. He concentrates upon the characteristic difference between romantic poetry and modern poetry. The former, Tate considers, is 'bad poetry,' though it is easy, simple, and emotional; whereas the latter is 'good poetry,' but it is baffling, complex, and untraditional. Modern poetry is quite a new type of poetry, because it makes a radical departure from the Romantic achievement. The reader considering it 'obscure' and 'ugly' rejects to accept it, because he is neither trained nor educated for it. He is so badly conditioned with the romantic school of poetry and poetics that he is prepared neither in perception nor in intellect to read modern poetry. He, therefore, refuses the "kind of poetry that does not offer him the familiar poetical objects alongside the familiar poetical truths." [25]

The Romantics, particularly Wordsworth, Tate blames, lack critical methods and principles. With their limited view of life, they fail to observe and experience it in its entirety. Every romantic poem is either a unique expression of personality or a response to an environment. The weakness of romantic sensibility is that it has "predigested perceptions"—poetized objects. It categorically instructs as to which objects are poetical and which are not, prescribing some particular ways to respond to them emotionally. This conditioning theory makes the reader passive, inert, or opiate, and he only responds to the poems; and the poems become only stimuli. However, the conditioning theory of education may be good enough for animals in zoo, but not good enough for human beings. "If a reader makes only responses to poems, he is not doing more than a chimpanzee or yahoo would be doing" (p.93). It is a chaotic state of democratic theory that conditions the reader to cherish bundles of reflexes without intelligence. Tate has a very serious objection to this type of theory which invokes an affective state in the mind of the reader. But his fury is limited to dull and decadent Romanticism, not the great Romantic poets like Keats.

Conversely, the modern poets see the chaotic, confusing, and disintegrating life in its holistic form. They do not confine the poetic material within a particular fold; for them any experience, any object, and any event may be suitable and potential subject-matters for poetry—not merely the pretty and the agreeable. They realize that "poetry is not a special package tied up in pink ribbon" (p.84). Modern poetry is an epitome of what men think, feel, and behave; and it makes possible know the world closely. But it is not an easy business to know the complexity of the world. Modern poetry, therefore, becomes a very difficult affair, demanding both in its writing and reading all the intellectual power. Tate observes:

> ...it is very hard for people to apply their minds to poetry, since it is one of our assumptions that come down from the early nineteenth century that our intellects are for mathematics and science, our emotions for poetry" (p.84).

Tate gets deeply disturbed, as he finds poetry totally transformed in biography and history. It is the "study" of the sexual life of the poet, of the history of his age, or anything else that the scholar desires. He usually studies anything but poetry. But Tate does not completely rule out the biographical and historical criticism. Of course, he dispenses with it when it becomes pernicious "only when some ham actor in an English department uses it to wring tears from the Sophomores by reciting the sad death of Percy Shelley" (p.90). Tate explores this weakness not in the Romantic Movement, but goes farther back when, for the first time in Western art, the belief was introduced that "poetry is chiefly or even wholly an emotional experience" (p.93).

Modern Poetry, Tate discovers, appears to be difficult. because the reader has lost the art of reading poetry. He "has been pampered by bad education, expects to lie down and be passive when he is reading poetry (p.92). He considers that genuine poetry is that that reads itself to him—something is being done to it, he is not doing himself. Caught in "an impressionistic debouch," the reader is a victim of "passive conditioning." He thinks that poetic comprehension does not involve anything i.e. technique, diction analysis, and the other. In short, these things are supposed to be irrelevant in reading poetry. Consequently, the reader fails to understand modern poetry. The fundamental problem before him is that he is quite unaware that poetry needs a hard work and perspiration. He no longer exerts his intellectual power to read poetry, because it demands an act of intelligence, knowing, and of cognition. In conditioning theory, there is no cognition because there is no intelligence. It is an irrelevant point to know as to what the subject matter of the poem is; *whatness* is not important. If a poem has to be considered a relevant thing, it should be something else than the stimulation i.e. *howness* of the poem. As a formal object, the poem should be looked at, studied, and construed. It requires of the reader the fullest co-operation of all his intellectual resources, all his knowledge of the world, and all the persistence and alertness that he now thinks only of giving to scientific studies. There needs a proper education of reading poetry, not the conditioning education. Now it is the duty of the critic to correct the taste of the reader as Eliot also suggests in his "The Function of Criticism." Modern poetry must invite to have the direct and active participation of the reader.

References:

1. William Doreski, *The Years of Our Friendship: Robert Lowell and Allen Tate* (Jackson & London: University Press of Mississippi, 1990), p. 14.
2. Monroe K. Spears, *Dionysus and the City: Modernism in Twentieth Century* (New York: Oxford University Press, 1970), p. 167.
3. Paul Binding, *Separate Country: A Literary Journey Through the American South* (New York & London: Paddington Press Ltd., 1979), p. 122.
4. George Hemphill, *Allen Tate* (Minneapolis: University of Minnesota Press, 1964), p. 30.

5. Leonard Greenbaum, *The Hound & Horn: The History of A Literary Quarterly* (London: Mouton & Co. 1966), p.142.
6. Robert S. Dupree, *Allen Tate and the Augustinian Imagination: A Study of the Poetry* (Baton Rouge and London: Louisiana State University Press, 1983), p. 3.
7. Quoted in *The Years of Our Friendship*, p. 21.
8. George Hemphill, *Allen Tate*, p.16.
9. Louis Cowan, *The Southern Critics*, p. 42.
10. George Hemphill, *Allen Tate and the Augustiniam Imagination: A Study of the Poetry*, p.14.
11. Louis Cowan, *The Southern Critics*, p. 43.
12. Allen Tate, *Collected Essays,* p. 298.
13. Allen Tate, *On the Limits of Poetry* (New York, 1948), p.15.
14. *Ibid.,* p. 276.
15. "The Hovering Fly," in *On the Limits of Poetry*, p.154.
16. Allen Tate, *Collected Essays* (Denever, 1959), p. 240.
17. *Ibid.*, p. 240.
18. *Ibid.*, p. 57.
19. Monoe K. Spears, *Modernism in Twentieth-Century Poetry*, p.165.
20. William Doreski, *The Years of Our Friendship*, p.16.
21. Quoted in *The Years of Our Friendship*, p.16.
22. Robert H. Brinkmeyer, Jr., *Three Catholic Writers of the Modern South* (Jackson: University Press of Mississippi, 1985), p.6.
23. Allen Tate, *Reason in Madness* (New York: G. P. Patnam's Sons, 1941), p. 3. Further references of the essay will be mentioned in parenthesis after the page no. of the same edition.
24. *Reason in Madness* p. 72. Further references of the essay will be mentioned in parenthesis after the page no. of the same edition.
25. *Reason in Madness* p. 83. Further references of the essay will be mentioned in parenthesis after the page no. of the same edition.

5

Cleanth Brooks

With his "invariably superb" scholarship, Cleanth Brooks (1906-1994) is positioned on a high pedestal in the history of the twentieth century literary criticism. Considered as a key figure to the New Criticism, he revolutionized the method of reading and teaching of literature in America, rejecting the biographical and impressionistic mode of criticism. He is also regarded as "the Critic of Critics," and wins huge commendation from many towering critics including his own teacher, John Crowe Ransom, who comments that Brooks "is very likely most expert living reader or interpreter of difficult verse."[1] Louise Cowan is of the view that he "is one of the most highly accomplished textual readers in the language."[2] Poetry, Brooks holds, uses a special kind of language and imparts a special kind of knowledge. It embodies the most complete knowledge of human experience to sustain the health of culture. With his unyielding aims and objectives, Brooks remains a champion of the formalist approach of criticism throughout his life, exploring "the interior life of the poem."[3] Metaphor, paradox, intellect, irony, and wit are the main tools in his concept of poetry. Despite his tremendous talent and sharp critical sensibility, Brooks's personality, gifted with numerous virtues, holds a glorious confluence of a wonderful man, an ideal teacher, a modest critic, and a humble scholar.

Brooks, the founder of the *Southern Review*, achieves success with two important books *Modern Poetry and the Tradition* (1939) and *The Well Wrought Urn: Studies in the Structure of Poetry* (1947), but his other text books *Understanding Poetry* (1938) and *Understanding Fiction* (1943) in collaboration with Robert Pen Warren and *Understanding Drama* (1947) with Robert Hielman prove to be a turning point in American education. These books pose a challenge and topple the long cherished tradition of reading and teaching of literature in the classroom.

Understanding Poetry is a tremendous success, a kind of revelation, and a classic statement on the exact method of reading and teaching of a poem in the classroom. It wins glowing tributes from the prominent personalities such as Bradbury, Sutton, Arthur, Mizener, John A. Meyers, Ransom, George Core, and T. D. Young. They unanimously subscribe to the view that the book brings a sea change in critical theory breaking a new ground of teaching poetry. "The authors taught the new generations of students how to read poems of all periods."[4] The book prescribes the technique of focusing upon a poem as language rather than history or biography or morality. Brooks and Warren undermine the "paraphrase of logical and narrative content," the "study of biographical and historical materials," and the "inspirational and didactic interpretation." Though they do not completely rule out the relevance of paraphrase, yet it may be helpful as a preliminary step to read a poem; the biographical and historical background may clarify interpretation, but things should be consulted as means not as ends.[5] Brooks and Warren analyze the effects of words, rhythms, structures, and poetic techniques on the total meaning of the poems chosen for interpretations. The method of understanding or reading a poem is undoubtedly complex. They first and foremost consider a poem a literary object and nothing else. It is a self-sufficient entity; it proves its effect by itself; that is why a consistent attention should be on the poem itself. A poem not only combines various elements but also maintains an organic unity in which all the elements are interrelated and integrated. Any of the poetic qualities taken in isolation has no meaning unless or until all the parts are inseparably and organically fused together. The materials treated by science are quite different from that done by poetry. Poetry aims at precise statement of attitudes, feelings, and interpretations, while the ordinary treatment of objects is vague and blurred. Poetry regulates words and entices the reader's imagination by its recurrent rhythms.

Understanding Poetry is a text book of a group of selected individual poems with a detail introduction. It also contains a glossary of the literary terms such as *verse*, *abstract*, *dramatic*, *imagery*, *irony*, *paradox*, *structure*, *symbol* etc. They all converge on the one point—concreteness as a poetic language. Though it is a useful book, yet not free of its defects and lopsidedness. It deals with more vigorously and enthusiastically the seventeenth century poets like Marvell and Donne than the romantics and even Shakespeare. Among the romantics, Keats enjoys a high position because of his sensuousness and concreteness and is placed over Shelley. Shelley suffers a lot in the hands of the New Critics because of his abstraction, vagueness, sentimentality, and absence of a logical integration of his images.

In *Understanding Poetry* Brooks condemns the three long established notions, which are supposed to be the crux of poetry. The first erroneous belief is that poetry is the quintessence of "the best realizations of the best mind." This misconception sets both the reader and the critics to dig ideas, message, and philosophy out of poetry. This approach of reading poetry is, of course, not the true function of literature. Brooks's second charge is that poetry is not a substitute for an actual emotional experience. Many critios, who fail to explore the statement of ideas, arrives at this conclusion that poetry is not an expression of ideas but of pure emotion. It is "an expression of a moment of pure realization of being." Brooks refutes the third fallacy: poetry is "a beautiful statement of some high truth" combined in a mechanical way. This notion tries to justify the characteristics of poetry—its rhythmical language, figures of speech, beautiful images, dramatic situation etc. But Brooks in one stroke brushes aside all these approaches and argues that the true function of literary criticism is neither message-hunting, emotion-catching, nor explaining the beauty in terms of the characteristics of poetry. Then, a question is raised as to what is the real function of criticism. Brooks propounds the concept of 'organic nature of poetry.' In his view, the various elements of poetry—noble thoughts, vivid images, diction, music, rhythmic movement and well-chosen rhyme—are not poetic in themselves. Conversely, poetry, he thinks, can have disagreeable ideas, grotesque images, unmusical sound, and faltering rhythm. The real criticism is an exploration and analysis of the internal relationship of the various elements, irrespective of their beauty or ugliness. The soul of poetry, Brooks considers, is the organic organization of the parts.

Modern Poetry and the Tradition (1939), an outcome of the synthesis of various ideas about poetry, is "the most satisfactory single statement of aesthetic formalist critical doctrine thus far produced."[6] Here Brooks appears as an advocate of modern poetry, explicating the poetry of Eliot, Ransom, Tate, Frost, Auden, Yeats, and other twentieth century poetry. He also expresses a sense of indebtedness to them in the preface to this book. He finds their poetry endowed with the load of high seriousness, the essential irony, tension, private myth, personal conceit, concrete metaphor, and the happy marriage of intellectual and emotional qualities in the paradoxical conceits of the metaphysical school. In his essay entitled "The Waste Land: Critique of the Myth" Brooks presents a matchless analysis of Eliot's "The Waste Land." Arnold L. Goldsmith remarks:

> Brooks' critique of Eliot's "The Waste Land" in *Modern Poetry and the Tradition* (1939) is an excellent example of the New Criticism at its best.[7]

Brooks admits the complexity and the revolution of critical sensibility embodied in modernist poetry. It tends to be bewildering and baffling because Eliot, Yeats, Pound and others introduce a novel poetic idiom and language and a selection of 'another metaphor' to render the deeply troubled psyche of the modern man after the holocaust of the World War I. Undoubtedly, their poetry, Brooks considers, appears to be difficult, obscure, and very complex to interpret, but refutes the charge of incomprehensibility. Modern poetry appears difficult for the many modern readers because they are fond of reading romantic poetry known for its decorative imagery, simplicity, idealism, clarity, sentimentality, and beauty. Romantic concept of poetry also divides words and objects into two groups—poetic and unpoetic, and emotional faculty is appreciated, whereas intellectual one underestimated. But the traditional poetry, Brooks upholds, also abounds in wit, irony, functional metaphor, and complication, which are the properties of modern poetry. These traits only get eclipsed in the nineteenth century. The romantics and Victorians think poetry an expression of some higher truth and keep intellect away from mingling with emotions. In this way, they do not nourish a healthy environment to the development of English poetry. W. H. Auden recapitulates Brooks's arguments in the following Words:

1. The Augustan neoclassicists regarded metaphor only as a decoration of thought. This is false; in poetry idea and image are one.

2. The Romantics ranked wit and fancy below imagination, intellect below emotion and considered irony below their dignity.

This is false; wit and irony are essential elements in serious poetry.

3. Both, Augustans and Romantics, regarded poetry as an elevated way of expressing elevated beliefs. This is false; the truth or error of beliefs expressed in poetry is immaterial; indeed, great poetry can be written without any beliefs.
4. In returning to metaphysical and iconic style of writing poetry, modern poets like Eliot, Yeats, Auden and Allen Tate are returning to the true tradition of English poetry, from which the Augustans and Romantics were heretical deviators.[8]

On the other hand, metaphysical poetry accommodates diverse experiences, discordant impulses, concrete metaphors, irony, paradox, dramatic tension, wit, stark intellect, conceit and the fusion of thought and emotion. Modern poetry carries forward this tradition of poetry very powerfully. According to Brooks, traditional poetry and modern poetry, on the surface, appears to be poles apart, moving into two different directions, but it is not so. On a closer examination, we discover that there is an interrelationship between the two. Therefore, it is quite imperative to have knowledge of traditional poetry to understand modern one. Brooks attempts to establish a relationship, a 'tradition' of English poetry by synthesizing both traditional poetry and modern poetry.

Brooks's idea of 'tradition' is mainly ingrained in the two chapters of *Modern Poetry and the Tradition.* They are: (i) Metaphor and the Tradition and (ii) The Modern Poet and the Tradition. But Brooks's concept of 'tradition' is quite different from that of Eliot, though both believe in it. In "Notes for a Revised History of English Poetry," Brooks strongly recommends a revised history of English poetry, being dissatisfied with the existing norms, values, practices, and judgments of English poetry. He calls for "the principles of poetic organization, developed to their logical conclusion."[9]

The readers, who are familiar with traditional poetry, face a good deal of difficulty in reading modern English and American poets. It is because of the change of metaphorical diction. Romantic metaphors and similes, A.E. Houseman concludes, are "things inessential to poetry," mere "accessories," "illustration," and "ornament," whereas the metaphors of T.S. Eliot, W. H. Auden, Allen Tate, W.B. Yeats, and Ransom are caused by a selection of 'another metaphor.' Their comparisons, unlike romantics, are characterized by ingenuity, intellect, and prosaic diction. In the fifth chapter of *Modern Poetry and the Tradition*, Brooks remarks that modern poetry is 'untraditional' and revolts against "lifeless conventions." The whole chapter devoted to modern American poets condemns the past practices, clichés, stereotype, worn out poetic object, Victorian didacticism, prudery, and priggishness. Lindsay, Edgar Lee, Masters, Sandburg etc. write about American scenes, American things, and American people, introducing "the legitimacy of experiment and innovation in subject matter and versification."[10] Modern poetry involves 'structure of inclusions', whereas Victorian poetry is 'a poetry of sharp exclusions.' The poetry of the New Critics—Ransom, Tate, and R.P. Warren beckons the third revolution in English poetry.

In the last chapter entitled "Notes for Revised History of English Poetry," Brooks issues certain prescription for the good of poetry. Subscribing to Allen Tate's view in his "Note on Elizabethan Satire," Brooks contends that poetry should have 'a dramatic context,' which exists in the Elizabethan poetry, and is later furthered by metaphysical poets and Shakespeare. He also determines the 'tradition of wit'[11] or 'a poetry of wit' in Donne, Ben Jonson, Cavalier poets like Herrick and Pope, though his wit is dominated by satire for the social and political purpose. The poetry of romantic precursors—Gray, Collins, Cooper, and Thomson—is not much different from the neo-classical. Romantic poetry heavily suffers the wrath of the modernists because of its simplicity, 'lucidity of emotion,' pastoral metaphors, musicality, abstraction, and sentimentality. But Keats and Coleridge escape from their acid test and receive a warm welcome for their sensuousness, concreteness, absence of didacticism, and complexity of experience. Victorian poetry—a poetry of message, a poetry of ideas, and a poetry of escapism—is marked by dull and sometimes "pompous didacticism" and "incredible sentimentality."[12] Though Browning's poetry in a way is much better than Tennyson's for his 'unpoetic', 'unexpected', and dramatic tension. Hopkins, Dickinson, and Thomas Hardy sow the seeds of modernism, and finally the emergence of T.S. Eliot, Ezra Pound, W.B. Yeats, and a plethora of others tolls the knell of Victorian poetry of religion and philosophy occasioned by the scientific discoveries.

Brooks exhibits a vogue, a 'tradition of wit' in English poetry right from the Elizabethans through Donne, Pope, and Hardy to the modernists. Modern poetry is in the line of this established tradition. Wit, the only true channel of poetic communication, is a continued tradition of English poetry. Therefore, in the revised history of English literature, the focus should be given on the 'tradition of wit.' Here it should be noted that Eliot's concept of tradition is different from that of Brooks. Both of them agree to the basic characteristics of modern poetry—difficulty, obscurity, method of indirection, artistic intensity, dramatic tension, blending of seriousness and levity; all these create "variety", "complexity," "shifts of tone", and wit coloured with the verve and vitality of metaphor. Eliot's concept of 'tradition' defines 'the historical sense' and 'the living past' right from the ancient European literature and culture to the modern. It is this guiding principle which controls poetic feelings and emotions and lends objectivity, impersonality, and depersonalization. Brooks's idea of tradition is limited and revolves round the narrow circumference of English poetry only.

Cleanth Brooks's tradition of English poetry is in terms of the poetic language— a language which is special and characterized by paradox, irony, wit, ambiguity, dramatization of experience, organic interrelationship and complexity. His deep concern is the debased and deteriorating condition of the language of poetry. He expresses his worry: "I am concerned with what is happening to our language."[13] This happens because of the decay of modern society. Language and society, Brooks argues, are interdependent and complementary to each other. Both run parallel; language reads the pulse of society. The key to a polished, value-laden, and aesthetically elegant society is vital, living, and concrete individual language. If a society is without values and a culture without direction, it is quite inevitable that the language will get deeply affected. Brooks finds both language and society chaotic, disordered, and anemic. "In any case our generation inherits a language that has lost its hold on concrete reality; that is slack and imprecise, and reflects a culture that lacks any commonly accepted value-system."[14] If a society is content with a language which is abstract, complicated, imprecise, and cliché-ridden, it means that there is "hardening of the arteries of thought and feeling in this culture which has slipped back towards the barbarism of civilization."[15] In such a sick culture, literature is an effective remedy. It can restore the private happiness, dignity, and sensibility of the modern man befuddled with the disastrous effect of industrialism and scientism. The power of literature tries to "to peal off the dead skin and callosities from the language." There is a close connection "between the state of language and the state of mind." There needs a transfusion of the blood of language to preserve the social and spiritual health. Brooks writes: "The dying flesh of language may produce a spiritual gangrene. One of the uses of literature is to keep our language alive—to keep the blood circulating through the tissues of the body politic. There can scarcely be a more vital function."[16]

Inspired by Coleridge, Eliot, Richards, Yeats and Auden, Brooks expounds the nature and function of poetry and the role of a poet. To him, poetry is an art and a poet is an artist, who seeks an order and meaningful pattern in the discordant and heterogeneous experience of the world. The materials of poetry—language, literary convention, ideas, personal experience—do not affect the nature of poetry, because they are conditioned and reshaped by the imagination and experience of the poet. But Brooks does not altogether deny the importance of biographical, moral, or social aspects; they should be the means not the end of the poem. In the poetic process, the poet does not follow a logical process like a carpenter or an architect. His approach is completely organic. Brooks argues that "he cannot transfer it [poem] into words in a mechanical fashion, corresponding to a builder's work on house." He is perpetually engaged in exploration, experimentation, imagination, and language. He unifies each and every item—the words, images, rhythm, local ideas, events etc. into the whole and the whole leads to a single thing. He is "constantly discovering for us a pattern in what we had taken to be mere confusion or something exciting in what we had thought banal, or the dark underside of what we had supposed to be innocent and smiling."[17] In this respect, a poet differs from a scientist, or historian, rhetorician or propagandist. Brooks says: "It is not enough for the poet to analyze his experiences as the scientist does, breaking it up to parts, distinguishing part from part, classifying the various parts. His task is finally to unify experience. He must return to us the unity of the experience itself as man knows in his own experience."[18]

Brooks underlies that a poet's job is not only to present "certain truths eloquently and persuasively in terms of rich images and resonant harmonies,"[19] but also to render a total situation and the artistic vision of reality with the help of his language and imaginative sympathy. His duty is to neither give a sermon nor perpetuate propaganda nor pour out his own emotions. As an active and responsible member of society, he has to arouse the people from the "drugged and benumbed" state into "full consciousness of their condition to let them see where they are."[20] A poet is purely an artist who bears the responsibility of his society and presents the truth in general.

Brooks considers a poem an independent 'structure.' All poems possess some common structural properties—'metaphor,' 'paradox,' 'irony,' 'tone,' and 'attitude.' He distinguishes 'structure' from 'form.' In the traditional sense, 'form' means poetic forms such as lyric, elegy, ode, ballad, sonnet etc. They are just like envelopes in which 'content' is contained. Rejecting this concept of form, Brooks suggests examining a poem in terms of structure, not of content or subject matter. An examination of content deprives of judging the beauty of the poem. Brooks further contends that content and structure of the poem are inseparable; they are always merged together. Dismissing Ransom's dualistic theory of structure and texture, Brooks maintains that structure embodies an organic unity or harmony and the total context. The entire poems taken for study should be analyzed to reveal a relationship between various parts and aspects—between word and word, between phrase and phrase, between line and line, between image and image, and between idea and idea. It is this relationship in which various parts of the poem unite together which Brooks calls structure.

Unity is achieved through psychological, imaginative, and dramatic process; logic and reason have no place for the total unity of the poem. Brooks's contention is that "The essence of poetry is metaphor, and metaphor is finally ontological rather than logical."[21] This leads to another very important aspect of Brooks's poetic structure i.e. a poem cannot be paraphrased at all. Since a poem is an organic whole like a plant or human body. How can then it be translated or paraphrased? Paraphrase means the demolition of parts as well as the whole of the poem; its metaphor, irony, ambiguity, tone, attitude as well as the total experience of the poet embodied in the poem get disintegrated. They do not convey meaning outside the poem; they cannot be dealt with in isolation. There is a great difference between the paraphrased prose content and the real core of meaning contained in the structure of the poem. Paraphrase cannot preserve complete meaning or convey its total effect because the poem has its own autonomy, anatomy, dramatic propriety, and organism.

Now Brooks's three very important essays—"The Language of Paradox," "The Heresy of Paraphrase," and "Irony as the Principle of Structure" have been taken up to discuss in details. They embrace the main marrow of the language and structure of his poetic theory.

The Language of Paradox

Traditional theorists describe paradox as a figure of speech, but twentieth century critics, particularly Cleanth Brooks, extend the scope and application of the term to encompass all surprising deviations from common perception. They elevate it to a higher position as a mode of understanding in poetry. Like Brooks, other critics have also felt its deep relevance:

> Both Friederich Schlegel and Thomas de Quincey argue that paradox is a vital element in poetry, reflecting the paradoxical nature of the world which poetry imitates.[22]

Cleanth Brooks commences the essay "The Language of Paradox" with the various objections and negative views held by the people apropos of paradox. He regrets that critics are not very enthusiastic to give much value to it, because they do not consider it a very effective device in writing poetry. But, despite all prejudices and discouraging approach towards paradox, Brooks exhibits his confidence and determination that "the language of poetry is the language of paradox."[23]

Though paradox literally means the assertion of the union of opposites, yet it has, Brooks contends, a great function. It lends a dramatization of experience. A poet's experiences are often diverse, discordant, crude, common, and complex. He can neither present them in the form of statement nor in that of abstraction as a scientist. He adopts an indirect method to unify the complexity of human experiences into oneness to give an impression of total experience. He wields the weapon of paradox to unify the opposites into one entity. Thus, paradox becomes "the language appropriate and inevitable to poetry" (p.292). A poet cannot escape from its use because paradox springs from the very nature of poetry consciously or unconsciously.

Brooks makes an unmistakable distinction between the language of science and that of poetry. A scientist expresses the truth through a language which is quite direct, clear, and shorn of all figures and paradox—"a language purged of every trace of paradox" (p.292), but a poet, on the other hand, discovers the truth only in terms of paradox. Brooks reads the poems very closely line by line and arrives at this conclusion that paradox is one of their common structural properties. He finds the richness, depth, and power of the poems issuing from the paradoxical situations on which they are based. This powerful device rejects the fallacy of its cheap and artificial function and, therefore, justifies Brooks's fury to those who deprive paradox of its naturalness. He says: "our prejudices force us to regard paradox as intellectual rather than emotional, clever rather than profound, rational rather than divinely irrational" (p.292).

Brooks finds Wordsworth's poetry teemed with many examples of the language of paradox. To justify his dogma, he first analyses his [Wordsworth's] two sonnets. Usually, Wordsworth's poetry is characterized by directness, simplicity, and unsophistication. And yet the typical Wordsworth poem is based on a paradoxical situation. For instance, in the following sonnet:

> It is a beauteous evening, calm and free
> The holy time is quite as Nun
> Breathless with adoration...

Wordsworth is in deep mood of adoration, but the small girl walking along with him is unaware of it. She should also keep tune with the holy time, and become like the evening, nunlike. Even she is less worshipful than inanimate nature itself. Yet in the next stanza, the poet notices:

> If thou appear untouched by solemn thought,
> Thy nature is not therefore less divine:
> Thou liest in Abraham's bosom all the year;
> And worship'st at the Temple's inner shrine,
> God being with thee when we know it not.

In these lines, there runs a deep current of paradox. It is fully necessary to note it even for those enthusiastic readers who are unconscious of it. The innocent girl is filled with deeper worship than the self-conscious poet, because she has a secret communion with or sympathy for nature throughout the year, reminding Coleridge's message in *The Rime of the Ancient Mariner*

He prayeth best, who loveth best
All things both great and small.

With her innocence, she is very close to God, whereas the poet is far off the glory of God; and even his prayer is "sporadic and momentary." In the sonnet, paradox does not stop here, but it has another dimension of paradox. It is quite obvious that the tranquility of the evening denotes 'worship' even to the dull witted and insensitive. It also reveals the external religious show of the nun, visible to all. It shows not only holiness but also the show of holiness, which is in direct contrast to the careless innocence of the girl, who cherishes a continual secret prayer for God.

Wordsworth's another sonnet *Composed Upon Westminister Bridge*, Brook holds, is a good and successful poem. But its greatness neither lies in the noble feelings nor in the brilliant images. Moreover, the sonnet contains a very flat writing with hackneyed similes. Even there is no graphic delineation, except a cluster of items: towers, ships, domes, theatres, temples, etc. All the objects of nature, places, and buildings twinkling in the morning light give a hazy impression. The poetic meaning or the power of the poem lies in its paradoxical situation. The beauty of the poem reveals an incongruity between the unattractive, noisy, smoky, and industrial city and the splendour of the morning in the "smokeless air."

Never did sun more beautifully steep
In his first splendour, valley, rock, or hill...

There is a contrast between the actual mechanical, robot-like and rigid disciplined life of London and the freshness and glory of the morning images, and the gliding river in a natural and gentle way in a zigzag motion. The poet gets shocked and amazed watching such a paradoxical picture and life existing in the city of London. Under the semblance of death, it acquires the organic life of 'nature.' Further the poem ends with the concluding couplet:

Dear God! the very houses seem asleep;
And all that mighty heart is lying still!

The poet always considered the houses inanimate and dead but in the morning beauty they appear to be 'asleep,' and will come into life; and in addition to that London, the city of cut-throat competition, is also silent with the "mighty heart." Brooks explores the real charm of the poem in its paradoxical images, thoughts, and treatments.

Wordsworth's statement in his preface to the second edition of the *Lyrical Ballads* also underlines the romantic paradoxes. His general intention is "to choose incidents and situations from common life," but they should be coloured in such a way that "ordinary things should be preserved to the mind in an unusual aspect." Later, Coleridge classifies this statement that Wordsworth aims at lending "the charm of novelty to things of every day," and exciting a feeling of the super-natural awe and wonder. The mind, which slumbers and remains dormant in the effete and dull social customs and conventions, opens an avenue of "the loveliness and the wonders of the world before us...." In other words, it is a studied attempt of Wordsworth to formulate his paradoxical attitude that "the common was really uncommon, the prosaic was really poetic." The romantics are primarily concerned with creating the wonder, the surprise, the revelation, "which puts the tarnished familiar world in a new light." This is the reason for existence of most Romantic paradoxes, yet the neo-classical poetry also abounds in paradox. In it the paradoxes depend on irony rather than on wonder. Brooks cites an extract from Alexander Pope's *The Essay on Man*:

In doubt his Mind or Body to prefer;
Born but to die, and reasoning but to err;
Alike in ignorance, his Reason such,
Whether he thinks too little, or too much...

Created half to rise, and half to fall;
Great Lord of all things, yet a Prey to all;
Sole Jude of Truth, in endless Error hurl'd;
The Glory, Jest, and Riddle to the world!

Pope also treats common objects, e.g. man, to awaken his mind to know himself in "a new and blinding light." Just as one gets a tinge of irony implied in Wordsworth's sonnets, so in Pope's poetry also there is a touch of awed wonder. Though in these two poets both irony and wonder never occur simultaneously, yet in the lyrics of Blake and *The Rime of Ancient Mariner* of Coleridge these two characteristics merge together. Like Wordsworth, Gray also broods in his *Elegy* the fate of the peasants against the pastoral setting. The elegy is steeped in paradox, but paradox is more inclined towards irony than wonder. Brooks quotes the following quatrain to show the ironic revelation and justify that "the paradoxes spring from the very nature of the poet's language: it is a language in which the connotations play as great a part as the denotations" (p.295).

> Can storied urn or animated bust
> Back to its mansion call the fleeting breath?
> Can Honour's voice provoke the silent dust?
> Or Flatt'ry sooth the dull cold ear of Death?

The poet, Brooks spells out, never uses notation like the scientist but, within his limits, he gives a literary colour to his language, while composing a poem.

Brooks draws a distinction between the language of science and the language of poetry. He observes that scientific language containing notation is essentially prone to fix and freeze the terms and words into exact denotation, whereas the poetic language is disruptive. The poetic terms and diction all the time modify each other, violating their dictionary meaning. T. S. Eliot also comments that there is a "perpetual slight alteration of language, words perpetually juxtaposed in new and sudden combinations," in poetry. This verbal process is continuous and becomes the nature of a poem. Unlike the scientist, the poet directs and controls the dictionary words according to their own way, disturbing their normal meanings.

The critic, Brook argues, should develop a critical faculty to evaluate how the poetic language works. To express the subtler states and shades of emotion, the poet urgently requires metaphors, as I. A. Richards also points out. He takes the help of analogies, but the metaphors "do not lie in the same plane or fit neatly edge to edge. There is a continual fitting of the planes; necessary overlappings, discrepancies, contradictions. Even the most direct and simple poet is forced into paradoxes for more often than we think...." (p.296). The dictionary meaning is violated by qualification." Analogy is the tool with which the poet proceeds in his work. The scientific language is direct and functions like notation. The method of art is never direct, but always indirect. Brooks quotes Shakespeare's figure:

> ... with essays of bias
> By indirections find directions out.

Even the most simple and straightforward poet is forced into paradoxes by the nature of his instrument. The main task of the poet is to employ paradox consciously to gain a compression and precision otherwise unobtainable. The method is an extension of the normal language of poetry, not a perversion of it. The device of paradox enables the poet to say what direct statement could never convey. He liberates the terms from the stabilizing influence of scientific thinking and allows them to escape into unexpected connotational novelties.

Brooks demonstrates that paradox is specially cultivated as a central device in metaphysical poetry. John Donne, who writes a collection of *Paradoxes and Problems* in prose, exploited this device very skillfully in "The Canonizations." Brooks interprets it in detail to show paradox as the very structure of the poem. The poem contains a metaphor in a form of paradox, which is very well reflected in the title of the poem. Donne treats very boldly the profane love of the two lovers as if it were divine love of a pair of holy hermits who renounce the world and the flesh. The poet justifies that the two true lovers also do the same and achieve a more intense world and are regarded as saints. The poem is fraught with a plenty of fantastic comparisons and the basic metaphor of the saint is carried on till the end of the poem. It is also characterized by a modulation of tone, dramatization, ironical tenderness, and brilliant paradox. Thus, "The Canonization" epitomizes Brooks's all the ingredients of his poetic theory of structure, in which paradox seeks a formula or category to identify the special character of literary language. But Brooks is very much conscious of the tendency of modern man also who hardly understands the paradoxical, ironical, and indirect language, because he is habituated to "an easy yes or no....He refuses to accept the paradox as a serious rhetorical device; and since he is able to accept it only as a cheap trick, he is forced into this dilemma" (p.297).

The Heresy of Paraphrase

When Cleanth Brooks appears on the literary critical landscape, he witnesses, after his personal evaluation, the mind of the people deeply preoccupied with certain heretical notions. He, therefore, prepares himself to fight against them to prescribe the correct perspective of criticism. He points out the right method of reading, analyzing, and teaching poetry. The function of criticism, Brooks holds, is not to dig out certain truth, or rational or logical or prose structure or formulations or remarks about the poem, which is traditionally supposed to be the "essential core of the poem itself."[24] They are rather contaminants to criticism. The critic's concern should not be with the *whatness* but *howness* of the poem i.e. the role of language as to how it functions and plays to express certain ideas. If a critic gets tempted towards statements, he contaminates criticism. This misconception acquires more force when a poem is used as a tool for propaganda. Like T. S. Eliot and Ransom, Brooks also condemns this mode of criticism.

"The Heresy of Paraphrase," the terminal essay in Brooks's *The Well Wrought Urn*, purposes to point out as to why he makes a thorough interpretation of ten poems selecting from different movements and ages ranging from Metaphysical poet, John Donne through Wordsworth and Tennyson to W. B. Yeats and T. S. Eliot. The poems chosen are representative of their own age and tradition. They have been held in admiration in their own historical periods and are still admired. The book commences with Donne's "Canonization" and ends with the moderns. The metaphysical and the modern have common poetic tradition, but the rest of the other masterpieces taken from different poetic modes of utterance can also be read in the same tradition. The intention of the inclusion of the ten poems is never "to express a common theme or to display some particular style or to share a social set of symbols" (192) but to show how the different types of poetry have a common feature i.e. structure. Of course, there is similarity of certain items in some of the poems. But it is a sheer co-incidence to come across some items they do have in common. For example, the light symbolism in Milton's "L'Allegro-Il Penseroso" and Wordsworth's "Immortality Ode;" or death as a metaphor of sex in "The Canonization" and *The Rape of the Lock*; or the likeness of theme and problem in the "Immortality Ode" and "Among School Children." Moreover, the startling point is that the ten poems without having much in common are very "close to the central stream of the tradition" (p.192) of English poetry.

Brooks argues how the undertaken poems in *The Well Wrought Urn* "are surely in the main stream of tradition" (p.192). He discovers that the common goodness of poetry cannot be stated in terms of "content" or "subject matter," but in terms of structure. The meaning or beauty of a poem never lies in its paraphrasable content or statement, diction, or imagery, but in its structure. Poetry can be studied only in terms of structure. But it is a misfortune of the traditional poetry, particularly romantic and classical, that it is read as statements, while only Metaphysical and modern poetry through analytical technique. It is the general tendency of the people to paraphrase the traditional poetry to understand and take out its meanings; they ignored the real meaning of poetry of all types. This method of reading poetry was so deeply rooted in American Universities and colleges that the teachers strongly protested against Brooks's *Understanding Poetry* and *The Well Wrought Urn* to be introduced into curriculum. However, later on they realized the value of these books, which change the whole approach towards poetry. Brooks advocates that even the traditional poetry has much more in it than its paraphrasable content, because the basic quality of the language of all poetry is paradox and irony. Therefore, classical and romantic poetry should also be read with the same analytical technique as Metaphysical and modern poetry is done. In this way, a common similarity or tradition can be discovered in all types of poetry including Metaphysical and modern. Thus, to paraphrase romantic and classical poetry means to miss the real meaning of poetry. In their *The Theory of Literature* (1949), Rene Wellek and Austin Warren discuss the various factors contributing to the real meaning of poetry besides the parapharasable content.

> The meaning of poetry is contextual: a word carries with it not its dictionary meaning but an aura of synonyms and homonyms. Words not only have a meaning but evoke the meanings of words related either in sound or in sense, or in derivation—or even words which are contrasted or excluded.[25]

Sound plays a very key role in determining human mind and behaviour. The patterning sounds, pauses and rhythm of the language of poetry also condition and control and create various mental waves, psychological states, and emotional feelings, whereas the paraphrasable content fails to yield such characteristics. Wellek and Warren further wave the act of paraphrase aside because

> Metre organizes the sound character of language. It regulates the rhythm of prose, approximating it to isochronism, and thus simplifying the relation between syllable lengths. It slows up the tempo, prolonging the vowels, in order to exhibit their overtones or tone colour (timber). It simplifies and regularizes intonation, the melody of speech. The influence of meter is, then, to actualize words: to point them and to direct attention to their sound.[25]

These two quotations cited here are just to reinforce Brooks's credo that poetry must be described in terms of structure, and that the paraphrasable content of poetry never contains the real meaning. The meaning of poetry depends upon structure and structure itself depends upon irony or paradox or ambiguity or complex of attitudes. Structure is far more internal than the metrical pattern, or than the sequence of images.

> The structure obviously is everywhere conditioned by the nature of the material which goes into the poem. The nature of the material sets the problem to be solved, and the solution is the ordering of the material (p. 194).

Here it is very essential to bear two points in the mind regarding the term structure. First, Brooks's concept of structure entirely differs from that of J. C. Ransom. To the later, structure means the argument or content of the poem. It always remains separable from texture and forms a dualism in the poem. It is never used in the same sense as Brooks has done. Secondly, structure also never denotes the meaning of 'form' in traditional sense. It is not just as a kind of envelop which "contains" the "content," nor is it a form like ode, elegy, sonnet etc. in which ideas or subject matter is dressed. That is why the structure of *The Rape of the Lock* is definitely not the heroic couplet as such, or the canto arrangement, or the mock-epic convention. The structure of a poem lies in attitude i.e. ironical and paradoxical attitude. Brooks remarks:

> The structure meant is a structure of meanings, evaluations, and interpretations; and the principle of unity which informs it seems to be one of balancing and harmonizing connotations, attitudes, and meanings (195).

Through the studies of the undertaken ten poems, Brooks concludes that the core meaning of the poem depends upon the structure, and further structure depends upon "paradox," "irony," "ambiguity," and "complex of attitude."

Most of the common heresies about poetry are born when the critic forms his misconception that the poem constitutes a "statement." It is totally misleading. His business is not to explore message—political, scientific or philosophical truth. Nor is his concern at all whether the statement in the poem is true or false, described clearly or vaguely, or eloquently or beautifully. Brooks dwells upon his view that "any good poem sets up against all attempts to paraphrase it" (p.196). Here it is to be noted that it does never mean that the critic cannot describe adequately or accurately the general effect or about the poem. For instance, *The Rape of the Lock* is about the follies and foibles of the eighteenth century society lady. The effect of "Corrina's going a-Maying" is one of gaiety tempered by the poignancy of the transience of youth. Paraphrase can be used as a pointer and a shorthand reference. It is an initial stage or the first step to what the critic is going to do. It cannot be the end of criticism.

The poem, Brooks considers, has a structure and structure has "a positive unity" and "an achieved harmony." It combines the conflicting ideas or opposites and discordant elements in the poem, producing an organic whole. That is why he firmly remarks: "The relation between all the elements must surely be an organic one—there can be no question about that" (p.200). The various elements are not arranged into uniform groupings of the same qualities, but the structure "unites the like with the unlike" (195). The organic unity is not achieved by the reduction and simplification of attitudes. Brooks further explains:

> It does not unite them, however, by the simple process of allowing one connotation to cancel out another nor does it reduce the contradictory attitude to harmony by a process of subtraction (p. 195).

Brooks makes a sharp distinction between the beauty of any particular item as such and the beauty of the poem taken as a whole. The latter is the effect of a total pattern. It is a kind of pattern which can integrate within itself intrinsically beautiful or ugly, attractive or repulsive. Brooks remarks: "Unless one asserts the primacy of the pattern, a poem becomes merely a bouquet of intrinsically beautiful items" (194).

Brooks's contention is quite clear that form and content in the poem are related inseparably. Neither form alone nor content alone is the real poem. Form and content or content and medium of expression exist together. It is impossible to express in different language what the poem reveals in its intuitive way. Brooks upholds W. M. Urban's remarks in *Language and Reality*:

> The artist does not first intuit his object and then find the appropriate medium. It is rather in and through his medium that he intuits the object (199).

If critics like Yvor Winters think that the traditional meaning of the form comes first and embellishments later, it means they "negate the function and meaning of the symbol" (pp. 199-200). Brooks holds that the "rational statement" or "rational meaning" is not intrinsic part of the poem but something extraneous to it. The universal and ideal relations cannot adequately be expressed directly but is expressed indirectly by means of the poetic intuition. Thus, the poem cannot be paraphrased, because when any statement, which incorporates the 'meaning' of the poem, is taken out, "immediately the imagery and the rhythm seem to set up tensions with it, warping and twisting it, qualifying and revising it" (p.197).

Brooks advises that a poem's reading reduced to a formulation is not a right method of reading poetry. The recapitulations of the poem are just like "scaffoldings" placed around the building, though with a sense of purpose. But it would be a sheer mistake to consider such formulations as the essence of the poem, because they "lead away from the centre of the poem—not toward it" (p.199). The "prose sense" of the poem cannot reveal its internal and essential structure. It does not represent the "inner" structure or the "essential" structure or the "real" structure of the poem. Of course, the formulations may turn out to be one of the parts of the poem, not the organic whole. Generally, the act of the paraphrasing, Brooks believes, inveigles the critic into leading astray from the main track of criticism. If the critic considers paraphrase the structure of the poem, he misses to taste the kernel of the poem, and treats something outside the poem. This assumption engenders a great "violence to internal order of the poem itself" (p. 202). It also raises the question of truth and the problem of belief. By doing this the function of metaphor and metre is totally misconceived and badly ignored. The statement of the poem unnecessarily is put into an unusual competition with science or philosophy or theology.

The positive theory of poetry claims that the poetic structure is highly relevant because it has an imaginative coherence, whereas the paraphrasable content, which is sometimes irrelevant, demands a logical coherence. Being ever tended toward the "barren logic-chopping," if a critic fails to obtain any statement, he concludes that it exists either in an "Ivory tower" or in a "free balloon." To him, no statement means no meaning in the poem. But Brooks repeatedly reacts such criticism and remarks:

> ...one can never measure a poem against the scientific or philosophical yardstick for the reason that the poem, when laid along the yardstick, is never the "full poem" but an abstraction from the poem—a transparent dodge (pp. 202-203).

There always exists a clear distinction between poetic truth and the truth of a scientific or historical or philosophical statement.

According to Cleanth Brooks, the positive account of what a poem is or does tell that the essential structure of a poem is quite different from that of the rational or logical structure of the "statement." The structure of the former is compared with that of architecture or painting or more closer to that of ballet or musical composition. "It is a pattern of resolutions and balances and harmonizations, developed through a temporal scheme" (p. 203). It is a pattern of resolved stresses. Brooks finally seeks an appropriate resemblance of the structure of a poem with the structure of a drama. He thinks it the most suitable analogy between the two because both of them use words. The drama cannot be reduced to a statement because of its very nature based on action through conflict rather than on a statement about action. Similarly, the poem which moves in its dimension includes attitudes and dramatic propriety. The dimension has surely an idea, but it will be always an abstracted idea. An idea is always steeped in abstraction. The precise meaning and significance of the poem lies in its relation to the total context of the poem.

> The relationship between the intellectual and the non-intellectual elements in a poem is actually far more intimate than the conventional accounts would represent it to be: the relationship is not that of an idea "wrapped in emotion" or a "prose-sense decorated by sensuous imagery" (p. 204).

Brooks argues that any proposition stated in a poem is not always in abstraction, but is justified in terms of the poem—in terms of a principle, which is quite similar to that of dramatic propriety. It is very well illustrated in Keats's "Beauty is truth, truth beauty." This proposition is valid or meaningful when it is studied in relation to the total context of the poem. It is meaningless and flat, when read in isolation or in itself or in terms of its scientific or historical or philosophical truth. But it should also be noted, Brooks contends, that a poem cannot be reduced to a proposition and then that proposition is elaborated in details to state exactly what the poem says as a poem, no more no less. First, if a poet forms a proposition beforehand, he cannot write a poem. Secondly, the reader may also make an effort to frame a proposition from a poem to understand it; there is no harm in doing so, but he should not think it "the inner core of the poem" (p. 206). Therefore, the conclusions of poems like Keats's "Ode on a Grecian Urn" and Wordsworth's "Immortality Ode" have their value only in the context of all the items that contribute to the organic whole of the poem: taken in isolation, they may sound as sentimental nonsense or trite reflection on life.

The poet has to grapple with his experience to give an order, a unity, and coherence to the poem. It never allows the rule of linearity or any formula, which results in a logical sequence, but pivots on a dramatic process. The poet unifies his attitudes into a hierarchical order, and finally subordinates them under the total and controlling attitude. This unity of the poem represents equilibrium of diverse forces. The conclusion of the poem is achieved when the various tensions are resolved and balanced harmoniously. These tensions are generated by propositions, metaphors, and symbols. Brooks remarks:

> The unity is achieved by a dramatic process, not a logical; it represents equilibrium of forces, not a formula. It is proved as a dramatic conclusion is proved: by its ability to resolve the conflicts which have been accepted as the donnees of the drama (p. 207).

This process of unity and coherence is applied to even those poems which may "accidentally possess a logical unity as well as this poetic unity" (p. 207).

The poet avoids expressing his ideas in plain, direct, simple, and discursive way, but "continually engaged in blurring out distinctions, effecting compromises, or at the best, coming to his conclusions only after provoking and unnecessary delays" (p. 208). It is a general conception that these meanderings—twists and turns—of poetry are negative, but, in fact, they have positive function and give birth to a structure—a structure of "gestures" or attitudes. Brooks remarks:

> The truth is that the apparent irrelevancies which metrical pattern and metaphor introduce do become relevant when we realize that they function in a good poem to modify, qualify, and develop the total attitude which we are to take in coming to terms with the total situation (p.209).

It is this structure which is found common in the ten poems studied in *The Well Wrought Urn*. The essential structure of poetry is not logical, but a structure of order—a structure of tensions, complex of attitudes, and dramatization—with recurring use of paradox and irony. In this way a poem written in an ironical and paradoxical mode cannot be paraphrased. The noticeable point to be noted here is that the meanings of these two terms 'paradox,' and 'irony,' should not be taken in their traditional sense, but in the sense to be derived from their use by poets like Donne, Wordsworth, Tennyson, Pope, and Keats, who have made use of irony and paradox as devices in the structuring of their poems. In the traditional sense irony is associated with "intellectual poetries" and satire to correct the follies and foibles of the society. But to Brooks, irony is the most general term in poetry to point out the recognition of incongruities. It has also "the kind of qualification which the various elements in a context receive from the context" (p. 209). This kind of qualification is of tremendous importance in all types of poetry.

The scientific terms are abstract symbols, pure denotations, and already defined. They cannot change their meanings in any circumstances or under the pressure of context. They cannot acquire any new meanings, because of their fixed, limited, and predetermined meanings. From logical point of view, like the scientific vocabulary, "the ideal language would contain one term for each meaning, and the relation between term and meaning would be constant" (p.210). But there exists no dictionary which contains the terms of a poem. The word a poet uses is conceived not "as a discrete particle of meaning, but as a potential of meaning, a nexus or cluster of meanings" (p.210). T. S. Eliot also contends that the business of a poet is "to dislocate language into meaning." Therefore a critic cannot consider a poem as primarily a rational statement, but it is described in an ironic mode. Brooks comments very aptly:

> When we consider the statement immersed in the poem, it presents itself to us, like the stick immersed in the pool of water, warped and bent. Indeed, whatever the statement, it will always show itself as deflected away from a positive, straightforward formulation (p.211).

To write a poem, the poet chooses paraphernalia of ambiguity, paradox, irony, complex of attitudes, metaphor, dramatization, ironic shock and wonder, and the assertion of the union of opposites. All these characteristics woven organically in the poem cannot be paraphrased. Nor does he adopt plain and discursive simplicity. Like a scientist, he cannot analyze his experience, dissecting into bits and pieces, distinguishing part from part, classifying the various parts. The poet's business is finally to write and dramatize the oneness of experience, despite its diversity. He not only decorates a poem with a superficially and mystifying rhetoric, but also imparts the insight preserving the unity of experience, as a man knows it in his own experience. The unity of experience, at his higher and more serious levels, dominates the apparently contradictory and conflicting elements of experience by unifying them into a new pattern. The poem is not a statement about experience or an abstraction from experience. It is an imitation of experience—"a simulacrum of reality."

One of the heresies according to Brooks, is the dualism about content and form which compels the critic to judge a poem either in terms of the truth and excellence of the statement on philosophical, or moral, or political, scientific ground, or in terms of its form, style, etc. The constitution of the concept of structure for paraphrase saves the critic from this dualism, because under the concept of structure, form and content become one. Whatever the content or meaning of the poem, it arises from the form in the sense of the relationship in which various parts of the poem are seen to stand to each other when we analyze ironies, paradoxes, and ambiguities in it.

Irony as a Principle of Structure

In "Irony as a Principle of Structure" Cleanth Brooks highlights the four aspects of his poetic theory: (i) the function of metaphor, (ii) an organic theory of form and content, (iii) irony as a principle of structure in the poem and its tradition in English poetry, and (iv) the role and pressure of the context. First, he holds that "the most essential of [poetic] devices is metaphor,"[27] unraveling its complex and magnetic properties. Through and through he brushes off its traditional concept—its decorative and fundamental approach. It has grown anemic. The critics of the eighteenth and nineteenth century regarded metaphor as "a kind of rhetorical gilding"[28] and "accessories." It is reduced to be "a mere surrogate way of saying something, not the necessary and inevitable way."[29] This "unnatural, strained, merely decorative and superfluous" [30] way of holding metaphor forces the modern critics, particularly Brooks, to bring a great revolution in the poetic language and metaphor.

In twentieth century literary criticism, the concept of metaphor undergoes a sea-change. Brooks extends its scope and recognizes it as a "natural—even essential way to expression,"[31] "the only verbal structure,"[32] and "the microcosm of the poem."[33] Metaphor "is frequently, the only means available if the (poet) is to write at all...."[34] Brooks gives his plea that "the metaphor is finally, the main body of the content."35 In "Literary Criticism: Poet, Poem and Reader," he points out that it is not like term A being compared to term B, or term B with term A. If a metaphor is used as mere decoration, it means much of the value of poetry is lost. "After all, we must not forget how much our discovery of the truth—scientific as well as poetic—is gained through metaphor."[36] Sharing with Robert Frost, Brooks makes a point that "poetry is fundamentally metaphor." These views removing the conventional misconception of metaphor lays deep emphasis on its functional aspect. It contributes to the total effect or appeals to the whole context, and builds the total meaning. It discovers a pattern in the jostling and often heterogeneous elements of poet's experience. It not only unifies the experience but also makes sense out of it. However, metaphor may be ingenious, unpleasant, and far-fetched, it must be justified in terms of total context. Brooks fusing the universal and the particular suggests that metaphor should be functional—the very essence of all poetry. With full devotion, he, therefore, sets the focus on the healthy function of metaphor and gives a new energy, a new dimension, and a new life to it. It achieves a new meaning, which is quite different from the eighteenth and nineteenth century notion of metaphor.

At the very outset of the essay, Brooks lays emphasis on the central doctrine of the inseparability of form and content. Propounding his theory of poetic technique, he fails to subscribe to the traditional notion that the poet first chooses an abstract theme and then he decorates it with concrete details. On the contrary, he is totally controlled by the particulars. Brooks suggests: "...he must establish the details, must abide by the details, and through his realization of the details attain to whatever general meaning he can attain. The meaning must issue from the particulars."[37] It must not be arbitrarily imposed upon the particulars. The traditional handling of language has to be reversed when the poet comes to deal with poetry. "For here it is the tail that wags the dog" (p. 59). Brooks, illustrating an example of the kite, intends to clear the concept that the concrete details, which always seem to hinder to reveal the meaning of the poet directly and clearly, are essential to the poem. The poet does not state anything directly and forthrightly. He takes only the help of metaphors. Through the introduction of metaphors, he takes a risk that he may fail to state his idea clearly and directly. He encounters a risk of saying it partially and obscurely. But the poet accepts this challenge and handles metaphors, because "direct statement leads to abstraction and threatens to take us out of poetry altogether" (p.59). The poet loads a poem with particular details, though they seem to negate the universal to which he aspires to remove abstraction from the poem. The tail of the kite seems to negate the kite's function, but it weighs something down to rise. The tail of the kite is functional and helps it fly upward. The tail that renders the kite more than a frame of paper is blown crazily down the wind. It warrants one to cite the judicious remark to Mark Schorer:

> When we speak of technique, then, we speak of nearly everything. For technique is the means by which the writer's experience, which is his subject-matter, compels him to attend to it; technique is the only means he has of discovering, exploring, developing his subject, of conveying its meaning, and finally, of evaluating it. And surely it follows that certain techniques are sharper tools than others, and will discover more; that the writer capable of the most exacting technical scrutiny of his subject mater will produce works with the most satisfying content, works with thickness and resonance; works which reverberate, works with maximum meaning.[38]

A great deal of energy is spent on metaphor, which generates "a principle of indirection." Related to particular images and statements, metaphor also sets forth "a principle of organic relationship." Brooks, as Rene Wellek notes, borrowed the metaphor 'organism' from Coleridge. He declares that "a poem is a unified construct, a psychological whole...."[39] Therefore, the poem is not a collection of beautiful or poetic images or objects, decorative pieces of figures, and statements which have no inter-connection or interdependence. The images having mere similarity with objects cannot be a poem. But it should have an organic growth like a plant. Just as the parts of a plant are organically related and each part contributes to the beauty of the whole, so the parts of a poem have an organic relation to each other and add to the beauty of the whole. Brooks presents a lovely metaphorical example:

> For in that case, one might arrange bouquets of these poetic images and thus create poems by formula. But the elements of a poem are related to each other, not as blossoms juxtaposed in a bouquet, but as the blossoms are related to the other parts of a growing plant. The beauty of the poem is the flowering of the whole plant, and needs the stalk, the leaf, and the hidden roots (p. 60).

To stress the organic relations of various parts of the poem and their imaginative unity in the total context, Brooks presents analogy after analogy, now to painting, architecture, music, and now more precisely to drama. He states: "the poem is like a drama." In the drama, all the elements interrelated with each other yields the total effect and unity. In "a good drama there is no waste motion." Similarly, in a good poem there are no superfluous parts. It has an organic growth and whole and beauty. St. Augustine also aptly remarks:

> Any beautiful object whatsoever is more worthy of praise in its totality as a whole than in any one of its parts. So great is the power of integrity and unity that what pleases as a part pleases much more in a unified whole.[40]

Brooks reacts to the concept of the neoclassical and romantic concept of poetry. The neoclassical critics like Dr. Johnson emphasize the logical unity of a poem. Since it was an age of logical bigotry, words in a poem tended to be "fixities, hard definite cores of meaning linked one to another in accordance with fairly exact laws."[41] They were quite unknown to the plasticity of words and the organic nature of their relationship. In the hands of the romantics, poetry turned into a spontaneous overflow of poet's personality. Focus gets shifted from the poem to the poet. But Brooks insists on the organicity of a poem marked by the imaginative unity. The poem is not an expression of the poet's personality, but is architecture—"an architecture in which stresses are balanced against each other and internal strains are reciprocated."[42]

While pointing out the importance or significance of the organic whole of the poem, Brooks explains the role of *context*. Each and every poem is written in a particular context. It derives its poetic quality from its ordinary word "never" repeated five times becomes one of the most poignant lines in *Lear*, but it becomes so because of the supporting context. Even the meaning of any particular item is modified by the context. For what is said is said in a particular situation and by a particular dramatic character. The particular word or image or statement becomes forceful, significant, and effective, when it is qualified by the context. Images with a new life acquire form of symbol, and statements attain dramatic utterances. The context also leaves its impact on the part. The part is modified by the pressure of the context. Any statement in the organic whole is not justified because of its logical or scientific truth; it must admit the pressure of context, whether it is 'ironical,' or merely callow, glib, and sentimental.[43]

The warping, turning, and twisting of a statement by the context creates a quality of irony. Brooks cites a very simple line to reveal the meaning of context: "this is the fine state of affairs." In a certain contexts, the statement means quite the opposite of what it purports to say literally. This is called sarcasm—the most obvious kind of irony. Here the meaning is produced quite apposite: produced by the content and pointed by the tone of voice. But the most important irony is what is devoid of both sarcasm and the tonal effect. The tone of irony can be produced by the accomplished disposition of the context. Brooks cites a quatrain from Gray's famous *Elegy:*

> Can storied urn or animated bust
> Back to its mansion call the fleeting breath?
> Can Honour's voice provoke the silent dust?
> Or Flatt'ry sooth the dull cold ear of death?

In its context, the stanza contains rhetorical question very clearly, but the answer is suggested in "the characterization of the breath as fleeting and of the ear of dead as dull and cold." In fact, here there is no question asked, but it is emphasized that nothing can bring the dead into life again.

Illustrating numerous instances, Brooks shows that all poetry is written in an ironical mode. Many of Thomas Hardy's poems and nearly all of Housman's reveal quite definite and overt irony. Irony comprises a whole variety of modes: tragic irony, self-irony, playful, arch, mocking or gentle irony, etc. These types of irony can be found in both dramatic and non-dramatic poetry. It is not confined only to satirical and dramatic poetry. "The basic principle of irony is the same, however, whether in tragedy or the lyric." Brooks considers it the most important device which becomes a principle of structure to qualify the meaning of poetry. He says: "Irony, then in this further sense, is not only an acknowledgement of the pressures of context. Invulnerability to irony is the stability of a context in which the internal pressures balance and mutually support each other. The stability is like that of the arch: the very forces which are calculated to drag the stones to the ground actually provide the principle of support—a principle in which thrust and counter-thrust become the means of stability."[44] There are twofold functions of irony: (i) the pressure of context and (ii) the stability of context. In this way, poetry of all ages, particularly modern, is characterized by irony.

If a statement is shorn of an ironic potential and without any qualification of context, it will be purely a mathematical equation like "two plus two equals four." The meaning of such statements is unqualified by a context. If they are true, they are equally true in any possible context. These statements are, in fact, abstract and their terms are pure denotations. If "two" or "four" actually happened to have connotations for the imaginative minded, they would be quite irrelevant. They do not participate in the meaningful structure of the statements. Statements made in the poem bear the pressure of the context and have their meaning modified by the context. Brooks argues: "Their relevance, their propriety, their rhetorical force, and even their meaning, cannot be divorced from the context in which they are embedded" (p.61).

It is through irony that the straight and linear denotation of scientific language becomes a warped statement in poetry, and it is also through irony that the gust of romantic emotion can be curbed into a more responsible and dialectical expression. For Warren, irony is a device of reference by which the poet's vision "can survive reference to the complexities and contradictions of experience."[45] The repeated emphasis on "paradox," "irony," and "tension" defines not only the characteristic nature of poetic structure, but also expresses the peculiar sensibility of the present age. It is pointed out time and again that the modern poet and the critic, unable to find coherence and order in the world of experience, seeks it in the coherence of artistic structure. Brooks's strongly fortified theories of structured unity in literary works may be considered as the projection of a spiritual need.

The importance of the term irony in modern criticism has been overused or rather abused. Brooks thinks that it has been almost the only term available to point a general and important aspect of poetry. That is why it has been overstretched too much. He cites an example taken from Matthew Arnold's poem "Dover Beach." The speaker in the poem expresses his reaction to the world, "which seems to lie before us like a land of dreams...hath really neither joy nor love nor light...." This statement is like the speech of the hero of a typical Hemingway story or novel, who speaks almost in the same way, though in a different idiom. However, different readers read the poem in their own way. To some it is just a trite statement; to others it seems false or at least highly questionable. The truth of this statement cannot be proved or validated in any case, sociologically, scientifically, and metaphorically. If it is done, the reader will move away from the problems of the poem, and from the justification of the poem. It can only be justified in terms of the context. In other words, the statement in the poem should grow properly out of a context. In the poem, the truism issues in the pressures of the context. It is not merely direct, immature, and sentimental statement. It is not just like a naked proposition. Brooks argues, the statement, by testifying T. S. Eliot's yardstick, proves to be coherent, mature, and based on the facts of experience. I. A. Richards also theorizes that poetry is capable enough to fuse the irrelevant and discordant, and never omits what is apparently hostile its dominant tone.

In the essay, "Irony As a Principle of Structure," Brooks studies the poems of Shakespeare, Wordsworth and Randall Jarrell to point out as to how irony plays its role in the poetic structure. First, here is very simple song of Shakespeare:

> Who is Silvia: What is she
> That all our swains commend her?
> Holy, fair, and wise is she;
> The heavens such grace did lend her,
> That she might admired be.
>
> Then to Silvia let us sing,
> That Silvia is excelling;
> She excels each mortal thing
> Upon the dull earth dwelling:
> To her let us garlands bring.

This song reveals as to who Silvia is. She is extolled hugely because she is endowed with angelic virtues and celestial gifts—holiness, wisdom, beauty, and grace. She is heaven's darling, excelling each moral thing on this monotonous and unattractive world compared to her own splendour. Laying finger on Silvia's grace,

Brooks deduces that her grace—the grace of her movement gifted by "heavens"—has theological overtones. Being aware of these overtones, the critic gets a delightful richness—richness very close to irony. Here the bestowal of grace on Silvia is for no other purpose than to admire her, which is quite strongly untheological. What more incongruous is Cupid, the pagan god of love, who lives in her eyes. He gets help from them, but it is not Christian "charity."

> Love doth to her eyes repair,
> To help him of his blindness,
> And, being help'd, inhabit there.

With this awareness, the second stanza acquires another layer of meaning. "For beauty lives with kindness" connotes not only the charm but also cruelty of the beautiful mistress, as Shakespeare knows the Petrarchan lover. This line also, in this context, means that the love god lives with the kind Silvia, and indeed has taken these eyes that sparkle with kindness for his own. Brooks finds a happy marriage between pagan myth and Christian theology. He thinks that it may be a blunder by Shakespeare, but it is a happy blunder—a kind of playful irony. On the whole, the song is telling and delightful. The touch is light; there is a lyric grace, but the tone is complex, incorporating an ironic complexity of the metaphysical poets.

In almost all successful lyrics of Wordsworth, Brooks discovers ironic potential created by his [Wordsworth's] method of simple juxtaposition. Brooks demonstrates irony from Lucy poems—the more innocent and, therefore, more convincing examples:

> She dwelt among the untrodden ways
> Beside the Spring of Dove,
> A maid whom there were none to praise
>
> A very few to love;
> A violet by a mossy stone
> Half hidden from the eye!
> Fair as a star, whom only one
> Is shining in the sky.
>
> She lived unknown, and few could know
> When Lucy ceased to be;
> But she is in her grave, and oh,
> The difference to me.

Lucy is compared to a violet and a star. The violet, half hidden under the mossy stone, lovely but unnoticed by the people, is ultimately hidden in the grave for ever. Her loss moves none but to the poet. The second star simile alludes that she is a solitary star to her lover's eyes. She has no rival nor does any idea of rivalry occur to her. In this way, the violet and the star balance each other, defining the situation themselves. From the great world point of view, Lucy is modest, shy, unnoticed and half-hidden from the eye, but from the lover's point of view, a lovely star, completely dominating that world, not arrogantly like the sun, but sweetly and modestly like the star. Such implicit contrast is more strikingly exploited by Donne in his poem, developing irony.

Brooks quoting another Lucy poem displays a great fascination for Wordsworth and Donne because their poems are based on a similar structure—dynamic structure—the pattern of thrust and counterthrust. In their work the relation between part and part is organic, which means that each modifies and is modified by the whole. One point is to be entertained of Wordsworth i.e. two words about his poetry—*simple* and *spontaneous*. They have become catchwords of the nineteenth century. *Simplicity* and *spontaneity*, Brooks argues, never mean that Wordsworth's poetry lacks complexities and ironical potential, but the reader will have to be attentive while reading the poem.

Keeping in view the pressures of context, Brooks discovers a tradition of irony in English poetry in all the ages and even in simple lyrical poetry. But in the modern age, irony becomes the most powerful vehicle and strategy of poetry, and is profusely used in it. There are various striking reasons for this. First, the common and traditional symbols fail to render the modern complexities; secondly, a loss of faith in the universals; thirdly, the most important reason is the "depletion and corruption of the very language itself" (p.67). Language in the course of time gets worn out and loses its vitality and freshness. In the modern time, advertising, the mass produced arts of radio, the moving picture, and pulp fiction—they are responsible for the corruption and aenima of language. That is why the responsibiiity and the accountability of the modern poet get more and more acute to restore and rehabilitate "a tired and drained language so that it can convey meanings once more with force and with exactitude. This task of qualifying and modifying language is perennial; but it is imposed on the modern poet as a special burden" (p.67). T. S. Eliot is also of opinion that after a certain period, there should be a complete overhauling of language to get it more effective, infallible and energized. The ironic techniques, the critics hold, are the result of the modern poet's own "bloodless sophistication and tired skepticism." But Brooks, rejecting this charge, argues that the modern potential readers are responsible, because their taste is corrupted by Hollywood and the Book of the Month Club. For the modern poet, it is not an easy task o address the reader of this age, because they are not simple primitive people but a public sophisticated and fully aware of the commercial art. So, the modern poet uses "his ironic techniques to win through clarity and passion" (p.67).

References:

1. Quoted in Lewis P. Simpson, ed., *The Possibilities of Order: Cleanth Brooks and His Work* (Boston: Lousiana State University Press, 1976), p.183.
2. Louise Cowan, *The Southern Critics* (Texas: University of Dellas Press, 1971), p. 66.
3. Vincent B. Leitch, *American Literary Criticism from Thirties to Eighties* (New York: Columbia University Press, 1988), p. 201.
4. Arnold L. Goldsmith, *American Literary Criticism: 1950- 1965* (Boston: Twayne, 1978), p. 110.
5. Cleanth Brooks, "In Search of New Criticism," *American Scholar*, 53: (1984), p. 43.
6. J. M. Bradbury, *The Fugitives: A Critical Account* (Chapel Hill: University of North Carolina Press, 1958), p. 238.
7. Arnold L. Goldsmith, p. 112.
8. W. H. Auden, "Against Romanticism," *New Republic*, 102 (February, 1940), p. 187.
9. Cleanth Brooks, "A Note on the Death of Elizabethan Tragedy," *Modern Poetry and the Tradition* (1939; New York: O.U.P., 1965), p. 218.
10. *Ibid.*, p. 72.

11. Cleanth Brooks, "Notes for a Revised History of English Poetry," *Modern Poetry and the Tradition*, p. 220.
12. *Ibid.*, p. 240.
13. "Telling it like it is in the Tower of Babel," *Sewanee Review* (Winter 1971), p. 137.
14. Cleanth Brooks, *A Shaping Joy*, p. 2.
15. *Ibid.*, p. 14.
16. *Ibid.*, p. 16.
17. Cleanth Brooks, "In Search of the New Criticism," *The American Scholar*, 53 (1984), p. 47.
18. Cleanth Brooks, *The Well Wrought Urn*, (1947), pp. 212-213.
19. Cleanth Brooks, "Organic Theory of Poetry," *English Institute Essays*, (1957), p. 54.
20. Cleanth Brooks, *A Shaping Joy*, p. 43.
21. Cleanth Brooks, *The Well Wrought Urn*, p. 248.
22. *Princeton Encyclopedia of Poetry and Poetics*, p. 598.
23. Cleanth Brooks, "The Language of Paradox," *20th Century Literary Criticism*, ed., David Lodge, p. 292. Hereafter the consequent reference will be mentioned in paranthesis of the same edition.
24. Cleanth Brooks, *The Well Wrought Urn: Studies in the Structure of poetry* (New York: Harcourt, Brace and Company, 1947), p. 199. Hereafter the subsequent references will be mentioned in parenthesis of the same edition.
25. Wellek and Warren, *Theory of Literature* (New York: Harcourt, Brace & Company, 1949), p.179.
26. *Ibid.*, p. 178.
27. Cleanth Brooks, "Literary Criticism: Poet, Poem, and Reader," *Varieties of Literary Experience: Eighteen Essays in World Literature* ed., Stanley Burnshaw (New York University Press, 1962), p. 99.
28. Cleanth Brooks, "Metaphor and the Function of Criticism," *Spiritual Problems in Contemporary Literature*, ed., S.R. Hopper (New York: Harper, 1952), p. 133.

29. *Understanding Poetry*, p. 133.
30. *Ibid.*, p. 3.
31. *Ibid.*, p. 44.
32. William Wimsatt & Cleanth Brooks, *Literary Criticism: A Short History* (New York: Knopf, 1957), p. 749.
33. Frank Lentricchia, "The Place of Cleanth Brooks," *Journal of Aesthetics and Art Criticism*, 29, No. 2 (Winter 1970), p. 245.
34. *Modern Poetry and Tradition* p. 26.
35. *Understanding Poetry*, p. 5.
36. Cleanth Brooks, "Literary Criticism: Poet, Poem, and Reader," p. 99.
37. Cleanth Brooks, "Irony as a Principle of Structure," *Twentieth Century Criticism: The Major Statements* (New Delhi: Light and Life Publishers, 1974) p. 59. Hereafter the consequent references will be mentioned in parenthesis of the same edition.
38. *20th Century Literary Criticism,* p. 387.
39. Brooks and Warren, "The Reading of Modern Poetry," *The American Review, 8, 4.* (1937).
40. *Literary Criticism: A Short History*, p. 653.
41. Brooks, "The Poem as Organism," *English Institute Essays,* (1940), p.23.
42. Brooks, "The Poem as Organism," *English Institute Essays,* (1940), p. 36.
43. Brooks, "Irony and Ironic Poetry," *College English*, 9, 5 (1943), p. 234.
44. M. D. Zabel, ed., *Literary Opinion in America* pp. 732-739.
45. R. P. Warren, "Pure and Impure Poetry," *Critique and Essays in Criticism*, ed., Stallman, p. 103.

6

Richard Palmer Blackmur

Richard Palmer Blackmur (1905-1965), a "shadowy figure, and a lonely one,"[1] faces all the facets of life without any grudge, despite his pessimistic perspective of life. A heroic personality steeped in vivacity, dynamism, and humour, he holds "frustration as a fundamental condition of life."[2] His mental landscape tinged with this enduring feeling creates an artistic sensibility, which isolates him from other New Critics, transcending the New Critical method. With his outstanding scholarship and overwhelming imagination, a sense of originality and penetrating vision, he approaches to appreciate literature and criticism, and emerges as a poet, critic, story-writer, novelist, and playwright. However, his reputation primarily rests on his critical output marked by gnomic, poetic, and lyric strain. He is a poet in his criticism because in "his prose, every sentence struggles to be poetry;" his prose "wears the poem's guise at last." In his essays, criticism "has become a part of literature or literature... has become a part of criticism." To Blackmur, both creation and criticism are works of art which present an organic expression of culture. Art and culture are, Blackmur says, interrelated with each other. The nature of art, therefore, should grow and change in relation to culture. That is why Blackmur, like Eliot, emphasizes that the act of criticism has to be done over and over again. He feels a throb of excitement in sharing Karl Shapiro's view: "A good work of criticism is a work of art about another work of art. Criticism is creation; it gives birth!" Blackmur's whole approach towards criticism pivots on this conviction.

Blackmur is perennially concerned with the power and precise use of language and its structure in the poem. He states: "Words, and their intimate arrangements...bring meaning to birth." He seeks to identify the character of the poetic words and wrestles as to how they could be used to achieve certain poetic effect. With his insistence on the concreteness of poetic language, he asserts that "when a word is used in a poem, it should be the sum of all its appropriate history made concrete and particular in the individual text." It is Blackmur's firm belief that the poet can get control over his material by employing the most appropriate words. Good poets always use words faithfully to their dictionary definitions, and avoid the blending and warping of words employed by Ransom and Brooks. He has a predilection neither for Cleanth Brooks's irony and paradox nor for Ransom's "companionship of structure and texture."[3] The technical aspect of the poem can be judged by showing how its words encounter other words and what tensions are produced among them, generating a new kind of language. In this way, the magic of words leads us to ecstasy by evocation and auguries. In his essay, "Notes on E. E. Cumming's Language," Blackmur notes: "The poet's genius is not shown in his private musing, but in giving to those musing the form of conventional language in such a way that the conventionality of the medium employed disappeared."[4] In his view, language goes beyond the denotative and connotative activity and takes the reader into the realm of myth, dream, history, religion, and even silence.

The analytical habit of Blackmur receives mixed remarks and comments from a number of critics. They call him "a botanist of the stanza, verse, phrase, even of the single word." He is gifted with "surgical skill" and makes his criticism "a demonstration of poetic dissection by a master anatomist." Alfred Kazin finds his "criticism so driven to a sensibility machine—taste, conscience, and mind working as gears, levers, and wheels." Paul Oppenheimer remarks: "the only modern critic to deal not with himself but with poetry." Edmund Wilson says that Blackmur "is nearly incomparable in modern criticism." Malcolm Cowley views: "As a line-for-line critic he was marvelous." According to Allen Tate, Blackmur is "a great master of explication of text." Russel Fraser estimates him as "without rival the critic as taxonomist."[5] In the words of Marriane Moore, Blackmur applies "the humility of complete attention." Despite such eulogies, it is quite unfortunate that Blackmur, in the history of contemporary American criticism, fails to achieve a due recognition because of various charges leveled on him. James T. Jones observes: "Blackmur is a fleshy critic with a frail skeleton."[6] Critics like Murray Krieger and Elizabeth Bruss deliberately exclude him from their studies on the ground that he is not a systematic theorist. However, his overwhelming consciousness of the possibilities of meaning of the single word makes "the sharpest and closest reader of poetry we have."

Blackmur's theory of creativity, although not systematically written, is based on the two faculties of mind—reason and imagination, which should be balanced and integrated. They should combine together to express felt experience of the poet. The function of the poet's reason is "the recognition and creation of order where disorder was."[7] The function of the poet's imagination is to make the mind's "discourse in images and idioms as meaningful as the original parallel experiences seemed when experienced in life."[8] Blackmur advocates that the artist should synthesize his experiences into an organic whole. It is this unified sensibility which is required for both the creative work and the work of criticism. The artist, blessed with a "talent for significant experience,"[9] receives the sense experience from outside and gives an order, control, pattern, and unity to it through reason. Like all the modernists, particularly the poets and novelists, Blackmur also admits the power of the irrational and, therefore, gives equal importance to the irrational expression of his experience. Through the amalgam of the irrational and the rational, he wants that criticism should also touch the same plane as the modernist artists did in painting, music, poetry, and novel. His intention is that criticism should be experience, not to point to an experience. In this way, he extends the scope and form of literary criticism. He makes it the emotional part of the critical essays. He mainly adopts the device of analogical form to express the irrational. The artist chooses some symbol or images to portray their feeling of disorder, alienation, and isolation i.e. an interior state of feeling by harmonizing disparate images into an organic whole. Through imagination, the artist perceives his felt experience in images and symbols, whereas through reason he controls, orders, and patterns them in an organic and artistic design. This unified sensibility makes sense experience of the artist intelligible and communicable.

With the maturity of mind, Blackmur cultivates a holistic view towards life, "the complete attitude towards life."[10] To realize this, he focuses his attention on primitive culture, magic, fairy-tales, and the contemporary social condition. They are an essential part of education for the modern mind. Being a student of Jung, he is preoccupied with the psychology of the poet. Celebrating some of the elements of romanticism, Blackmur hails expression of personal moods, emotions, and experiences, but never allows them to express directly to the readers, because the direct expression lacks reason. He recommends the romantic interior states of mind or subject-matter without allowing them the romantic methodology for expressing them. He thinks that poetry is not a direct communication of abstract ideas to the reader, but an expression of experience objectifying with the concrete and sensual images and symbols. The unbridled romantic effusions must be controlled, patterned, and ordered by reason. Pannick is of the view that the best poetry "has a rational structure which controls, orders, and composes in external or objective form the material of which it is made; and that effect it is dependent only upon the limits of language."[11] According to Blackmur, every poem should have a rational structure to organize feeling or the material of poetry into form.

Blackmur, although grouped among the New Critics, makes a marked departure from the New Criticism. He is more than a New Critic because he is quite conscious of the empty methodology of the New Criticism: "I fear that if new growth is not undertaken there may be only a false sterile life." Robert Boyers also finds its limitations: "The New Critics have relied upon their considerable linguistic skills as if these were adequate for all of the critical tasks to be performed."[12] While concentrating on the power of words, gestural language, and technical devices, and various approaches to literary criticism, he establishes a nexus between literature and society and the social responsibility of the critic. His interest in poetry also extends to the mind of the poet and to the place of the poet in society, which are inextricably interrelated. It is society that conditions the psychology of the poet.

The spiritual health of society plays an important role in Blackmur's criticism of poetry. He focuses his critical attention on the condition of society which makes a very gloomy and moribund world-view. For a serious artist, the ordinary or commonplace life he lives cannot yield proper subject-matter for his poetic creation. He has to cherish "always either a literal faith, an imaginative faith or as in Shakespeare a mind full of many provisional faiths." The contemporary life,

Blackmur observes, is rudderless, meaningless, and cheerless; it is marked by moral chaos, religious decline, and spiritual sterility. All values and traditional institutions appear to be crumbling down, because of "the lack of order in contemporary culture."[13] There is no intellectual strength to uphold the Western culture. Blackmur introduces the phrase "techniques of trouble" to describe the plight and predicament of modern man. "Techniques" means "new knowledges" of psychology, anthropology, sociology, and psychiatry; and "trouble" means self-in-crisis or the fragmented self. The "new knowledges" split the self into pieces reducing it to "an almost undecipherable jargon." In such a bewildering environment, a serious artist cannot explore his subject-matter. Therefore, "it must be a life with a leaning, life with tendency to shape itself only in certain forms; to afford its most lucid revelations only in certain lights." The poet creates a body of belief, some principle of life, his own world-view, and his own spiritual health of a society. John Paul Pritchard comments that "the poet must create some personal belief like Yeats, revive some belief from the past, or seek some present but hidden system"[14] to order, organize, and cohere his experience to explain society to the reader.

Blackmur's criticism of poetry reveals that the poem cannot exist in isolation. It is not a self-contained autonomous entity but has a serious social nexus between the poet and his society, social institution, and reader. In the poem, he reflects the motives of his psychology and mental activity. Gerald Pannick views: "Blackmur is a romantic because his fundamental insight was that all arts, artists, societies, cultures, and social forms were part of a complex interrelation of living, indeterminate, and endlessly changing components."[15] This romantic emphass on the psychology of the poet leads Blackmur to study the conditions of the society which moulds the mind of the poet. And the poem becomes a social phenomenon, an expression of the collective mind of the society, and a communication with social significance.

With a unique style to express his ideas, Blackmur also deals with other literary problems which are beyond the purview of the New Criticism. Deeply influenced by Henry Adams, in the later phase of his career, he shifts his concentration from the artwork to the artist, the function of the artist in mass society, and to the role of the critic who plays a part of a mediator between art and the public. These issues widen his literary critical scope distracting him from the main tracks of the New Criticism. In this way, Blackmur's criticism differs from the other New Critics.

Surprisingly, Blackmur, throughout his life, preaching a precept of precision, clarity, and exactness in poetic language, could become so abstruse, obscure, and awry in his critical essays. His style is "too crude," difficult, synoptic, and oracular. Perhaps he does so "to impress the less intelligent reader" and to make him "think he is reading first rate criticism." Yvor Winters criticizes him as "obscuranist" and "unintelligible." John Wain also finds his critical essays very difficult:

> Now what disturbs me in reading Mr. Blackmur is the feeling I so frequently get that he is deliberately refusing to reduce his meaning to simple terms—that, on the contrary, he is inflating it, surrounding it with a nimbus of uncaught and uncatchable meaning.[16]

In a nut-shell, Blackmur is a balanced critic, incorporating neo-classical, romantic, and modernist elements in the whole body of literary criticism. Avoiding extremity, he assimilates all the valuable points from different sources in his critical essays. His critical canon is marked by a happy blend of the traditional and the modern. Hankering after the "complete criticism," he establishes a critical method tempered with scientific rigour, yet at the same time he fails to seek critical conclusion that would be universally valid. Giving due place to all the approaches to criticism, he gives a new dimension to criticism by elevating it to a plane of art, in which both the rational and the irrational play an equal and vital role as they do in other creative arts—painting, poetry, novel and music. He also opens a new avenue to the social function and relevance of literary criticism avoiding the dogmatic difficulties, and using the best in sights and virtues of the New Criticism.

Blackmur's critical insights are distilled through his essays, particularly through these four essays: "A Critic's Job of Work," "Language As Gesture," "A Burden for Critics," and "A Featherbed for Critics." In this chapter an attempt now has been made to elucidate and interpret them. The first two essays deal with the critical process, whereas the last two with the social role of the critic.

A Critic's Job of Work

Blackmur's "A Critic's Job of Work," a kind of a manifesto of the New Criticism, is an exposition of the nature and function of literary criticism. He discovers that criticism is an art. It is a ceaseless process, dealing with literature from any number of relative points of view. In his opinion "any rational approach is valid to literature and may properly be called critical which fastens at any point upon the work itself." He conscientiously weighs each of them and gives a due place. With his liberal outlook, he, therefore, lambastes a dogmatic or single approach in literary criticism. He begins the essay with the oft-quoted statement that "criticism is the formal discourse of an amateur,"[17] imbued with both reason and imagination. In this essay, Blackmur deals with the rational aspect of the critical act, while the imaginative role in criticism is testified in the next essay "Language As Gesture." He continues his essay with comments on six representative methods. Without any dogmatic gesture, he proposes his own critical method called as 'technical approach.' Blackmur also recommends culling some other points through inferences. In brief, Blackmur's conception of criticism evinces both factual materials and technical devices. That is why he upholds the ulterior purpose in arts and criticism, but once it becomes a kind of fanaticism, he rejects it downright.

Blackmur frowns upon the kind of critics who are sheer conventionalists. Once they happen upon any doctrine, they cling to it very poorly, considering it the consummation and termination of that doctrinal mode of thinking. They refuse to budge from the worn out approach, even if it starts tottering and losing its relevance and appropriateness. Moreover, it is undeniable fact that all doctrines in one way or the other ultimately collapse to debility and commonplace. All knowledge is discovered in the particular time and circumstances. If taken literally, it cannot last forever. Blackmur remarks:

> ...every formula of knowledge must fall the moment too much weight is laid upon it—the moment, it becomes omnivorous and pretends to be omnipotent—the moment, in short, it is taken literally (p.20).

He deplores fanaticism of the kind of critics who think of any one critical method sufficient and final. This whimsical attitude deserves full condemnation in literary criticism. Such scholarship becomes "dead knowledge" (p.20). Therefore, an anxiety, a critical tumult, and a kind of bewilderment should start to sharpen the mental perception, and apply any new "concept that seems propitious or helpful in getting over gaps" (p.20). But the new critical method should be introduced very consciously, provisionally, speculatively, and dramatically. The critics should cultivate flexibility, humility, and generosity to achieve real scholarship and get rid of their pet fads, embracing new modes of thinking and coping up with new situations and times. Gerald J. Pannik thinks that "different critical methods tend to restore vitality to individual perception."[18] But it is not easily attainable. "The end-virtue of humility comes only after a long train of humiliation; and the chief labor of humbling is the constant, resourceful restoration of ignorance" (pp.20-21).

The glaring examples of such orthodoxy are the use and misuse of Freud and Marx. Their shadows always loom large in any piece of work. They get more honour and scope in the artistic imagination and literary criticism than in their own disciplines. Freud's impetus is so might that a school of critics appears "with all the mad consequence of schism and heresy and fundamentalism" (p.21). So the economic insights of Marx encroach upon the subject and value of the arts. Though they offer only a limited field of interest in literature and criticism, yet are stretched to an irrelevant purpose. The theoretical terms and concepts of Freud and Marx percolate through all the modes of thinking. But the terms of any critical method, Blackmur argues, should be employed "for their own sake alone and with only a pious or ritualistic regard for the doctrines in which they are clothed" (p.21). All doctrines, virtually, appear to be propagandas crying for their validity. None of them is free of the illogic and inconsistencies. Blackmur observes:

> All banners are wrong-headed, but they make rallying points, free the impulse to cry out, and give meaning to the cry itself simply by making it seem appropriate (p.23).

In literary criticism, the critic leaving his obstinacy should exercise his discretion, while applying the terms and concepts from other disciplines. When borrowed without due consideration, they produce "false dilemmas like solipsism and infant damnation" (p.22). He should take the kernel and leave the husk. Sometimes, a few champions and supporters of fallible doctrines get entangled in them and take a good deal of time to get out of it. The critic should develop a free disposition like that of Plato and Montaigne. Their minds are not conditioned by any fixed doctrine or enmeshed in any formula. With their "unindoctrinate thinking," they are blessed with imaginative skepticism and dramatic irony, which keep "the mind athletic and the spirit on the stretch." In the early writings of Plato, he wins admiration for his conflicting ideas in shifting balance, presenting them in contest and evolution. Montaigne also, on the other hand, throughout his life, keeps his mental horizons open to receive new ideas steeped in ironic sense. He always suggests "a third for provisional" (p.22). With their vivid questing outlook, they borrow ideas and improvise them according to their requirements. Blackmur observes: "Any single insight is good only at and up to a certain point of development and not beyond, which is to say that it is a provisional and tentative and highly selective approach to its field" (p.25). No observation ever tells the whole story. There is always room for something quite untouched. In this way, Blackmur suggests, terms borrowed from other doctrines never become stultifying dogma. Rather, through this approach—a rational approach—there ushers in the multiplication of doctrine, and "arrogant technologies" with the huge body of critical thinking. Therefore, the critic should cherish a receptive mind instead of succumbing to a particular idea with great rigidity. It is the negative or tragic aspect of thought. "Thought is a beacon not a life-raft" (p.23). Each has its own function. There should not be any confusion between the two.

Blackmur further quotes a list of writers and poets—Shakespeare, Shaw, Shelley, Dante, Baudelaire, Dostoevsky, and Pascal—who demonstrate both flexibility and commitment in their thinking. The critic has to be sagacious as to which aspect of these writers is to be highlighted. Of course, their dogmatic aspect should be underrated. In the case of Andre Gide, for example, the critic never calls attention to the advocacy of homosexuality and the political conversion to communism, but to his (Gide's) acutely scrupulous ethical sensibility. It is a true job of the critic.

Blackmur compares the act of criticism with that of walking. Both are almost a universal art, and require a constant intricate shifting and catching of balance. But a few know how to perform either very well. None likes to follow a new terrain. It is fatiguing and awkward. In the modern age, the critic prefers some "easy theory" or "outmastering dogma." He is unwilling to tax his mind. He lacks the generality of the mind and confines himself within a single approach, whereas critics like Kenneth Burke and T. S. Eliot adopt a studied complex approach by establishing parallel of reference. There is more flexible, more available, and more stimulating standard of judgment than a single approach. The great flaw of a single approach in literary criticism is that it becomes highly passionate, confused, controversial, and stultified. In Blackmur's opinion, these feats are fastened to Irving Babbitt, the champion of a particular critical methodology called humanism.

Once a body of criticism is governed by a fixed idea, the evil of fanaticism, "falsification," "arrogant irrationality," and barbarism emerge on the critical landscape. This type of criticism becomes tendentious, self-proved, and absolutely assertive. Its bane is very much distinct in Maritain, Massis and Nardau. But Blackmur paradoxically explores a tinge of legitimacy and worth even in the worst order of such criticism. Irving Babbitt, a great dogmatic critic, works with his critical approach without an awareness of its methodological limitations. Hence, there occurs a gross distortion and vitiation in his criticism. Despite these serious vices of his critical approach reflected in modern literature, Blackmur, however, finds some relevance and value in Babbitt's criticism. His two paramount notions—the inner check and higher will—manifest the massive erudition and acute observation leaving a lasting imprint on his works.

On this ground, Blackmur also sanctions those orders of criticism also which have an ulterior purpose. Criticism cannot be condemned merely on this count. Moreover, no criticism is autonomous. It is a process of elucidation and probes ceaselessly ulterior purpose within it. But the critic has to be alert to distinguish between good and bad ulterior purpose. The same feat is also applied to arts, because they cannot exist without any functions. They yield order, meaning, and value. Art, without any ulterior purpose, Blackmur explains, is like the function of a handsaw hanging above a bench and to cut wood is to belittle it. But an artist's mind remains pregnant with various purposes, and sometimes he fails to design them in his årts. It becomes the responsibility of the critic, if he is inclined to them, to concern himself with those purposes. But "he must be certain to distinguish between what is genuinely ulterior to the works he examines and what is merely irrelevant" (p.27). He must further not take for granted that after his criticism no other ulterior purposes are left. His is not the final. With all these contrasting notions, Blackmur, however, arrives at this conclusion that the best criticism is dependent finally on the critic's strength of mind.

> A good critic keeps his criticism from becoming either instinctive or vicarious, and the labor of his understanding is always specific, like the art which he examines; and he knows that the sum of his best work comes only to the pedagogy of elucidation and appreciation. He observes facts and he delights in discriminations. The object remains, and should remain, itself, only made more available and seen in a clear light (p.25).

In contemporary literary criticism, Blackmur exhibits three different approaches mainly dealing with the ulterior purposes in literature. They are the serious defects and unchastened virtues of this kind of criticism. The first example centre's upon Santayana's essay on Lucritius in *The Three Philosophical Poets*. His critical method transcending thė realm of the special responsibility of poetry ventures into philosophy. The essay is a document of ulterior motives rather than "a poetic ordering of nature" (p.28). Its representation is so convincing, complete, copious, and commanding that Lucretius himself appears to be receding from his own station—from his own moral bias. It is an epitome of the philosophical insight, the moral scope, and the influence of Democritan's atomism. Santayana's moral and philosophical criticism of the essay is a good substitute for the poem, but he misses one thing very vital that "Poetry is idiom, a special and fresh saying, and cannot for its life be said otherwise; and there is, finally, as much difference between words used about a poem and the poem as there is between words used about a painting and the painting. The gap is absolute" (p.28). Whatever may be his function of criticism, but it is sure that it has no concern with the poetic aspect of the poem. However, Blackmur does not completely rule out the relevance and meaning of Santayana's philosophical criticism. No doubt, his criticism is of deep philosophical nature, but Lucretius's poem also reveals the facts of an ulterior purpose ingrained in it. The poet and the critic both are concerned with moralism. But the former is ever conscious of the poetic canons—imaginative richness, picturesqueness, and special idiom with nuances of meaning. Whereas the latter becomes fully dogmatic, shifting his attention from the poetry of the poem to merely its philosophy.

The second order of criticism is psycho-sociological. Getting from bad to worse, it is a conversion from literary to biographical values. In *Pilgrimage of Henry James*, Van Wyck Brooks submits neither the ulterior purpose nor the artistic aspect of Henry James's novels, but studies his plight and predicament in life. Through the investigation of the biography, the society, and the age of the novelist, Brooks argues how they become the governing factors reflected in James's novels. Brooks picks up his personal tragedy and failure and "raises it to an obsession, an omnivorous concept, under which all other themes can be subsumed" (p.29). Consequently, James's work is made typical and universal, which is completely distorted. Hence, Brooks's main focus is on the artist and the cultural situation of America, not on the art. "Art is not taken as the objectification or mirroring of social experience but as a personal expression and escape-fantasy of the artist's personal life in dramatic extension" (p.29). This critical approach may be of great importance to understand the life of Henry James, but it cannot, Blackmur holds, be called literary criticism in any way.

In *The Great Tradition*, Granville Hicks presents a fanatic approach of Marxist economic theory in literary criticism. He examines the whole body of literature in the light of class struggle, and establishes its tradition in American literature since the Civil War. A victim of this obsessive idea, he reduces criticism to a formula, twisting the whole complexion of American literature. Hicks has two categories of writers: (i) the upholders of the Marxist theory and (ii) the opponents of this ideology. The former are eulogized, while the latter slandered and dismissed, and even their works are held pseudo and fraudulent. Great arts, though sometimes used as a vehicle to interpret religious, moral, and psychological insights, are hardly handled as propaganda, as Hicks does so defiantly. His strong recommendation is that American literature should delineate the class struggle from a Marxist viewpoint goading to political action. Blackmur condemns this kind of criticism permeated with ulterior motive. It has nothing to do with literary criticism, because such a critic "is not writing criticism at all; he is writing a fanatic's history and a casuist's polemic" (p31).

The three aforementioned critics have different critical approaches—philosophical, biographical, and political—to literature. There is a common defect in them, because they all analyze and interpret literature with a deep overtone of ulterior motives. They sift out the content from literature, and lay a great stress on it, without considering the sense of intimacy between the content and structure. Content can be expressed without any specific setting and particular form, but stated directly like this, it looks like a skeleton. It cannot lend aesthetic sense or a unique pleasure unless it is fashioned into a structure. This inner contact is absent in these three critical methods. That is why, they cannot function the job of literary criticism. Blackmur suggests developing "sustained contact" with literature.

> We have constantly—if our interest is really in literature—to prod ourselves back, to remind ourselves that there was a poem, a play, or a novel of some initial and we hope terminal concern, or we have to falsify facts and set up fictions to the effect that no matter what we are saying we are really talking about art after all (p.32).

Blackmur further cautions those critics who have continuous intimacy with the artistic aspect of literature. They develop another kind of defect which is visible in their own criticism. Their approaches to criticism are quite different, free of ulterior purpose, but are not free of "limiting features." With their own inherent mental weakness, though quite unaware of it, they become lop-sided and indulge in only one particular aspect of literature, and neglect other very essential ones deliberately, bringing a distortion in literary criticism. Their approach is not all-embracing, but skeletal devoid of flesh and blood. Blackmur again demonstrates this drawback by examining the character, scope, and value of the works of other three critics—I. A. Richards, Kenneth Burke, and S. Foster Damon. He is not concerned here with their objective validity, as it always exists in such criticism, but with the strength of objective criticism, whether it reaches into aesthetic theories or not.

Richards's position as a literary critic bobbing on the waves of commendation and condemnation ultimately receives a serious setback in the hand of Blackmur. With his profound love and knowledge for poetry, Richards, no doubt, an admirable critic, shrinks his weight and dominion, because he spends his whole energy on a particular aspect of literary criticism. He unnecessarily lays too much stress on the scientific principle and statistical method stuffed with various types of thought. His theoretical mechanism is very mammoth, mazy, and inclusive, but the amount of actual literary criticism is so meagre that it seems almost a by-product instead of a central product. Blackmur blames: "The point of Mr. Richards's book is the impossibility of understanding…the mechanism of meaning in even a small body of work" (3).

Literary criticism is not a science, but "Richards places the whole burden of criticism in the application of a scientific approach, and asserts it to be an implement for the judgment of poetry" (p.37). Science can handle only the language and its words but cannot touch the imaginative product of the words which is poetry. It is an object revealed by criticism. Richards's bias towards the psychological and linguistic methods of criticism reduces the scope of his literary criticism. This narrow and limited approach to literary criticism stultifies the power of imaginative apprehension and co-ordination of varied and separate elements. His method is for its own sake and not for literature, because it fails to respond to the questions literary criticism would put. Even it does not fulfill the very practical purpose of analyzing the use, meaning, and value of the language in a particular poetry. Richards exhausts all his resources in preparing the framework of criticism, instead of getting into poetry itself. That is why Blackmur, like Ransom, inflicting caustic comments on Richards spurns him to consider a critic at all, because "few would care to emulate him for any purpose of literary criticism" (36). Richards investigates the problems of belief, of meaning, of communication, of the nature of controversy, and of poetic language as the supreme mode of imagination. His theoretical framework includes the pedagogy of sensibility and the practice of literary criticism.

Richards's wide and penetrating insight, different levels of sensibility, sheer excitement, the profundity of the problems of knowledge, and the seminal value and stimulus of his work stimulate the mind of critics. No critic can escape his influence. Certainly, he has made genuine problems at least for the readers of poetry. From the point of view of a psychological theory, Richards's criticism is integral, integrating, and unheretical, but from that of literary criticism, Blackmur holds, it has a profound heresy—even more distorting than the heresies of Santayana, Brooks, and Hicks. He transforms literary criticism into the sciences of linguistic and psychology. When feeling is taken into consideration, the importance of science is thrown into the background. No scientific description can either explain or underrate a poem unless the description is translated back to the imaginative feeling. On the whole, Blackmur considers that criticism must be concerned, first and last, with the poem itself as it is read. Just as no amount of physics and physiology can explain the feeling of things so no amount of linguistic analysis can explain the feeling or existence of a poem.

Blackmur is very ruthless to Kenneth Burke because of his critical methods applied to only certain aspects of literature. He adopts the psychological and linguistic approach to literary criticism with greater profundity than Richards. That is why Blackmur states:

> As Mr. Richards in fact uses literature as a springboard or source for a scientific method of a philosophy of value, Mr. Burke uses literature, not only as a springboard but also as a resort or home, for a philosophy or psychology of moral possibility (p.39).

Burke's keen interest lies in the right meanings of words and the wrong meaning, showing that the right meanings maintain a balance to the wrong meanings. His main contribution is the presentation of the types of ways the mind works in the written word. "He is more interested in the psychological means of meaning, and how it might mean (and often really does) something else, that the meaning itself" (pp.39-40). Like Richards, Burke is engaged largely in the meaning of meaning and is, therefore, deeply devoted to considerations of language. However, he uses literature as a tool of philosophy, psychology, and linguistic, instead of keeping his critical focus on the work and on its possible meanings. He cannot go beyond this. Literature is more than these things. The reality in literature, Blackmur, argues is an object of feeling "like the reality of a picture or a cathedral" (p.40). It is not a methodology or principle or speculation:

> Mr. Burke's essays become as pertinent to literary criticism as they are to the general ethical play of the mind. Otherwise they become too much a methodology for its own sake on the one hand, and too much a philosophy at one remove on the other (p.40).

After examining the philosophical, the sociological or historical, the tendentious, the semasiological, and the psychological approaches to criticism, Blackmur arrives at the scholarly criticism discussed in S. Foster Damon's *William Blake*. He defines scholarship as "the collection, arrangement, and scrutiny of facts" (p.41). In "The Function of Criticism," T. S. Eliot also used the term "facts," but in the sense of the technical devices, while Blackmur's term refers to the mode of the artist's thinking, of his reading, and of his strange mystic faith and belief. Gerald J. Pannick clears the meaning of facts very aptly: "A fact is anything that may be stated about a work—its structure, its theme, its meaning, its rhythm, and so on."[19] And then these facts are applied to his work. Damon does this scholarly work on Blake's poetry. Piecing together all the facts, he presents a picture of Blake as a consistent, logical, and systematic poet, while in real sense he is not like that. Rather his value and potential rests upon his inconsistencies.

With a tacit predilection for the scholarly criticism, Blackmur holds it the mainspring of all other forms of literary criticism. He states: "Upon scholarship all other forms of literary criticism depend... in much the same way that architecture depends on engineering" (pp. 40-41). But as a critical method, scholarship also has its own merit and demerit. Its "positive advantage" is that it is a cooperative effort; it is neither complete nor final. It can be, therefore, modified, re-arranged, complemented, and corrected by later scholars. The "negative advantage" is that it dredges out only the factual materials. Once this work is done, the critic thinks that his job is over. He does not further explain the facts to associate with other aspects of work. The scholarly criticism never penetrates into the kernel of the work and fails "to investigate the mysteries of meaning or to connect literature with other departments of life" (p.41). But one thing is here notable that scholarship never distorts the meaning of the work because of being less concerned with it.

The scholarly criticism should not be confined only to the kind of Blake's poetry, but must exhume the facts in all orders of poetry, particularly in contemporary poetry. Simple, self-evident, and supererogatory poetry goes unnoticed because everything of the artist appears to be on the surface. Therefore, the critic does not feel any need to be on the surface. It is totally misleading; "self-evident facts are paradoxically the hardest to come by" (p.42). The scholarly criticism prepares the ground for interpretation of the work, which cannot develop itself to the full without the facts. The different layers of its meaning, its final value, and its created emotion—all are grounded in the factual meaning. Despite this, Blackmur is quite conscious of its limitation. Though the scholarly criticism is a worth adopting approach, it never embraces all the aspects of an analytical method applied to the poem. "It is only the basis and perhaps ultimately the residue of all the other stories" (p.43).

Pointing out one by one the defects of the six types of critical methodologies, Blackmur finally elucidates his own critical approach called the technical one. It is also not free of its limitation because it "does not tell the whole story either; the reader is conscientiously left with the poem with the real work yet to do" (p.43). Assimilating the critical prescription laid down by Blackmur, the reader has to apply his own discretion, his own analytical method, and his own critical faculty, exploring the true nature of literary criticism. However, Blackmur's critical approach is mainly through the technique. He uses the term 'technique' in a sense more inclusive and wider way than has generally been used by the New Critics. To him, the term 'technique' is to be used in linguistic, intellectual, emotional, and philosophical sense. He defines the term "technique on the plane of words and even of linguistics in Mr. Richards' sense, but also technique on the plane of intellectual and emotional patterns in Mr. Burke's sense, and technique, too, in that there is a technique of securing and arranging and representing a fundamental view of life" (p.43). Blackmur takes the philosophical aspects of literary criticism as the proper business of the critic.

Blackmur thinks of technique as indispensable because it analyses only literary aspects, penetrating into "the heart of the literature." He enumerates its two fold advantages. First, it welcomes and assimilates other approaches and is ever ready to be complemented and modified by them, incorporating the technical aspect of whatever is discovered in a poem. It, thus, exemplifies that the interpretative and evaluative functions of criticism are possible only through the technical approach. Its second advantage is that it reduces a poem to a literary fact. Once the critic ascertains facts and the technical devices, he exerts a good deal of labour in searching for exacting standard of vocabulary or critical idiom to communicate or accommodate the facts appropriately. In the work of art, facts are not easily perceptible, nor do they all occur to one mind. It may connote different things to different people. No single approach is sufficient. Therefore, the technical approach is a cooperative venture.

Blackmur's conception of criticism achieves completion when the technical approach is infused with direct or imaginative apprehension. Essentially a relevant part of the critical act, it plays a very vital role, as it is recognized greater than technique. Therefore, without imaginative apprehension, the technical analysis never completes the critical act. The real work of the critic as well as the reader is the imaginative apprehension of the essence of the meaning that comes after the conscious gathering of facts, which can be talked about in the critical analysis. After the conscious critical activity, there starts imaginative procedure, which cannot be discussed or examined, but known or intuited. Blackmur defines the terms 'imaginative apprehension' as the preconscious—some irrational principle of the mind. Raising a volley of questions, he wants to know the enigmatic process in criticism whether concepts, words, images occur to the critic's mind in the same order as they appear on the print. It is the preconscious that forms the mixture of a word, an image and a notion mysteriously. It is achieved through intuition. It is an adventure in the preconscious free of all doubts of meaning. In such a state, the critic envisions the total work as "the living, expanding, prescient substance" (p.45) without anything of the conscious critical act. In this way, criticism reveals "the modes of making the preconscious consciously available" (p.45). Attuned to the preconscious apprehension of the intermingling of words, images, and notions, the critic takes another responsibility to make the realization of the preconscious in conscious terms so that others should use and understand. Thus, both the creative work and the work of criticism have to undergo the same mysterious process. They are two orders of reality. The job of a critic is to isolate them creating his own categories of approach.

Language As Gesture

Blackmur's "Language As Gesture," one of the finest fruits of formalism, places him on the high pedestal of literary criticism. This essay is a sequel to his "A Critic's Job of Work." He theorizes that a critical object has two parts—"facts" and "gesture." The former is concerned with reason while the latter with imagination. If "A Critic's Job of Work" discusses the conscious critical act of the critic, "Language As Gesture" examines the role of imagination in the critical act. These two levels in the critical act are complementary or interdependent. Gesture is 'moored' in the facts of a work. Blackmur defines gesture as a quality—an added meaningfulness to words. Hinging his poetic theory on gesture, he perpetually lays emphasis on the power of words. They, he argues, should have vibration with their full life—"the full life being modified and made unique by the qualifications the words perform upon one another in the poem." Through this process, language gets layered with multidimensional potentiality and acquires poetic meaning. Blackmur, basically, takes a hold of words of the poem and asks a very important question. Do these words represent a genuine fact, condition, or feeling? The direct parts—sentences, phrases, single words—are the main object of his attention. The way in which they combine is sometimes an afterthought.

However, Blackmur's poetic theory finds its best expression in his "Language As Gesture." He contends that the real meanings of the dictionary words are entirely different from the real meanings of the words employed in the poem. In the poetic use, language acquires new dimensions, depths, and nuances, while the language used in the common life or the dictionary definitions of words lack these qualities. A dictionary is just like a huge graveyard where each and every word is dormant and embedded in the ground; as the poet in his frenzy, like the Creator, chooses a word, it comes into life like a dead body on the Day of Judgment Blackmur views that language is made of words, and gesture is made of motion. Apparently, there is a paradoxical relationship between language and gesture, and so how could language be taken as gesture? But on a second and careful look, words are found to be made of motion—action or response. When the language of words becomes helpless to convey the exact meaning, we take help from the language of gesture. This is common knowledge, but what is not sufficient realized is that language deprived of gesture becomes insipid and like dead wood. Blackmur presents one of the best examples by citing a line from Othello: "I understand a fury in your words but not the words." This sentence pregnant with the force of gesture reveals that without incorporating some quality of gesture within it language cannot be made of highest use:

> How without it could the novelist make his dialogue ring? How could the poet make his cry lyric, his incongruity comic, or his perspective tragic? The great part of our knowledge of life and of nature—perhaps all our knowledge of their play and interplay—comes to us as gesture, and we are masters of the skill of that knowledge before we can ever make a rhyme or a pun, or even a simple sentence. Nor can we master language purposefully without re-mastering gesture within it.[20]

Blackmur asserts that the great or perhaps all parts of the knowledge of life and nature is understood through gesture. He holds that language is a dramatic and concrete externalization of the inner intentions and unvoiced feelings. Like Brooks's paradoxical and metaphorical aspects of language, he also focuses his attention on words, which remain inert but gets active and conspicuous when a poet handles it. When a writer remains incapable of clothing his words with gesture, he cannot embody his feelings or experiences in words in the exact manner he wants. His condition becomes like a stenographer, who only notes down the words of his boss, but not his gestures—the various impressions created, intentions revealed through the rise and fall of voice, pauses between words, or intonations. He confronts with this difficulty all the time. Therefore, a writer's duty is to charge his words with gesture to portray not only his feelings and thoughts, but also to concretize the abstract and the theoretical contents which he wants to set forth. This end can be achieved by loading words with extra meaning. Blackmur states that words transformed into gesture change their properties and "carry the load, wield the load, lighten the load, and leap beyond the load of meaning" (p.20).

In "Language As Gesture" Blackmur reveals that gesture is one of the basic components of the suggestiveness of all arts—architecture, sculpture, painting, dancing, acting, and music. Poetry also takes part in all the six parts, and, therefore, must be vested with gesture. Poetry is the meaning of meaning and in the finest specimen of poetry

> ...the words sound with music, make images which are visual, seem solid like sculpture and spacious like architecture, repeat themselves like the movements in a dance, call for a kind of mummery in the voice when read, and turn upon themselves like nothing but the written word. Yet it is the fury in the words which we understand, and not the words themselves (p.12)

Gesture is a highly subjective procedure; it is something very mysterious, indefineable, and inexpressible. It depends on the working of the imaginative faculty of the artist, who undergoes a deep sense of agony and anguish. Pannick comments very aptly:

> ...gesture indicates its spiritual existence... gesture is not something tangible that can be objectively proven to exist; it is something intangible that may only be asserted to exist. Gesture is felt or intuited psychically just as one can sometimes intuit which horse will win before a race. That part of the mind which deals with these psychological predilections, in Blackmur's scheme, is the imagination.[21]

In Blackmurian terms gesture is called "imaginative skepticism." In modernist movement, a welter of artistic, architectural, and visual techniques—expressionism, Dadaism, surrealism etc. and fresh idioms, critical vocabulary, and huge experimentation—they all are nothing but a source of releasing gestures from language. They deliberately obliterate the normal modes of meaning from the context. Similarly, the critic resorts to his own imagination to analyze gesture in the work of art, "although it can be circumstantially 'proven' to be present by reference to compositional techniques and syntactic strategies."[22]

There are no fixed formulas to invest language with gesture, because numerous poetic and artistic techniques are adopted to create that added meaningfulness, although some of them are pointed out in the essay. The devices are—simple repetition, complex repetition of words, punning, frenzy of the poet, alliteration with rhyme, refrain, metre by ordering accounts, and lastly the device of evocation and imperative, though not discussed by Blackmur. Meaningful and meaningless words, if repeated, create unforeseen impressions. This impact is the result of a special organization of words, rather than their meanings. In this way, the quality of the language and style constitute the worth of the poem.

In a sense any word or congeries of words can be pushed to the condition of gesture either by simple repetition or by a combination of repetition and varied repetition. Macbeth's "Tomorrow and tomorrow and tomorrow" or Lear's "Never Never Never" have been cited by Blackmur as examples of simple repetition which change the nature of the most familiar into the most pervasive gesture. Blackmur explains that the meaning of words does not count so much as the meaning that repetition in a given situation makes them take on.

The verbal sound arrests the attention of Blackmur perennially. The sound created by the repetition of words is the mighty means to generate gestures in them. Different devices are handled to create various types of repetition of the sound. The commonest and the most effective of them—punning, rhyme, alliteration, etc.—are injected to create special sounds to endow the words with gestures, so that they could dance with meaning energetically. Pun is a play of words acting one like another. Rhyme and alliteration are the terminal and the initial form of punning. But pun, in its fullest gamut as gesture, is extremely pervasive, because it combines the perceptions of different sense into a single sensation. Punning is the onomatopoeia; it has a nexus between sound and meaning; it is taken as both sound and meaning, because the sound of words or lines presses into meaning and the meaning is pressed into sound. Pun is the very gesture that the elements of sound themselves reveal the elements of meaning. To justify this motive, Blackmur cites three illustrations from the three different sources of Shakespeare—*Hamlet, Macbeth* and his sonnet.

But I wish to explain only one, as an example, taken from *Hamlet.* The phrase "In the dead vast and middle of the night," uttered by Horatio to Hamlet about the ghost of his father contains a word 'vast.' It is printed in different forms in different texts i.e. 'wast,' 'waste,' or 'waist.' It makes no difference as to which one is correct. Once the word is invested with gesture, all the other different senses automatically appear at once, uniting into one sense. Here the gesture of the play "upon and within words constitutes the revelation of the sum or product of all the meanings possible within the focus of the words played upon, even though we did not know what all these meanings were." (p.19)

Blackmur also cites two lines from Wallace Stevens's poem "Bontam in Pine-Woods" to show the maximum case of alliteration and rhyme reduced to pun—pun both of sound and meaning.

> Chieftain Iffucan of Azcan in caftan
> Of tan with henna hackles, halt! (p.19)

The sounds of words are so predominant that the reader ceases to know as to what they mean. For the time being, the words get deprived of their normal meanings just as they go beyond their normal meanings and also tend to become gesture.

With his ceaseless effort and full recognition, Blackmur intends to unfold the hidden power of a word or a combination of words. No doubt, words generally get worn out by the time poets use them, but it is their duty to handle the words seriously and make them novel, fresh, strange, and impressive by cultivating a sense to the value, precision, exactness, and infallibility of words. Quite conscious of the value of careful concentrated reading, Blackmur tells that it is not only the poet who should know his job precisely; the reader should also be able to determine the exact sense of the poet. In his essay, "Example of Wallace Stevens," Blackmur points out that the artists can achieve "excellence even by writing an existing language as if it were their own invention." They can create originality being faithful to the words as they appear in dictionary. In this way, a reading of poetry produces a shocking recognition if they know the exact meaning of the word; and a window to knowledge gets opened before them. In "The Expense of Greatness" he states very clearly: "To the individual artist the use of word is an adventure in discovery."[23] It will be unscholarly and churlish to degrade the word to the level of mere keeping up appearance. Blackmur is a Newton who unearths the gravity of a word—its gesture, its unknown perception, its various layers, its definite character and its complexity.

Blackmur observes that all sorts of effect—timely effect—and meaning must be rendered by words and their adequate internal relationship in written as well as spoken arts. In "The Expense of Greatness" he states: "Words, and their intimate arrangements, must be ultimate as well as immediate sources of every effect in the written or spoken arts."[24] After making an adventure into the reality of words, the artists become capable of handling them in precise and impressive way, and can differentiate a word charged with intensity from that devoid of it. He further comments the relation of thoughts and words in the essay "W. B. Yeats: Between Myth and Philosophy." He says that it is true that while analyzing critically the structure of a poem, its thought becomes "irrelevant" because it may be "taken as felt assertion."

Blackmur establishes his relationship with Kenneth Burke sharing his view that "the language of poetry may be regarded as symbolic action" (p.3). The difference between the two is that Burke is mainly "concerned with setting up methods for analyzing the actions as they are expressed in the symbol," while Blackmur emphasizes "the created or dead-end symbol." He explores the puzzle of the language in the process of becoming symbolic. His main object is "to show how the symbol invests the language with poetic actuality. Mr. Burke legislates; I would judge; the executive is between us" (pp.3-4). When language is used as gesture, a symbol is created, which is defined by Blackmur as something that is used to express "meaningfulness in a permanent way which cannot be expressed in direct word or formulas of word with any completeness; a symbol is a cumulus of meaning which, once established, attracts further meaning to it..." (p.16). On the whole, in "Language As Gesture" Blackmur epitomizes the significance of gesture in the following remarks:

> It is a poem which, using symbol, and making, playing upon its words alliteration and rhyme and meter and refrain, using as it runs, escapes all the mere meaning in words and reaches the pure meaningfulness of gesture (p.23).

Blackmur approaches a work of art through the technique and holds that technique and substance, form and content are inseparable. Each is relative to the other and cannot exist, in its particular quality, without the other. Ignore one and the other begins to look. Technique and substance have concrete inter-weaving. But Blackmur uses the term 'technique in a sense more inclusive and wider way than has generally been used by the New Critics. 'Technique' refers to what Blackmur calls the "new knowledges" of psychology, anthropology, sociology, and psychiatry. The term 'technique' is to be used in linguistic, intellectual, emotional, and philosophical sense. Ultimately, we judge a poem genuine because by means of words it discovers the truth of a fact, representing a fundamental view of life. However, in "A Burden for Critics," he has come round to accept that the critics should not confine themselves to the superficial and mechanical executive techniques, but they should pay adequate attention to the major conditions, obsessions, and intuitions of the poet which go a long way in shaping the literary constructs.

A Featherbed for Critics

Fraught with bald advice and overt moral lessons, the essay, "A Featherbed for Critics" (1940), opens with a firm belief, hope, and purpose of Blackmur in the matter of the profession of writing. He discovers the general impact of writing in America very despairing and disheartening. This sorry state of affairs generates "the feelings of stress and unease" [25] and provokes him to write this essay. Imbued with the spirit of a concentrated social commitment, and expressing a deep dissatisfaction at the existing anemic conditions of writers, he formulates certain prescriptions for the resuscitation of the profession of writing. He is confident enough that his voice will not fall on deaf ears. Rather, it will definitely constrain the reader, the critic, the writer, and the society to brood over the fate of the profession of writing in America. Blackmur gives an equal concentration to all of them held responsible for the decay of the profession of writing. Blackmur's precepts laid down in the essay are not concerned with the extraordinary, the great, and the fanatic who hold prestigious chairs at Harvard, because their professional position is secured. However, these chairs are not going to strengthen the profession of writing itself. To warrant his thesis, he exposes the weakness of society and mentions a host of writers and critics—D. H. Lawrence, T. S. Eliot, Balzac, Dante, Thomas Hardy, W. B. Yeats, James Joyce etc.—illustrating their merits and demerits.

Blackmur deems that writing is a profession with "a living, growing institution" (p.277), but the problem is that the mentality of the reader as well as the society has undergone so badly changed that they are not ready to pay a due respect and value to the profession of writing. In this way, the writer receives a depleted and discouraging response from them. However, the writer also fails to function the social role with responsibility and sides the society in perpetuating evils and viciousness such as war. Society and the writer are the representative of the whole society, and their motto should be the same, because "the profession of society, and the profession of writing are the same" (p.227). Unfortunately, both act from a defect of professional responsibility and insincerity beyond their means—moral, intellectual, and emotional.

Under this crucial situation, the role and responsibility of a critic gets more intense and serious; he has to play a role of a mediator between the writer and the society. His duty is to exert his potential to establish and recognize "the idea of the writer as a man with a profession" (p.277). Gerald J. Pannick remarks: "Blackmur is more concerned with what the critic can do for writers and all artists who lack a spiritually sustaining and nourishing response from their societies."[26] The critic, a responsible person with a very serious social role, has to inculcate awareness in the writer that his business is to write; writing is his profession. This role is to make him realize his position and relevance, and value in the society as to where he is necessarily going. The critic must recall the writer to be extra-careful and sensitive and

> ...keep himself in a steady startled state: as if one were about to be haunted; as if one were never to get used to, and hence never to let down, one's powers of vision, one's resources of feeling (p.302).

The critic educates the writer in the tradition of literature, and after reading the works of a particular writer, he (the critic) could then discover the latent attitude to life manifested in the work and make it known to the writer himself to produce high level writing. Between the writer and the society

> ...a deep collaboration is necessary, a collaboration in which the forces are autonomous and may never consciously cooperate, but which is marked by the unity they make together and by culture which the individual, by the art of his convicted imagination, brings to light (p.303).

Blackmur, therefore, chastises both the writer and the society for not performing their duties and responsibilities satisfactorily. The society is neither ready to assure respect for the writer nor the writer is true and sincere to his profession. "The fact is, that writers devote very little of their ability exclusively to writing; ...society neither requires nor perhaps permits more than the least devotion" (p.280). Blackmur, therefore, repeatedly holds society responsible for the dissipation and distraction of energies of writers by offering the job of teaching, lecturing, publishing, editing etc. It compels and entices them to accept such offers by exposing the sheer necessity of livelihood or a living. Of course, livelihood is the first requirement of writers, but the itch or the ability to write seriously and gradually is rubbed out by accepting such "subtle and brutal" jobs in quasi-public life. Even the creative energy of a serious writer gets drained into an exhausting and irrelevant direction.

Society always plays a very vital role in shaping the fate of the profession of literature. It always flourishes best in connection with institution of society. When "society leaves off the preservation, maintenance, and insemination" (p.285) of the profession of letters, the university or a college, Blackmur suggests, has to take care of it and pursue the liberal education. In the twentieth century, under the forms of capitalist democracy, there is no public institution of the state itself able to afford an integral connection for the profession of writing. Only a few serious writers can make a living entirely writing. That is why Blackmur suggests, the rest of the promising lot of writers should be attached either to a university or a college, because teaching is more suitable than any supine forms of work, even the government job for a living. The big academic institutions furnish better than average subsistence and provide better than average opportunity for what is called leisure to write. Therefore, writers should also, without any complaint, express a sense of gratitude to a university.

As a critic, Blackmur's sincere effort is not to save a few individuals, but to secure and elevate the profession, to save and improve the professional habit of the whole possible band of serious writers. The university comes in, at least indirectly, to help reestablish the writer as an effective force in his profession. In this way, the university not only provides him with leisure to write, but buy some of his leisure actually to write, because the writer as a teacher has a plenty of leisure in the university.

According to Blackmur, in some good medical and scientific schools, some of their doctors, physicists, and chemists in their leisure, teach the art—the quality of the profession of the medicine, physics, and chemistry, instead of physiology, crystallography, and tar compounds. In the same way, the university teachers, who are also creative writers, should teach the profession of writing in leisure. In consequence, they can restore the lost glory and respect of the literary figures of the eighteenth and the nineteenth centuries. And then there will be a race of men of letters—educated and handy in their profession. But Blackmur is also conscious of the limitation of the university because it cannot fully assure or furnish the ideal guarantee of writer's profession. Therefore, they should have to participate in some living institution, not limited to the profession of writing, in order to endure at all, but more especially to achieve their own coherence and secure their own aims.

The critic's business is to tell the function and role of the writer, whose primary work is to write and through his writing to affect society. Essentially, gifted with a prophetic vision, he is susceptible of playing his vital role at the most appropriate time under any conditions and circumstances. He has to play a great responsibility to give a direction and shape to the society because his relation to the society is positive. In this way, he can prove to secure the maximum responsibility in his work, but the effect of his irresponsibility may also leave a very negative effect on the society. Therefore, he has to be extremely careful and try to analyze, dissect, and asses his ideas before presenting to the society. The position of the imaginative writer is also supreme if he succeeds to change the general moral fibre and restore the damage done to the society, and alter the fibre by a simple change of heart or shuffle of the will.

Blackmur is also aware of the predicament of the incredibility of intellectuality and the crisis of faith the writer encounters in the modern time. He lacks an institutional source of belief like the Church and, therefore, faces difficulty in identifying his views and experiences or rather his "conviction" derived from within himself, because they do not have any institutional sanction. His sensibility is the joint product of his talent, education, and the general sensibility of his time. Consequently, he has to employ a different type of writing i.e. writing steeped in rational preoccupation. The writer should also know about those factors which constitute his accomplishment or "inward mastery," which alone makes his work powerful, authoritative, objective, and lasting. It always develops through his "conviction." Here conviction means, according to Blackmur, what the writer selects his experiences to communicate in accordance with his view or attitude of life. A modern writer suffers this problem, because he is without his convictions. With his perpetual reflection, the writer must be conscious of his role, while communicating his ideas in the work. The critic's responsibility is to bring into notice that the writer is "performing the most arduous critical act of which he is capable" (p.278). In addition to this, his personality is also reflected in the life of his society.

Along with the artistic accomplishments, the writer has also to cherish the attributes of publicist, the moralist, the preacher, the district leader, philosopher, and the social reformer to withstand the convulsions of his society. He has to play the social roles to create value while telling an amusing story or composing a musical poem. Indeed, every person—a doctor, lawyer, mason, carpenter, and mechanic—bears his responsibility. But a writer's responsibility is more than anybody else in the society; he is pushed forward as the scapegoat of general necessity, because he is gifted with an art as to how to dabble with words. The administrative moral authority of the imaginative writer stems from his craft. A society fracturing and falling morally always tends "to make the writer…deliberately a false god, and then calls him responsible." To feel responsibility is to feel the pang of experience, and to act from responsibility is to put that pang into one's writing. It can be here added the savory of Yeats's remark to the effect that good poets write with difficulty what bad poets write easily.

The great and successful writer looks and acts like a businessman whose business is nothing but writing. For a while, he may get indulged in petty affairs, but is never distracted from his main target. Like the best lawyers, actors, and mechanics, he remains fully committed to his profession i.e. writing. On the other hand, the average successful writer catering to the taste of the book stores and magazines only fulfills the tricks of his trade, and pay a little attention to the existence of his profession. Such type of the writer neither deserves blame nor appreciation from the society. He fails to hold the position which amounts to criticism and gives enjoyment. Rather, his writings never come within the periphery of literary criteria; he becomes a tool in the hands of society and is guided by it. He listens to the dictates of the cheap social requirements. The shapes of his works are wrought or inflated by social pressure. The social demand of fact, excitement, and urgency has overwhelmed the high seriousness in writing. Blackmur states: "the demand together with the capacity for informed seriousness in high level popular novels has fallen off" (p.281). Though writers like Balzac, George Sand, and Christina Rossetti also write under the pressure of the society but they intend to ameliorate it and give values to society rather than supply the need of the pot-boilers. Despite the talent of writers, the quality of the operative force of the whole institutions plays a very seminal role in writing. The contemporary writers disregarding the profit motive should take inspiration from a band of serious writers, who face both a theme and a living excruciatingly. To search for an adequate theme is as slow and hard as to find a living.

The writer discovers that good and evil are inextricable in the world of value, and cherishes the dream of absolute freedom of imagination and the utter moral independence. These are the most haunting and illuminating heresies that the writer can entertain. The writer lives in the society and cannot escape from being influenced by it. He has to exert enormous powers to paint and portray the actual without being deluded by illusion. His obligation towards society is to be honest in distinguishing the actual. It is perfidy to the actual that weakens a writer, and disintegrates his writing, and it is fidelity to the actual that strengthens him and gives his writing a force to leave an effect on society. In addition to conceptual honesty, act of vision or mechanism, the writer must muster his talent.

A Burden for Critic

An imaginative skeptic, R.P.Blackmur, like T.S.Eliot, expresses his deep fury at the chaotic and corrupted state of current criticism. He feels a dire need of such criticism as it not only corrects the taste of the audience but also connects the arts with the society. Modern criticism, buried under unwieldy masses of obscuring commentary, needs vitality, reformation and possibilities. Though Blackmur begins, "A Burden for Critics" (1948) with a modest remark: "This essay does not introduce a system of criticism,"[27] yet he has a serious and momentous intention to improve and invigorate the enervated condition of criticism. A serious and conscious social critic, he has a perpetual concern as to how a critic can play a social role. The position, importance, and value of the critic hinge on his sense of responsibility to his society. In relation to it, he gets work done; and out of relation to it, he gets nothing done. Blackmur, therefore, knows the function of criticism; it always compels the critic to be conscious of his role and responsibility to the society. And this consciousness the way the critic feels becomes his burden. Blackmur remarks:

> ...criticism makes us conscious of what we have done, and sometimes makes us conscious of what can be done next, or done again (p.198).

In this essay, Blackmur introduces his personal three new terms—*momentum*, *performance*, and *aesthetic*—that are essential to an understanding of the concepts of criticism and the critic's literary and social responsibilities. It warrants me, before proceeding further, to clarify the concepts of these terms. First, *momentum* means the dynamic and ever-changing state of society; everything in society is moving, shifting, and swapping—all in a state of flux. The portrayal of this condition of society, Blackmur calls, momentum. Secondly, *performance* deals with the critical act of the critic trying to establish a relationship between the society and the arts. Thirdly, *aesthetic* discusses the judgment and standard of criticism. These terms rationally woven together converge on the importance of the critic who is conscious of the social responsibilities. The terms are further elucidated as the essay heads for a fuller analysis and interpretation.

Blackmur, ruthlessly critical to his own society, exposes its anarchic and topsy-turvy condition i.e. "in corruption the best is the worst" (p.200). He reminds Matthew Arnold's anxiety in "Dover Beach" where he encounters a world which:

> Hath really neither joy, nor love, nor light,
> Nor certitude, nor peace, nor help for pain;
> And we are here as on a darkling plain
> Swept with confused alarms of struggle and flight,
> Where ignorant armies clash by night.
> (Dover Beach)

Also, W. B. Yeats laments in the same tone in his "The Second Coming":

> Things fall apart; the centre cannot hold;
> Mere anarchy is loosed upon the world,
> The blood-dimmed tide is loosed and everywhere
> The ceremony of innocence is drowned;
> The best lack all conviction, while the worst
> Are full of passionate intensity...

Blackmur discovers that the modern man has lost the power of using his mind to look into the true nature of a thing or situation. If he exercises his mind to see the truth or reality of a particular thing, he spurns to acknowledge all the visions of value with which it is at variance. The modern culture has made:

> ...the best in us the worst when we have either pushed an insight beyond its field or refused, when using one insight, to acknowledge the pressure of all those insight—those visions of value—which it is in conflict (p.200).

Consequently, man has lost the feeling of richness, the sense of relation, and the power of judgment. Being dispossessed with these values, a critic fails to bring his experience of literature to actual performance. He remains shrouded in the fog of confusion and indecision, and knows "neither what to bring, nor what to look for" (p.200). It has become a general phenomenon of the modern world.

Against this cultural backdrop, the modern society, Blackmur continues, witnesses the disappearance of tradition, and the decay of the power of conviction and mastery. Overwhelmed by the accidents of his massive ignorance, man is also indulged in his individual subjectivity. In an age of engineers and anarchs, he has lost the field of common reference and dwindles in his ability to think symbolically. The old unconscious skills disappear without any apparent means of developing new unconscious skills. The age yields a whole series of highly conscious skills, but they are dubious and precarious, ingrained in the sciences of psychology, anthropology, and sociology. And this tremendous confusion of the practices of these sciences is running with urbanization. All modern scientific and technological techniques developed in the lines of highly conscious skills "discover trouble, undermine purpose, blight consciousness and prevent decision; they promote uncertainty, insecurity, anxiety, and incoherence" (p.203).They provide barriers between man and access to his common enterprise. The unwieldy and unmanipulable fact of urbanization does more of the damage than the conscious techniques. In comparison to the old culture, the modern one appears to be barren, violent, and anti intellectual. It is based on law and rational wisdom, and general craft in which there is felt a kind of total responsibility to total disorder. There is an invoked anarchy at both levels—in the world and in the individual personality. There are chances of growing misunderstanding everyday with each other. On the whole, it is a world alive and moving but does not understand itself.

This massive change in the structure of society revolutionizing the artistic sensibility gets more emphatic in the school of arts and criticism. It causes an eruption of a plethora of techniques and *ism*: hedonism, naturalism, impressionism, naturalistic relativism, aestheticism, symbolism, Imagism, futurism, expressionism, Dadaism, surrealism, Art of Art, the private mind, free verse, dream literature, spontaneous or automatic form, anti-intellectual form, the stream of unconsciousness, the revolution of the word, and the new cult of the word. The modern world is caught up with such trains of ideas, images, trends, habits, and tendencies. All these paraphernalia portray an intolerable, disintegrating, irrational world; a world nevertheless serving, throwing up value after value with inexhaustible energy but without a principle in sight.

In this maddening and muddling state of modern world, the new arts, throwing up the values, are produced. But they are extremely difficult to understand because of the gigantic and tumultuous urban society, affecting both the audience and the artist at his work. The institutions, the conceptions, and the experience of culture get into arts bringing a deep change. The relationship between the society and the arts in America gets badly shifted. Thus, in this new form of culture, "almost the whole job of culture has been dumped on the artist's hands" (p.206). At this crucial juncture, the role of the critic becomes more serious and he has to play a very vital role through the responsibility of his criticism. He remains concerned with "choice, not prescription, with equity, not law; never with the dead hand, always with the vital purpose" (p.199). The critic is rather the relativist of insight, aspiration, and vision. He is a relativist, because he believes that the things like truth and moral change depending upon a particular culture and situation. That is why, Blackmur undermines that the critical act is a dynamic act: "what is permanent is what always fresh, and it can be fresh only in performance—that is in reading and seeing and hearing what is actually in it at this place and this time." (p.199) It is in performance the critic finds out relation to momentum.

In an age of anarchy, social chaos, moral decline, and cultural disorder, religious sterility, the New Critics fail to perform the true function of criticism. With "a distaste for dogma and the doctrinaire mind,"[28] he discovers its limitations and shortcomings. Despite its exactness of analysis, its expertness of elucidation, and its ramifying specialization of detail, the New Criticism has been, Blackmur holds, very "facile" and "natural." Though he is generally grouped with the New Critics and does embrace certain tenets of the New Criticism, yet never indulges in bigotry to it. That is why sharing with Yvor Winters and the other New Critics, he joins a attack on Brooks and specifies that the monistic interpretation of literature is impossible:

> It is a criticism…which has dealt almost exclusively either with the executive techniques of poetry (and only a part of that) or with the general verbal techniques of language (p.206).

The New Criticism is created to cope with and develop the kind of poetry illustrated by Eliot's *The Waste Land* and Yeats's *Tower.* It is eminently suited for the initial stages of criticism, not for the later ones. Moreover, it is suited for only *some* older poetry; for the other older, the later seventeenth, and all the eighteenth century poetry, it is nothing but a little piece of information, and, therefore, "made misjudgments when applied" (p.207). It is ineffective for Dante, Chaucer, Goethe, or Racine, and disfiguring if applied to drama.

Yet, in the absence of positive culture outside poetry, the New Criticism has to be introduced and applied, because there was no other way of "creating a verbal sensibility capable of coping with the poetry at all" (p.207). With a shared culture, capable of convictions, masteries, and vital dogmas, the stable and structured society in the past did not require much criticism either to order or to create culture. The artist's main function was to express the continuity of culture and the turbulence that underlay it. That is why the history of criticism is so much concerned with matters of decorum: conformity, elegance, rhetoric, or metrics, which are generally now considered in the review. But the modern fractured and falling society feels an urgent need of criticism—social criticism. It is so unfamiliar and so extensive that the maximum and multiple burdens, in its full swing, fall on criticism to bring the art to full performance. The artists are now left holding the whole cultural bag. In such a demanding situation in which the culture has broken down, the linguistic emphasis of the New Criticism is not enough; it cannot play a therapeutic role. "Its service is only preliminary to filling the needs of the time."[29] Rather there is a need of a reintegration of values and a judgment of culture in Arnoldian sense. The artists must dramatize at once both the culture and turbulence to control and create the very symbolic substance of the culture.

To achieve this end, Blackmur suggests both the artists and the critics to bear shared responsibilities. The artists' duty is to utilize the residual old available tradition—whether in language, culture, or institutions of their society—to maintain a continuity of cultural values; and it becomes their liability to picture the actual in their day. As honest writers, keeping themselves free of the grosser hallucination, they must present the criticism of life as Matthew Arnold suggested. Artists and critics must consider art a solution, a panacea to restore culture. Blackmur, therefore, finds that "art is...a human increment to creation" (p.202).

On the other hand, the role of the critic is "to make bridges between the society and the arts: to prepare the audience for its art and to prepare arts for their artists" (p.206). This function was not performed by the New Criticism. But now as an instructor, the critic must train the readers to develop the early forgotten practice and "skill of symbolic thinking" (206). Through his performance—the critical act—he must explain the meaning of symbols introduced in a work, because the common readers have lost the ability to do so. But only the interpretation of symbols is not enough. Blackmur remarks:

> Besides analysis, elucidation, and comparison, which Eliot once listed as the functions of criticism, criticism in our time must also come to judgment (206).

Blackmur differs from T. S. Eliot in the sense of "performance." Eliot's critical act is the "labour of shifting, combining, constructing, expunging, correcting, testing,"[30] but Blackmur's is to broaden the social relevance and base of criticism. It is done through both the inculcation of the "skill of symbolic thinking" in the readers and the aesthetic judgment of the arts. The critic must compare and judge as well as analyze and elucidate. It is his duty to know "not only what people are reading, but also...what they are reading about" (p.207).

Blackmur unlike the New Critics attaches the value of the aesthetic judgment to criticism. To enlarge and achieve it, the critic has to first liberate himself from the cramping damage done to it. For example, psychology turns aesthetic into the mechanics of perception, scientific logic turns it into semasiology, and the technical philosophers turn it into a branch of epistemology. These studies, like the social sciences, the spread of universal education and the rapid industrial development generate extraneous and puzzling problems and give a great blow to both the culture and aesthetics, introducing a "New Illiteracy" in modern society. To get rid of the destructive effect of this massive bewildering knowledge, the critic must create aesthetic experience to restore the culture and aesthetics. The excellence of arts lies in the aesthetic experience, exploring the representations in art of what is actually going on in society. Blackmur uses the term aesthetic in a technical sense, and laying a deep emphasis on it he argues vehemently:

> I see no reason why all forms of the word aesthetic cannot be restored to good society among literary critics by remembering its origin in a Greek word meaning to perceive, and remembering also its gradual historical limitation to what is perceived or felt—that is, what is actually there—in the arts (208).

Blackmur's critical judgment is based on the aesthetic standard, which becomes the measurement of the arts. He explains:

> ...for the literary critic aesthetics comprises the study of superficial and mechanical executive techniques, partly in themselves, but also and mainly in relation to the ulterior techniques of conceptual form and of symbolic form (p.209).

In this statement, there emerge the three elements determining the aesthetic judgment: (i) executive, (ii) conceptual, and (iii) symbolic techniques. Executive techniques mean "the whole rationale of management and manipulation" (p.209). Its simple meaning is the artistic arbitrary devices, or facts, or form of the work. In the modern times, these devices being difficult and agitating lapse into a state of oblivion. Blackmur, being a traditionalist in many of his attitudes, wants them now to be argued, redeemed, and turned into strength by their use. The main study of executive techniques is related with the ulterior techniques of conceptual and symbolic form. Secondly, conceptual techniques deal with "the rationale of what the artist does with his dominant convictions, or obsessions, or insights, or visions, and how they are translated into major stresses of human relations as they are actually experienced" (p.210). Its simple meaning is the content of the work.

These two techniques lead the critic into the territory of the third—the symbolic techniques meaning the artist's attitude or opinion about his experience of life in the arts. This term reveals the hidden cause or meaning i.e. what happens in the arts that retains the quality of timeless and universality as long as they are read. It operates in the arts as sustaining force, "invokable forces," "raw forces," or the force of reality pressing into the actual experience of symbolic form. It gives the reader an illusion of distance and control. All the three elements—executive, conceptual, and symbolic techniques—rationally woven together prepare the grounds for the discovery of life. The act of an aesthetic judgment is the complete critical act of the critic. Through the aesthetic experience, the reader repeatedly discovers, and, discovers again what his life and culture are in the current society. Through the use of the aesthetic judgment, the critic not only judges the art but also its life, its morality, its culture, its identity, and its meaning. A critic becomes more than a critic—an explorer of and eye-opener to the present society.

In an age of deculturization, without knowledge or standard of art, ignorant of aesthetic, and lacking a religious tradition, the critic's best recognition rests on the aesthetic judgment. He, therefore, must promote rational intent, rational statement, and rational technique in art through his rational judgment. Along with exposition, analysis, and comparison of the arts, he has to focus his attention to judgment—aesthetic judgment to determine the identity of the present society. So, with a greater degree of conscious, the critic must put the audience into maximum relation to the burden of their social dynamics.

References

1. Alfred Alvarez, "R.P.Blackmur (1904-1965)," *Review: A Magazine of Poetry and Criticism* 18 (1968): 21.
2. Russell Fraser, *A Mingled Yarn: The Life of R.P.Blackmur* (New York & London: Harcourt Brace Javanovich, 1981), p. 277.
3. Denish Donoghue, ed., "Introduction," *Selected Essays of R.P.Blackmur* (New York: Ecco Press, 1986), p.4.
4. R.P.Blackmur, *The Double Agent: Essay in Craft and Elucidation* (Gloucester, Mass.: Peter Smith, 1962), p. 21.
5. Russell Fraster, *A Mingled Yarn*, p. 273.
6. James T. Jones, *Wayward Skeptic: The Theories of R.P.Blackmur* (Urbana & Chicago: University of Illinois Press, 1986), p. 3.
7. "The Great Grasp of Unreason," *A Primer of Ignorance, ed.* Joseph Frank (New York: Hartcourt, 1967), p.4.
8. R.P.Blackmur, "Notes on Four Categories in Criticism," *The Lion and the Honeycomb* (New York: Harcourt, Brace & World, Inc., 1955), p.218.
9. "T. S. Eliot: II," *Hound and Horn* 1 (1928): 304.

10. "T. S. Eliot: II," *Hound and Horn* 1 (1928): 315.
11. D. H. Lawrence and Expressive Form," *The Double Agent,* p. 104.
12. Robert Boyers, *R. P. Blackmur: Poet-Critic* (Columbia & London: University of Missouri Press, 1980), p.7.
13. Walter Suttan, American *Literary Criticism*, p. 135.
14. John Paul Pritchard, *Criticism in America*, p. 259.
15. Gerald J. Pannick, *Richard Palmer Blackmur* (Boston: Twayne Publishers, 1981), p. 155.
16. John Wain, *Essays On Literature and Ideas* (London: Macmillan & Co. Ltd., 1964), p.146.
17. Denis Donoghue, ed., *Selected Essays of R.P.Blackmur* (New York: The Ecco Press, 1985), p.19. The subsequent references will be mentioned in parenthesis after the page number of the same edition.
18. Gerald J. Pannick, *Richard Palmer Blackmur*, p.57.
19. *Ibid.,* p. 56.
20. R.P.Blackmur, *Language As Gesture: Essays in Poetry* (London: George Allen & Unwin, 1961) p.6. The subsequent references will be mentioned in parenthesis after the page number of the same edition.
21. Gerald J. Pannick, *Richard Palmer Blackmur*, p.71.
22. *Ibid.*, p.6
23. R.P.Blackmur, *The Expenses of Greatness* (Gloucester: Peter Smith, p.1940), pp.221-222.
24. *Ibid.*, P.222.
25. R.P.Blackmur, *The Expenses of Greatness*, p. 277. The subsequent references will be mentioned in parenthesis after the page number of the same edition.
26. Gerald J. Pannick, *Richard Palmer Blackmur,* p.75.
27. R.P.Blackmur, *The Lion and the Honeycomb* (New York: Harcourt Brace & World Inc., 1955), p.198. The subsequent references will

be mentioned in parenthesis after the page number of the same edition.

28. Walter Suttan, *Modern American Criticism*, p. 135.
29. John Paul Pritchard, *Criticism in America*, p.261.
30. T.S.Eliot, *Selected Essays* (London: Faber & Faber Lmt., 1972), p.30.

7

W. K. Wimsatt, Jr.

W. K. Wimsatt, Jr. (1907-1975), a leading apologist and theoretician of formalist criticism, is ignored unjustifiably by the critical scholars. He fails to occupy a due place in the history of the New Criticism. Even J. P. Pritchard denies him to accommodate in his book *Criticism in America.* However, Wimsatt strives earnestly to establish a level of legitimacy in English studies. Drawing inspiration from both the ancient critics (such as Aristotle and Longinus) and the contemporary (such as T. S. Eliot and Chicago School), he formulates his theories. A Professor of English at Yale University, he lays a stress on objective approach to criticism decrying affective theory as "less a scientific view of literature than a prerogative." Affective theory is a purely psychological method which is interested in exploring the mind and the intention of the poet and the effect of the poem on the reader. Wimsatt strongly argues to disregard these factors while analyzing and evaluating a poem. Since both the reader and the poet are outside the poem, their implications will be an importation of meaning from outside. Therefore, such type of literary interpretation is quite irrelevant, if not completely meaningless, and distracting, whereas the words on the page are all that matter. Primarily known for his studies of eighteenth century literature, Wimsatt produces the three important books—*The Verbal Icon: Studies in the Meaning of Poetry* (1954), *Hateful Contraries* (1965), and *Literary Criticism: A Short History* (1957) in collaboration with Cleanth Brooks. His detailed "grammar of criticism" is discussed in *Hateful Contraries* right from diction, imagery, metaphor to paradox, ambiguity, irony, theme, myth and genre.

The Intentional Fallacy

Wimsatt's *The Verbal Icon* (1954), a group of seventeen critical essays compartmentalized into four sections, is a milestone in the history of objective form of literary criticism in America. It reflects his critical canvas to its fullest extent, embracing the various dimensions and consistent approach to the literary problem at different levels. The essays are produced "out of several critical preoccupations and occasions."[1] *The Verbal Icon* opens with the two much anthologized and always cohabiting critical essays—"The Intentional Fallacy" and "The Affective Fallacy." These stimulating essays, co-authored with his young philosopher friend, Monroe Beardsley, pose the same perpetually recurring questions as to what poetry is and how it should be interpreted. Though these haunting questions are already tackled by Eliot, Hulme, Pound, and other critics of the school of the New Criticism, yet it is these critics who propound more critical and sharper tools and idioms than anyone else in the realm of literary criticism.

The essay "The Intentional Fallacy" first published in 1946 is again included in *The Verbal Icon* in 1954. It is not quite novel what Wimsatt and Beardsley discuss in it. Some of the critics have already touched upon that the critic should focus his attention on the poem, not on the poet. In his seminal essay "Tradition and Individual Talent" (1919), T.S. Eliot suggests that "Honest criticism and sensitive appreciation are directed not upon the poet but upon the poetry."[2] The critics C. S. Lewis and E. M. W. Tillyard argue the same issue in the *The Personal Heresy* (1939); in *The Picture of Dorian Gray* (1891) Oscar Wilde remarks "To reveal art and conceal artist is art's aim;" and D. H. Lawrence writes in "The Spirit of the Place": "Never trust the artist. Trust the tale. The proper function of a critic is to save the tale from the artist who created it."[3] It is quite evident that all these critics advocate an objective approach towards literary criticism. The personality of the artist, like God, should be hidden in his work. The poet should not reflect it nor it be interpreted by the critic. Wimsatt and Beardsley continue this tradition in a more forceful and argumentative manner and thus the essay becomes a cornerstone in the history of American literary criticism in the 1940s and 50s.

The critical dispute between intentionalists and anti-intentionalists has been the basic issue of the New Criticism. The former believe in the pure linguistic artifact, ' a verbal icon' as the authors termed it. Raising a very serious issue of the intention of the poet in literary criticism, they contend that it has been a vogue to explore the mind of the poet to judge or evaluate his performance or quality in a work of art. Intentionalism is deeply rooted in the tradition and history of literary criticism. The critics determine the meaning of a work in the origin of the poet's mind or his intention. It is sheer unfortunate; the modern objective school of criticism downright dismisses this romantic conception. They argue that "the design or intention of the author is neither available nor desirable as a standard for judging the success of a work of literary art"[4] (p.334). In another essay, they termed "The Intentional Fallacy" as "The Genetic Fallacy," which is "a confusion between the poem and its origin"[5] (p.345). Peter Lamarque explains:

> A fallacy is an invalid mode of reasoning, and Wimsatt and Beardsley claimed that it is fallacious to base a critical judgment about the meaning or value of a literary work on 'external evidence' concerning the author's intentions.[6]

The main contention of the present authors is that a poem is not a product of inspiration nor a fit. It is related with the intellect, not with the heart. "The designing intellect," therefore, plays an active and decisive role in the creation of a poem. It has its own autonomy and anatomy, purely based on the verbal structure. It has nothing to do with the biographical, historical, social or any other external circumstances. A critic's business is not to look for all these things, while making a literary analysis of the poem. Professor Stoll also remarks very clearly that a poem is not "a will," "a contract," or "constitution." It is an aesthetic artifact. The American poet Archibald MacLeish's statement: "A poem should not mean but be," aptly accords with what the authors explain the meaning of a poem: "A poem can *be* only through its meaning—since its medium is words – yet it *is*, simply *is*, in the sense that we have no excuse for requiring what part is intended or meant" (p.335). No doubt, the poet is possessed with his own personal feelings and emotions, but they should be expressed through dramatic persona, as Eliot talks about in his very famous "objective correlative" theory.

It is very well argued by the authors that when a poem is produced, it goes beyond the control of the creator. Now it is neither the property of the poet not the critic. It becomes a public property—open to all to judge in terms of purely verbal structure. "It is embodied in language, the peculiar possession of the public, and it is about human being, an object of public knowledge" (p.335). The artist has no claim over his language or the words outside the poem cannot be held authentic. It acquires an objective existence and the artist's original ideas are thrown into the background. The reader should bank upon and apply his own knowledge of linguistics and literary components to arrive at the conclusion about the thematic centrality and unity of the work.

Wimsatt and Beardsley discover that a huge quantity of criticism has proceeded from the poets themselves. The third section of the essay opens with a series of quotations of Plato, Keats, Byron, Wordsworth, Housman, Edward Young, Carlyle, and Pater regarding the nature, definition, and production of poetry. In terms of these poets, genesis, inspiration, imagination, emotion, spontaneity, recollection, tranquility, and truth to oneself are the cardinal elements in the poetic creation. The authors hold that the inspirational or romantic strain of poetry infects easily the young persons and, therefore, it prevails upon them to reveal "the lava of the imagination." The definitions and precepts expounded by the romantics may be "inspiring" and "exciting" and "excellent" advice for writing poetry, but Wimsatt and Beardsley consider it "what a child can do." This view, of course, touches the extreme end, because intentionalist creation cannot be lowered to that position. However, they categorically differentiate the art of producing poetry from that of criticism. Poetic creation is "an art separate form criticism (p.338). Criticism is "the public art of evaluating poems" (p.338); it is the judgment of poems. Poetic creation belongs "to a psychological discipline, a system of self-development, a yoga" (338). Production of art and criticism are two different disciplines.

The key words of the intentional school are: 'sincerity,' 'fidelity,' 'spontaneity,' 'authenticity,' 'genuineness,' 'originality.' The authors suggest to replace these words with 'integrity,' 'relevance,' 'unity,' 'function,' 'maturity,' 'subtlety,' 'adequacy.' The latter are concerned with the aesthetic aspect of the work. A critic should give least importance to the psychology or content in the examination or evaluation of the poem. His main emphasis should be on expression. Only through 'expression,' aesthetic value can be achieved, which resides in the intrinsic part of the poem. "Aesthetic art," says Professor Curt Ducasse, "is the conscious objectification of feelings" (338). The touchstone of a piece of art rests on the objectification of the artist's emotions. A successful objectification of a self is an element in the definition of art. "The evaluation of the work of art remains public; the work is measured against something outside the author" (p.338).

Wimsatt and Beardsley explain the difference between the external and internal evidence for the meaning of a poem. The internal evidence deals with the poem, while the external with the poet. The real meaning of a poem exists in the internal study, not the external. But in the realm of literary scholarship, there is a good deal of confusion among the critics. They fail to draw a clear-cut distinction between the personal studies and poetic studies. Generally, they study the personality of the poet and think as if it were poetic. Though the personal studies are an attractive one in itself as Professor Tillyard argues, yet it is "a derogatory purpose." Certainly, the critics should not study the personal life of the author. If they attempt to explore authorial intentionality, they really do not find what they are looking for. The intentional fallacy is a historically based literary biography—a romantic idea.

Wimsatt and Beardsley categorize three possible types of evidence, which are generally applied to study literature. But all the three are not equally useful for literary criticism. The first most agreeable and accessible type of evidence for the meaning of a poem is "internal evidence." It is

> ...discovered through the semantics and syntax of a poem, through our habitual knowledge of all the literature which is the source of dictionaries, in general through all that makes a language and culture (p.339).

Internal evidence, a poetic study, interprets the anatomy of the poem; it studies the verbal interrelationship, images, symbols, and the organizing principle forming the complex organic structure of the work. It is these internal components which determine the meaning of a literary product. These characteristics found within the text are to be discovered. The analysis of the internal evidence is exposed to the public, not to the individual, which can be verified by anyone.

The second type of evidence is the "external" one. Letters of the author, interviews, introductions, writer's journal, manuscripts, correspondence, biographical data, social and biographical contexts, linguistic change, and the author's commentary are called the external evidence. In the analysis and interpretation of a literary text, these things are "private or idiosyncratic" and, therefore, should be fully avoided. They are held to be the error of evaluating a work, because they distract the critic from the actual text. The sole value or meaning of the text is an independent entity, a separate thing, an autonomous object, finished and freestanding, and independent of any references outside it. It is autotelic, as Eliot also holds the same view in his "The Function of Criticism." The author's intention whether himself stated or supposed does not play an important role in evaluating the text. The external evidence is not easily available nor "a part of the work as a linguistic fact" (p.339). However, the author's intention may be taken into consideration after a close-study of the text is done.

The third type of evidence is "intermediate" evidence. It is also related with the "private" experience of the author, but helps understand the linguistic facts of literature. This evidence is "about the character of an author or about private or semiprivate meanings attached to words or topics by an author" (p.339). The personal information of the author does not mean to give rise to intentionalism; instead it tries to clarify the meanings of the words; the nuances of imagery within the text. David Richter states:

> ...knowing how an author is apt to use a word or phrase may be beneficial in finding unifying structures and themes in a piece of literature. Being aware of how the word(s) work for an author may give the reader a better understanding of how the word(s) work in the text [7]

The critic while evaluating a text can combine intermediate evidence along with the internal one. In this way, he will produce a quite different judgment of the text; it will be a text-oriented analysis. But it is to be noted that there is a great danger of overlapping or merging of the intermediate with the external evidence that entails intentionalism. There is a great possibility that intermediate evidence may distort the primary internal evidence of a text. Therefore, it becomes very difficult to separate these two from each other.

Wimsatt and Beardsley illustrate two examples to justify the theory of evidence. First, John Livingstone Lowe's noted work *The Road to Xanadu* on Coleridge's "Kubla Khan" is purely devoted to the external evidence of the second and third types. In terms of poetic studies, nothing can be detracted from this book. With associationist preoccupations and intentionalist bias, Lowes boldly wanders in the land of romanticism. He clusters all the information very systematically without being attentive to the words of the poem. His extensive study of the sources of imagery and language in Coleridge's poem is another version of the Intentional Fallacy. Digging out such sources of literary material in the personal or cultural life of the author provides little or no aid to understand the meaning of the poem. Wimsatt and Beardsley contend that there are several external factors which are responsible for the production of a work of art, but it is not essential to study all of them, because they are in no way going to help make poetic studies. The outside is cut off to focus the inside. They spell out:

> There is a gross body of life, of sensory and mental experience, which lies behind and in some sense causes every poem, but can never be and need not be known in the verbal and hence intellectual composition which is the poem. For all the objects of our manifold experience, for every unity, there is an action of the mind which cuts off roots— (p.340).

Another example drawn from John Donne's "A Valediction: Forbidding Mourning" shows how the intermediate evidence lapses into the external evidence. In one quatrain, the poet uses astronomical language, "trepidation of the spheres" which may reflect changing Renaissance attitude towards science. A critic starts arguing Donne's deep knowledge or interest in astronomy instead of analyzing the significance of these words in terms of poetic studies; their meaning in terms of imagery, conceit, and metaphor. It matters little whether or

Donne knows astronomy, the important thing is as to how in terms of astronomy, these words function in the texture of the poem. But the critic is tempted "to prefer private evidence to public, external to internal" (p.341).

In the final section of "The Intentional Fallacy" the authors discuss the crucial question of the poetic use of "allusions" and "notes" in the end of the modernist poetry. T.S. Eliot, Ezra Pound, and others extensively introduce literary allusions to enhance the depth, intensity, and suggestiveness, emerging as a challenge and important issue to the objective literary analysis. It may become a different version of romantic expressivism. There is a danger that the critic may indulge in a different job "where a false judgment is likely to involve the intentional fallacy" (p.342). He assumes that without reading the sources of allusions he cannot know what the poet wants to say. Generally, it happens that instead of integrating the allusions and notes with the poetic meaning, the critic delves deep into the sources where the poet draws from. Consequently, the analysis or criticism gets "redolent with intentional implication." M. A. R. Habib holds his view: "As far as allusions are concerned, we must be able to justify their use in terms of their objectively discerned function in the poem…."[8] Allusions create irony, paradox, condensation of thought, integrity, and the integral structure of the poem. The notes given by the poet in the end of the poem, as Eliot does in *The Waste Land*, should be studied as the integral parts of the poem and be analyzed in the light of poetic studies. The authors argue:

> Ultimately, the inquiry must focus on the integrity of such notes as part of the poem, for where they constitute special information about the meaning of phrases in the poem, they ought to be subject to the same scrutiny as any of the words in which it is written (pp.342-343).

Allusions and notes should be studied within the framework of the verbal expression, not the oracle of the poet. If not careful, these notes can become external evidence. A reader may be misled into going outside of the original text in order to gain information that may or may not be revealed the author's intention.

The Affective Fallacy

Another very popular essay, written in collaboration between Wimsatt and Beardsley, "The Affective Fallacy," is a critical document of affective psychology. It automatically claims to co-exist with "The Intentional Fallacy." Both fallacies, they argue, are the long cherished obstacles to objective approach of criticism. Generally, critics and scholars always shun talking against these two strands of romantic expressivism: the 'intention' of the poet and the 'affection' of the reader. The intention means the historical, biographical, social, or any other external sources related to the poet outside the poem. The affection means the feelings, emotions, mental state or disposition of the reader after reading the poem. This term, which is first used by philosophers, deals with the psychological effect of the poem leading to impressionism and relativism. Such a criterion of criticism becomes a purely subjective rather than objective activity. Habib remarks that it is a "discourse about the subject (the reader) rather than the object."[9] Wimsatt and Beardsley, therefore, hold that the affective fallacy is an erroneous way of analyzing a work because the critic or reader lays too much emphasis on his personal, emotional, and psychological bias influencing the interpretation of the work. In this way, the objectivity of the work gets confused with its subjective colouring. The affective fallacy is "confusion between the poem and the results (what it is and what it does)."[10] The two fallacies have actually undermined both poetry and criticism as an art.

The authors dwell upon the laws of emotion and venture to recount some generalities about objects, emotions, and words. They mention a host of critics such as Count Korizybski, Hayakawa, Walpole, Lee, and Richards, who upholds affective criticism, but the authors mainly concentrate their attention on C. L. Stevenson's *Ethics and Language*. Just as Richards tells the two uses of language i.e. referential and emotive, so does Stevenson. He makes a distinction "between what a word means and what it suggests" (p.346). The former refers to a "linguistic role." Its role is to fix responses to a word. It is also called the *descriptive* or *cognitive* function of words. It gives only the literary meaning of a word. For example, the word 'athlete' may be said to mean one who is interested in sports, among other things, but merely to suggest a tall man. The linguistic rule is that athletes are necessarily interested in sports, but may or may not be tall.

The second main function of words is emotive. There is no linguistic rule to stabilize responses. The main tendency of Stevenson's argument is that emotive meaning is something noncorrelative. It is independent of descriptive meaning. Hence, emotive 'meaning' is said to survive sharp changes in descriptive meaning. Words with the same descriptive meaning are said to have quite different or opposite emotive 'meaning.' Wimsatt and Beardsley expose the shortcomings of both Stevenson and Richards that they never tell that the meaning of emotive language depends upon descriptive language. It is a fact that the term 'emotive meaning' and 'feeling' do not refer to any such cognitive meaning as that conveyed by the name of an emotion—'anger' or 'love.' Rather, these key terms refer to the expression of emotive states. Since the term 'meaning' has been traditionally and usefully assigned to the descriptive functions of language, it would have been better to use the term 'import.' It will be a happy choice. There should be the difference between grounds of emotion and emotions themselves, between what is immediately meant by words and what is evoked by the meaning of words.

C. L. Stevenson believes that there are certain words such as expletives which do not have descriptive meaning. They have only emotive meaning. But at the same time, these words also have only the vaguest emotive 'import,' something raw, unarticulated, and imprecise. 'Oh' (surprise and related feelings) 'Ah' (regret), and 'Ugh' (distaste). It demands more descriptive reference to specify the feeling. Wimsatt and Beardsley underscore one important point missed by the semanticists that "a large and obvious area of emotive import depends directly upon descriptive meaning" (p.347). Secondly, a great deal of emotive import which does not depend on descriptive meaning does depend on descriptive suggestion.

Wimsatt and Beardsley contend that the relation of language to objects of emotion is about the status of emotions themselves. They quote the citation from Westermarck's *Ethical Relativity* that difference of emotion 'largely originates in different measures of knowledge, based on experience of the consequences of conduct and in different beliefs.' In certain culture and society, a particular object of emotion produces a definite emotion, but the same object of emotion in different culture and society may produce another or no emotion. They may be a part of its custom and tradition. For example, Westermarck in his *Ethical Relativity* writes that

> ...the custom of eliminating of the aged and unproductive has been practised among certain primitive tribes and nomadic races. Other customs, that of exposing babies, that of suicide, that of showing hospitality to strangers—or the contrary custom of eating them—seem to have enjoyed in some cultures a degree of approval unknown or at least unusual in our own (p.348).

Objects of emotion vary from one culture to another, one place to another, and from one time to another. They are subject to change of time and place.

Wimsatt and Beardsley argue that there is no role of affectivism in the interpretation of a work of art, yet a large number of affective critics emerge on the literary scene who offer argument after argument on scientific bias in favour of the doctrine of emotive meaning. They lay emphasis on the measurement of poetic value by the degree of feeling felt by the reader. So affective criticism, though in its personal or impressionistic form it meets with strong dislike from scholars, yet in its theoretical or scientific form finds strong support from the same quarter.

The authors detail the growth, development, and the result of a long tradition of 'affection' deeply rooted in the history of literary criticism. Enunciating various types of impressionist champions, the authors give a long list of the affective approach. They believe that the reader's response to a work of art is the only yardstick for evaluating its worth. Plato, Aristotle, and Longinus are the early examples of affective theory. Plato holds that "not only art does the poet sing, but by power divine." He feeds on the divine inspiration and speaks the divine truth in a state of frenzy. Poetry is not a craft, a conscious and considered judgment; it is the result of irrational, the impulsive, and the mysterious, coming from the super rational source outside the personality of the poet. It comes out spontaneously like a fountain. Aristotle's theory of *Catharsis* defines that the function of tragedy is to arouse the emotions of pity and fear in the reader or audience and then to offer an emotional cure from these emotions. Longinus's theory of sublime discusses that the effect of the art is to elevate and transport the reader to another world. The reader achieves an emotional ecstasy. Poets like Wordsworth, Keats, and Housman etc. have a firm and sincere belief in author psychology. They are "soul cultivators." In the modern time, I. A. Richards is the pioneer of affective theory—the theory of value—expounded in *The Principles of Literary Criticism.* Wimsatt and Beardsley further explain that affective theory has been an unscientific approach towards literature. It is simply "the soul adventuring among masterpieces."

When art, says Wimsatt and Beardsley, leaves its effect not only on the mind, but also on the body, it achieves "the physiological form of affective criticism. "A poem," says Hans Zinsser, "means nothing to me unless it can carry me away with the gentle or passionate pace of its emotion, over obstacles of reality into meadows and converts of illusion…" (p.351). Emily Dickinson asserts in her letter: "If I feel physically as if the top of my head were taken off I know that is poetry." According to Burke, "Beauty is something which "acts by relaxing the solids of the whole system." Housman feels the 'shiver down the spine' and the sensation in 'the pit of the stomach.' In the opening paragraph of his essay on John Galsworthy, David Lodge comments:

> Literary criticism can be no more than a reasoned account of the feeling produced upon the critic by the book he is criticizing. Criticism can never be a science: it is in the first place too much personal, and the second, it is concerned with values which science ignores. The touchstone is emotion, not reason. We judge a work by its effects on our sincere and vital emotion, and nothing else. All the critical twiddle-twaddle about style and form, all this pseudo-scientific classifying and analyzing of books in imitation—botanical fashion, is mere impertinence and usually dull jargon.

The advanced version of affective theory is hallucination. It is created by the neo-classicists, who observe the unities of time and place. The action of the drama should be within the single revolution of the sun, and there should not be any shift of location. These unities are designed to convince that the action is realistic or probable. And thus they cast a hallucinatory effect on the audience or reader. In Coleridgean phrase, it is called "willing suspension of disbelief" and "a temporary half faith." E. D. Synder also perpetuates this theory more intensely by presenting his hypothesis of hypnosis. In this regard, Wimsatt and Beardsley have a very serious objection and give an acrid remark:

> As this form of affective theory is the least theoretical in detail, has the least content, and makes the least claim on critical intelligence, so it is in its most concrete instances not a theory but a fiction or a fact—of no critical significance (p.351).

In the course of their study, Wimsatt and Beardsley become more pungent to the affective critic. In their satirical tone they remark that the "affective critic is today actually able, if he wishes, to measure the 'psychogalvanic reflex' of persons subjected to a given moving picture" (p.359). The affective critic not only explores the effect of the poem on the mind of the reader but also measures the changes taking place in his body after reading the poem. The authors seriously censor such type of criticism. That is why they underrate Aristotle's theory of catharsis, Longinus's sublime, and Richards's synaesthesis. The purely affective criticism is too physiological or it is too vague. Hence, at the literary level general affective theory "produced little actual criticism" (p.352).

Wimsatt and Beardsley suggest that the critic should avoid both the physiological and the abstractly psychological form of criticism. Subjective affections drown the concreteness, hardness, precision of emotion and reduce its 'thinginess' or ontology into "a circle of the utmost abstraction" (p.353). On the other hand, the criticism of a poem or story which induces vivid images, intense feelings or heightened consciousness in the critic is neither anything which can be refuted nor anything which is possible for the objective critic to take into account. When a critic is free of his private feelings and associations, vivid images emerge.Vividness and abstraction are poles apart in criticism. The former refers to classical objectivity and the latter to romantic reader psychology. There is a vast difference between emotive criticism and cognitive criticism. The authors prefer the latter because the more the emotion of the critic induced by a poem will be specific, controlled, and logical, the more it will be reliable to the readers. The critic should respond to them, instead of talking of tears, prickles, or other physiological symptoms, or vague states of emotional disturbances.

The authors quote Thomas Mann: "Art is a cold sphere." It alludes to Immanuel Kant. Art should be considered an autonomous realm, when the critic maintains an aesthetic distance. Rather he never gets involved in his own personal feelings. An act of literary criticism resembles Kantian aesthetic judgment in its coldness. At the same time, Wimsatt and Beardsley are also aware that psychological theories of aesthetic distance, detachment or disinterestedness. A criticism on these principles has already taken important steps towards objectivity. The authors epitomize the main thesis:

> The critic is not a contributor to statistically countable reports about the poem, but a teacher or explicator of meanings. His readers...will not be content to take what he says as testimony, but will scrutinize it as teaching (p.354).

In the concluding part of the essay, Wimsatt and Beardsley subscribe to the views of Eliot, Richards, Winters, and Ransom that there are two uses of language—logical and emotive. Poetic language is always emotive. It preserves and respects emotions by embodying in formal or dramatic structure. It is not a sheer expression of ideas. While dealing with the relationship among the three—emotion, idea, and object, the authors refute Arnold's notion that "poetry attaches the emotion to the idea." They believe that poetry cannot make ideas "thick and concentrated" (p.354). It cannot be stated, expressed, or commented. Poetry tends to be a formula of emotion embodied in hard, concrete, clear, and concentrated images and objects. It should be in a suggestive language.

Like Eliot's theory of objective correlative, Wimsatt and Beardsley present their thesis that the poet should not communicate his emotions directly to the reader "like an infection or disease, not inflicted mechanically like a bullet or knife wound, not administered like a poison, not simply expressed as by expletives or grimaces or rhythms...." (p.356). Emotions should be expressed through certain objective correlatives or emotive objects. They state:

> Poetry is a way of fixing emotions or making them more permanently perceptible when objects have undergone a functional change from culture to culture or when as simple facts of history they have lost emotive value with the loss of immediacy (p.356).

While speaking of Macbeth, the authors say that "poetry of pure emotion is an illusion." It is about both emotions and objects.

Wimsatt and Beardsley contend that poetry should be in suggestive language, and suggestiveness is born out of emotive objects. They point out two types of objects which carry emotive quality—(i) the objects which are the reasons for human emotion and (ii) objects which by some kind of association suggest either the reasons or the resulting emotion. These two types of objects are used through the simile, the metaphor, and various other figurative devices. But it is the metaphor—"the wrong way of saying something" (p.355)—which operates the main function to describe an emotion in poetry. The metaphor brings together and unifies all sorts of meanings concerned with emotions and makes the poetic discourse suggestive. It is also true that emotions become associated with certain objects in a given social, cultural, and historical context, but poetry keeps open a space for the preservation and understanding of universal feeling. The job of a literary critic is to deal with poetic emotion without being influenced or affected. He should disengage emotion from the object and maintain criticism as a logical, impersonal, and precise enterprise. He should avoid looking directly to other disciplines to explain it. A poem embodies emotion and ideas in its unified and intelligible structure and the critic should analyze that structure on its own terms.

Explication as Criticism

Explication means a formal, structural, or textual criticism or analysis. It examines poetry for knowledge of each part in the direction of the total value i.e. whole. Its attempt is to reveal ironies, ambiguities, paradoxes, structural unity, complexity of language, and autonomy of the poem. Wimsatt holds that explication is itself an act of criticism and hence of evaluation. Arising in America during the 1930s, the school of explication, which lays an energetic claim to a superior understanding of a poem, reveals literary value by keeping off the historical or biographical knowledge of the poet. Wimsatt observes that explication is "a kind of practical test of how well aesthetic theories of order and wholeness do apply to literary works."[11] It serves "as the basis of literary criticism and history,"[12] though, Wimsatt thinks, the extreme theory of explicative criticism cuts apart understanding and value. The critic should find an escape from the two extremes of sheer affectivism and sheer scientific neutralism. He writes very obviously:

> A theory of poetic wholeness and coherence need not proceed to the extreme—either idealistic or positivistic—of making the only kind of untruth the unmeanigful. The kind of truth found in poetry (if either our poetry or our criticism is to survive) will have to be more than the satisfaction aroused by the contemplation of a system of symbols (pp.10-11).

Deeply influenced by Coleridge's theory of organic unity of a poem, Wimsatt believes that the poem is an organized whole, and wholeness is achieved through diverse but reconciled parts. All the different parts are blent harmoniously, and this act of organization establishes wholeness. The part-whole relationship is a perpetual matter of discussion. The parts of a pattern can have beauty only in virtue of their relation to the whole; they do have value only as interacting and making whole. Explication, says Wimsatt, has affinity with holism because both are concerned with organization, wholeness, and structure, not only with the particular parts. Both demand a perfect fusion or assimilation of the two polarities—part and whole. Coleridge, "the father of holism in English criticism,"[13] defines that a poem is a composition which proposes "to itself such delight from the whole, as is compatible with a distinct gratification from each component part."[14] Inside the poem, there are only parts and whole, which should be studied very closely. The value of the whole poem, while always keeping in view the parts, has to grow out of parts which are themselves valuable. According to Wimsatt, poetry is the art which most readily goes beyond the simple pleasure principle of the romantic school and illustrates the principle of structure and harmonious tension. He quotes:

> Poetry is a complex kind of verbal construction in which the dimension of coherence is by various techniques of complication greatly enhanced and thus generates an extra dimension of correspondence to reality, the symbolic or analogical (p.9).

In a poetic composition, Wimsatt, studying Aristotle's *Rhetoric*, dwells upon the complex verbal artifice or style at formal and implicit levels. His focus is on the howness rather than whatness of expression. A critic's function is to demonstrate specific merit or demerit of a poetic composition. Wimsatt is of the view that "the critic's job is never to judge a poem…but only to place the poem in its historical context and to elucidate, to compare, and to analyse" (p.17). T. S. Eliot always lays emphasis on the facts— the technical aspect of a work of art. Therefore, the chief validity and advantage of a fully explicative criticism is that it never corrupts the taste of the reader, and avoids making personal whimsical judgment. Eliot further states:

> The critic must not coerce, and he must not make judgments of worse or better. He must simply elucidate: the reader will form the correct judgment for himself.[15]

When the organic form has been established in its self-sufficiency and complexity, a judgment upon the relationship quite naturally follows.

While explicating a poem, Wimsatt says, the critic should not be rigid to his own critical canons. He should welcome and accommodate others' views. Wimsatt never believes in "a form of monistic expressionism,"[16] though in "Explication as Criticism," he talks about a "'monism' of criticism or evaluation, but it will insist at the same time on certain other principles" (p.1). In the Introduction to *The Verbal Icon*, he says:

> I believe in the integration of literary meaning but at the same time in different kinds and levels of meaning. It is surely true that in a certain sense no two different words or different phrases ever mean fully the same. That is the literary sense.

Wimsatt allows for a certain degree of variation in the analysis of poetry. He does not necessarily contend that there is only one possible reading for any given poem. The critic, therefore, should deal with "the general issues of expression rather a canonical concept of poetry." Wimsatt holds that "the fully evaluative expressions are to be taken as provisional...but never as fixed rules of thumb , or heading on a score sheet of evaluation" (xiv). He is quite conscious that serious studies have not been made on the purely verbal style or complexity. He epitomizes that "the general anatomy of verbal powers is less widely understood than the most obvious anatomy of the human body" (p.xiv).

Unlike other new critics, Wimsatt gives equal emphasis on the content and the technique. However genius the poet is he has to cultivate or train himself for the technique. The technique calls for education. Both the poet's genius and training contribute to both the content and technique of his poem. Their relationship is complementary with each other. The poem is considered "as both expression and artifact." Therefore, the relationship between the content and technique represents the axis and reciprocal motion of all cognative literary criticism.

Organic Form: Some Questions about a Metaphor

Wimsatt's "Organic Form: Some Questions about a Metaphor," an exceptionally critical document, is a mosaic of philosophical ideas, theories, and principles of a crowd of aestheticians, theorists, nature philosophers, historians, poets, and dramatists. It unveils the profundity of his knowledge about the various facets of criticism and aesthetics. The essay primarily hinging on the critical discussion of the two scholars—(i) Phillip G. Ritterbush, a historian and nature philosopher and (ii) G. N. G. Orsini, an imposing critic and idealist aesthetician—poses a critical question of organicism. Wimsatt gives an array of arguments in favour of the theory of organicism in poetry, paintings, and visual arts, because they embody an organic order, aesthetic beauty, and secret life of the creative human spirit. In this essay, Wimsatt discusses the three issues: (i) whether the poem presents biological imagery; (ii) whether the process of its growth in the mind resembles the growth of a tree; and (iii) whether the poem is the hyperstatized verbal and mental act and itself looks like an animal or vegetable.

Numerous analogies have been used for poetry, but it is the human body which is supposed to be more appropriate. The metaphor of human body or mechanism, a great wonder, Wimsatt argues, is generally compared to the organic form in the poem. Its parts—nerves, bones, veins, arteries, lung, heart, liver, and all the other organs—are built very symmetrically and systematically and function so accurately and automatically that there seems something truly mysterious in them. This organic beauty leads an artist to burst out with such an utterance: "What a piece of work is man!" Wimsatt holds the human body good enough to formulate his arguments about the organic whole in the poem. Though the larger versions of organicism also appear in the cosmic unity and the social and ethical harmonies, yet they are not within the purview of discussion in this essay. Wimsatt confines himself only to the metaphor of human body that has an organic order and aesthetic beauty. This analogy is found not only in the poem but also in visual arts in which we get the presence of organic and artistic form. It is repeatedly and emphatically discussed in the modern organistic literary theory. In visual art, both representational and abstract paintings are artistic forms, and hence by idealist definition, they must be organic forms, yet the latter lacks life-like organic growth. It is a crystal or mere lifeless mechanical form.

Wimsatt encompasses in his discussion another very important metaphor for the poem—the metaphor of the plant life. Romantic poets always make an extensive and lavish use of nature. Though they talk very little about the organic form in their essays, yet their treatment of nature is a healthy sign to the development of English poetry. Wimsatt states:

> Yet, by and large, the prevalence of nature, especially landscape and botanical nature, in English poetry during about two centuries does suggest a kind of latent equation in the poetic mind: Themes or images of organic life in poetry confer upon that poetry the poetic life of organic form.[17]

Coleridge, the most important translator of German organic idealism to English scene, speaks with his critical insight in his essay: "If the artist copies the mere nature, the *natura naturata*, what idle rivalry."[17] He explores a deep overtone in the visible image of nature, which yields moral reflections: "nature is thought, and thought nature" (207). It is the "mystery of genius in the Fine Arts."[18] Bernard Blackstone rightly holds:

> ...there is no English Romantic poet better than Keats for showing us the genial swell of organic forms, the unfolded buds, the ripening fruit, the loaded blessing of the vines, the swollen gourd, the plumped hazel shells, and for making such images symbolize a transcendent experience of beauty—even beauty like that of a Gracian Urn (p.207).

The textbooks of Goethe and the treatises of other nature philosophers and scientists are fraught with pictures and scientific modules on organic life, but they failed to lend anything for aesthetic purpose. Their approach is totally analytical and scientific. Wimsatt discovers a good organic analogy between a plant and a human body. To validate his intent, he cites Gustave Geffroy:

> A flower—...Free and growing out of the earth, or captive in a vase, it presents an artist with the perfect example of the universal creative force—in it he may find form, colour and even expression, a mysterious expression composed of stillness, silence, and the fugitive beauty of things which are born to die in the same moment.[19]

Romantic Germans highly preoccupied with organic form, as Rene Wellek argues in the first two volumes of *History of Modern Criticism*, leaves a deep imprint on Coleridge. He believes that a poem grows in the mind like a plant. In *Biographia Literaria* he focuses his attention on the poetic principle which is located in the psychology of the poet than in the poems. He, therefore, searches the organic depth of the mind of the creator. His most striking and deliberate statements about organic form occur in his lectures on Shakespeare's power as a poet, his imagination, and his judgment so happily wedded to his genius.

Wimsatt conceives the theory of organic form with the help of M. H. Abrams's clear exposition in his *The Mirror and the Lamp* (1953). Abrams enumerates that five properties of plant life enter into the analogy between plants and poems. Construed from Coleridge's letters, notes, treatises, and conversations, the five principles arranged in order are: (1) the whole, the priority of the whole; without the whole, the parts are nothing; (2) Growth, "the evolution and extension of the plant;" (3) Assimilation; the plant converts or assimilates diverse materials into its own substance; (4) Internality; the plant is the spontaneous source of its own energy; it is not shaped from outside ; and (5) Interdependence, between parts and parts, and parts and whole.

These overlapping principles in a nut-shell is called "Organic Form." They have a close affinity with "the favorite Coleridgean concept of the tension and reconciliation of manifold opposites which it is the peculiar power of artistic genius to accomplish" (p.211). Coleridge's principles, Wimsatt holds, unite a measure of poetic structuralism or objective doctrine regarding poetic form—a form that bears a genetic overtone. Orsini says: "It is only the finished product that we can apply the concept of organic unity."[20] But Wimsatt at one respect tries to place the superiority of the physical as well as botanical organism over the human poetic consciousness:

> There is at least one respect in which the physical organism, either growing plant or animal, is immeasurably surpassed by the human poetic consciousness. I mean, in its capacity for self-revision, rearrangement, mending. Plants renew leaves and flowers; animal moult in several ways; a lobster can lose a claw and regrow it; the human body heals cuts and regrows a finger nail (211).

At the same time, Wimsatt hastens to add that there is a great difference between the power of mind and action of any physical organism. The action of physical organism has its own limitation because it cannot revise or recast the power of human mind or reaffirm or cancel a little bit something done earlier by the mind. Human mind has got a spiritual power. The poem, "the finished product," is "a moment of spiritual activity, hypostatized, remembered, recorded, repeated. The human psyche makes the poem out of itself, or offers a remembered action of itself as the poem" (212). This is a difference between a tree and the human mind. A tree offers nothing but appears as the necessary product of the process which is itself. Therefore, in the analysis of the poem, there is no role of "intentional" fallacy.

Wimsatt makes a distinction between the romantic concept of poetry and that of the eighteenth century nature philosophers. The romantics believe in unconscious, indeliberate, and "unpremeditated art" and intend to make poetry as radically spontaneous as possible. On this ground, they justify the analogy between plant life and poetic creation and tend to that of vegetable. Some theorists hold that Shakespeare creates his Hamlet "as a bird weaves a nest." Schiller urges that "a poet should be a plant." On the other hand, eighteenth century thinkers draw plant life closer to human consciousness i.e. plants are conscious. Wimsatt observes that despite its revisions, prunings, and reviewings, a poem finally achieves an organic unity. "The moment presented as the poem is a contrived moment" (212). The ultimate end of a piece of work should look organic and spontaneous, though it passes through the poet's awareness and consciousness at the verbal and mental act. Some artists affirm the first impulses, and any revision of the first draft consider an "aesthetic sin" or lack of genius. But Shakespeare, Coleridge opines, never writes anything without conscious design. W. B. Yeats also knows that the hours of stitching and unstitching are a normal course. He states:

> A line will take us hours may be,
> Yet if it does not seem a moment's thought,
> Our stitching and unstitching has been nought.[21]

Like Coleridge, Wimsatt never talks about the consciousness of the poet but lays emphasis on the poem itself. He defines that the poem is "the hypostatized verbal and mental act," and has an organic growth like a human body or plant life. It is an objectified act, a poetic object. But along with other theorists, Kant observes that a work of human art differs a natural organism. The latter is self-organizing and can itself repair when damaged. Wimsatt finds the verbal work of art superior to the natural organism in the capacity of self-organization, as one of the characters of the poetic organization. Plato expounds that a composition should be like a living being with foot, body, and head.[22] Aristotle contends that it ought to be a unity like an organisim.[23] Orsini suggests not to extend the simile or metaphor of the physical organism too far, nor to take it literally, because it is not essential to the concept of aesthetic organic unity. The aesthetic unity is "generated by the Kantian a priori synthetic idea, the human reason's glorious power of nonempirical creative unifying vision." The art work has indeed, and literally, an organic form, a synthetic unity in multiplicity.

The aesthetic organicist, Wimsatt advises, not to dwell for a long time on the analogy between a poem and the ragged and crude physical organism. He should be content to confine his appeal to a much purified post-Kantian version of the aesthetic properties:

> ... the individuality and uniqueness of each aesthetic whole, the priority of the whole to the parts, the congruence and interdependence of parts with parts and of parts with the whole, the uniqueness and irrepalacability of parts and their nonexistence prior to the aesthetic whole or outside it (pp.214-15).

Whimsatt is quite sure that no literary critic is likely to rebel against these ideas, whatever school of criticism he belongs to. He must repose his faith in them. In this respect, the theory of organic form is very much indebted to the doctrine of Romantic organism. The New Critics are fortunate enough to receive the well-established theory, the metaphor of human body or plant life, and the literal idealist doctrine. All these conceptions help them understand the poetry of a poem.

Wimsatt places superiority of plant organism to physical organism. If a leaf is plucked from the tree, it gets withered, damaged, and died. Still it may be pressed between the pages of a book and treasured it years later. It has a kind of superiority to certain parts of other and higher organism. For example, an ear cut from a vanquished bull and a human finger chopped off are preserved in formaldehyde. Jean Paul, John Keats, and Coleridge—they all support the notion that the aesthetic beauty of a work lies in the whole as well as in the part. Jean Paul confidently states: "the spirit of a work like the *Iliad* is manifest both in the whole and in the smallest syllable."[24] Coleridge explains that poetry offers a "pleasure from the whole consistent with a consciousness of a pleasure from the component parts," and that it communicates "from each part of the greatest sum of pleasure compatible with the largest sum of pleasure of the whole." It is true that the poem is all knowable; it is all knowledge, through and through. It is transnoetic, an act or a possible act of self-reflexive consciousness. There is no substitution of one part without the whole, and no life in the part without the whole.

Wimsatt discovers that parts detached from the whole bear as much beauty as the whole. The head of many a marble statue has survived truncation and has been admired for centuries in a garden or museum. Feathers of any birds either put in a hat or lapel or preserved in a vase appear to be beautiful, because there is an implicit sustaining context within which such relics are admired. The same is also applicable to certain fragmentary, sketchy, or partly abstracted representational forms of arts—for instance, a single fleeting leg in a sculpture entitled "Runner" by Leon Underwood. These parts have an aesthetic significance in the contexts of a habitual consciousness of their relation to the rest of the visible surface of a bird or a human body. Parts, of course, are equally important as the whole.

Wimsatt is also conscious that necessity in the relation of parts to parts and parts to whole differs very widely with different parts. If someone goes into a movie just in time to see the last part, he will likely experience a nearly maximum loss of meaning and aesthetic quality in a part deprived of its whole. If he arrives at the beginning of the movie or reads the first chapter of almost any novel, he will likely have the opposite experience. However, it is an undeniable fact that symmetry is one of the necessary conditions of the beautiful. Plotinus remarks:

> Only a compound can be beautiful, never anything devoid of parts.... Yet beauty in an aggregate demand beauty in details; it cannot be constructed out of ugliness; its law must run throughout.[25]

The Kantian aesthetics also hold that the interdependence of parts in the organically unified poem is so close that to remove any part is to damage the whole and that no part is replaceable by any other conceivable part. But Wimsett comes across a paradox of these two propositions. Many poets keep revising their poems assiduously, removing parts, adding others, replacing others even to the last breath. Editors, compositors, critics, theoretical producers, and actors make many inspired changes in works, either purposely or accidently. Even a corrupt text, edited and emended through critical speculation, has been gratefully accepted. Wimsatt's intention is not to aim at genetic or textual problems, but to point out certain embarrassing aesthetic dubieties. Five-act plays and epic narratives are generally lumpy.

Producers of plays can cope with that lumpiness, but aestheticians may have to close their eyes while exploring an organic order. Catherine Lord, a Professor of aesthetics, argues that too close a degree of organic unity unnecessary defeats the episodic and multifarious nature of such extended literary works. It is, Harry Berger notices, the "conspicuous irrelevance" of descriptive detail. Even various types of open-ended or multiple choice fictions are well established feature of the literary scene. Such terms as "indeterminacy," "irrelevance," and "nonstructure" begin to appeal to the critics.

Wimsatt subscribing to the Kantian proposition makes a very frank confession that a critic's business is to "interpret the aesthetic object in his best frame of mind" (p.220). What the work is and says is an ideal work of art; what makes clearly better sense has the superior claim. Hamlet, as F. W. Baterson has sensibly affirmed, yearned not that "this too, too sullied flesh," but that "this too, too solid flesh would melt, thaw, and resolve itself into a dew." The latter reading makes a good sense. It is possible through "the best frame of mind," which demands common sense, practical approach, and convincing acceptability. It is not a matter of aesthetic perfection, but of better sense. The neo-Kantians appear to be right to some extent, when they claim that perfection in this world is hard to achieve.

Wimsatt is optimistic of and pleased to the direction of modern literary theory. The critics have now realized the urgency of reading the poem by applying the organistic formula. They are quite aware of a loose, stretchable, and adjustable kind of organic form in the organic structure of the poem. Therefore, they think of their prime duty of the well knit organized conception of poetic organicism. They focus their attention on the extremely subtle, intimate and manifold "interanimation" of parts in a poem. This doctrine of organcity creates the dialectic of literary theory and helps analyze the organization of the poems. Wimsatt admits the contribution of the critics who have adopted structural method in analyzing and interpreting the poems. Their structural commentary upon English lyrics reinforces that explication of poems is "one of the termini of literary criticism" (p.221). In the hands of the critics, the poems

> ...are subjected to extremes of analysis under the rigorous structural technique, and they yield no doubt some secrets

of "the grammar of poetry and the poetry of grammar" (p.212).

They take a deep interest in such logical and grammatical commonplaces as "Unity and Division, Likeness and Difference" and in such various multiple occurrences of pattern as "Formal, Logical, Syntactical," "Rhetorical," "Phonetic" and "Lexical." Wimsatt appreciates the structural approach of criticism which lends a sense of gratification and integrity of the poem. While explicating the parts of the work, the critic's experience about the work does not come to end abruptly, but he should be capable of re-experiencing the entire work. It should not be as a succession of events, but as an integral design, just as we see a painting or a piece of sculpture.

With all its pros and cons, Wimsatt deduces that "neither the organicism of the extreme biological analogy nor that of the priori or transcendental or absolute assertion is likely to encourage superior readings of poetry. The American critics adopt a golden mean. They are preoccupied with the homelier and humbler sort of organicism based on "empirical, tentative, analytic, psychological, grammatical, lexicographic" (p.223).

References:

1. W. K. Wimsatt, Jr., *The Verbal Icon* (New York: The Noonday Press, 1954),
2. T. S. Eliot. *The Selected Essays*, p. 17.
3. D. H. Lawrence, "The Spirit of Place," David Lodge, ed., *20th Century Literary Criticism: A Reader* (Longman Group Ltd.: London 1972), p. 123.
4. "Affective Fallacy," in David Lodge, ed., *20th Century Literary Criticism: A Reader*, p. 334.
5. "Intentional Fallacy," in David Lodge, ed., *20th Century Literary Criticism: A Reader*, p. 345. The subsequent references will be mentioned in parenthesis after the page number of the same edition.
6. Patricia Waugh ed., *Literary Theory and Practice* (Oxford University Press, 2006), p.177.
7. David H. Richter ed., *The Critical Tradition: Classic Texts and Contemporary Trends* (Boston: Bedford, 1998), p. 750.

8. M. A. R. Habib, *A History of Literary Criticism and Theory*, p. 625.
9. *Ibid.*,
10. David Lodge, ed., *20th Century Literary Criticism: A Reader* (Longman Group Ltd.: London 1972), p.345. The subsequent references will be mentioned in parenthesis after the page number of the same edition.
11. W. K. Wimsatt ed., *Explication as Criticism* (New York: Columbia University Press, 1963), p.1.
12. *Princeton Encyclopedia of Poetry and Poetics*, p. 265.
13. Explication as Criticism, p.5.
14. Cited *in Explication as Criticism*, p. 6.
15. T. S. Eliot, "The Perfect Critic," *The Sacred Wood* (New York, 1930), p.11.
16. W. K. Wimsatt, *The Vebal Icon*, p.xii.
17. *Day of Leopards*, (New Haven and London: Yale University Press, 1976) p. 207.
18. J. Shawcross, ed., *Biographia Literaria* (London, 1939,II) p. 257.
19. *Ibid.*, pp. 253-254.
20. Cited in *Day of Leopards*, (New Haven and London: Yale University Press, 1976) p. 208.
21. G. N. G. Orsini, "The Organic Concepts in Aesthetics," *Comparative Literature* 21 (Winter 1969):5
22. "Adam's Curse," *The Collected Poems of W. B. Yeats* (New York, 1959), p.78.
23. Plato, *Phaedrus,* p.265.
24. Aristotle, *Poetics,* VIII4:XXIII.z.
25. Cited in *Day of the Leopards*, p. 215.
26. *Ibid.*, pp.217-218.

Bibliography

Abrams, M.H., "Review: Anatomy of Criticism," *University of Toronto Quarterly*, XXVIII, No. 2 (Jan.): 190-96, 1959.

———,*A Glossary of Literary Terms*, Delhi: MacMillan. 6th ed., 1993, New York: Harcourt, Brace, Jovanovich College Publishers, 1971.

———,*The Mirror and the Lamp*, New York: Oxford University Press, 1976.

Adams, Hazard, *The Interest of Criticism: An Introduction to Literary Theory*, New York: Harcourt, 1969.

Alvarez, A., *The Shaping Spirit*, London: Chatto and Windus, 1958.

Anderson, Quentin, "New Critic Back Down South," *New York Times Book Review*, 21 May: 7, 31-32, 1978.

Arc, Jonathan, *The Yale Critics, Deconstruction in America*, University of Minnesota Press, 1983.

Auden, W. H., "Against Romantics," *The New Republic*, 102 (Feb. 5), 187, 1940.

Barry, Peter, *Beginning Theory*, Manchester: Viva Books Private Ltd., 1988.

Barthes, Ronald, "The Structuralist Activity," *Critical Essays,* trans., R. Howard, III North Western University Press, 1972.

Beaver, Hartold, *American Critical Essays: Twentieth Century*, London: Oxford University Press, 1961.

Berman, Art, *From the New Criticism to Deconstruction: The Reception of Structuralism and Post Structuralism*, Urbana and Chicago: University of Illinois Press, 1988.

Binding, Paul, *Separate Country: A Literary Journey Through the American South*, New York & London: Paddington Press Ltd., 1979.

Blackmur, R. P., *Language as Gesture: Essays in Poetry*, London: Allen, 1954.

———,A Critic's Job of Work," *American Literary Criticism,* ed., Charles J. Glicksberg, New York, 1951.

———,*The Double Agent: The Essays in Craft and Elucidation*, Gloucester, Mass., Peter Smith, 1962.

———,*The Lion and the Honeycomb*, New York, Harcourt, Brace & World, Inc.,1955.

———,*The Expense of Greatness,* Gloucester: Peter Smith,1940.

Blamires, Harry, *A History of Literary Criticism*, London: Macmillan Education Ltd., 1991.

Blanken, Lind, "Cleanth Brooks: Fourteenth Jefferson Lecturer in the Humanities," *Humanities* (April), 4, 1985.

Booth, Wayne, C., *Critical Understanding: The Powers and Limits of Pluralism*, Chicago: University of Chicago Press, 1979.

———,"What is not old about the New Critics." *Humanities,* 6.2 (April), 7-8, 1985.

———,"R. S. Crane: Criticism as Inquiry; or, The Perils of the High Priori Road," *Twentieth Century Literary Theory,* ed., K. M. Newton, New York: St. Martin Press, 1988.

Borklund, Elmer, *Contemporary Literary Critics*, Detroit, Michigan: Gale Research, 1982.

Boyers, Robert, *R. P. Blackmur: Poet-Critic*, Columbia & London: University of Missouri Press, 1980.

Bradbury, J. M., *The Fugitives: A Critical Account*, Chapel Hill: University of North Caro, 1958.

Brinmeyer, Jr., H. Robert, *Three Catholic Writers of the Modern South,* Jackson: University Press of Mississippi, 1985.

Brooks, Cleanth, *Modern Poetry and the Tradition*, New York: OUP, 1965.

————,*The Well Wrought Urn: Studies in the Structure of Poetry,* New York: Harcourt, Brace and Company,1947.

Brooks, C., Robert Penn Warren, *Understanding Poetry*, New York: Henry Holt, 1938.

Bromwich, David, "Revising the New Critics," *Commentary,* 54.5 (Nov), 1972.

Burke, Kenneth, "The Problem of the Intrinsic," *Accent*, 3: 86-94, 1943.

———,*Language as Symbolic Action,* Berkeley: University of North California Press, 1966.

———,*The Philosophy of Literary Form*, Berkeley, California: University of North California Press, 1973.

Cain, William, *The Critics in Criticism*, Baltimore: The Johns Hopkins University Press, 1984.

Carritt, E. F., *The Philosophy of Beauty Oxford*, University Press, 1952.

Clair, John, "Donne's Canonization," *PMLA*, Vol. LXXX, No. 3, 300-2, 1965.

Clark, William Bedford, "Cleanth Brooks: Mr. Eliot's Christian Critic," *Southern Review*, 18 (1982).

Coleridge, S. T., *Philosophical Lectures*, London: Faber & Faber Ltd., 1932.

Cookson, William, ed., *Selected Prose,* 1909-1965, New Directions, 1973.

Coughlin, Sister Phyllis, "Aspect of Literary Form in Three Contemporary Theories: Cleanth Brooks, R.S. Crane and W.K. Wimsatt, Jr." Dissertation Abstract, 34, 8: 5096A. Fordham, 1973.

Cowan, Louise, *The Southern Critics*, Texas: The University of Dallas Press, 1972.

Crane, R.S., ed., *Critics and Criticism: Ancient and Modern,* Chicago: University of Chicago Press, 1952.

———,"The Critical Monism of Cleanth Brooks."

———,*The Language of Criticism and the Structure of Poetry*, Toronto: Toronto University Press, 1953.

———,*The Idea of Humanities and Other Essays: Critical and Historical*, Chicago: University of Chicago Press, 1967.

Cross, J. Shaw, ed., *Biographia Literaria*, London: Oxford University Press, 1962.

Culler, Jonathan, *Structuralist Poetics: Structuralism Linguistics and the Study of Literature*, London: Routledge and Kegan Paul, 1975.

———,*On Deconstruction: Theory and Criticism after Structuralism*, Ithaca: Cornell University, 1982.

Daiches, David, *Critical Approaches to Literature*, II ed., Orient Longman Ltd., 1956.

———,"The New Criticism," *In A Time of Harvest: American Literary Literature 1910-1960*, ed. Robert Spiller Ernest. New York: Hill and Wang, 1962.

Davis, R.C. et al., *Literary Criticism and Theory: The Greek to Present*, New York: Longman, 1989.

Day, Douglas, "The Background of the New Criticism," *The Journal of Aesthetics of Art Criticism*, 24.3 (Spring), 1966.

Denham, Robert D., "R. S. Crane's Critical Method and Theory of Poetic Form," *Connecticut Review*, 5.2 (April), 46-55, 1972.

———,*Northrop Frye and Critical Method*, University Park: Pennsylvania State University Press, 1978.

Dictionary of Literary Biography. Modern American Critics since 1955. Vol. 67, 1988. Detroit, Gale Research.

Dolan, Paul Joseph, "Tradition in Modern Literary Criticism," *Dissertation Abstract*, Vol. 28, 4130, 1966.

Doreski, William, *The Year of Our Friendship: Robert Lowell and Allen Tate*, Jackson & London: University Press of Mississippi, 1990.

Donoghue, Denish, ed., *Selected Essays of R. P. Blackmur*, New York: Eco Press, 1986.

Dupree, S. Robert, *Allen Tate and the Augustan Imagination: A Study of the Poetry*, Baton Rouge and London: Louisiana State University Press, 1983.

Eisenstein, Sergie, *The Film Sense*, New York: Harcourt. Brace, 1957.

Eliot, T.S., *The Sacred Wood: Essays on Poetry and Criticism,* London: Methuen, 1920.

———,"The Frontiers of Criticism," in *On Poetry and Poets*, New York: Farrar, Straus and Cudahy, 1957, 113-31, 1956.

———,"Tradition and the Individual Talent," *English Critical Texts*, ed. D.J. Enright, Delhi: Oxford University Press, 1962.•

———,*Selected Essays*, London: Faber and Faber, 1963.

Empson, William, *Seven Types of Ambiguity*, London: Penguin, 1961.

Fekete, John, *The Critical Twilight*, London: Routledge and Kegan Paul, 1977.

Fish, Stanley, *Is There a Text in This Class*? Cambridge, Mass: Harvard University Press, 1980.

Foster, Richard, *The New Romantics: A Reappraisal of the New Criticism,* Bloomington: Indiana University Press, 1962.

Fowler, Roger, *A Dictionary of Modern Critical Terms,* London: Routledge and Kegan Paul, 1973.

Rank, Joseph, ed., *A Primer of Ignorance*, New York: Harcourt, 1967.

Fraser, Russell, *A Mingled Yarn: The Life of R. P. Blackmur*, New York & London: Harcourt, Brace, Javanovich, 1981.

Freund, Elizabeth, *The Return of the Reader: Reader Response Criticism*, London and New York: Methuen, 1987.

Frye, Northrop, "The Archetypes of Literature," *Fables and Identity,* New York: Harcourt, Brace, 1951.

———,*Anatomy of Criticism: Four Essays, Princeton*, N.J. Gebhard, Patricia, 1957.

———,"The New Criticism as an Aesthetic Theory." *The Western Humanities Review*, 17, 1963.

Goldsmith, Arnold, *American Literary Criticism: 1905-65*, Bostan: Twayne, 1979.

Goodheart, Eugene, *The Skeptical Disposition in Contemporary Criticism,* Princeton University Press, 1984.

Graff, Gerald, "Cleanth Brooks: New Critical Organism," *In Poetical Statement and Critical Dogma,* Evanston III: North Western University Press, 87-111, 1971.

Graff, Gerald, *Literature Against Itself,* Chicago, 1979.

Greenbaum, Leonard, *The Hound & Horn: The History of a Literary Quarterly*, London: Mouton & Co., 1966.

Guerin, Wilford L. et al, *Literature and Interpretive Techniques*, New York: Harper and Row, 1986.

Habib, M. A. R., *A History of Literary Criticism and Theory*, Blackwell Publishing, 2008.

Handy, J. E., "The Achievement of Cleanth Brooks," *Hopkins Review* 6: 148-61, 1953.

Hardin, Richard F., "Archetypal Criticism," *In The Contemporary Literary Theory,* ed., Douglas Atkins and Laura Morrow, Amherst: Univ. of Massachusetts Press, 1989.

Hartman, Geoffery H., *Beyond Formalism*, New Haven: Yale University Press, 1970.

———,*Criticism in the Wilderness*, New Haven: Yale University Press, 1980.

———,*Easy Pieces*, New York: Columbia University Press, 1985.

Hassan, Ihab, *The Postmodern Turn: Essay in Postmodern Theory and Culture,* Chicago State University Press, 1987.

Heilman, Robert B., "The Critics who made us: Cleanth Brooks and The Well Wrought Urn," *The Sewanee Review,* 91.2 (Spring), 322-33, 1983.

Hemphill, George, *Allen Tate*, Minneapolis: University of Minnesota, 1964.

Hoffman, H. J., *The Twenties,* New York: Collier Holloway, John. 1955.

———,"The New and Newer Critics." *Essays in Criticism* (5 Nov.), 1962.

Hopper, S.R., ed., *Spiritual Problems in Contemporary Literature*, New York: Harper, 1952.

Hulme, T.E., "Romanticism and Classism," in *Speculations: Essays on Humanism and Philosophy of Art,* ed., Herbert Read. London: Routledge and Kegan Paul, 1977.

Hutcheon, Linda, *The Politics of Postmodernism*, Routledge, 1988.

Hyman, Stanley Edger, *The Armed Vision: A Study in the Methods of Modern Literary Criticism*, New York: Vintage Book, 1955.

Indra, C. T., "A Correspondence with Cleanth Brooks," *Indian Journal of American Studies*, 13/1 (January), 3-22.

Jauss, Hans Robert, *Towards an Aesthetic of Reception*, University of Minnesota Press, 1982.

Jay, Gregory S., ed., *Modern American Criticism Since 1955*, Gal, 1988.

Jones, T. James, *Wayward Skeptic: The Theories of R. P. Blackmur,* Urbana & Chicago: University of Illinois Press, 1986.

Kermode, Frank, *Romantic Image*, London: Routledge and Kegan Paul, 1957.

Krieger, Murray, *The New Apologists for Poetry*, Minneapolis: University of Minnesota Press, 1956.

———"Post-New Criticism Fashion in Theory," *Critical Essays,* ed., S. Viswanathan et al, Madras: Macmillan, 1987.

Lane, Michael, ed., Structuralism*: A Reader*, London: Jonathan cape, 1970.

Lawal, Sarah, *Critics of Consciousness*, Cambridge: Harvard University Press, 1963.

Leary, Lewis, and John Prichard, *American Literature and Research Guide,* New York: M. Thomas Inge St. Martin's Press, 1976.

Leavis, F.R, *New Bearings in English Poetry. A Study in Contemporary Situation*, London: Chatto and Windus, 1961.

————,*Common Pursuit*, London, 1952.

Lee, Brian, "The New Criticism and the Language of Poetry," *Essays on Style and Language*, ed., Roger Fowler. London: Routledge and Kegan Paul, 1966.

Leggett, B.J., "Notes for a Revised History of the New Criticism: An Interview with Cleanth Brooks," *Tennessee Studies in Literature*, 24, 1-35, 1979.

Leitch, Vincent B., *American Literary Criticism from Thirties to Eighties,* New York: Columbia University Press, 1988.

Lemon, Lee T., *The Partial Critics*, New York: Oxford University Press, 1965.

Lentricchia, Frank, "The Place of C B," *Journal of Aesthetics and Art Criticism*, 29: 235-51, 1970.

——— *After the New Criticism,* Chicago: The University of Chicago Press, 1980.

Levin, Harry, *Review of Literary Criticism: A Short History, Modern Language Notes*, 73 (1958), 155-60.

Lodge, David, ed., *20th Century Criticism: A Reader*, London: Longman, 1972.

Martin, Linda-Wagner, "Review of Cleanth Brooks's On Prejudices Predilections and Firm Beliefs of William Faulkner," *Studies in Fiction*, 25.3 (Summer), 356, 1988.

Matthiessen, F.O., *The Responsibilities of the Critic*, New York: Oxford University Press, 1952.

Maxwell, D.E.S., *The Poetry of T.S. Eliot*, London: Routledge and Kegan Paul, 1966.

Miller, David M., *The Net of Hephaestus: A Study of Modern Criticism and Metaphysical Metaphor*, Paris: Mounton: The Hague, 1971.

Muecke, D.C., *Irony: The Critical Idiom*, London: Methuen, 1970.

Mukherjee, Tuntun, *The Chicago Critics: An Evaluation,* Delhi: Academic Foundation, 1991.

Munir, *An Autopsy on English Literature*, New Delhi: Adhyayan Publishers and Distributors, 2009.

Murry, J. M., 'Metaphor,' *Countries of the Mind*, London, 1931.

Narasimhaiah, C.D. 1968. "New Criticism: An Assessment," *Indian Essays in American Literature*, ed., Sujit Mukherjee and V.K. Raghavacryulu. Bombay: Asia, 1968.

Norris, Christopher, *Deconstruction: Theory and Practice,* London and New York: Methuen, 1982.

O'Connor, William Van, *An Age of Criticism 1900-1950,* Chicago: Henry Regenery Company,1950.

Olson, Elder, "William Empson, Contemporary Criticism and Poetic Language." *In Crane,* 1952.

Orsini, G. N. G., "Organic Concepts in Aesthetics," *Comparative Literature* 21 (Winter 1965):5

Pannick, J. Gerald, *Richard Palmer Blackmur*, Boston: Twayne Publishers, 1981.

Pole, David, "C B and the New Criticism," *British Journal of Aesthetics*, 9: 285-97, 1964.

Pound, Ezra, "How to Read," *Polite Essays*, Norfolk: Conn, 1929.

———,*The Spirit of Romance*, London, 1910.

Preminger, Alex, ed., *Princeton Encyclopedia of Poetry and Poetics*, London: The Macmillan Press Ltd., 1974.

Pritchard, J.P., Criticism *in American*, Oklahoma University Press, 1956.

Pulos C.E., "C B" in *The New Critics and the Language of Poetry*, Lincoln Nebraska: University of Nebraska Studies, 72-82, 1958.

Rackin, R.P., *Poetry without Paradox: The Limitation of the New Criticism of the Lyric*, Ph.D. Thesis, Graduate College of the Illinois, 1962.

Ransom, J. C. *The New Criticism,* Norfolk, Conn., 1941.

———,*God Without Thunder: An Orthodox Defense of Orthodoxy*, New York: Harcourt, Brace and Co., 1930.

———,*The World's Body*, Baton Rouge, 1968.

———,"The Concrete Universal: Observation on the Understanding of Poetry," *The Kenyon Review*, 16 (1954).

Richards, I. A., *The Philosophy of Rhetoric*, New York: OUP, 1965.

———,*The Principles of Literary Criticism*, London: Kegan Paul, Trench, Trubner & Co., Ltd., 1934.

Richter, H. David, *The Critical Tradition: Classic Texts and Contemporary Trends*, Boston: Bedford, 1998.

Rylance, Rick, ed., "New Criticism," *Encyclopedia of Literature and Criticism*, London: Routledge, 1991.

Shwross, John, ed., *Coleridge's Shakespearean Criticism*, 1930.

Sipson, P., ed., *The Possibilities of Order: Cleanth Brooks and His Work*, Boston: Louisiana State University Press, 1976.

Spears, K. Monroe, *Modernism in Twentieth Century Poetry*, New York: OUP, 1970.

Spingarn, Joel, "Introduction: Criticism in America," *Literary Opinion in America,* New York: Harper Torchbooks, 1962.

Stallman, R. W., ed., *Critique and Essays in Criticism 1920-1948,* New York: Ronald Press, 1949.

Stamiris, Yiannis, *Main Currents in Twentieth Century Criticism: A Critical Study*, New York: Whitson Publishing Co., 1986.

Stewart, L. John, *John Crowe Ransom*, Minneapolis: University of Minnesota Press, 1962.

Suttan, Walter, *Modrn American Criticism*, Englewood Cliff, N. J., Prince Hall, 1963

Tak, A. H., *Coleridge and Modern Criticism*, Delhi: R P Publishing Corporation, 1985.

Tate, Allen, *On the Limits of Poetry*, New York, 1948.

———, *Reason in Madness*, New York: G. P. Patnam's Sons, 1941.

———, *Collected Essays* (Denver, 1959).

Wain, John, *Essays on Literature and Ideas*, London: Macmillan & Co., 1964.

Ward, A. C., *Twentieth Century Literature 1901-1950*, W. C.: EIBS Methuen, 1963.

Waugh, Patricia, ed., *Literary Theory and Practice,* Oxford University Press, 2006.

Wellek, R. & Warren, A. *Theory of Literature*, London: Jonathan Cape, 1948.

Wimsatt, W. K., *Day of the Leopards,* New Haven and London: Yale University Press, 1976.

————, ed., *Explication as Criticism*, New York: Columbia University Press, 1963.

Wimsatt, W. K., & Beardsley, M. C., *The Verbal Icon,* New York: The Noonday Press, 1954.

Wimsatt, W. K. & Brooks C., *Literary Criticism: A Short History*, New Delhi: Oxford & IBH Publishing Co. Ltd., 1962.

Wren, C. L., *Word and Symbol*, London, Longmans, 1967.

Zabel, M. D., ed., *Literary Opinion in America*, New York, 1951.

INDEX